Slip

Slip

a novel

TANYA SAVKO

KOVA

Kova Publishing
Phoenix, Oregon

Copyright © 2010 by Tanya Savko
Cover design and photograph by Tanya Savko

Published in the United States by Kova Publishing, Phoenix, Oregon

www.kovapublishing.com

Library of Congress Control Number: 2008904808

ISBN 10: 0-9817868-0-4

ISBN 13: 978-0-9817868-0-3

Printed in Canada

For Nigel and Aidan

Acknowledgments

I wish to thank early reader Dan Latham for being willing to take on the formidable task of critiquing a first manuscript written by someone he didn't previously know. His unbiased comments were invaluable, and I look forward to returning the favor.

Thanks are also in order to my family members who agreed to read a big box of paper (i.e. the book before publication): my father, Michael Savko, my sister, Anastasia Savko, and my brother, Alexis Savko, who essentially wrote the back cover copy.

Thanks to my other family members who gave endless support during the writing of this book: my sons, Nigel and Aidan, my mother, Madeline Rose, and my sister, Macrina Lesniak.

Thanks to Sharon of Rogue Books, Kelly Howell of Brain Sync, and Genevieve Athens of the Autism Society of Oregon for their generous quotes.

Thanks to Jan Hale of The Wright Fulfillment Company for her encouragement and friendship, and for her therapeutic dogs.

One

I always wanted to be a librarian when I grew up," Andrew answered his wife as he turned on the faucet and began to draw a bath. He'd said it with the incredulity of one who had abandoned a fledgling dream early on, before it had even taken hold, so long ago that even he himself had forgotten it. They had been discussing his future employment plans as they realized that, mentally as well as financially speaking, he would need to go back to work soon. Being a stay-at-home parent for the past three years was not what he had planned for himself when he had graduated from college at the age of twenty-three. He was supposed to have traveled the world by now, published a book, bought a house. It was 1997.

"Really?" Erica said with a small laugh. "You never told me that before! You're the first guy I know who wanted to be a *librarian* when he grew up." She pushed a lock of her chin-length black hair behind her ear as she entered the small bathroom of their home.

"I know. It's not the typical fireman or baseball player answer."

He reached down and tested the temperature of the water, then stood back up and blotted his hand on his jeans. "I'm sure you never wanted to be a ballerina."

Erica laughed again, this time her short *Ha!* burst that always unnerved him if he wasn't expecting it. A guffaw, really. "No, but at some point I did want to be a veterinarian, which is another 'girl' thing to want to be. Then I discovered I was allergic to cats, which was a bummer."

Funny how we can get so far from where we thought we wanted to be, Andrew thought. He had obtained his bachelor's degree in English, and, aside from the occasional résumé written for a friend, he had not had many opportunities to utilize his education. The only writing he did was the infrequent, boring journal entry. His goal of being a freelance writer had

good

been shelved along with his record collection; he was not sure when he would be able to enjoy either one again. Having small children precluded the achievement of lofty goals, including the purchase of new stereo equipment. And, by not working, he certainly wasn't contributing to household expenses. "But we save on childcare costs with you staying at home," Erica had said. "And we know the kids will always be safe." Erica attended the local university studying graphic design and worked nights as a bartender. Andrew suspected she did not realize his growing resentment about his isolation, home alone with two toddlers, and, he felt, his mental stagnation. Not to mention their growing debt. Andrew looked at her. "So. Do you want to tell him or should I?"

"I told him last time."

"All right, I'll do it," Andrew said.

"Maybe we should do Eileen first, and then tell him."

"Okay. I'll get her." Andrew walked out behind his wife's lean frame. She was as tall as he was, which, even though he was devoted to her, was an issue with him. A small issue, at least. He would never tell her, of course, but he wished she were a little shorter. Or maybe if he were a little taller—but not really. He was comfortable with his own average height, his blond surfer-type good looks. But, aside from that, he thought that Erica was perfect for him, and the issue of her height was so minor that he rarely thought about it. He often had to defend her decision to not take his last name, however. His rather conservative parents believed that it somehow made Erica less loyal, less "married," perhaps. But Andrew completely understood her desire to maintain her recognizable name. Erica Hudson just sounded better than Erica Pavel. He accepted it without any difficulty. It made her seem stronger, more independent, and that appealed to him. He also liked the fact that his wife was two years his senior. He would always be younger, which comforted him somehow. As the eldest of three children, he had sometimes wished for an older sibling to share some of his responsibilities.

Andrew walked down the short hallway of his two-bedroom duplex. They had lived there for two years now, and neither of them had put anything up on the white walls of the rental. They figured if they didn't make themselves too comfortable there that they would be more motivated to save money to buy a home. It was a notch on Erica's success meter, but to Andrew, owning a home was not a means to an end, it was an end in itself. As a child he used to pore over Sears catalogs and pick out electronics, appliances, and furnishings that he thought he would like to have when he was an adult and owned his own home. His Spartan rental did not achieve the desired effect. It depressed Andrew far more than it motivated him. How can you save money when you're not making any?

But Andrew smiled when he found his younger child, fifteen-month-old Eileen, dancing in the living room to the song coming from the TV. Her short, straight, wispy blond hair bounced with her movements, like it had a mind of its own. His older child, three-year-old Nathan, sat on the old, dark red velveteen couch and sucked both his forefinger and middle finger of his right hand while he watched the TV, and, with his other hand, tugged on and twisted a lock of short, wavy, dark blond hair near the whorl at the top rear of his head. He seemed oblivious to his sister, and to their father entering the room. Andrew goose-stepped over several errant toys and stuffed animals, including the old pull-string telephone with the eyes that rolled back and forth when it was pulled across the room.

"Hi, Nathan! What are you watching?" *I have to try,* Andrew thought. *Maybe one of these days he'll tell me. Maybe he'll just decide that it's time to talk.*

Nathan continued sucking his fingers and twirling his hair and did not respond. Speaking and interacting were not high priorities for him, as much as Andrew could tell. Sometimes it seemed that, when not upset by something, his son existed in a semi-trance state, regarding any interaction as an intrusion. Andrew turned to Eileen.

"Guess what! It's time for a bath! You can watch more *Lion King* when the bath is over. Come on with Dad," he said as he picked her up and leaned over to turn off the TV. Nathan yelled, which prompted Eileen to protest by whining and kicking her legs against Andrew's abdomen.

"I thought this was supposed to be easier doing Eileen first!" he called down the hall, over the din of his children. He held Eileen closer, restraining her, as he walked to the bathroom.

"You know it will be," Erica said. She rolled up the sleeves of her sweatshirt and began undressing a suddenly more compliant Eileen while Andrew walked back to get Nathan.

What's so wrong with a nice, warm bath? he thought. *Why is it always so traumatic for him?* Andrew sat down next to him on the couch where he sat staring at the blank TV screen, still sucking his fingers and tugging his hair, only now a bit harder, sensing the tension. Andrew put his arm around him and pulled Nathan to him.

"Nathan," he began. "Let's go watch Eileen take a nice bath."

"Leen," Nathan said in his usual rote tone. He removed his fingers just long enough to say his sister's name, noting that *she* would take the bath, then replaced them.

"Yes, come with Dad," Andrew said, holding out his hand to him. Nathan did not move, so Andrew picked him up and carried him. He was a healthy child, dense-boned and muscular, solid. Large for his age, taking after Erica's side. "The bath is nice and warm. You can watch Mom wash Eileen's hair. She likes it," he said, hoping that might coax him into the tub. He didn't want to tell him yet that he would be next or he would shriek and scare Eileen.

Erica had just laid a now-placid Eileen back on her left arm and with her right hand slowly poured a cup of water over Eileen's head as Andrew walked in with Nathan. Nathan watched, glad that he was still clothed. Once the clothes came off, he knew there was no turning back.

"See?" Andrew said to him. "Mom is just wetting Eileen's hair. She's okay. The water feels good. Now she's putting shampoo in her hair to clean it. Now she's going to rinse the shampoo out. See? Mom is holding her. Now all the soap is out of her hair and she's all finished. Now she can get out and watch more *Lion King*!"

Erica wrapped Eileen in a big yellow towel and carried her out into the living room. She seated her on the couch and turned the TV and VCR back on and came back to the bathroom, saying, "Now it's your turn to wash hair, Nathan!"

"Aaahhhh! Aaaahhh!" he yelled, kicking Andrew as he set him down and undressed him. Erica shut the door. Together they lifted him into the tub. Erica held his legs while Andrew went through the same hair washing motions that Erica had with Eileen, only at a much faster pace. It was quite a feat, considering the fact that Nathan's hair was thicker than Eileen's and he thrashed so violently. Nathan fought and yelled. Water sloshed everywhere as his arms flailed. Andrew finished as quickly as possible, pulled his hysterical son out of the tub and onto the bathmat, and wrapped him up.

"I'm going to check on Eileen," Erica said, blotting herself with a towel.

Andrew began to dry Nathan's body and hair, a routine his son actually seemed to enjoy. "I don't know why you scream, Nathan. No screaming or hitting or kicking, remember? You're okay. Nothing happened to you. We just washed your hair. This screaming over the hair-washing is just a bit too much." Sometimes he felt like he was talking to a wall, but he wanted to believe that Nathan heard him and understood. They knew he could hear quite well; several times he had come running from the bedroom all the way out to the kitchen when he heard the faint scrape of the ceramic cookie jar lid being lifted. They also knew he was incredibly smart. Six months earlier, Andrew's mother had brought over two wooden puzzles, one of the alphabet and the other of numbers zero to nine. They told Nathan the names of all the letters and numbers just a few times, and by the end of the afternoon he had them memorized. Every single one he knew, at the age of two and a half. He had also had no difficulty with fitting the puzzle pieces where they belonged. Andrew wrapped the towel around him again and hugged him. "Come on, let's go get your pajamas on."

He guided Nathan into the kids' bedroom, which was the only room in the house with anything on the walls. Eileen's white wooden crib had baby Mickey, Minnie, and Donald all over the sheets, and Nathan's low toddler bed had *Lion King* sheets on it. Andrew and Erica were both Disney fans and adorned their children's room accordingly. During childhood, Andrew had gone to Disneyland several times with his family. Erica had not been able to go at all as a child (her usually single mother had not been able to afford it), but at the age of nineteen she began working there as a food server. She had liked to tell neighborhood kids that she went to Disneyland every day, just to see the surprise and admiration on their faces.

Together they dressed their children for bed, Andrew thankful for the one evening a week that Erica was home and he didn't have to do it alone. Aside from the bath trauma, which they reserved for that one night a week, it wasn't too difficult getting the kids ready for bed, but the lack of adult interaction was driving him crazy. And it was good to feel like a family, to do something all together, even if it was just getting ready for bed, and even if it did include an episode of shrieking hysteria. The older gentleman who shared their duplex was hard of hearing, much to their relief.

After they had brushed the toddlers' teeth (another element of personal hygiene that Nathan protested, but with tolerance, since it occurred more often), they sat on the couch with them and read a Winnie the Pooh book and then carried them to their beds. Eileen was finally out of the stage that required half-hour rocking sessions before she fell asleep and allowed the rocker, usually Andrew, to slip her into her bed without waking. Andrew had to coax his children into just about everything, even sleep. He felt like a reluctant Tom Sawyer, making every activity sound worthwhile, enviable, desirable.

Exhausted, he collapsed on the old-but-still-in-good-shape couch that had belonged to his parents. It looked like something from an estate sale with its tufted camel back and curved wooden legs exposed.

"*X-Files* tonight," Erica announced, coming out of the bathroom and walking over to turn on the TV. She had watched the show since its first season in 1993, and Andrew began watching the following year when Nathan was a baby. He often would watch an entire episode with Nathan sleeping on his shoulder, gently rocking him, while Erica was at work. The show's unconventional subject matter of two FBI agents investigating strange crimes and bizarre phenomena appealed to both Erica and Andrew, so Erica began scheduling her nights off when the show was on because they enjoyed watching it together. This was their "date night." Their scheduled alone-together time in a marriage full of crabby, problematic toddlers, empty bank accounts, unrealized goals and abandoned dreams. This was their distraction, as much from the stress that filled their lives as from a marriage with little life in it, although Andrew couldn't see that. They laughed and talked about their children; they went through the motions. They "communicated," or so Andrew thought. And he had no doubt that he loved her, that they would always be together. That their marriage was the one thing he could count on.

Erica sat down on the springy couch beside Andrew, who laid his bent legs sideways on the couch so that his feet rested under his left hand. He hadn't responded to her announcement; he just absentmindedly began picking at an old callous on his left foot, slowly peeling the dead skin away as he watched the show.

Two DAYS LATER, Andrew pulled into the Southern Oregon Mental Health parking lot just in time for his appointment. He had been seeing a counselor for about two months regarding his depression and anxiety, once a week for the first month, and now every other week. He couldn't really tell if it was helping or not. It was good to get out of the house, to talk to another adult, to try to work through some of his issues, but he still felt like throwing his head through the glass window in his dining room whenever he felt the anxiety well up within him. The build-up of agitation created an unbearable combination of rage and depression. What was wrong? What was making him feel this way? He knew it had a lot to do with the fact that he had been home with the kids for three years, and he sorely needed to go back to work, but he didn't have a job to go back to. He had worked as a shift manager at Payless Drugstore when Nathan was born, and he felt that going back there would not be the best choice (nor had he had any offers to come back), but he didn't know what else to do. Three weeks ago, he had gone to an interview at a real estate office to be an assistant for one of the brokers: certainly not a dream job, but at least it was an office job. All seemed to have gone well, but two weeks later he realized that it was the first job for which he had applied and not been hired, and that didn't sit well with him. Now Erica was well into her term at school, so he would have to wait until December to start looking again, when the term ended. He couldn't take much more of being home alone with the kids.

He jogged from his car through the rain into the single-story brick building, gave his name to the receptionist, and looked around for a place to sit. The room smelled of disinfectant used to camouflage the smell of vomit. He took in a shallow breath, sat down on a vinyl-covered, thinly upholstered bench as far away from the two other people in the room as he could be, and avoided eye contact with them. Across from Andrew sat a plump, middle-aged woman, wearing a hairnet and clutching a plastic trash bag, who began hacking without resolve. Then Andrew glanced at the teenage girl in the corner, fidgeting, digging through her purse, her long, stringy brown hair falling in her face. He looked away quickly when he saw her arms with the track marks and stitches on her wrist. Andrew shuddered mentally. *Should I really be here?* he wondered. But he couldn't afford a private practice, so this would have to do. He needed something.

Moments later, Jim Beckman, the clinical psychologist he had been seeing, opened the door and called Andrew in. Jim, a gangly man in his fifties, was dressed in a light blue oxford cloth shirt, a pair of khakis, and brown loafers. Andrew wore what he called his "At-home Dad uniform:" blue jeans and a crewneck shirt (today it was striped with primary colors of varying widths), and black Converse Hi-top sneakers. He followed Jim into his small office. Its narrow walls were lined with shelves of books, and it had barely enough room for a desk with a computer on it, two thinly upholstered green chairs in front of it, and Jim's black swivel chair behind it.

"So, Andrew, how are you feeling?" came Jim's typically subdued voice.

Andrew often wondered whether Jim was tired, preoccupied, or just bored, which only added to Andrew's anxiety. Jim's face, even first thing in the morning, was greasy and off-putting, and Andrew found himself feeling uncomfortable looking into his counselor's gray, uninviting eyes, like standing at the mouth of a cold, dark cave and hesitating to go in out of the rain.

"I'm about the same as last time: not really feeling much better. I'm still peeling the skin off the bottoms of my feet, even when I don't realize I'm doing it."

"Have you tried wearing socks all the time?"

"Yes, but I just pull them off. I can't seem to stop the peeling. It feels good, but then I go too far and make my feet bleed and it hurts to walk on the parts that I peeled." But the peeling felt good, so primal, reptilian. He didn't know why he liked it, why it fascinated and obsessed him. It also seemed to soothe him somehow.

"Of course it hurts. Maybe you need to try something to distract yourself when you feel a desire to peel skin off your feet, like doing jumping jacks until the urge passes."

"Okay. I could try that." *Yeah, I'll put that on my To-Do List. Jumping jacks, for Christ's sake. I want an epiphany. Something that will snap me out of this pseudo-depression I'm in. Maybe one day while we're all away for the day the house will burn down and we can just start over.*

Jim leaned forward and continued, reminding Andrew of strategies they had discussed during previous sessions: taking walks twice a week, writing in his journal, going out dancing, which was something Andrew had said he liked to do and hadn't done for a long time. "Have you been implementing these activities into your life again?"

Andrew explained how hard it was to carve out time for himself, with Erica working five nights a week and going to school during the day, compounded by the fact that his children, especially Nathan, would not do well with a babysitter because of behavioral problems. Even Eileen was not without her issues. Since infancy, she seemed to be extremely sensitive to various stimuli. If they were carrying her and they walked into a room that was too bright, too dim, or with too many people, even if it was quiet, she would begin wailing and would not stop, even when removed from whatever had disturbed her. She would cry for two hours even while being held. They could never figure out what set her off. She cried even harder if they put her down. Now, as a toddler, the crying jags had given way to incessant whining and tantrums. It was no wonder none of their friends and relatives offered to babysit.

"I thought you were going to switch and she was going to stay home with the children for a while and you were going to get a job," Jim said, leaning back in his chair while lacing his fingers. He blotted his face with a dirty handkerchief.

"Yes, the last one I applied for I didn't get, and now Erica needs to finish out this term, so maybe around Christmas time, but no one's really hiring then."

Jim asked if Andrew had tried the breathing exercises they talked about.

The breathing exercises Jim suggested reminded Andrew of the birthing classes he went to with Erica and trying to implement them during Nathan's birth. He tried to breathe with her, to coach her, and she'd ended up shrieking at him to stop breathing on her, shrieking with each wave of labor that overpowered her. The breathing exercises were as useless to her then as they were to Andrew now: they offered no relief. But he told Jim they helped a little, although he was still constantly rearranging the chairs around the kitchen table. He would catch himself doing it every fifteen minutes sometimes, even when he didn't want to do it. He would look over and see them out of alignment and feel forced to go over and fix them, lining them up with the wood grain of the oak table. He probably did it at least twenty times a day. "I don't get mad at the kids over it; it doesn't really have anything to do with them."

"Well," Jim said, adjusting his seat. "They're toddlers, so I'm sure they move the chairs a bit throughout the day."

"I guess so. And my oldest knocks the chairs backward and lets them crash to the floor whenever he gets upset or frustrated about something."

"Like a temper tantrum?" Jim tapped his pen on his desk. Andrew bristled at the convenient, thoughtless label Jim stuck on a function of a developmental delay. A symptom. *You have a Masters in psychology and that's the best you can come up with? It's just a fucking temper tantrum? Come on.*

"Not really. He just gets so frustrated when he can't communicate with us." *It was never like a temper tantrum. It was more like a cry for help.*

Jim asked how the testing was coming along, and Andrew explained that they were still in the initial six-week diagnostic period. They'd been to the Early Childhood Development Center office a few times for tests, and the therapists had come to the house for home observations and interviews.

There would be a meeting in a couple of weeks to go over what services they could provide for Nathan.

Jim commended him for being proactive about having Nathan tested early, instead of waiting to see if he'd catch up. He suggested that once Nathan began receiving speech therapy, it would alleviate Andrew's own anxiety and depression.

Jim shifted in his seat again and cleared his throat. He then went on to discuss the subject of parentification, how Andrew had previously told him that he often took care of his brother and sister while growing up, and asked him to describe how he felt about it, how it related to him now being a parent.

He hadn't really stopped to think about it. That was just what was expected of him. He loved his baby sister to no end, guarded her like a precious heirloom. He remembered, though he was only eight years old when she was born, noticing the contours of Bernadette's cherubic face while he cradled her in his arms. This was his baby sister. He loved her before she was born, imagining her crawling on the floor, remembering how his parents had smiled at each other when they saw that their pregnancy announcement had been so well received. Solomon, who was five at the time, was also excited. They crawled around on the floor together that night, pretending to be babies, anticipating the arrival of their younger sibling. All Andrew told Jim was how old he'd been when Bernadette was born, and that he'd babysat her a lot. "She's always felt like more of a niece than a sister."

Jim said that it was common for adults who had been parentified as children to think of their younger siblings as nieces or nephews. "How old was she when you started taking care of her?"

"She was just one month old the first time."

"Your parents left an eight-year-old alone with a one-month-old?!" It was the most emotion he'd seen from Jim, the bulging eyes and shocked tone.

Andrew explained that there was a twelve-year-old babysitter there, a girl who didn't know anything about babies. She used to go upstairs into his mother's bathroom and play with her makeup. His sister started crying and the babysitter didn't know what to do, so Andrew started rocking her to comfort her. A few months later, his mother had him changing Bernadette's cloth diapers.

"That's parentification—placing too much responsibility on children too young to take care of younger siblings. You had also mentioned that you had migraines as a child?"

Andrew confirmed that he had, around ages eleven and twelve. He received frequent chiropractic treatments for about a year, and hadn't had any migraines since. He'd definitely had headaches throughout his teens and adulthood, but not the throbbing, relentless pain of the migraines, so intense he felt as if his skull would burst.

Jim then steered the discussion toward comparing Andrew's past status as a child-parent to his current status as a stay-at-home parent. He suggested that Andrew's identity had suffered as a result.

"Andrew, you need to start scheduling time for yourself; it's not going to happen on its own. Also, are you still against medication? You had mentioned wanting to avoid that, although I think you should consider it."

Andrew sighed. This was not the first counselor in his life who had recommended antidepressants, and he never wanted to become a statistic, didn't want to become dependent on them, so he had always refused. Jim had brought it up before, and Andrew had told him he wanted to try a non-medicated approach, but he was starting to think he might need the medication. He told Jim that nothing had really changed with doing the breathing exercises. "I still pull strands of hair off my head, still peel the skin around my fingernails and my feet, still rearrange the chairs around the table all day long. Still feel agitated and depressed all the time; I hate it. And I've been starting to have some episodes of insomnia, really having a hard time falling asleep. But I just don't want anything that's going to knock me out. I have to be able to function and take care of the kids if they get up during the night."

"I think you should talk to Dr. Taylor. She can prescribe a low dosage of something that would help you feel better. It doesn't have to be long-term, and she can answer all your questions about it. Put your mind at ease."

Andrew sighed again. "Okay. I think I'm ready for that." *At this point, I'll try anything.*

THAT NIGHT, ALONE on the couch, his children in bed, Andrew tried to find some answers. He set aside his thoughts about his own potential diagnosis (obsessive compulsive disorder, Jim had mentioned as probable, and, after he researched it, Andrew felt a dreaded certainty of it) and focused on his nagging concern about Nathan. Something was different about him, beyond his developmental delay in speech, but Andrew couldn't figure out what it was. He sat on the couch and thumbed through his copy of *What to Expect the Toddler Years*, published in 1994. He glanced at all of the topics under the heading "Some Chronic Health Problems," focused on mental retardation briefly (*No! He knew the entire alphabet! At three!*), and then checked the index for various sections on language development. "Language development: delayed, at 13 months; delayed, at 19 months; evaluating, at 19 months; factors affecting; frustration and; intelligence and." He knew that his son was severely delayed in that area. But if he was smart enough to learn the alphabet, and his hearing seemed fine, why couldn't he talk? Why wouldn't he talk? Andrew recalled pointing to a robin in the backyard last month as he crouched near Nathan. "Bird, Nathan. Say 'bird.' Can you say 'bird?'" And Nathan, unimpressed and unresponsive, had stared blankly at the robin while he sucked his fingers.

Andrew looked back at the "Some Chronic Health Problems" section. He had heard of autism when he was nine years old and read about it in his father's *Encyclopaedia Brittanica*. He didn't remember much about it, only that autistic people seemed to be in their own world. But, according to the description in *What to Expect the Toddler Years*, children with autism were not affectionate and did not make eye contact. Nathan was affectionate enough with family members and sometimes made eye contact with them. He just didn't talk. That alone did not mean he had autism. So . . . what, then? What about the screaming?

The ringing phone jolted Andrew off the couch. He made a mad dash to grab it before it woke up the kids.

"Hi, Andrew," he heard his mother's pensive voice. He could see the crease in her forehead deepen as she greeted him and then sighed with a hint of impatience. Andrew instantly felt impatient too. He finally gets the kids in bed, collapses on the couch to relax, and she calls. It was a familial love that he felt for her, tolerant, detached even. He had never been at risk for being branded a mama's boy. Too independent for that. His mother had always said he'd never been the cuddly type anyway. "Did I catch you at a bad time?"

Andrew listened a moment for a crabby whimper, almost wishing there was one to necessitate postponing the phone call, but the duplex was silent. All he could hear was the rain tapping on the roof. He had been looking forward to some free time. "No, this is fine. The kids are in bed, and I was just reading."

"Erica at work?"

"Yeah, she's closing tonight," Andrew said. "She probably won't be home until about 3:30. Friday and Saturday nights are the busiest."

"Well," his mother began, "I need to talk to you about something important." She almost sounded business-like, as if she were a manager confronting him about sales dropping in his department.

Like I don't have enough to deal with in my own life, Andrew thought. He mentally groaned, but he decided to sound supportive for her sake. "What's that?"

"Um, I'm not quite sure where to start." She paused, then tentatively continued. "Well, you know your father and I have been sleeping in separate rooms for the past several months, right? Has Bernadette mentioned that to you?" She mentioned his sister's name as if she were an ally of sorts.

How the hell would Bernadette know? Andrew wondered. She had been away at college for the past several months, but his brother had stayed there last year. "Actually, Sol mentioned something about that a few months ago before he moved." No big deal. After twenty-seven years of marriage, a break might be a good idea. Probably even necessary.

"Well, I've just been dealing with a lot of past issues in your father's and my marriage, and I needed some space to figure some things out. I don't know if this will surprise you, but we haven't had the happiest marriage."

Andrew sensed where this was going. His ears began ringing, and he felt a hollowness in his chest. "Didn't you love him?"

His mother switched to a pacifying tone. "Yes, yes, of course, honey. I loved him then and I still love him. I was blindly in love, in fact. I didn't see the signs when we were dating that he might not be right for me."

"What do you mean?" Andrew asked.

His mother sounded almost as if she were reciting a list, defending herself. She told Andrew that his father had talked about wanting children, but when the time came he had no idea or inclination of how to interact with them or take care of them. He figured that he was the breadwinner, and that was all he had to be, like most of his contemporaries in the 1970s. He was the head of his Catholic household, he paid the bills, took his family to church every Sunday, didn't cheat on his wife or beat his kids, and he expected to come home to a clean house with dinner on the table. That was the arrangement. She had her role and he had his.

Andrew thought of his father, just about to retire from thirty years of city government administrative work, coming home wearing a suit and carrying his hard leather briefcase every night, all those years. "I remember he took Sol and me to bowling tournaments," he said quietly.

"That was after years of dealing with him spending all of his free time somewhere else instead of with his family. First it was night school or the library, while he was getting his Masters. Then he got into bowling. He used to come home from work, shovel down whatever I had prepared for a nice dinner, and then run out the door to go bowling, two, sometimes three times a week. It caused years of dissent in our marriage, Andrew. It wasn't right. And there were other issues as well. Our sex life was, well, it was often lacking. Many times your father was impotent, and angry about it. And I, of course, always tried to be understanding and supportive—"

"Mom! I really don't want to hear about Dad's and your sex life! Just because I'm an adult doesn't mean it's something I'm comfortable listening to you talk about!"

"Sorry. You're right. I probably shouldn't have said that to you." His mother sighed. "It's just years of not being respected, not feeling like I had a partner, not being listened to. Twenty-seven years of marriage is a long time to have issues build up. Issues that have caused years of resentment and anger. I haven't decided yet what I really want to do. But I do know that your father and I definitely need marriage counseling, and I need to be separated from him in order to have a clear perspective while we're going through it."

"So you and Dad are separating? Is that what you're saying?" The hollowness returned to Andrew's chest.

"Yes, Andrew. I really feel that's what I need while we're in counseling."

Andrew took a deep breath. "Well, I certainly agree that you both need counseling. I just don't understand why you need to separate, right before the holidays. Is it because Dad's retiring early and he'd be spending more time at home now?"

His mother sighed, exasperated. "It really doesn't have anything to do with that. It's just been building up for years, and I need to make some changes. I can't continue with things the way they are any longer. I know it's right before the holidays, but I have to do this." Andrew noticed a pleading tone in her voice.

"It's okay, Mom. I'll deal with it. I know this is hard for you, and I'm sure it's not a decision you've made lightly. It just seems so strange. I don't really know how I feel. I don't resent you for it. I want you to know I'm supportive of whatever you feel you need to do. I just need to think, maybe," Andrew said. He felt an urge to get off the phone; this was Big. He assured her that he wasn't upset and that they would talk again soon, relieved to have averted the imminent guilt trip by cutting the conversation short. Placating his mother was something he'd learned early on, as if to some extent he'd had to take care of her, too: meeting her emotional needs that his father apparently didn't.

Andrew hung up the phone and stood in the kitchen a moment. *So,* he thought as he walked around the kitchen table straightening the chairs, *my parents are no longer the "united front." Never really were.*

Andrew shook his head as he walked to the bathroom. He felt like he had been tricked, somehow. It all seemed so hypocritical. He had thought his parents would always be together. Of course, probably all children thought that. But now he was an adult. He wondered how other adults felt when their parents divorced. What were common reactions? He had no idea. All of his friends whose parents had divorced did so when the kids were kids, not adults.

Can't believe she told me he was impotent. You don't tell your son that about his father!

Andrew brushed his teeth, peed, and walked into his bedroom. It was small; they had given the larger bedroom to the kids. There was barely room for the queen-sized bed that was a wedding gift from his parents (*Oh, the irony!* he thought) and the gleaming dark cherry wooden dresser he had bought himself as a college graduation present with the money his grandmother had given him. The bed sheets and down comforter were a light cream color, magnifying the starkness of the bare white walls. The one shared wall in the duplex was at the head of their bed, and they often heard their neighbor's snores. On Andrew's dresser was a black and white artsy-looking 8 x 10 photo of Erica and him on their wedding day, walking through a grove of birch trees in a local park. The digital clock glowed 12:30 as he climbed into bed.

Andrew's thoughts first focused on his father, and the sad fact that, aside from the occasional bowling games and family camping trips, he really hadn't been that close to him, he admitted. He never felt that "buddy" father-son relationship that so many of his friends seemed to have with their fathers. His father just never talked to him, never asked him how he felt about things, or what he thought. Neither had his mother, for that matter. Solomon felt the same way, and he felt sure it was even worse for Bernadette. She had never even gone bowling with them. Andrew could remember his dad going bowling a lot, usually without them. He never thought much of it as a child; that was just what his dad did. It was the way things were. How could he have known it should have been different? But their dad loved them, in his own imperfect way. On the rare nights when he was home before they went to bed, he would read to them—short picture books that could be finished in one sitting—and kiss them goodnight. He just had his own agenda and fit them in from time to time. They didn't think to yearn for more, becoming emotional camels, a little every now and then tiding them over.

Andrew couldn't sleep. *Insomnia again, at least three nights a week now.* He remembered how on Saturdays he and Sol would sit in the family room and watch cartoons on their little thirteen-inch color TV while Dad would mow the lawn of their quarter-acre, suburban middle-class home. Once, before Bernadette was born, he distinctly recalled they were watching *The Donny and Marie Show*, and they noticed their father gritting his teeth and cursing as he shoved the push mower around the yard, their spooked tabby cat dashing off to the neighbor's yard, ears back. Andrew and Sol rolled on the floor with laughter, and then hid and watched their father some more, traversing the entire yard in that manner.

Mom was probably masturbating somewhere.

Then their father would come in, comment how he was sweating like a pig out there, look at them with disdain, as if at the ages of four and six, they should be the ones mowing the lawn, and then grab a big, frosty glass with the Coors logo painted on it out of the freezer and pour himself a beer. *What happened to those Coors glasses? Maybe Sol has them.*

Andrew's mind kept turning as much as his body did. Finally he dared to look again at the clock, which read 3:13, and he felt comforted realizing that Erica should be getting home soon. The rain had abated.

Why can't I sleep? he thought, for the eighteenth time. *At least the kids sleep through the night now. Oh, the irony. Now that they can, I can't.*

TWO

Erica pulled up the long asphalt driveway of her home. After her busy day, it felt like the last stretch of a marathon. She was home and she could go to sleep. The duplex was situated back from the street, another thing that she and Andrew liked about it. Not only was it quieter, there was also less of a chance that Nathan could run out into the street. They could probably catch him before he reached it, escape artist that he had become.

It was 11:30 on a Saturday night, a good four hours earlier than she usually came home on Saturday nights, but she was still tired. She had made it through another long week: five days of school, five days of work, seven days of fitting in homework and time with her family. She found that bartending fit in with her school schedule better than most jobs, and, being the bar manager, she could choose which nights to work the dinner shift and which nights to work the late-night shift. She usually worked the late-night shifts on Friday and Saturday because she didn't have class the next day, but that night she had only worked the dinner shift and had hoped to be home by 9:30 to spend some time with the kids before they went to bed. Sometimes, *often*, she felt like the ghost parent. Barely there. An occasional presence. Part of her envied Andrew, not only because he spent more time with the children, but also because he had finished college before they were born. Well, with two months to spare, so only just. But he was done. He could rest on his laurels. She had so much farther to go it wasn't even worth figuring out at this point. It would take this side of forever.

She grabbed her purse and got out of her little white mid-eighties, four-door car, which she had owned for five years. It wasn't an exciting car, but it got her to class and work, grocery shopping, and the kids to doctor appointments. They had sold Andrew's little pick-up truck about two years ago to pay off some bills. "And besides," she had told Andrew, "we won't all be able to fit in there in eight months!" Andrew had looked at her, smiling. "You're pregnant?!" She nodded as he threw his arms around her. "I can't wait!" he said. Erica shook her head as she realized that she rarely heard exuberance in her husband's voice any more.

She walked through the front door and saw Andrew on the couch, reading. "Hi," she said. Andrew just looked at her with a sullen face and went back to his book. Erica could hardly remember a time when he wasn't like this—unresponsive unless agitated. She found her husband insufferable. Maybe that was why she insisted on working and going to school: to spend as little time as possible in his negative presence. It darkened the house even on the brightest summer day and now, nearing winter, it cast an unbearable bleakness. Andrew had been depressed for so long that it didn't seem like he could ever get back to being the spontaneous guy with the dreams of living in the south of France, the one who had planned fun little weekend outings for them, like to the coast or Crater Lake. The one who liked to surprise her by baking chocolate chip cookies or bringing home flowers for no reason. Yes, he had done those things. Where was that person? Erica could hardly remember him now and had stopped trying. It was all she could do just to get through the day.

As she walked across the living room he blurted out, "Thought you were only working the dinner shift tonight so we could spend some time together before the kids went to bed."

Please. Not now. Please just let him get swallowed up by that couch. "Yes, Andrew, that was the plan. Then Rick came in late, and I had to keep working until he got there. It happens sometimes! I'm the manager, so I have to cover when someone's late!"

"You could have called!"

"It was too busy! It's Saturday night, Andrew! You know I'm at work. I'm not at your beck and call!" *Why can't he be more understanding?*

"We're married, Erica. Look, I know no one else you work with is married, but that's what you do when you're married: call to let me know you'll be late. It's common courtesy!"

She didn't like feeling so defensive, didn't like the way he made the anger well up in her so that she almost wished she could smack him. Sometimes she hated him. "I have enough stress from my job and school, and I don't need it from you!"

"Then let me work!" Andrew said.

"Then find a job!"

"For a decent-paying office job, I will have to work days, and you're in school during the day, so how the hell is that supposed to work?"

"Andrew, we've discussed this! I don't want to talk about this now! Jesus, I just got home! Can I take a shower, please?!" Erica said as she went into the bathroom.

She shut the door, set down her purse, and ran the fingers of both hands over the top of her head. She breathed deeply, turned on the water in the shower, and began removing her "work clothes." She wore a black knit shirt, fitted but not too revealing, since she had worked the dinner shift and needed to look more professional than she did for the nightclub hours. Late night bartending called for cleavage. Not that she had more than most, but she had learned to make the most of what she had. The better she looked, the better her tips. She removed her sterling silver Celtic knot on the black leather choker, her chunky black platform loafers, her black lace miniskirt. She caught a glimpse of her wide-set shoulder blades framing her tattoo of an ethereal crescent moon that was nearly ten years old. It was hard to pick out a favorite of the three that she had. The others were on her upper arms—a wolf on one and a Celtic knot on the other, both even older than the moon. At sixteen she had marched herself into her tattoo-artist uncle's parlor and asked for some ink. Willy—"Wild Willy" as he was called—thought it was a great idea: two big tattoos on a sixteen-year-old girl's upper arms. Well, even though she was young when she got them, she had no regrets as an adult. Uncle Willy did good work, the first artist in the family. To create, to render something so beautiful it made people gasp and stare, that was Erica's dream. She wondered if Uncle Willy ever felt that way. He couldn't have done it just because it was cool. His work was too exquisite, the gray wolf with its knowing eyes that pierced you, dared you to change, to feel, to believe, to dream. The Celtic knot with its intricate spirals, endlessly entwined, drawing you in, to be connected to something greater than yourself: eternal life.

Erica tested the spray of water and stepped over the side of the tub. She loved steamy showers and closed her eyes as the water poured over her face and hair. She turned around to soak the back of her neck and shoulders. She thought of her Great Aunt Maggie, who had taught her to take showers. Aunt Maggie had also taught her to brush her teeth, tie her shoes, bake bread, wash the clothes, and many other things. Auntie, as Erica called her, had taken care of her for the first five years of her life while her hippie parents, she later learned, were running drugs from Mexico. She remembered one summer at age thirteen when she was visiting Auntie for a few weeks how she had overheard a conversation between Uncle Willy and her grandfather, Maggie's brother-in-law, who, Erica realized in retrospect, was probably drunk. He had been drunk every day since his wife Jeanette had died in a car accident before Erica was born. She had, presumably, fallen asleep at the wheel and hit a cement mixer head-on. Erica overheard Uncle Willy saying something like, "No, Dad, Raquel was only sixteen when Erica was born. Remember she wanted to give her up for adoption and Aunt Maggie wouldn't let her?" Erica recalled the sting she felt when she first learned that her mother hadn't wanted her. Her mother had explained/rationalized, "We were just too young to have you when you came along," as if she, Erica, had insisted upon it. She didn't really feel any resentment as an adult, and now as a mother herself, who had also dealt with an unplanned pregnancy, she realized how young her mother truly had been. Giving her up for adoption probably would have been the most responsible choice, except that Aunt Maggie had stepped in. Aunt Maggie's teenage daughter had been killed in the car accident with Erica's grandmother, who was Maggie's sister. One year later, Erica was born, and Erica wasn't sure if her presence had helped to fill the emptiness of the loss of Maggie's only child, or if she just served as a distraction from constant grief. But Erica did know that Auntie loved her. A resentful divorcée whose husband had run off with a much younger flower child in 1967, Maggie had never remarried. She was full-blooded Miwok, proud, independent, and feisty. And she was the one who had always encouraged Erica's love of art and her talent for drawing.

MONDAY MORNING, ERICA walked briskly across the campus of Southern Oregon University on her way to class. She and Andrew had argued again that morning about the car, how it would be a good idea to have it home in case of an emergency with the kids and he needed to get to the hospital. Erica pointed out that they were literally one block away from the hospital, and that an ambulance could be at the house in less than five minutes. She, however, could not rely on the bus service, which only came along every half hour and might cause her to be late for class or work. Besides, she often got off work way too late to take the bus home. She needed her car.

Erica hurried to class, to avoid being late as much as to get in out of the cold wind. The sprawling campus was located in the foothills of the Siskiyou Mountains and had been landscaped like a park with many trees and bushes and benches along the asphalt paths curving around the buildings, the oldest of which dated back to the 1920s, its Italian Renaissance architecture still stately and elegant. Erica had photographed it for one of her classes last year. The school's enrollment of just over five thousand made up one-fourth of the population of the city of Ashland, and, it being on the small side as universities go, Erica frequently ran into people she knew.

As she rounded a corner headed toward the art building, she nearly crashed into her friend and previous co-worker, Gavin. One second she saw brick and the next second she saw a wall of plaid flannel in front of her face.

"Oh, my God, Erica!" Gavin exclaimed, stopping short. He grinned slowly, and she could tell right away that he was stoned, but that was the norm.

"Gavin! Hi! I was just running to class!"

"Me too! How are you?" Gavin spread his arms to give her a hug. He was a good six inches taller than Erica, and broad, with shoulder length brown hair and a somewhat chubby face that hadn't been shaved in about two weeks. He was a sociology major on what he called an eight-year plan. She found it absurd that he was taking so long when he didn't have to work his way through school, as she did. His parents were footing the bill; he bartended one night a week for the social perks of it. He'd met his girlfriend Simone, Erica's best friend, when she leaned across the bar and crooned that she'd have a Screaming Orgasm.

"Oh, fine. Just tired with work, school, and toddlers to take care of," she said quickly. *But you wouldn't care to hear about that.*

Gavin said it must be tough, and Erica noticed his glazed eyes trying to feign concern, trying to function through the warbling effects of his vice. That was the real reason why it was taking him so long to get through his undergraduate work.

"Yeah," she said, "especially now because we've been short-handed at work and I've had to put in a lot of hours." Gavin hadn't worked for six months, and Erica figured he was too stoned to pick up on her hint, but she threw it out there anyway.

"Oh, hey, that reminds me, I just met this girl who moved into town and is looking for work. She seems cool, and I know she won't screw you over. She really wants to make a good impression because she just got out of prison in California," Gavin said.

"Just got out, huh? Drugs?"

"Yeah, but she moved here so she wouldn't get back into it. She's living with relatives, and they have kids, so she should be all right. Her name's Brooke; she's about our age."

"Okay, I'll talk to her. I'm off tonight, but tell her to come in around 4:30 any other night this week," Erica said, starting to move away. "I gotta run!"

"Okay, thanks, Erica! Give us a call so we can go for a hike or something!" Gavin called over his hunched shoulder.

"I will!" *Since I have so much free time*, Erica thought. Well, maybe hiring someone else would help, once she was fully trained. Trained! Like circus animals. But her life felt like a circus, so that wasn't too far from the truth. She hurried on into the building and slipped through the back door of her art history classroom just as the professor walked up to his podium to begin.

ERICA RETURNED HOME that afternoon to a clean house (if her husband *did* have obsessive-compulsive disorder, at least it was not without benefits) and warm chocolate chip cookies. Andrew had loved to bake; he had worked as a baker for about a year and a half during college and had told her that he always helped his mom bake while he was growing up. *A cookie-baking mom instead of a pot-selling one.* She often marveled at the vast differences in their upbringing.

"You make the best cookies," she told him, biting into one, so surprised at the treat. It had probably been a year since Andrew had baked anything. She felt a glimmer of hope. This was a good sign, something he hadn't done for a long time. At least he might be in a good mood today, not antagonistic. *Dark.* She sat down at the table and glanced at her children in the living room as they watched a video.

"Thanks. I'm glad you like them," Andrew said as he wiped down the kitchen counter where he had made them. There was something testy about his voice, and Erica's small hope deflated. It was like he baked the cookies just to prove to her that he still could. Not in a loving, generous way. In a spiteful, defensive way.

She did not have the mental energy to combat him, to be mired. *Relax, Andrew,* she wanted to tell him, begging him. In a tired, non-threatening I'll-talk-to-you-but-don't-pick-a-fight tone she asked how his day was.

"Oh, fine. Nothing unusual. We played in the backyard for a while, had lunch, and played with blocks."

"That's good. Home visit tomorrow?" Erica asked. *We might as well be commenting on the weather. And who knows, we might have to resort to that at this rate, at this level of non-intimacy.*

"Yeah, at two o'clock." Andrew laid the washcloth over the faucet and came over and leaned on the table. "Do you think we could all go for a walk this afternoon? After you relax for a bit?"

She had diffused it. He sounded genuine. *At least for now.*

Erica grew so weary of his mood swings, trying to second-guess him. It was enough to have to do that with Nathan every time they were in an environment that was potentially problematic for him, like the grocery store. "Sure. We could go right now, if you want. I'm game." Erica stood up. Taking a walk was something they could do together and, barring any sudden noises that would send Nathan into hysterics, they might enjoy themselves. It happened a few times a month. Occasionally someone would fire up a lawn mower right as they were passing by and Nathan would shriek inconsolably and they would have to go home, neighbors staring the entire way. At least he didn't protest the next time they attempted to go for a walk. There must have been something about them that Nathan liked.

"Yeah, that sounds great," Andrew said. "I'll get the backpacks." He walked through the living room back to their bedroom, saying, "Guys, we're going to go for a walk now!"

Erica went into the living room and said, "Come on, Nathan, let's go tinkle before we go for our walk." She put her hand on his shoulder and guided him, without any opposition, to the bathroom and helped him pull down his pants. He sat on the toilet, and Erica heard a trickle.

"Good job," she said. *At least he's potty trained,* Erica thought. She went into the kids' room to get hats and jackets.

Andrew walked by with the child carriers. "You want me to take Nate?"

"No, I can take him. Probably by spring he'll be too heavy for me, but this is short enough around the block, so I'll be fine," Erica said. She handed Eileen's hat and jacket to Andrew.

"Okay, if you're sure."

"Yeah, you take Eileen." Erica led Nathan out of the bathroom and put on his dark green fleece hooded jacket. Then she picked him up and put his legs through the openings of the larger child carrier that Andrew had set up against the couch. She fastened the straps on Nathan and then sat down in front of the carrier while she put her own arms through the padded straps and then stood up. "Man, Nate, you are getting heavy," she muttered as she fastened the hip belt and distributed Nathan's weight.

She stood waiting for Andrew as he tried to fasten the straps on Eileen's shoulders and chest while she sat in the carrier. Erica mentally sighed as she realized that Andrew had slipped back into his negative state. It was like tip-toeing through broken glass with him. She could sense his frustration and walked over to see what the problem was. The straps were twisted, tangled, and stuck under one of Eileen's legs, but Andrew became so agitated, huffing and gritting his teeth, that Erica couldn't stand it.

Relax, Andrew! she mentally pleaded. *It's not that big of a deal!*

Finally Andrew muttered, "Damn this thing," and pulled Eileen out of the pack and set her on the floor while he ripped the straps out so he could straighten them, sucking in his breath.

"It's all messed up," Andrew said through gritted teeth, still looking at the straps and tugging on them.

"Forget it!" Erica said, disgusted. She stormed out the front door and shut it behind her, Nathan on her back.

I try so hard to be in a good mood around him, to do things he wants to do, to be positive, even though I'm tired and I have homework to do. Tangled straps are not worth freaking out about. We were just taking a walk! Everything is so complicated with him. It's not even worth it most of the time. I can't even stand to be around him now. I can't deal with his negativity. I can't continue to be happy for both of us with all the stress I'm under! He has really changed. He's not the same person at all.

Erica pounded the pavement without noticing her surroundings. Low clouds blanketed the nearby mountains and blocked the sun. She walked up the hill they lived on, passing a few old Victorian homes, a few Crafts-man bungalows, and some tract homes from the 1960s all mixed together. Most of the houses were kept up, but a few were run down or just in terrible need of a paint job. Then she turned left at the street that ran perpendicular between hers and the street that the hospital was on.

Erica wondered if Nathan had noticed the turn of events regarding the family walk. Although he rarely spoke, he was an intuitive child. She recalled one afternoon almost a year ago while Andrew was at the grocery store and she was home alone with the kids. It was close to Christmas, and they had all of the presents hidden in their closet. While she was breastfeeding Eileen, Nathan had been exploring, and Erica heard him in the closet. She got up out of the rocking chair, balancing Eileen in her left arm, still on the breast (Erica was amazed at her own ability to do that), and walked down the hall and into their room. Nathan stood in front of the open closet door, looking at its contents, and stated in a flat voice, "Toys." Erica, stunned that he had spoken, gently shut the closet door and led Nathan out of the room. "Yes, those are toys," she said. "And they are for Christmas. So if you open them now, then you won't have any toys for Christmas. So we're not going to have those toys right now, okay?" Nathan somehow seemed to understand; he did not protest, and he never went in the closet again.

Andrew appeared to not be coming after them, which was fine with Erica. She thought about how much Andrew had changed since she first met him at Payless Drugstore four years earlier. She was usually attracted to men taller than herself (although she would never tell him that), but she was still attracted to his charming, friendly demeanor, his sun-kissed good looks (she always liked blond surfer-types), and his intelligence. He was two terms away from getting his BA in English when they met, and she liked the fact that he was a writer. They talked a lot while at work, which was the only time they saw each other. She was still living with Rob, her boyfriend who had moved up with her from Weed, California, where she had been living with her mother and taking classes at College of the Siskiyous. She transferred to Southern Oregon University (then called Southern Oregon State College) in the fall of 1993, and Rob had moved up with her. He lasted five months in Ashland and decided that he missed all his drinking buddies in Weed, so he moved back. Erica was glad. She didn't miss having to sleep next to him after he passed out nearly every night ("There's nothing to do in this town!" he routinely complained. *Try getting a job*, Erica wanted to tell him. *That'll give you something to do. Try reading a book.*) and snored, and even peed in the bed a few times. *Nothing like waking up in cold urine, especially someone else's.*

Erica wasted no time in asking Andrew out as soon as Rob had moved. As they were counting their tills one night, closing up, she said to him, "We're all going to The Pub tonight after work for a drink. Want to come along?" And then when Andrew showed up and found her sitting alone at the table, she casually said, "I wonder where everyone else is. Billy and Josh said they were both coming." Andrew figured out her little scam a few months later, and they both had a good laugh over it.

She loved talking with him. He was smart; she practically hung on every word he said. They talked about books they both liked, bands they'd both seen, foods they both hated, and the fact that they both feared spiders and had been nude artist models for art classes while in college, an unusual thing to have in common. They were clicking so well on their first "date" that Erica felt comfortable telling him that she had had cysts on her ovaries when she was twenty and couldn't have children. "That's okay," Andrew had said. "I'm not ready to have kids yet, anyway. And we can always adopt!" He'd said it in a jovial tone, as if to displace the awkwardness of discussing that topic on a first date. But Erica hadn't felt any awkwardness. She felt comfortable bringing it up with him. He talked like he wanted to have a future with her, and she craved the stability that he seemed to possess.

The next day at work, she found a card inside her locker that had been slipped through one of the vents on her locker door. "Erica" was scrawled across the yellow envelope. She opened it and pulled out a card with a little cartoon guy waving at a little house as he was walking away. Inside was printed, "Thanks for the lovely time!" and Andrew had written underneath it, "I really enjoyed your company last night. I hope you don't think it too presumptuous of me, but I wish I could have kissed you goodnight. Maybe next time!" Erica melted. How did he know how much she loved getting cards? Flowers were nice, but to a reader, cards were the best. She had a whole shoebox-full in her closet, some she had bought for herself, just because she liked them.

Two days later, they went out to lunch together and she told him about a store in Redding, California, that sold rock band T-shirts and memorabilia and cool studded belts and jewelry. She mentioned a black leather wrist band with silver hoops on it that she liked. Andrew suggested that since they both had the day off, they drive down there and see if the store still had it. He was willing to drive four hours round-trip for a bracelet for her! By the time they got to the store and he actually bought it for her, she thought she was in love.

Andrew gave her cards at least once a month for the first year. Then he cut back to just her birthday, Valentine's Day, and Mother's Day. As if directly related to that, at the same time Andrew became sullen, negative, and almost constantly agitated. What had happened to the spontaneous, generous man she thought she fell in love with? It didn't matter anymore. All the cards in the world couldn't change the undeniable fact that she had fallen out of love with him. And for a while, she thought, maybe she never really was in love to begin with. Maybe she only thought she was in love with Andrew because she truly wanted to be. Or thought she should be. Maybe she had been in love for a little while, a glimmering. But if it had been there at all, Andrew killed it. By sinking further into that couch every night, further into his dark depression, he took the love with him, until she no longer felt any of it. *Because it really wasn't about the cards. It wasn't about driving to Redding for a bracelet. It was the love.* She knew that he loved her more than anyone ever had and that was all she thought she needed. Aunt Maggie always told her, "Honey, you gotta marry a man who loves you more than you love him." So she did.

Three

Actually, we have a history of early talkers in my family," Andrew said to Sally McIntyre, Nathan's caseworker from Early Childhood Development Center. Sally made it seem so easy, like everything would be all right. Her voice and her presence felt comforting to Andrew, and trustworthy. He wanted to believe in her.

She was short but hardy, with short curly blond hair and bright green eyes, so vibrant that Andrew figured they were colored contact lenses. They reflected an energy in her that Andrew lacked, vitality combined with serenity, and wisdom. Was that peace? He wished he knew.

Sally, along with two assistants, had come for the twice-weekly home visits in the continuing six-week diagnostic period to determine Nathan's needs and assess his development. She asked Andrew questions from a pediatric evaluation questionnaire while the others "played" with Nathan, and Eileen had joined in as well.

"Oh, that's interesting," Sally said as she wrote something on her clipboard. Her pleasant demeanor and warm smile put Andrew at ease. He figured she was probably about Erica's age. He wondered how many years of school she had needed to become a caseworker. The two assistants who had come with her were both older.

"Yes, my mother claims I started saying single words at seven months, and my siblings started talking early as well."

"That *is* early," Sally said. "Now what about ear infections?"

"He's only had one." Andrew recalled how Nathan was only two weeks old and he had taken him in to check his weight and make sure the jaundice had subsided, and the doctor checked his ears and then glared at Andrew when she said that Nathan had an ear infection. As if he had left him out on the back porch all night long or something, and that had caused it.

Sally then asked about Nathan reaching gross motor milestones: rolling over, sitting up, crawling, pulling up to stand, walking. Andrew told her that he did everything right when the book said he should.

"He started walking at ten months and was running by thirteen."

"Yes, his gross motor skills seem to be great; he looks very active."

"Oh, he is! If he wants something on the kitchen counter, he'll just push a chair over and get it himself!" *This is easy enough*, Andrew thought. They went on to discuss sleep patterns and appetite, mostly inconsequential topics that Nathan didn't have any notable problems with.

"Is he able to show and receive affection?"

"Oh, yes, he's very affectionate with family members and extended family," Andrew said. He felt relief at being able to say it.

"That's good. How does he do interacting with peers?"

"Well, aside from Eileen, he doesn't have too many opportunities to interact with other children, and when I take him to a park, he doesn't seem to know what to do with them. One time a friend came over with her son, who's about the same age, and Nathan just kept bumping him with his body and laughing. It was like he was trying to play but didn't know how. And the other little boy got upset and thought Nathan was being mean."

"Well, we have a few different programs that can help with socialization skills. We'll have a meeting in two weeks to discuss Nathan's placement, and we'll be sure to put him in a program that will address all of his needs," Sally said. "Now, if you could please fill out this last questionnaire. It's just part of the diagnostic profile to assess his skills: things he can do, things he can't do, words he says, things that bother him, stuff like that. I'll go and jot down a few more observations while you're working on that." Sally got up from the kitchen table and walked over to Nathan, who was sitting on the couch facing the back of it where he had lined up a series of small toy cars end to end on the back of the couch. He was laying his head to one side at the end of the line of cars to stare at them while he sucked his fingers, something Andrew saw him do quite often.

"Hi, Nathan, what are you doing?" Sally asked.

Nathan removed his fingers long enough to repeat "What are you doing?" without looking at Sally.

Great, the eye contact thing, Andrew thought. *The mimicking thing.* The easy part was over too soon. He glanced over at Eileen, who was trying to put together a Mr. Potato Head toy and getting frustrated. One of the assistants, a middle-aged woman with long brown hair, helped her with it. Andrew turned his attention to the questionnaire.

The questions were as Sally had described. He began filling them out, mentally groaning as he saw the long list of words that most thirty-six month olds typically say, knowing that Nathan did not even say one-fourth of that list.

Nathan let out a sharp squeal and Andrew snapped his head in that direction. Sally held a primary-colored mechanical pen, and the low whirring noise of the motor had upset Nathan.

"I'm sorry!" Sally said. "I didn't know that would bother him!" She put the pen in her bag.

"You should hear him when I turn on the vacuum cleaner," Andrew said. "Mechanical sounds really seem to upset him."

"I'll remember that," Sally said. Andrew was impressed by her combination of professionalism and concern.

He finished up with the list of words. *That didn't take long,* he thought with sadness, and he started on the self-care section. *Dresses self?* Sometimes. *Feeds self?* Uses fork, but not spoon. *Reaction to bathing?* Distress while shampooing hair. Andrew went on to the behavior section. *Does the child engage in any repetitive calming behavior?* Sucks fingers, twirls hair at back of head. *Does the child bang his/her head?* Yes. Andrew thought about how often Nathan banged his head on the low windows in their living room. He didn't do it hard, but he did it frequently. He also liked to bang his head on Andrew's back while he was sitting on the floor, and he always sucked his fingers whenever he banged his head.

He kept thinking of Nathan when he was a baby, how much he held him, rocked him, carried him around everywhere, showing him everything about their life together. He remembered how he would hold him facing outward so he could look at things, and, swaying gently and humming, he would stand in front of the baby Mickey and Minnie Mouse pictures on the wall of Nathan's bedroom. Then he would slowly, slowly walk down the stairs of the two-story duplex they had lived in at the time, and Nathan would stiffen his little body and fling his arms out to his side as if he felt he were falling, even though Andrew held him close to his chest. *My precious baby boy.* He remembered how he would think that every day, overcome with emotion because this was *his* child, *his* son. Because he couldn't believe it was possible to love someone so much.

Erica was home, and it was time to vacuum. It seemed crazy to Andrew that they had to schedule certain household necessities for the few times that they were both home together (*but then, I'm always home*, he thought). He had to wait for Erica to be home so that he could do the grocery shopping (Nathan got upset too easily in stores). Both of them had to be there to wash Nathan's hair. And of course, vacuuming was not without problems. There were times when just standing too long in front of the closet door in the hallway (where the vacuum was kept) was enough to send Nathan screaming through the house. Woe to any guests who opened the closet door just to hang up their coats. The resulting trauma often made Andrew prefer sweeping the rug with a broom. After all, the indoor-outdoor carpeting certainly didn't create much drag, and it was worth avoiding another episode of Nathan's hysteria.

But sweeping the carpet could only get it so clean, and Erica was home, so Andrew announced that it was time to vacuum. Nathan ran to his room wailing, and Eileen, who enjoyed imitating her older brother, joined him.

"Come on, guys, let's go play outside. Then you won't hear the vacuum," Erica said as she walked into their room. She picked up Nathan, still thrashing and wailing, and carried him back through the house and out the door in the kitchen that led to the backyard, with Eileen following.

As soon as they were outside, Andrew heard Nathan's yells diminish, and he went to get out the vacuum cleaner and begin. He had inherited his parents' twenty-seven-year-old Eureka upright, which, he thought as he rolled his eyes, had probably been a wedding gift in 1970. Was it a bad omen for his own marriage that he'd inherited one of his parents' wedding gifts, now that his parents were separating? It was also probably louder than newer vacuum cleaners, he guessed, and hoped they could buy a new one soon that might be less stressful for Nathan. When Andrew finished, he unplugged the old machine and wound the cord around the hooks on the back of it. He put it away and opened the door to announce that the reign of terror had ended.

Erica and the kids came back in the house a minute later, just as Andrew had straightened the last chair around the kitchen table. He and Erica hadn't said much to each other since the day they were supposed to go for a walk together. Each felt that the other had overreacted, and neither was willing to take responsibility by apologizing. They ended up deciding not to talk about it anymore, but they didn't talk about anything else either. Andrew felt Erica getting more and more distant and felt himself to be powerless. She had been the shot-caller in their marriage from day one. She'd held the emotional purse-strings long before the financial. He felt like a kid again, the sick feeling in his stomach when he knew he was in trouble with his parents but wasn't sure why.

So THIS IS what a psychiatrist's office looks like, Andrew thought when he had first entered the room. He had never been to see an actual "shrink" before, just counselors. Dr. Taylor, wearing a navy suit with a soft green silk shirt, barely looked thirty-five. She sat behind her large mahogany desk which faced two plush maroon chairs (Andrew sat in one) and took notes on a yellow legal pad as Andrew answered her questions. Off to the right was a couch upholstered in a floral print *(A psychiatrist with a couch in her office! Was that a requirement?)*, and to the left were several tall bookcases. Sunlight flooded the large, high-ceilinged office through a wall of windows behind Dr. Taylor's desk.

"Well, Andrew, it's obvious that you're in pain," she said as she looked him in the eye, with her hair, like Erica's except lighter and longer, softly framing her pretty face. She had an empathetic voice and spoke with authority. "You are exhibiting typical symptoms of depression and anxiety, compounded by symptoms of obsessive-compulsive disorder. Everything you've described - the low appetite, the weight loss, the insomnia, peeling skin, pulling out hair (which is called trichotillomania), compulsively arranging the chairs around the kitchen table - all point to the fact that, not only are you a good candidate for antidepressant medication, you would really benefit from it. I know you've resisted in the past, but that's probably because you, like many people, think of medication for mental issues in a negative light."

"Yes. I've always thought it was a sign of weakness," Andrew said.

"Many people do, and that's a sad misconception. Think about it: if you had a heart condition that required you to take medication, you would take it, right? You wouldn't think that was a sign of weakness. Most depression is caused by the brain not producing enough serotonin. Antidepressants help the brain to produce more serotonin to function better. It's medication for a physical condition. There's no reason why anyone should see it as a sign of weakness."

Andrew said he didn't want to get dependent on it and Dr. Taylor assured him that he could take it for however long he felt he needed it, then decrease his dosage more each week when they determined he was ready to stop taking it. She recommended Zoloft, starting with a low dosage that would increase depending on how he felt. She also offered to write him a prescription for something to help him sleep and looked at him expectantly.

Andrew agreed, feeling defeated. He never thought he'd be the type who needed antidepressants. He really did not want to take them, but he knew he needed some relief from his symptoms. The last time he had arranged the chairs around the kitchen table had actually reduced him to frustrated tears because he didn't want to be doing it, but he felt compelled to and couldn't stop himself. He hoped the medication would help in that area at least.

As he drove to the pharmacy near his home, he thought about the odd practice in modern society of paying money for the opportunity to divulge one's personal history to a complete stranger. He had just shaken hands with a woman he had never seen before, sat down across from her, and told her some things about his past that not even his wife knew. He had told Dr. Taylor how depressed he had been in junior high when kids picked on him because he was sensitive to it. One day when he was thirteen, he had actually pricked his wrist with a razor blade, just to see how bad it might feel. When he got to high school, he finally met some friends he fit in with, other studious types who liked to analyze literature and took advanced placement classes. He threw himself into his studies, which was what he did best, and turned to writing as his escape, which he did almost daily. He hadn't written anything since before Eileen had been born and realized that that was probably adding to his depressed, anxious state. He suddenly felt the absence of writing like friends long gone. Not dead, just out of his life, wondering what they looked like now, how their voices would sound, and longing to hear them.

TWO NIGHTS LATER, Andrew was lying in bed while Erica was at work. He hadn't taken the sleeping pills (actually hadn't even fulfilled that prescription, due to his fears about not being able to get up if anything was wrong with the kids), but it was his second day on Zoloft, and already he felt it.

It must be working, he thought with a smile. *No wonder antidepressants are so popular.* His serotonin level seemed so high he felt like he was on Ecstasy. He remembered one night during his first year of college (his "making up for lost time" year, his "I have one year left to be a teenager" year, his "now I can get high and not worry if my parents find out" year) when he and his roommate were driving out to Emigrant Lake, five miles outside of Ashland, looking for an Ecstasy party. It was not large, as lakes go, but being a man-made lake it had various coves that were separated from the main part of the lake. Both high school and college kids had their late-night parties there, and someone always got hurt jumping and diving off the rocks jutting out above the water, leaping into the darkness, drunk, frying on acid, or just taking a dare. After one death and a diagnosis of paralysis, most wisened up and nixed the nighttime diving antics. But they kept up the parties. Andrew had only been out to the lake twice before, and that was in daylight. It was ten o'clock at night now, and he had no idea where he was going. His roommate, Tom, who possessed an Ichabod Crane-like physique and moved with effeminate, highly entertaining mannerisms, mentioned that it was supposed to be around the back of the lake, so Andrew veered off the highway onto a dirt road and followed it around toward the back. The dirt road kept getting bumpier and bumpier, and all the while both of them were looking off to the side as best as they could in the dark for the bonfire that was supposed to mark the site of the party. At one point Andrew looked in front of the car and screamed: They were in the water! Tom screamed, "Back up!" Andrew backed up several feet and they were able to see that they had driven down an old boat launch into the lake, fortunately not too far to be able to back up. They sat in the car for a moment catching their breath and laughing at themselves and the fact that they had driven down a boat launch while sober. It had been such a shock to look up and see water all around them! They found the party soon after that and were not sober for much longer. Andrew, Tom, and their friends spent the rest of the night eating oranges, talking, rolling around in the dirt, and clenching their fists and teeth from the speed in the Ecstasy. Andrew felt so good he had said, "Why doesn't everyone take this all the time?!" and he felt the same way about Zoloft. Already, in just two days, he had stopped peeling the skin off the bottoms of his feet and no longer felt the urge to arrange the chairs around the kitchen table. Zoloft was the battery in his flashlight, the coins in his parking meter, the helium in his balloon. Why on earth had he ever resisted taking it?

Andrew turned on his left side and extended his legs diagonally in the bed, enjoying the cool softness of the sheets while he slowly, luxuriously moved his legs like scissors a few times. He felt like he did in a flying dream, like he was floating, hovering above the ground, suspended, moving slowly and peacefully above his life. There was Erica, looking up and blowing him a kiss, there was Nathan waving, actually looking at him, saying "Hi, Dad!" and Eileen calling out "I love you, Daddy!" There were his parents, smiling, their arms around each other. He kept ascending until he could no longer see any of them, and all was quiet and dark, and he was asleep.

Four

Erica tucked a small red fleece blanket around Nathan. It was four in the afternoon, and he was taking a rare nap at the same time as Eileen. They both slept on a sheet-covered futon on the floor in the living room that had been pulled out of their closet when Andrew's brother had visited a few months ago. The kids liked to play on the soft futon, so they decided to leave it out. Eileen often took her naps on it, and whenever she was home with them, Erica, exhausted from her work and school schedule, usually joined her while Nathan watched a video a few feet away. But today Erica curled up with both of them, while the last rays of the December sun broke through the clouds and into the living room window. She knew if she put her hand on the glass she would feel the penetrating cold from outside.

Andrew was at a meeting at the Early Childhood Development Center office in Medford, a nearby city of about eighty thousand people, to discuss their evaluation of Nathan's development. Erica gingerly touched her son's thick, wavy hair, so like her own.

Her pregnancy with Nathan had been fine until her seventh month, when her blood pressure began to rise. Erica attributed that to all the stress in her life: working full time on her feet in a check stand, taking as many summer school classes as she could, and planning a rushed wedding with a controlling soon-to-be mother-in-law. Her own mother was preoccupied with starting a new waitressing job and couldn't seem to make the time to drive up one hour and be involved, but Erica wasn't too surprised. Andrew's mother would come in to the store while she was working (which Erica had specifically asked her not to do) to ask what she had in mind for her colors and flowers because the reception was to be held at Andrew's parents' home. Erica had a line of customers behind her. "Elaine," she had said with as much patience as she could muster, "I really can't go into it now. How about if I call you tonight?" "Well, we really have to order the flowers in the next few days," Elaine said, in what Erica took to be a lecturing tone. She appreciated the fact that Andrew's parents agreed to help them pay for the wedding (her own mother could barely support herself, and her father was unreachable, backpacking somewhere in Mexico), but it was just so much to deal with. Full-time work, pregnancy, school, and planning a wedding. A week before the wedding, Erica was hospitalized with pre-term labor, eleven weeks before her due date. The doctor had been able to halt the contractions with a shot of Terbutaline, but, lying in the hospital bed with Andrew by her side, Erica realized that she desperately needed to slow down. Her classes had ended, and she decided to take a year off school to just work. She had insisted that Andrew be the stay-at-home parent, thinking that it would be easier for them when she did go back to school if they were already in that routine. And Andrew was looking forward to quitting the drugstore since he had worked there for over two years before Erica started, and he wanted to write. He had an idea for a novel, something about a case of mistaken identity. He'd finished a rough draft of it the year before and put in the closet, claiming it needed a lot of work before it was publishable. He had never showed it to Erica.

Erica, slowly opening her eyes, noticed her children still liked to sleep on their stomachs. When they brought Nathan home from the hospital, they put him to sleep on his back, which all the baby books of the 1990s had instructed new parents to do to avoid Sudden Infant Death Syndrome (SIDS). After two months of Nathan not sleeping for more than thirty minutes at a time, out of desperation Erica and Andrew committed the condemnable act of allowing their baby to sleep on his stomach. And he only woke up once during the night from that point on (to breastfeed). They took it one step further with Eileen, and from her first day of life to her seventh month, she slept in their bed with them every night. Everyone slept better that way, and Erica enjoyed experiencing "co-sleeping" again every now and then for an afternoon nap.

Her dreamy state ended by Andrew unlocking and opening the front door. Andrew was a quiet, unobtrusive, observant person, which she appreciated, and as soon as he noticed the kids asleep on the futon, he silently shut the door and tiptoed to the kitchen table. Erica gently rose and followed him. He had seemed better lately, less irritable, since he started taking Zoloft, and Erica was grateful for the reprieve. And she was glad for his sake that he wasn't so miserable. But it still didn't change her feelings about not being in love with him anymore. How could she tell him? What could she do? She didn't want to move out, but she didn't feel right about asking him to move out. She knew he would suggest counseling for them both, but that would do nothing for her. *Counseling,* she thought, *is for when you're having problems in your marriage and you* want *to work through them.* The truth was that she was no longer in love with him, and no longer wanted to be married to him. She wanted to be on her own. Her feelings for him, aside from caring about him as her children's father, were dead. She couldn't see how counseling would remedy that. She hadn't needed counseling to deal with her abandonment issues with her parents, and she didn't need counseling now. But she couldn't ignore the fact that she'd never felt so stuck in her life.

"How did the meeting go?" she asked in a low voice as she sat down.

Andrew, still standing, removed his gray fleece jacket, hung it on the back of his chair, and sat. He looked sad, defeated. "They believe that Nathan exhibits characteristics and symptoms of autism," he said, looking at the table, averting her eyes.

Autism! That's impossible, Erica thought. *There's no way that child has autism! People with autism sit in a corner and rock themselves all day and don't interact with anyone!* "Autism?" she asked. "How could it be autism? What are they basing that on?" She looked at Andrew, thinking, *Look at me! Look at my face when you say something like that to me!*

Andrew looked at his hands and slowly turned his silver Celtic-woven wedding band around his finger. "I know; that's what I thought at first, too. When they said that word—autism—I just froze. The whole rest of the meeting I felt numb. I think because deep down I believe their diagnosis is correct."

"But how? It doesn't make sense," Erica said. *They brainwashed you into believing that!*

"Erica, the book we have doesn't describe autism very well. It just mentions the stereotypical signs. They definitely said that Nathan shows potential. They think that, with an intensive therapy program, he should be able to attend a regular public school," Andrew said.

Erica thought, *Of course he'll go to a regular school! He's barely three and he knows the entire alphabet!* "So, because he's not talking, that's the reason they think it's autism? I still don't understand."

"It's a combination of factors, they said. Not talking is one of them, but also the way that he plays, how he lines things up and stares at them, how he just repeats what people say back to them, how he moves someone's hand to do something instead of pointing or gesturing or asking for help. And they said the fact that he shrieks while having his hair washed and that he's so sensitive to sounds, like the vacuum cleaner and the food processor, indicates sensory problems that are part of autism. They said they'd be glad to go over all of it with you and answer any questions that you have at the meeting on Monday to discuss his placement in their program. They're really helpful, caring, and professional, Erica. I think they're right about Nathan. If he didn't have all these other issues going on, and they had said autism just because of his speech delay, then I would question it. But I really think they're qualified to make that evaluation," Andrew said. "They work with lots of kids who have autism, so they know what the characteristics are." He finally looked at her, patronizing, almost pleading for her approval. She had seen that look enough times, especially lately. She could tell he sensed that they had drifted apart long ago and would never reconnect on the same level again, like a cloud slowly separating with the air currents, until it is unrecognizable from its original shape.

"Well, I trust your judgment, Andrew, but I still find it hard to believe." *He is not autistic! He loves when his family comes to visit, he gives hugs, he laughs and plays with them! There's no way!*

"It is hard to believe, I agree. It's a shock. I still feel like I'm on autopilot or something. I can't believe it, either," Andrew said. "He'll be okay, though. I think speech therapy will be a great help, and I think they have a preschool setting, so that will be good for him to be around other kids." Andrew reached across the table and put his hand over Erica's. "I think it'll work out."

Don't touch me, Erica thought, recoiling. *It's a little late for tenderness.* She stood up and closed the beige polyester drapes behind the kitchen table quickly, as if he had kept her from doing it by placing his hand over hers. Her voice was austere. "Let's get dinner started."

ERICA GLANCED AT Andrew hunched over the kitchen counter as he wrote a note of detailed instructions for his mother. She would be babysitting the kids for about two and a half hours that afternoon.

"I don't understand why you need to write so much. My God, the woman raised three children, Andrew! Can't she handle an afternoon with her two grandchildren? She doesn't even have to feed them dinner or put them to bed!"

"I know, I know," Andrew said. "If I don't have a note ready for her, she'll give me this look of panic and ask how she's supposed to entertain them. I tried writing less the last time she babysat, and apparently that wasn't enough. It's almost not worth the trouble, but we need her to babysit, like, four times a year, so I have to do this."

"Geez," Erica said under her breath. She had developed an irritated tolerance of her mother-in-law. Elaine was helpful and sincere, Erica admitted, but often so annoying with her idiosyncrasies. Erica recalled how she had taken Nathan with her to visit her mother and brother in northern California almost a year ago when the restaurant had been closed for cleaning and she had a weekend off. Her mother had only seen Nathan once before that, yet she eagerly babysat him while Erica and her brother went out to dinner one night during the visit. If Erica had written a note for her, she would have been insulted. "Don't you think I can take care of my own grandchild?!" she imagined her mother saying. She had no patience for her mother-in-law's apparent anxiety over watching her own grandchildren for two or three hours.

Erica went into the living room and sat on the couch with her children while they watched *The Lion King* video. It was at a point in the movie when Simba the cub hung onto a spindly tree branch during a wildebeest stampede and his father's bird advisor cried out that he was going to go for help. "Hurry!" Simba yelled to the bird as he flew off.

"Ur-ree!" Nathan yelled at the TV.

He talks, Erica thought. *He just doesn't talk like most three-year-olds. He's different; that's his personality. It doesn't mean he has autism.*

"Ur-ree!" Nathan yelled again, running around the room. Eileen got up and joined him.

Just then, Andrew's mother arrived and parked her car beside the house.

Of course, right as they're running around yelling like maniacs, Erica thought. "Okay, calm down now. Come sit on the couch. Grandma's here," she said.

They stopped running and went over to the living room window, which was only two feet off the floor, so it was easy for them to see out. They watched Elaine get out of the car and walk to the front door, carrying a plastic grocery bag. A few seconds later she knocked on the door, and Erica opened it. She greeted her mother-in-law with an obligatory hug.

Elaine was several inches shorter than Erica, trim and youthful looking with shoulder-length light brown hair and a broad, even smile. She wore a green Fair Isle patterned sweater with jeans and tennis shoes. Erica only chatted with Elaine when Elaine pursued it, which was not often. Erica didn't loathe her; Elaine just drove her to levels of irritation that she had never experienced before. Erica believed Elaine didn't like her, either, only politely tolerated her because she had married her son and given birth to her grandchildren.

Elaine set the bag down and held out her arms to them. "Hi, guys!" she said as she knelt to be at their eye level.

"H-A-B, 5-6-4," Nathan said in a flat tone, while he looked at his grandmother. Erica thought it sounded almost like a greeting.

"H-A-B, 5-6-4?" Elaine questioned. Then she looked at Erica. "My gosh, that's my license plate! He's memorized my license plate!" To Nathan she said, "Yes, honey, that's my license plate number. You know Grandma!" and gave him a hug, which Nathan accepted with a little stiffness.

"Hi, sweetie," she said to Eileen, hugging her. Then she stood up and looked at Andrew, who had walked into the room. "That's amazing," she said as she went toward him and hugged him.

"Hi, Mom," Andrew said. "Well, he likes letters and numbers."

"Yes, but that's amazing that he memorized my license plate."

"Yes, it is. Well, we need to get going, Mom. I wrote a list of things they like to do. We should be back around five, so you don't have to get them dinner or anything," Andrew said.

"Okay. And where is the diaper-changing stuff?"

"I wrote that down," Andrew said, getting on his coat. Erica picked up her keys and purse. *Same place it was last time you babysat*, she thought.

"Can you just show me real quick?" Elaine asked.

Give me a break, Erica thought.

Andrew walked quickly down the hall into the kids' bedroom as his mother followed. Erica led Nathan and Eileen back to the couch.

"Grandma is going to stay for a little while. Mom and Dad will be back soon, okay? You watch more *Lion King*," she told them and kissed their heads.

Andrew came back down the hall. "Bye, guys," he said.

Elaine sat down on the couch between them. "Say, 'Bye, Mommy! Bye, Daddy!'" she prompted. Nathan sucked his fingers and Eileen turned her little body around so she could slide off the couch to run after them.

"Let's go," Erica murmured to Andrew. They shut the door as they heard Eileen begin protesting, "No bye! No bye!" and crying.

"Great," Andrew muttered.

"She'll be fine," Erica said, getting in the car. "We've got to get going." *Get this over with*, she thought.

Andrew drove to the offices for Early Childhood Development Center. He had taken Nathan there before for some evaluations and testing, as well as the meeting the previous week when they had told him that he exhibited signs and characteristics of autism. Erica had tried to keep her true feelings about their evaluation to herself. She didn't believe it; she thought they were wrong. But she knew if she told Andrew that she felt that way, he would accuse her of being in denial, and she didn't want him thinking that. She had talked to her mother on the phone a few days earlier while Andrew had been at the grocery store, and her mother agreed with her. Nathan was affectionate! He was smart! He was aware of his surroundings; he didn't withdraw from them. There was no way he could have autism. Erica felt convinced it wasn't just her parental defenses thinking that. She wasn't in denial. The facts spoke for themselves. *He just needs speech therapy. Then he'd be able to communicate and wouldn't be so upset by things.*

As if reading her mind, Andrew said, "I know you disagree with their evaluation of autism, and I can understand that. But we both agree that he really needs speech therapy, so I think it would be best if we just go in there with an open mind and listen to what they have to say and what types of programs they have to offer. Does that sound reasonable?"

Of course it's reasonable. I've never been unreasonable, Andrew. "Yes, of course. I'm not going to put up a fight or anything, Andrew. I want him to receive speech therapy as much as you do; I just don't think he has autism. I don't want him to be labeled."

"I know, honey. I don't think they're trying to label him."

Erica bristled at being called *honey*. "Autism is a label!"

"They're just trying to understand his behavior so they can work with him. There are more issues other than his not talking," Andrew said in the patronizing tone again.

"I know that! Don't you think that once he can talk, he won't be so frustrated trying to communicate, and those other issues are probably related to that?"

"Could be. But the possibility exists that those other issues, like sensitivity to sound, could be caused by something other than his inability to communicate, and they're going to work with him further to find out. Okay?" Andrew asked, getting off the freeway and making a left turn.

"All right," Erica said, resigned. *It's almost like you want him to have autism,* she thought. She stared through the windshield and rode in silence the rest of the way to the office. Andrew did not say anymore either.

They pulled in the driveway of the ECDC building, a renovated Colonial-style home, parked in the front, and went inside. They signed in at the front desk and were directed down a hallway to the meeting room. Upon entering, they saw seven women seated around a long table, all with stacks of notepads and files in front of them.

Erica stiffened. *What are we doing here? He's only three years old. How could this be happening? I feel like I'm walking into a trap. Nathan's just a new project for these people.*

Andrew led the way, shaking hands with the various therapists and consultants, and Erica, in a daze, did the same. *How am I supposed to remember all these people?* she thought. Finally, after being introduced to the five new faces, which included a speech-language pathologist, an occupational therapist, the regional autism consultant, the center's preschool teacher, and the director of the center, they sat down and greeted the two individuals she had met before, the intake coordinator, who had long brown hair and giggled, Erica recalled, and the behavioral consultant, a petite Asian woman, who had both come to the house during the six-week evaluation period. Erica hadn't met Sally McIntyre yet, the preschool teacher who had come for the home visit.

The director, a fifty-something woman dressed in a navy suit, began. "Okay. Since I don't regularly attend meetings, I may have missed some of the recent changes, but don't we have to have them sign the consent—you know, how we all sign the statement that the child is eligible—shouldn't they have also signed their permission—"

"At the end," Donna, the intake coordinator, broke in.

"—to provide services?" the director concluded. "At the end?"

"Yeah," Donna said.

"Okay," the director said. Erica had already forgotten her name.

"It's the new rule," Donna said, giggling. *Already?* Erica thought, annoyed.

"Well, I have some questions to start with," said Esther, the woman who had been introduced as the regional autism consultant. She was the eldest one in the room, with oval glasses, short gray hair and a purple shawl, and although Erica felt like she should be wary of her labeling Nathan, something about Esther's quiet, non-confrontational demeanor put her at ease. "I just want to get a better sense of Nathan and his play skills. It sounds like there are a lot of things that he's interested in." Erica and Andrew nodded, and Esther continued, "How is his attention span to the toys he's interested in? And what kinds of things are you seeing in play? Does he actually play with the toys, kind of the way they were designed to be played with? Or does he have his own way of playing with them?"

Andrew described Nathan's own way of playing with things, how he would line up the Sesame Street cars and just lie down and look at them after he'd lined them up. "He likes to group things, and what he likes to do with crayons - I try to get him to scribble a little bit - but he likes to take them and he puts them in the track of the window, where the window slides along the track to open. He likes to line them up in there because they fit in there."

"Sounds like he has a pretty good attention span to be able to do that," Esther said. Erica liked the way she focused on Nathan's strengths, even though his behavior was different. "How about if you bring something?" Esther asked, looking at Erica this time, which she appreciated. "You bring a toy and sit down next to him, kind of leading his play? Will he attend to you and play with you with that toy?"

"Sometimes," Erica said. "He's got a little railroad track set and sometimes I'll try to build the tracks together, but he decides that all he's interested in is pushing the cars down the mountain that's part of the set. He doesn't seem interested in taking the train along the track at all. I've tried to get him interested in that, but maybe it's just part of his personality to want to do something else with it."

No one disagreed with her.

Sally, the preschool teacher, spoke next, her green eyes wide, excited. "Well, just some ideas I have . . . I think it would be good to get him to play with toys more as a sort of process, more organized, with a beginning, a middle, and an end. We call it 'engagement.' It's an engagement in the environment. And there are ways that we can teach that, and one way is using visual systems. It sounds like that's a strength for him? I understand he's learning letters and numbers already?"

"Yes," Erica and Andrew said in unison, nodding, and everyone seemed impressed.

Sally continued, "And the fact that he's examining things is very good. So maybe we could take those strengths and use some pictures or puppets to show the steps of an activity just to organize his play better. That way, when he gets older and moves to a different situation, he's appropriately playing with the materials."

Erica actually found herself agreeing with everything that had been said so far. And she was especially pleased that there had been no mention of autism yet. Maybe Andrew had been placing more emphasis on it than there actually was. She said, "Okay, that sounds good. That's helpful to know why it's important to guide his play. I hadn't thought of that before. I had thought that the fact that his play style is unusual is just because it's part of his personality, and that's his style of playing with things. But I realize now that he might need to be taught that there are other ways to play with something."

Sally pointed out that children learn through play, and if Nathan was only playing with toys in certain ways, then he might be blocking himself out to other learning and peer socialization that could be going on, which made sense to Erica. "If you know how to play with toys the same way that your peer is, you're going to be able to have more social interactions. And, from what you've told us, this is something that Nathan also needs more of," Sally said.

Erica and Andrew nodded again.

"And Andrew had previously said that Nathan has trouble with transitions?" Tessa, the behavioral consultant, asked. Seated directly across from Andrew, Tessa looked so small in the seat, like a child. It was the embodiment of how Erica had felt upon entering the room.

Andrew said, "Yes, but mostly I meant in new situations and with people he doesn't know. For instance, when we came here for his evaluation, he was very nervous and he was constantly moving. He wouldn't sit still or try to engage much in your activities that you were trying to get him to do in order to test him. And he does that with most new situations. He gets very nervous. We went over to Waldorf School's Pumpkin Festival and he just didn't know what to do. He was trying to run into the crowd, and doing this head-butting thing he does when he's upset, charging like a bull, and I was asking him to hold his grandmother's hand because I was holding Eileen, and he wouldn't do that. He got very upset and frustrated and finally he just started sobbing. I guess he couldn't understand why he was in this strange place with all these people, even though we were with him. We ended up having to leave. So that's tending to be a problem, especially now that he's three. I was a little more used to that when he was younger, but he still does it. And I'm not sure what type of behavioral problem that indicates, but it's some sort of adjustment problem he seems to have. He just threw himself on the ground, just laying there, kind of crying. And he's done that in other situations, too. He's very afraid of doctor's offices, stores, and restaurants, and it's something that we're concerned about because he won't be consoled." Erica just nodded along with what her husband said; all of it was undeniably true.

"Well," Jane, the occupational therapist began, "we can certainly do an OT eval and explore the possibility that the behavior you described could be related to sensory integration problems." Her hair was pulled back in a bun that matched her quick, business-like voice.

What does that mean? Erica thought. "I'm sorry, but what is that?"

"Many people with autism have difficulty with filtering all of their senses at once. Some have extreme sensitivity to sound, some to light, touch, or smell," Jane said in an authoritative tone. Erica felt it was condescending, like she should have known what an "OT eval" was.

"Yes, Nathan screams when we go anywhere near the vacuum cleaner. I always thought it was a fear of the machine itself, but maybe it's the sound that bothers him?" Erica said, trying to redeem herself, surprising herself that she cared what Jane thought of her.

"Most likely it is," Jane said. "We can test for that and, through therapy, teach him ways to filter sounds so that he doesn't go into overload."

"That sounds good," Erica said, and Andrew agreed. *The book's description of autism didn't say anything about that*, Erica thought.

The director spoke. "Well, let's get started on formulating these goals."

Sally suggested focusing on attention engagement for a cognitive goal, and Tessa specified attention to toys, by himself, and then attention to an adult-directed play. "Is that okay with everyone?" Sally asked. "I don't want to bombard him with too much at first." She seemed to care about Nathan already, Erica noted.

Erica said, "That's another one of my concerns because he tends to be overwhelmed by a lot of things."

"Well," the director said, "the whole idea is that we're supposed to, by law, create a plan approved by you. So anything that you don't agree with, we can change."

"Okay," Erica said. *At least there's that.*

Tessa, tiny yet effective, looked at both Andrew and Erica and said, "I want to make sure we didn't overlook anything as far as what goals to write."

Andrew described how Nathan was fine within their home with their day-to-day routine, but if they went somewhere he wasn't used to, he got very nervous and tried to run.

"So, for safety reasons also," Tessa said, "if we write a goal that he will transition with his parent or teacher to new activities—"

"—or a new environment—" Esther, the regional autism consultant, added.

"—or a new environment, that he can do that without stress," Tessa finished.

Karen, the pregnant speech-language pathologist with a round face and snappy blue eyes, said, "I'm wondering if we could incorporate something to do with speech. Part of what sounds like the problem is he doesn't know what to do, what to expect. He may not understand what you're telling him. He needs some way to understand how long he's going to be there, what happens next . . ."

Andrew explained that they try to prepare Nathan beforehand when they're going somewhere, try to describe it to him, but they don't know what it means to him.

"Visual cues might help with that."

"He's very visually oriented," Erica said.

"We have a lot of tricks that you'll really like," Karen said, and everyone laughed. "Basically, we use picture cues and visual cues called the Picture Exchange Communication System, PECS for short. We work with a lot of children like Nathan,"—Erica noticed that she didn't say "autistic children"—"and to them it's like you're speaking Greek and they're just not getting it. Hence, there's a big stress because of what's happening next, and there's a lot of trouble with sequencing things. So we show them a picture or a cue of what they're supposed to do, then they see it and they catch it so much faster. And you say the words with the cue, and pretty soon they understand the words alone."

"So did we come up with a goal?" the director asked, trying to keep the meeting on track.

"Transitioning to a new activity," Sally said.

"Without distress," Tessa added.

"I think I'd like to see the adult-led play goal being more of a social-type goal because the intent there is social," Esther said.

"That's what I was thinking," Karen said. Erica felt like her head might snap the way she had to turn back and forth to attend to each person speaking, like watching a ping pong game at close proximity.

Esther turned to Sally and said, "You can call it a social-cognitive goal."

"Okay," Sally said. "Let's write this." She, Tessa, and Karen began talking among themselves at their end of the table.

Donna turned to Erica and Andrew and said, "In some ways, this gets real picky and we're all doing these little things on the goal, but it's good, because the way the law requires it to be written, this makes us really clarify what we're going to do. Not just 'We want to make the kid better.' We describe what it is that we're aiming at so that all of us have a clear understanding of what we're going to tackle." Donna smiled, and Erica was afraid the giggle would follow, but she was lucky that time.

Then Jane turned to them and suggested adding something about fine motor skills, as in writing and copying shapes, which Andrew and Erica agreed would be important to do in the preschool. "Since he knows numbers and letters, he probably has a lot of potential in the area of writing," Jane said. "We have to give Nathan the benefit of the doubt; just because he hasn't done it yet doesn't mean he can't."

Erica suddenly realized that this wasn't about labeling at all. Even though she didn't know all the jargon that she heard, she could sense that they were just here to figure out what they could do to help her son. Somehow she felt that this was right, whether or not Nathan had autism.

Donna turned to Erica and Andrew and said, "Another page of the IFSP (the Individualized Family Service Plan) is called Family Outcomes. And this is just any other family concerns that you might have, things that we might be able to give you resources in the community for, reminders on here of things you might want to do. You might want to put down hearing screening, for example. Is that something you might want to pursue?"

"Yeah," Andrew said, "just to rule out any hearing problems."

"It's sort of a place to put all the little odds and ends down so we don't forget what we talked about. I like to work with the parents on helping to further identify what might be some of the causes—the whole question of personality versus disorder."

"Yes, I did have concerns if this therapy would go against Nathan's personality, if we would be disregarding if he has interest in this area and not enough interest in another area, and how it would affect interacting with people. And I realize now that it does affect his interaction with others," Erica said. "I thought that it might, but I wanted to know specifically how." She realized that she didn't even feel brainwashed, as she had been wary of before the meeting.

The three women who had been writing the goals began to laugh, and the director said, "You must be pleased with yourselves!"

"This is good!" Sally said. "We've never written one like this before!" And she read off the paper, "Nathan will transition to and attend to a variety of adult-led play activities demonstrating skills of imitation 3 out of 4 times. And it's broken down into . . . Nathan will transition to a variety of new activities using a visual system with prompt and then independently . . . He will attend to a variety of adult-led play activities demonstrating skills in imitation with adult assistance."

The director approved and Erica asked if it would be possible for them to get copies of the goals.

"Oh, yeah," Donna said. "We'll mail copies to you. So now we need to talk about services—what exactly we do to reach these goals. Most likely we'll still continue with the home visits so that we can create a level of consistency for him to be able to crossover what he learns in the school setting to be able to use at home. For instance, with the PECS visual cues that we mentioned we use, we can provide you with some to use at home. And because of the fact that he's not had a lot of peer involvement, we can start him off in what's called the Focus Group, which has only—how many kids are in it, Sally?"

"Four."

"So it's small, and we have assistants who work one on one with each child, so they can help him get used to being around the other kids."

"And we do want speech therapy," Karen interjected.

"Yes," Erica and Andrew said in unison.

Sally suggested having Nathan start the following week, and they discussed days and times for the Focus Group, home visits, and speech therapy sessions, and set a date for the occupational therapy evaluation. While that was being done, Esther and the director excused themselves saying they had other meetings to get to. The meeting seemed to be ending, and Erica was relieved. Her head felt full. There was so much new information to process. She hadn't even thought about the subject of cost, and she cringed when it was brought up. Donna assured her that if their private insurance didn't pay, which was through the state due to their low income, they would never be charged for any service. Erica instantly relaxed.

Donna then began handing them various forms to sign and date: the documentation of placement decision, the prior notice of consent for initial placement for early childhood special education (which Erica felt uncomfortable signing, but she knew she needed to for Nathan to receive the therapy), the page that listed the 'team'—everyone who had attended the meeting and their titles, and a 'report card' for her and Andrew to fill out indicating their opinion of the meeting and the process they'd gone through with the initial testing and home visits.

At the end, Donna turned to look at both of them, but her eyes rested on Erica as she said, "Feel comfortable?"

Erica was surprised to realize that, in spite of everything, she did. If this had to happen, if her child really did have special needs, this place wasn't so bad. "Yeah," she said. "Thanks."

Five

Andrew waited to make a left turn from the quiet street they lived on to the main highway that would take them to Medford and the Focus Group, which was at a different location than the main office where the meetings had been. Nathan sat in his car seat in the back, sucking his fingers and tugging on his hair. He seemed to sense something was up.

Andrew had the car in neutral, something he had to do whenever he slowed the car, or it would die while idling. Then he had to throw it back into drive as soon as the light changed or it was his turn to go at a stop sign. The car had an automatic transmission, but it was almost like driving a stick-shift car with all the switching back and forth between drive and neutral.

It was also inconvenient when waiting to make a left turn onto a busy street where there were no stoplights. Just as Andrew had put the car back in drive and started to go, another card came zooming around the curve to his left, and he had to slam on the brakes, causing the car to die.

"Damn it," he muttered, restarting the car.

"Damn it," Nathan echoed in a small voice.

He chooses the worst times to decide to talk, Andrew thought.

Finally Andrew was able to turn, and they were on their way. He wondered what this would be like, not just the Focus Group, but having a 'special needs' child. Having a child with autism. Having to deal with years of therapy appointments, meetings, the 'labels' that Erica was concerned about, her denial of the diagnosis of autism, and the future of their family.

Andrew glanced out at the scenery as he drove north on Interstate 5, the artery connecting Mexico and Canada and the three West Coast states in between. It passed through Los Angeles, Sacramento, Ashland, Portland, and Seattle, among other cities, for a total of 1375 miles. The landscape transformed from stretches of coastline into the urban sprawl of major cities, from flat agricultural areas into the higher altitudes of the Cascade and Siskiyou mountain ranges and the lush green of Washington. Andrew's favorite spot along the highway happened to be right where he was. He loved to gaze at the beautiful Rogue Valley he lived in, nestled between the Cascades and Siskiyous. Not a day passed that he didn't appreciate it. Except lately, now that he was looking for work. A small valley with a total population of one hundred thousand didn't instill him with much confidence of finding a great job in, say, the publishing industry.

In fact, the only thing Andrew felt confident about was Nathan receiving therapy through ECDC, as he and Erica referred to it. But every other issue in his life had caused his anxiety to surge so high that, on his own, he increased his Zoloft dosage (his counselor approved it after the fact). Their financial situation scared him, for one thing. For the past two weeks they'd had to buy their groceries with credit cards, and their meager Christmas would once again be on credit cards. Andrew hated living this way. He blamed himself since he was the one with the college degree and couldn't find a decent job. Sometimes he felt so hopeless.

His parents were getting a divorce, for another thing. He had to deal with constant phone calls from them. He figured it was because he was the only child living locally. Or maybe it was because he was the eldest. His sister was safely away at school and his brother was almost seven hundred miles away in Los Angeles, removed from the drama. Each parent would call Andrew and bad-mouth the other. *What a horrible example to set for your married adult child! As if the fact that I'm an adult makes me any less sensitive to the skirmishes of my parents' divorce.*

Andrew's own marriage did not seem healthy at all. He and Erica rarely talked. How was his anxiety and depression supposed to get better when he received no support from his partner? No encouragement? How could their marriage survive having a child with a disability when Erica was in denial about the diagnosis and wouldn't even talk about it? Or anything else for that matter? And she was also stressed about finals and busy at work. Not a good combination. Whenever Andrew tried to talk to her, she always said she was too tired to go into it.

As Andrew neared the Focus Group location, his thoughts again turned to Nathan. He had so much apprehension about his son's future and how having autism would affect him and the whole family. They had said he showed potential, but Andrew still felt daunted. There were no guarantees, no expectations. Will he read? Will he enjoy fiction? Will he converse? Will he converse about thoughts and ideas and feelings? How will Eileen be affected? How will Nathan do in school? In the workforce? Will he make friends? Be able to understand enough to play on team sports? *There is so much I want to share with him, so much life, and now I don't know if he will ever understand.*

Andrew parked the car and walked up to the single-story brick building with his son. Here was the place in which he was putting so much hope. Would it make a difference? Was it all just the lofty ideas of kind people who meant well? Autism had such a foreboding feel to it, a darkness that no light could penetrate. The shocking death sentence of developmental disabilities. In its presence, its shadow, hope was all they had.

On the far left of the building he saw a typical-looking playground, and when they entered the foyer, it was warm, quiet, and inviting with plants and soft chairs. The woman at the front desk directed them down the hall to the Focus Group. So far, Nathan did not protest. Was he curious? He sucked his fingers and held Andrew's hand.

The door to the classroom was cut in half, with the bottom half shut and the top half open. Andrew poked his head in and Sally greeted him warmly.

"Hi! Come on in!" She wore navy twill pants and a floral print button-up, long-sleeved knit shirt. She looked relaxed, yet professional, as she lowered herself to Nathan's height. "Hi, Nathan! I'm Sally, remember? We're going to have fun playing with toys, okay?" Then she stood back up and said to Andrew, "I'll give you a quick tour."

Andrew looked around at the brightly-colored, toy-filled classroom. At first glance, it seemed like any other pre-school classroom, but then the differences became apparent. Instead of the typical babbling of pre-schoolers mixed in with the occasional shouts of "Mine!", he mostly heard the praising and coaxing from the teachers as they guided the children in their activities. He noticed the classroom had a 1:1 student/teacher ratio, with all of the four other children either physically or developmentally disabled (or both). He could sense Nathan's anxiety with the new environment. He checked out a few toys and quickly crawled into a five-by-five foot pop-up tent filled with stuffed animals and beanbags, which he found off in a quiet corner.

"That's fine if he wants to stay in there for a while," Sally said. "This is a lot for him to take in." She began to walk around the room and Andrew followed. "Here are all of the kids' schedules. I've already made one for Nathan. Every day when they come in they can look at their schedule, and that way they'll know what order the activities will happen in. They know what to expect. Structure and routine are very important to them, and the schedules are made from the visual cue cards that we mentioned at the meeting."

Andrew looked at the vertical side-by-side schedules for the five children. At the top was a laminated picture of each child with his or her name written under it. Under that, each child had several laminated white cards, three by three inches in size, with black and white symbols on them and words printed at the bottom of each. The first one for each child said "Circle Time" with a circle and little chairs around it. The successive cards each featured different activities, including "outside," "snack," "choice," "OT," "work," and "leave" at the end. The cards were attached to the schedule by Velcro strips, and Andrew noticed little plastic baskets on the wall next to each schedule.

"Some of the children like to pull the card for each activity off the schedule after they've done it and put it in their basket. Sort of like crossing things off a to-do list. Then they are reminded what they need to do next because they're back here and they see it. They really come to enjoy their schedules," Sally said.

Andrew looked around while they walked through the room. One little boy cawed like a bird to communicate, a girl grunted, and two other boys were not saying words, but were loudly verbalizing sounds. He also noticed that those two boys were using more of the little laminated cards, handing them to the teachers who would help them go to the toilet, wash their hands, get the toy they wanted, or tell them it was not time to go outside.

"Here is where we give them their snacks," Sally said, indicating a C-shaped table with four small chairs around the outside of it. Andrew noticed that these were not the typical little plastic and metal pre-school/Kindergarten chairs. These were wooden, with arms on the sides and buckled straps at the waist.

"We offer a variety of fruit, crackers, yogurt, juice and milk, plus some other items that each child likes in particular. Let me know if Nathan has any favorites."

"Oh, he'll probably like most of what you have," Andrew said.

"Is he allergic to anything?"

"Not that I know of."

In the middle of the room was a rainbow-colored circular rug with the same kind of little wooden chairs around it. Sally indicated that it was where they have "Circle Time" and do various group activities, such as singing or reading stories.

"Right now everyone is having a 'Choice' time. It's when they can pick out whatever they want to do or play with. It's about the least structured thing we do here, but they still have to use the cue cards to ask for what they want, and we guide them through organizing their play and trying to interact with peers a little bit. After a few months, if they're doing well in the Focus Group, then we move them to the Focus Pre-School. There's a lot more peer interaction. There are eight children in that class, but Joey over there is about ready to move into it now, so it'll be nine. We try to keep the Focus Group to a maximum of four. The other thing with the Focus Pre-School is that we have a few typically-developing peers in it, so the kids with autism can learn from them."

Andrew nodded and said, "That sounds great. I think I'll go check on Nathan for a minute."

"Okay. I'm going to have the kids transition to snack time now, so you can observe how we do that when you're finished."

He found Nathan lying on his back inside the tent on a pile of beanbags, sucking his fingers and twirling his hair. Andrew poked his head inside. "How are you doing in here?"

Nathan removed his fingers to say, "Go," then replaced them. Andrew knew he wasn't telling him to go away. Nathan wanted to leave.

"We're not ready to go yet, Nate. You can stay in the tent with the animals, or you can come out and play with toys. We'll go later." Andrew wasn't sure what sort of response he would get, but Nathan did not move, so maybe he understood.

Andrew went back to observe the snack table. Sally was seated along the inside of the C, and the children were seated around the outside of it, across from her. Andrew noticed that all but one boy, the one ready to transition to the Focus Pre-School, were buckled in their chairs. The little girl, who seemed to have a physical disability as well, leaned to one side in her chair.

Sally asked each child what their choice was by offering a few laminated cue cards. The child would then pick a card, hand it to Sally, and she would give them what was on the card while praising them. "Good job choosing," she said.

Andrew could not deny that although these children could not talk, they had, through this program, learned to communicate and interact. The teachers here constantly worked with them to get them to focus, respond, make choices, name things, participate. It was full of purpose. He felt certain that Nathan would benefit from this environment.

Of course, that would require getting him to come out of the tent at some point.

ANDREW RECLINED ON the couch with his back against the arm so that he could stretch out his legs along the length of it. He read an astrology book as he waited for Erica to come home from work. He had noticed that things between them seemed even worse since Nathan's diagnosis, and whenever he asked Erica what was wrong, she would tell him nothing was. She finally agreed that they "need to talk," and said she would try to get off early that night. Andrew wondered if she really would make it happen or if she would just blow it off and stay at work until the time she usually finished, saying it had been too busy to leave earlier.

But Erica came home just before ten o'clock, which he took to be a good sign, although she looked exhausted. She acknowledged him and went straight to the bathroom to take a shower. Andrew wondered if maybe his mother, whom he had talked to on the phone an hour earlier, was right about Erica somehow blaming herself for Nathan's autism, and maybe that's why she was in denial.

Erica emerged from the bathroom, put some things in the bedroom, and came and sat next to Andrew on the couch. She was silent for what seemed like a full two minutes, deciding what to say, Andrew guessed. She wouldn't look at him. It was killing Andrew to try to figure out what she could possibly have to say that would take her so long to compose. He thought about his futile attempt to be playful and retain closeness the other afternoon when they were both home, and he had leaned over her while she sat at the kitchen table and said to her, "Plant one on me, baby," and she gave him an exasperated peck on the lips. How desperate of him. *Lame,* he thought afterward.

At last, Erica, still looking in her lap, said, "I'm not happy in this relationship."

Andrew envisioned a guillotine falling. A knot formed in his stomach. He immediately felt his blood go cold, and he tingled with nausea.

Not this. No, not this. Please, not this.

Andrew's head swam as Erica continued. "I'm sorry, Andrew, but I resent you. I no longer feel close to you. I don't feel like I can be myself with you; I've lost my sense of self. You changed, Andrew. You are so different from how you were when we met. You're unhappy and agitated all the time, and I can no longer be happy for both of us. I've been waiting for you to get back to your normal self, but I can't go on like this. You're not the person I married. I dread coming home from work because I'm afraid of getting a scowl from you because I can't control what time I get off. I don't want to bring friends over because of your irritable moods. I still care about you, but I can't be there for you emotionally. I can't offer you any more support. I have so much I'm dealing with, and I need to regain my sense of self."

Andrew tensed as he began to silently cry. Tears ran down his face as he thought about how depressed he had been as a stay-at-home parent for three years and how he had developed obsessive-compulsive disorder as a result of his isolation. Erica was right. It had started after Nathan was born and got even worse after Eileen. Erica was always trying to be happy for both of them. He could see it now, how hard it must have been, day after day, month after month.

Erica said, "I just want you to know, I'm not moving out or anything. At least not for a while. I just need some space, okay?"

"I'm sorry I'm crying. This just makes me so sad."

Erica enfolded him in her arms, and he sobbed. His body shook as he cried into her shoulder, and her words kept echoing in his head. *I'm not happy in this relationship.* He was so blind! So stupid! How could he have not sensed this?

She held him for a few minutes, and then she gently but firmly pulled away as Andrew clung to her. "I need to get some sleep; I've got a final tomorrow that I need to study for in the morning."

She walked down the hall and into their bedroom and emerged a moment later with her pillow. She went over to the futon and lay down, pulling a blanket over herself.

"You can still sleep with me," Andrew said, almost pleading.

God! How pathetic I sound!

"I think it would be better if I slept out here tonight," Erica said. She sounded calm, relieved to have finally gotten the difficult "talk" off her chest, he thought.

Andrew persisted. "But I'm not mad at you."

"I just think it would be better if I slept out here tonight. I'll sleep in the bed with you again, but not tonight."

"Okay," Andrew croaked. He could barely talk. He turned the living room light out and dragged himself to bed as relentless tears welled in his eyes again. He shut the bedroom door and blew his nose and wiped his eyes. He got into bed and began gasping into his pillow to muffle the sound. He didn't want her to hear him crying.

THE NEXT DAY, while Erica was at school, Nathan had a home visit with Sally and the ECDC staff. Andrew was still reeling from his 'talk' with Erica. His mind kept vacillating between despair and a weak hope that maybe it didn't really happen. When she wasn't home it was easier to pretend, but he could only keep that up for so long. He couldn't ignore the lump that he'd had in his throat the entire morning. And when he focused on that for a split second, the tears would start to come again.

Sally, cheerful, with excitement in her voice, began to tell Andrew how yesterday at school she had gotten Nathan to sit in a chair at Circle Time. He had to be much farther back than the others or he would start yelling, but it was a good start. He kept trying to undo the belt buckle on the chair, saying, "Open!" several times, but soon he accepted the fact that he was staying in the chair and just sucked his fingers while he observed.

Andrew tried hard to keep his composure, but his eyes watered uncontrollably, and Sally could see it.

"I'm sorry," she said, concerned. "If this isn't a good time for you, we can go. We can just skip this visit."

"I'm sorry," Andrew said. "I received some difficult family news yesterday, and I'm still dealing with it."

"It's okay; I understand."

"I hate for you to have come all this way just for me to cancel," Andrew said.

"It's not a problem. I know how hard things can be," she said softly. "Don't worry about us; it's fine. We'll come back on Thursday."

"Thank you," Andrew said. They probably dealt with this all the time: parents grieving over the diagnosis. That's probably what Sally thought it was. He felt terrible that the three of them drove twelve miles from north Medford for nothing. Not to mention the fact that he was disrupting Nathan's routine just as he was happily exploring a vinyl storyboard they had brought. Sally, who already seemed to understand his son so well, offered to leave it there for him because he would have been upset if they left with it so soon after he began to examine it. Andrew promised to bring it back to the school the next day.

After Sally and her assistants left, Andrew was overcome with emotion. Having someone be so genuinely empathetic somehow made him feel worse, even though he appreciated it so much. He put on a video to keep the kids occupied and went to his room.

'I'm not happy in this relationship.' 'Relationship?!' She couldn't even say marriage! It's not like I'm just her boyfriend that she's been seeing for a while. I'm her husband and we have two children together! It's not just another 'relationship!' Why couldn't she have talked to me sooner? Why did she wait until the point that she resents me and no longer feels close to me? She's talked a little, but it's about inconsequential things. She's been here physically, but not emotionally. She's so distant; it's like a vacant twin of her, a shell.

Andrew washed his face and walked out into the living room to check on the kids, who were fine. He thought about calling his mother, but he wasn't sure if he was ready to do that yet. She would, undoubtedly, launch into another barrage against his father, thinking that it was now acceptable to commiserate with Andrew because he was also having marital problems. Then he almost laughed as he realized how wrong they had been last night when they talked on the phone about what they thought was bothering Erica.

We were way off.

Six

Erica stopped along the trail and bent down to tie her shoe. Her friend Gavin had organized a hike up Table Rock, one of two flat-topped mesa buttes just north of Medford. Erica, Gavin, his girlfriend Simone, and their new friend Brooke were about half-way up the one-and-a-half-mile hike to reach the eight-hundred-foot summit. The trail, although a bit muddy with it being winter, was flanked by woodsy chaparral and white oak savanna as well as many old oak trees and some conifers.

Erica loved to be outside getting some air and exercise. She was glad to have somewhere to go; she had felt so awkward around Andrew since the night she finally told him how she felt about their relationship. She felt bad because she knew he was hurting, but she had been needing to make a change for a long time. And she was glad that the process had begun. She felt a little bit freer now, even though she knew full well that she and Andrew still had much to deal with. They had just talked that morning about their financial situation, with Andrew whining, sorry that he couldn't find a good job. Said he would put an ad in the paper for being a writing tutor, writing résumés and helping with papers as he had done while he was in college. Erica told him, *Never mind—that wouldn't help much anyway.* Her financial aid had already been approved for the next term, so she decided to do one more. Andrew said fine.

It was strange to think that, even though she viewed her current financial situation as pretty dire, they were almost comfortable compared to how she had lived growing up. When her mother had finally decided to be a mother and had quit stuffing Erica's diapers with drugs to get through airports, they were destitute. Erica recalled how, when she was seven, they had lived in a tent in some campground for about four months. Of course, things didn't get any better after that. They might have had a metal roof over their heads in her mother's new husband's trailer, but Darrel, a tall, greasy-haired, pastey-faced factory worker, must have hated Erica for entering his life with all the slaps and shoves she got from him. Several times Erica actually had to shield her baby brother, Caleb, from his blows. Finally, her mother came home from work early one night, witnessed her children being beaten with a belt, and had the strength to leave the pig. Erica shuddered, remembering how she had cowered behind the side of the couch, putting Caleb behind her, trying to stop that wretched, filthy man, who thought that a beating was acceptable punishment for a two-year-old who had knocked over his full beer that had been teetering on the edge of the coffee table. He blamed her for not "watching Caleb." She remembered the paralyzing terror, but in the back of her mind was also a tiny surge of disgust at this man's indecency as he relished removing his belt and coming at them with it. Erica had just been about to turn around and let her back take the brunt of the blows when their mother walked through the door. "Leave them alone!" she screamed as she pulled her husband away. Then he hit their mother, again and again. "Stop it!" Erica shrieked. Somehow she had the presence of mind to call the police. How did she know how? At nine? *How many nine-year-olds call the police to save their mother?* It had been a horrible night, the culmination of many horrible nights, which caused Erica to develop an intolerance of any fighting, verbal or physical. Maybe it was actually more of a phobia. Even in adulthood she avoided confrontations whenever possible.

It was back to the tent for three months while her mother saved up enough money to get a small apartment. At age eleven, Erica had to take care of her four-year-old brother every day after coming home from school and prepare dinner for the two of them while their mother waited tables at a Denny's. It was hard on Erica, but looking back, she didn't mind. They were out of that terrible man's trailer. It was the one time she ever felt proud of anything her mother did.

And that was better than she could say about her father. Before the age of seventeen she remembered seeing him once, when she was five, and he had come to the small trailer her mother was renting at the time. He was tall and large and looked like a lumberjack, like Paul Bunyan without his ax. He filled the doorway of the pink trailer that had been painted with regular house paint. Her mother greeted him warmly, in spite of the fact that he'd brought his girlfriend, a quiet but smiling Mexican girl. They went to a local park with a small lake and had a picnic lunch on an itchy wool blanket on the grass. Her mother had not gone; Erica figured abduction must not have been a possibility that crossed her mother's mind. Or perhaps it had and she was willing to take the risk. They ate bologna and cheese sandwiches and then walked out on the little fishing dock. Erica had worn cut-off shorts and a tank top because her father had said he wanted to teach her to swim and she didn't have a bathing suit. They got to the end of the wooden dock and he said, "Okay, hold your breath and kick to get back to the top," and then he threw her in. She still remembered the feeling of terror as she plunged into what she imagined was a hundred feet of dark water, wondering in her panicked state if she would sink all the way down. She kicked and flailed her little arms, not daring to open her eyes until she felt herself surface, gasping and spluttering. "Good! You're a swimmer!" she heard her father say as she frantically paddled back to the dock and he pulled her up. She hadn't even caught her breath long enough to say anything before he announced, "Okay, try it again!" and threw her back in.

Erica jogged to catch up with her friends. She stopped thinking about her father and thought about all the hikes she and Andrew had taken together on Grizzly Peak, another local hiking trail that offered stunning views of the valley they lived in. They put their children in backpack carriers, and within an hour, they'd be having lunch at the summit under cornflower skies. She wished she and her friends could have gone there today, but the elevation was more than three times higher than Table Rock and the road to the trailhead was inaccessible due to snow. Besides, this was her first time on Table Rock, and she had always wanted to hike it.

"So you're going to go another term?" Gavin asked her. He was her friend by association: first they had tended bar together, then he began dating her best friend. Erica liked him well enough, but she couldn't understand what Simone saw in him. He was a bit on the lazy side, Erica thought, with a slack jaw and no discernable muscle tone in any part of his body. He'd let himself go in the past six months, not that Erica found him very attractive to begin with. But she'd been told, and not just by Simone, that he knew his way around a bedroom, so she figured that was the pull.

Erica walked behind him, avoiding the little mud puddles created by his heavy footfalls on the squishy path. "Yeah," she said. "I'm still getting financial aid, and Andrew hasn't found a job yet, so he'll stay home with the kids."

Simone, a petite girl with short blond hair who looked out-of-sync walking beside Gavin, turned around and asked, "How's Nathan's therapy going?" Erica had met Simone two years earlier when she waited tables at the French restaurant where Erica bartended at the time.

Simone was now a photographer's assistant for the Medford newspaper and did a little freelance work on the side. A year ago she had taken the Pavel-Hudson family portrait with four-month-old Eileen crying non-stop, two-year-old Nathan sucking his fingers and staring blankly at the camera, and Andrew and Erica smiling a little too hard, forced even, convincing themselves that nothing was wrong. That they were happy.

Erica told Simone that Nathan's therapy seemed to be going okay, that she hadn't noticed a difference yet, but it had only been two weeks. She wished that Simone had asked her at some other time, not in front of a co-worker she barely knew. She didn't feel ready to discuss her son's developmental issues, especially since at the moment she wanted to forget them.

But of course Brooke asked, "Who's Nathan?" She was about Erica's age, with a slender build, shaggy, shoulder-length dark blond hair, and energetic blue eyes. She was shorter than Erica, but then, most women were. And she wasn't the brightest light on the porch, from what Erica could tell, but she had a good work ethic. A little clumsy with breaking glasses, but at least she was on time and worked hard. She thanked Erica for hiring her, giving her a chance.

"My son," she told Brooke.

"How old is he?"

"He's three." Erica looked away. How could she change the subject? She could comment on the sky clouding over, but that would be too obvious.

"What's he in therapy for?"

Erica knew she would ask. She wished Simone hadn't brought it up. Now she would have to explain something that even she didn't understand. "He's receiving speech therapy," she said, deciding to keep it simple.

"Oh, I thought you meant like, therapy, you know, like with a shrink!" Brooke said with a laugh.

No, that would be my husband, Erica thought. She continued goose-stepping over Gavin's sloshy footprints.

"Do they still think he has autism?" Gavin said.

"Yeah," Erica said, bristling at Gavin's nonchalance, his use of her son's diagnosis as a conversation booster. Autism was cool to him. She imagined him boasting to people in his psych classes that his friend's son had autism. It angered her how easily people were seduced by the novelty of someone else's problems. "I don't see how that's true, though. He's very affectionate and is always aware of his surroundings."

"Yeah, the way you've described him, he doesn't sound like anything I've read about autism in my psych classes. I need a break," Gavin said, stopping and pulling a water bottle out of his backpack. Simone stopped and began rotating her arms around like a windmill. Erica stretched out her calves.

"What's autism?" Brooke asked, reaching out to grab the water bottle that Gavin offered.

Taken aback, Erica wasn't sure where to begin. *How could anyone not have heard of autism?* "It's a disorder that affects language and social development." She really wanted to get off this topic.

"Oh," Brooke said. Gavin then asked her if she remembered the movie *Rain Man* and she didn't, so he suggested she rent it, mentioning that Tom Cruise was in it.

Erica thought about pointing out that the movie portrayed nothing of what it was like to have an autistic preschooler, or one who showed some signs of being autistic, since she didn't believe that Nathan was. She realized that maybe she had taken for granted the fact that Gavin knew about autism because he had taken psychology classes. She wondered if perhaps Brooke represented the general public in her lack of knowledge about autism. If so, and if Nathan did indeed have autism, how would anyone outside of his family and his therapists be able to have any understanding of his behavior?

She took a swig from her own water bottle as they continued up the trail. Then, much to Erica's relief, Simone began talking about having a little party at their place that night and asked her if she'd be able to go.

"Yeah, I've got the night off," Erica said. "I'll be there." She knew Andrew could stay home with the kids; he never had plans. It didn't even seem like he had any friends! She could see him, how he looked every time she walked in or out of the front door, a book in his lap, his mouth sullen, his eyes glaring.

ANDREW HAD JUST settled in for another mediocre night of reading on the couch when the phone rang. He jumped up to grab it so the kids would not be awakened, betting that it was probably one of his parents. Occasionally his brother or sister would call, but they were preoccupied with work and school most of the time. Erica certainly never called; she claimed it was because she was too busy, but Andrew thought it was because she wanted to pretend he didn't exist. Recently, a co-worker of hers had called looking for her, and when he had offered to take a message, the girl said, "Are you the babysitter?" Offended, Andrew said, "No, I'm her husband." "Oh. She never mentioned she had a husband." There was a tone in her voice that sounded like she thought it was funny. He wasn't too surprised to hear that. And of course he was forbidden to call Erica; "personal phone calls at work are unprofessional," she had told him.

"Hi, Andrew," the deep male voice said. It still took him a second to recognize his father's voice. Prior to that month, his father had only spoken to him on the phone once or twice before in his whole life. Gabriel Pavel loved his children, but it was still difficult for him to transition to interacting with them as adults. Andrew was convinced that his father still viewed them as extensions of himself, as he had when they were growing up. And before the recent separation, he could always hear about how his children were doing just by asking their mother. *Why was that enough for him?* Andrew wondered. At any rate, it was never his father's inclination to call up anyone just to shoot the breeze.

Andrew asked how he was, not really wanting to know, anticipating the mother-bashing. He wished they could go back to the days when all his father talked about with him was how his last bowling meet went.

"Oh, I'm just still trying to deal with this bomb your mother dropped on me. It just isn't right, what she's doing. And right when I'm about to retire! She doesn't even realize the financial ramifications of this!"

Andrew posed that it was probably not a decision she'd made lightly.

"Well, how do you feel about it?"

"Dad, I'm not taking sides."

"Well, I wasn't asking you to take sides. I just think that it's so ironic that now that I'm retiring, your mother decides that she wants a divorce. She made a vow, in the church, and now she won't uphold it! I would continue to even though I was unhappy in the marriage too. No one stops to think that maybe there were things that I didn't like in the marriage, what with her all of a sudden becoming frigid after we had you kids. But I was willing to overlook that! I never—"

Frigid! What is it with these people? "Dad! Even though I'm an adult, I'm still your child! I don't need to hear things like this about your marriage! Tell it to a counselor or your brothers. I mean, Dad, of course I care about you, but there are certain things that I don't feel comfortable discussing with you, okay?"

Gabriel apologized for burdening Andrew with his marital problems in light of the fact that Andrew was going through his own, and Andrew refuted that even if he wasn't having marital problems it still wouldn't be acceptable to bad-mouth his mother. Much to Andrew's relief, Gabriel conceded. Then he asked how things were with Erica.

"Things are not very good. She doesn't seem to want to have anything to do with me. Her work had planned a company Christmas party, and I said I would get a babysitter so we could go together, and she said not to bother because she didn't want to go. Then at the last minute, a half an hour before the party, she 'changed her mind' and went without me. She rarely talks to me; she says she needs to 'regain her sense of self,' which she does by hanging out with her friends from work. So I don't know. It doesn't look good."

"Well, I'm sorry to hear that. I hope she comes around soon," his father said.

"I don't think it's a matter of 'coming around.' Whenever I try to talk to her about it, she says not to push her and that I'm trying too hard. So I think I'll just do my own thing for a while. I'm hoping to find a job soon, and that will help. And tomorrow night Bernadette's coming over to babysit since she's in town for Christmas break, and I'm going to go out to a nightclub, which I haven't been able to do for a long time," Andrew said. He didn't bother mentioning the part about being on antidepressants. His father was in the camp that considered overcoming depression to be a matter of will; he would have told Andrew he needed to "think positive" and "snap out of it." Andrew could only imagine what his father's theories were on Nathan having autism. He probably believed it was God's retribution for Andrew siring a child out of wedlock.

At MIDNIGHT THE following night, Andrew found himself dancing to the hard, fast techno beat at Dogma, the restaurant and nightclub where Erica worked. He enjoyed dancing, but since he hadn't done it in so long, within twenty minutes he was out of breath and had a stitch in his side. He decided to take a break and get a beer.

Dogma, recently remodeled and under new ownership, was the hot spot for night life in Ashland. Its two-story floor plan offered plenty of table seating for the restaurant patrons, who enjoyed its Pan-Asian cuisine. The interior design, dubbed "city style" by several reviewers from the San Francisco Bay Area, Portland, and Seattle, featured exposed air ducts, Asian décor, and a cat walk connecting the main portion of the upper floor with the DJ booth. Upstairs along with several other dining tables was a pool table, and downstairs at the rear of the establishment was the dance floor, currently a mass of gyrating, sweaty bodies. Andrew was barely able to inch his way out.

Once off the dance floor, he weaved through a sea of people on his way to the bar, ducking as an aggressive cocktail waitress elbowed her way through while balancing a tray of drinks high above her head. "Coming through!" she yelled as she effectively safeguarded two full martini glasses and two pints of beer while fording the crowd. Andrew recognized her skinny frame and angry, black fox-like eyes that still looked as mean as they did seven years ago. She had worked as a dishwasher at the café where he had waited tables while in college. In fact, he had seen a lot of familiar faces that night since it was two days before Christmas and many people had come home for the holidays. Andrew had only been there a half an hour and had already run into several old co-workers and college friends. It was like a class reunion, complete with some who'd had too much to drink and puked in the bathroom.

Being at Dogma, Andrew got some small pleasure out of the fact that he was in Erica's space, and he could tell she wasn't comfortable with it. *Keep pretending I don't exist*, he thought as he leaned on the long concrete-topped bar. *It's hard to hide a husband in a small town.*

He stole a few glances at his wife. In truth, he loved to watch her work. She had a talent for bartending. She could handle people well, she knew her alcohol, and she could really fly filling the glasses: shaking, mixing, pouring. She raked in the tips, and she deserved them. Andrew admired how well she could perform under pressure; he thought she was the best bartender he had ever seen. And from his clubbing days he had seen, and dated, quite a few. It could even be said that he had a 'thing' for bartenders. "They have great timing and they're good with their hands," he used to say with a smirk to his college friends, co-workers at the café.

Erica didn't see him from the other end of the bar, but he could tell she was agitated because she knew he was there, on her turf. He ordered a pint of hefeweizen from the other bartender, a tall guy with long blond hair pulled back in a ponytail. The bartender smiled slyly at all the girls leaning on the bar in the conceited way of a guy who knew that all he had to do was say the word and any one of them would have gone home with him. Everyone called him Nick, and he kept strategically placing his hands on Erica's hips every time he had to pass behind her. Andrew also noticed Brooke, wearing an apron and looking flustered, backing the bar and hurrying by every few minutes with a dish rack of glasses to be washed or put away. He had met her a few days ago when Erica gave her a ride home after they returned from a hike. He couldn't blame Brooke for not acknowledging him at the bar; the afternoon he'd met her he was so mad at Erica that he didn't look at either one of them. He'd been less than welcoming, as a matter of fact. Erica walked through the door talking about going to a party that night when she'd already been gone all day, enjoying herself, and he'd been stuck home with the kids, as he had been for three and a half years. It was like she'd been flaunting her social prowess to him. In any case, he felt self-conscious now that he'd not made a good first impression on Brooke. He had a conscious goal of befriending Erica's friends and co-workers, a longing to be seen as a cool spouse, likable, congenial, estimable. Maybe with one-fourth the confidence and charisma of someone like Nick; Andrew knew he was nowhere near that category. He could always apologize to Brooke and tell her that he'd been sick that day they met. She responded well to Erica anyway, almost seemed to idolize her and hang on her every word. *Must be helping her to regain her sense of self,* Andrew thought. *Her own little fan club.*

He turned around to survey the bar and caught the eye of someone else who looked faintly familiar in the dim light. It was Isaac, a waiter whom Erica had worked with two years ago at the French restaurant in town. Erica had mentioned that he was now a bouncer at Dogma, although he wore dressy street clothes that night instead of the black "Security" T-shirts the other bouncers wore. Andrew had only met Isaac once before, but he recognized his big, dark eyes and his angular jaw, his long, straight Greek nose. He was several inches taller than Andrew, and big-boned, which seemed to be a prerequisite for being a bouncer.

"Andrew!" he called, as if they were old friends. Isaac walked over to him. "Hey, man, good to see you. It's been a while. How've you been?"

"Fine, and you?" Andrew raised his voice to compensate for the din of the bar.

"Can't complain," Isaac said.

"So, I heard you're a bouncer here?" Andrew said, for lack of anything else. He'd only met him once before, was surprised that Isaac even remembered him.

"Yeah, but I'm off tonight. My brother's visiting," Isaac said, then turned to a guy on his left. "Hey, Miles, this is Andrew, Erica's husband."

Andrew shook hands and exchanged "good-to-meet-you"s with Miles, who looked like an older and shorter version of his brother. Andrew saw Miles shoot Isaac a surprised look, but it was also, unless Andrew imagined it, reproachful. Miles shook Andrew's hand in an uneasy, reticent manner.

As if to detract from the awkward exchange, Isaac casually called over his shoulder, "Good seeing you!" as he and Miles turned and disappeared into the crowd.

Andrew shrugged and finished his beer. He was just glad that this time *he* hadn't been the strange, unsociable one. He made his way back to the dance floor and angled himself into a corner. Here, he had a mirrored wall in front of him, and he watched himself, his quick expert moves. At least he could still dance. It was here that he felt the same confidence that Nick exuded behind the bar. He felt eyes on him, some awed, some envious; all made him feel self-assured. Estimable, if only for those moments on the dance floor.

FOUR DAYS LATER, Andrew peered over the edge of the Bowl, a large glacier-like hollow on top of seven-and-a-half-thousand foot Mt. Ashland, where he and Bernadette had gone snowboarding for the day. He hadn't been snowboarding in three years and felt a little too rusty to attempt the vertical drop-down trail marked with black diamond signs. In fact, in all his college years of snowboarding on Mt. Ashland, just a half-hour drive from the city, he had never gotten up the nerve to attempt the Bowl. He would, in awe, watch his friends fly down into it and usually emerge unscathed, but he had also seen a few people fall and get hurt. It wasn't worth attempting today, especially with the current conditions. The wind whipped his face with snow flurries and visibility was poor. He certainly wished for one of those lucky-on-the-mountain days, with azure skies and, to the south, a view of majestic Mt. Shasta, sixty crow-flying miles away in northern California, and, looking back the other direction, all of the Rogue Valley spread out before him.

Today he was lucky if he could see sixty feet in front of him, and the Bowl was certainly not an option, especially since the lift operators had just made an announcement that they were closing the lift that went up to it. But he loved to watch the skilled skiers and snowboarders who mastered it, and one day he hoped that he could at least try.

He turned to Bernadette, teased her with a comment about how cute she looked in her powder-blue-and-gray name-brand women's snowboarding apparel, and suggested they go to the lodge for a break. Her face still looked cherubic, with her little button nose (red, at the moment) poking out underneath her goggles, and her bird-like lips forming a coy smile.

"Okay," she said, taking off down the run before he could.

"Be careful!" he called after her, doubtful that she heard. He still felt protective of her, probably always would. It seemed fitting, comforting, to Andrew that with all the time he spent babysitting his sister, she was now babysitting for him once in a while. Things had come full circle.

Andrew, excited to be getting back into snowboarding after his three-year hiatus, smoothly carved his way down the intermediate run, enjoying the rhythmic movements of the sport, the feeling of gliding, turning, picking up a little speed. It seemed poetic to him, and exhilarating. Balancing the edges of his board seemed symbolic of the need to balance his life: being a full-time parent of toddlers, one of whom had autism, dealing with being separated from his wife but still living with her, trying to find a decent job, and fitting in a little free time to relax and do the things he enjoyed. *Balance is hard to create,* he thought, *and even more difficult to maintain, especially through rough spots. But when you do, it's a perfect ride.*

He and Bernadette both had perfect rides down to the lodge. Andrew watched his little sister as she schussed down the straight run. She had just finished her first term of college, but since she had spent more of her growing up years in Ashland, she hadn't wanted to go to college there, like Andrew and Solomon had. She attended the University of Oregon in Eugene, a three hours' drive north, where she enjoyed dorm life and being away from their feuding parents.

Andrew hadn't been as close to Bernadette growing up as he was to Sol, but as they got older they began to get to know each other better, and he began to relate to her as more of a sister and less of a niece. She was more of a contemporary now. Snowboarding was one thing they had in common; Sol never could get the hang of it. Andrew and Bernadette also enjoyed camping, hiking, and rafting, while Sol, not being very outdoorsy, preferred to participate in local community theater projects, focusing on set design. He obtained his Bachelor's degree in Theater Arts from Southern Oregon University two years ago and moved to Los Angeles to try to get a job in the film industry, which was easier dreamed than done. He had recently found a job as an usher at the Ahmanson Theater and hoped to move up from there. *At least he's working in his field,* Andrew had thought, reminding himself that he was not.

When they reached the lodge, they paid a dollar to put their boards in a secure holding area, then went inside the warm, alpine-styled building. This was one of Andrew's favorite sensations: coming in out of the cold. A quick, primeval sense of relief, good fortune, ease and comfort. In the center of the lodge a tall stone fireplace surrounded by wooden benches beckoned patrons to sit down and thaw out. Behind the fireplace was a wide wooden staircase, upon which echoed the clumping footfalls of ski and snowboarding boots, still heard above the din of the grill and all the people seated at the tables and milling around the lodge.

Andrew pulled his black fleece neck gaiter down and took off his gloves. "Do you mind if I go upstairs to the bar and have a beer?"

"No, go ahead," Bernadette said. "I'll go to the cafeteria and get a snack. I'll just wait for you there."

Andrew walked over to the split-level staircase. As he ascended he could see out the high windows that the conditions were not yet improving, but it was still early and he hoped to get in a few more good runs before calling it a day.

From the entrance to the bar, he could hear a sports event playing on the TV, and small groups of people talked and laughed at their tables. He walked up to the bar and ordered a Corona. After a few minutes, he glanced around to see if he knew anyone and realized that Brooke, seated a few tables away, was waving at him. He stood up and walked over, feeling a little sheepish since the first time he had met her he hadn't been very gracious.

He smiled and said, "Hi, Brooke."

"Hi, Andrew!" she said with enthusiasm. He thought she looked like she'd had a few drinks already, which added to his surprise that she remembered his name. But it seemed to make her remember him in a more positive light. She asked if he skied or snowboarded.

"Snowboard. I'm here with my sister; she's visiting from Eugene."

"That's cool," Brooke said, then introduced him to Mandy, the twenty-something girl on her right, and then to a big guy seated across from them. It was Erica's friend Gavin.

Andrew tried not to show his surprise. "Hi, Mandy," he said, glancing her way politely, and then reached out his hand to Gavin. "Hey, Gavin, I've heard a lot about you. It's good to meet you finally."

"Yeah, you too, Andrew. I think my girlfriend Simone's over at your house right now hanging out with Erica," Gavin said, reaching across the table and shaking his hand.

"Yeah, Erica mentioned that she was going to come over today." *So this is Gavin,* Andrew thought. He hadn't really pictured him before, and it was good to be able to put a face with the name. He looked a bit oafish, not in a stupid way, but in a big, clumsy way. He didn't appear to be participating in any winter sports that day, and neither did Brooke. Mandy was the only one who had a pair of goggles pushed up on her forehead. Many people came up the mountain with friends or family who spent the day on the slopes while they relaxed and waited in the lodge all day. Andrew thought that Gavin seemed to be the latter type. He was friendly enough, at least. Andrew thought he could like him.

"I saw you out at Dogma the other night," Brooke said to Andrew. He said he had seen her that night, and that she looked busy. He commented on how he had seen a lot of people there that night from his college days who were back in town for Christmas, and he and Gavin talked about a few people they discovered that they knew mutually.

When Andrew had drained his bottle, he announced that he was going to find his sister and see if they could get in a few more runs. Hearty, insincere goodbyes were said, and he walked out of the bar and back down the stairs. He smirked as he thought about the fact that he had just had a beer with Erica's friends. As he was getting out little by little, the gap between his world and her world seemed to be closing, even though their emotional gap was widening. He shook off the sense of hopeless resignation and began looking for Bernadette.

He caught a glimpse of her chartreuse fleece hat where she sat in the eating area, surrounded by some friends. He approached and smiled as she introduced him to several recent high school graduates.

"Shall we try to get in a few more runs?" he said.

"Sure," Bernadette said. "Hang on just a second." She turned to finish up with her friends, and then she and Andrew walked out together.

It was still windy and snowing as they put on their gloves, buckled their bindings, and took off back down the hill to the lifts, about a hundred yards away. Andrew figured they'd only be able to get in about three more runs, unless the weather improved.

He followed his sister to the loading area where they stopped to unbuckle their back binding and drag their boards, still attached at their front binding, to get in line for the lift. He had seen other snowboarders push their boards in front of them and put their loose right foot on the board and glide up to the line, like they were skateboarding. It looked cooler than limping along on your right foot, dragging your board that was attached to your left foot. Andrew decided to try it.

He flung the board in front of himself and quickly tried to place his right foot on the other side of the empty binding, but he missed, lost his balance, fell backward, and sat down hard on the upright back of the binding. He had also seen other snowboarders bend the back support of the binding down whenever they unbuckled it and pulled their right foot out of it, and this had to be one reason why. As the top edge of the hard plastic binding made contact with his testicles, a searing pain tore through that region and all he could do was gasp in shock. He had never experienced pain like that before. It was incredible. He immediately dragged himself off to the side and sat in the snow, hoping to numb the pain, which was still shooting through his groin. He began salivating like he was going to throw up when he saw Bernadette looking around for him. He put his arm in the air and waved her over, hoping that he wouldn't throw up, but not really caring if he did.

"What are you doing?" Bernadette asked with impatience as she looked down at him.

He slowly stood up. "Bern, I just hurt myself really bad. I accidentally fell backward and sat down hard on my binding, and I'm in a lot of pain. I need to go back to the lodge to check on it."

Bernadette's expression immediately changed to one of concern. "Oh, my God!" She took his arm. "I'm going with you. Let's get back on the lift."

Andrew dragged his board behind him (*Oh, the irony!* he thought) and got on the short lift, which fortunately did not have a line. As he sat down on the chair, the pain jolted him, and he leaned on his left buttock to ease the pressure. He laughed a little as he explained to Bernadette what he had been trying to do that caused the accident.

As they got off the lift, Andrew realized that he was in such throbbing pain that he would not be able to snowboard back down to get to the lodge.

"I'm going to have to walk," he told Bernadette as he unbuckled his other binding and put the board under his arm.

She told him she'd wait for him at the front door and took off slowly.

Andrew walked as bow-legged as he could, trying not to focus on the pain. Fortunately the lodge was only about a hundred yards away, but it was enough time to think about how ridiculous he had been, trying to look cool, how he would never forget to fold his binding down whenever he took his boot out of it, and to obsess about the prognosis of his injury.

He finally came hobbling up to Bernadette and handed her his board. "I'm just going to go in the bathroom and check on it," he said, panting.

What he saw when he stuck his head between his legs alarmed him almost as much as the initial pain. His sack had swollen to the size of a small, dark purple cantaloupe. There was a small bleeding cut where his skin had split at the point of impact with the edge of the binding. He felt faint as he stood upright and pulled up his pants. This was not good.

"Um, Bern, I'm gonna have to go to the hospital. It's pretty bad. It's like I now have three nuts and all three of them are the size of tennis balls, and I am in so much pain."

"Andrew! I'm so sorry that happened! Do you want me to drive your car?"

Andrew envisioned the car stalling every time Bernadette had to break. "No, I'll drive. My car's really temperamental. But thanks." *God, this is gonna suck.*

Bernadette hiked back to the rental shop to return the boards. She met him back at the car a few minutes later and they began the slow drive home through the increasing snow. Andrew prayed he wouldn't have to stop and put chains on; he hoped that the studded tires on his front-wheel drive car would provide enough traction. He was thankful that the car was an automatic and he didn't need both feet to work a clutch, because there would be no way he could have managed it with the position he was in. He had to lean so far on his left buttock that he was practically on his hip.

Bernadette looked at him. "Are you sure you're okay to drive?"

"Yeah. I can do it. I know it looks weird, but I have to do it this way."

"Okay. Just let me know if I can do anything."

"It'll be all right. I'll drop you off at Mom's and then go to the hospital."

They continued down the winding road to the bottom of the mountain, then got on I-5, which wound its way down the Siskiyou Pass in hard curves for the remaining seven miles into Ashland. Andrew could barely breathe he was in so much pain. It was also difficult to balance so far on his left side like he was and be able to drive. And by the time they reached their mother's house, there was no circulation in his left leg from leaning so far on his hip. He extricated himself from the car and limped into the house.

Their parents, with the help of an architect, had designed the lovely three-and-a-half-thousand square foot home themselves. The living room, or 'great room,' as Elaine preferred to call it, had vaulted ceilings which made the wall of ten-foot-high windows seem even taller. The windows framed a gorgeous view of the south end of Ashland with the Siskiyou Mountains behind it. A six-foot-high flagstone fireplace filled the wall to the left of the windows, and on the wall to the right were eight-foot-high custom-made bookshelves. Their parents had furnished the room with a baby grand piano that only Bernadette knew how to play, a pool table, and a tan Italian leather sofa with a matching chair and ottoman facing the fireplace. Glossy wood floors ran the entire length of the first floor, from the guest wing at the north end, through the great room, all the way down to the kitchen at the south end.

"Hi, guys!" Elaine called as they walked into the kitchen. The white cabinets were contemporary and in good taste, however, Andrew didn't care for the lavender tile countertop and flowery wallpaper. But she had designed it herself, so he never commented negatively on it. "I'm glad you're back safe. The weather's looking awful!"

"Yeah, it's not ideal," Andrew said. He then told her about his injury.

"Andrew! That sounds horrible! Do you want me to drive you to the hospital?"

"No, thanks; I can manage. I just want to call Erica and let her know what happened, and then I'll go."

Andrew picked up the lavender phone and dialed. When Erica answered, she sounded like she had just been laughing.

"Hi, it's me," Andrew said.

"Oh. Hi."

"Um, I just wanted to let you know that I'll be home a little later than I expected. I injured myself pretty bad while snowboarding and I'm going to go to the hospital and have them look at it. I'm at my mom's now; I just dropped off Bernadette and I'm on my way to the hospital, so I don't know how long it'll take there. I hope to be home in an hour or two."

"Okay. Whatever it takes."

Whatever it takes? What's that supposed to mean? "Don't you want to hear what happened?"

Andrew could hear someone laughing in the background. "Well, I'm hanging out with Simone right now, so just tell me when you get home."

It felt like a slap. "Okay. Bye," he said and hung up the phone.

She doesn't even care that I've been hurt! She'd rather hang out with her little fan club! I'm going to the fucking hospital, and all she can say is 'Okay, whatever it takes'! She could have at least pretended to care. Would that have been so hard? It's not like I'm her husband or the father of her children or anyone important.

He waddled out to the living room and said goodbye to his mother and sister, the two people he knew who really did care, and tried not to think about the one who should.

Seven

Erica bet that the ridiculous position Andrew was lying in was a sympathy ploy to get her to cancel her overnight trip to Shasta.

Dream on, Andrew! she said to herself as she stuffed her backpack with a couple of long-sleeved shirts, thermal underwear, socks, and snowboarding gear. Gavin and Simone were coming in a few minutes to pick her up for the ninety-minute drive to Mt. Shasta City, where they would spend the night and go to the Mt. Shasta Board and Ski Park the next morning. They were meeting a few other co-workers there at a small hotel. She looked forward to having a night and a day off with her friends. Andrew was driving her crazy.

She zipped up her pack, laced up her hiking boots, and walked out to the living room to put her pack by the front door. Sure enough, Andrew was still lying upside-down on the couch with his legs outstretched up against the wall, his head hanging over the front edge of the cushions, as he had been doing all day every day when he wasn't eating, in the bathroom, or doing something for the kids. Eileen thought it was funny that Daddy was upside-down, and Nathan would walk by and try to stick his fingers in Andrew's nostrils. Now Nathan sat next to him watching Disney's *Toy Story* and sucking his fingers.

"Andrew, I think that after five days of being upside-down like that, it's not going to start swelling up again."

"The doctor said to elevate my pelvis as much as possible for a week. And it *is* still swollen. And it still hurts. When I have to sit on it, it feels like I'm sitting on an inflatable pillow, like one of those donut things for hemorrhoids. Hey! Maybe I should get one of those," he said with a goofy laugh.

Maybe you should lay off the Vicodin, Erica thought. She knew she should feel sorry for him, especially with his injury, but the truth was that she couldn't stand to be around him, and everything he said or did irritated her. She would have taken off her wedding ring, but it came in handy, being a bartender, to have an excuse when drunk guys hit on her. All she had to do was flash her hand and say, "Sorry!" But she realized that by keeping it on she was sending the wrong message to Andrew, whose desperate attempts to keep their relationship going, like getting his mother to babysit so they could go to a pub and throw darts together, exasperated her. She couldn't wait to get out of the house.

As if on cue, a pair of headlights came up the driveway, and she hugged and kissed Nathan and Eileen good-bye.

"I'll see you tomorrow night!" she called on her way out the door. She climbed in the back seat of Gavin's red mid-size SUV, sat next to Brooke, and greeted everyone. Gavin was driving, and Erica was glad to see that he wasn't stoned. Brooke, however, appeared to be, with her blood-shot, heavy-lidded eyes. At least she had enough sense never to come to work stoned; she was dependable. Erica was glad she had hired her. Simone was probably sober. She was focused on her photography career and didn't want to jeopardize her job. Erica admired her for that, especially since she lived with a pothead. Erica could never understand how Simone could tolerate Gavin's almost constant pot smoking. Maybe Simone had gotten into a rut as well; Erica could identify with that. But it was so much harder to break out of a rut when you had children. Simone didn't! What was holding her back? It seemed so unlike her, as driven as she was, and independent.

As they got on the freeway, Erica felt sheepish about the giddiness she felt; she couldn't wait to see Nick, who was meeting them there with Isaac. She did her best to squelch the tinge of guilt in the back of her mind. After all, she had told Andrew that she wanted to be separated. If they had enough money, she would have already moved out. They were no longer together. They hadn't even had sex in over a month! There was no reason why, if the attraction she had to Nick turned out to be mutual, she should keep herself from acting on it. *There.* Satisfied with her justification, she decided to ponder something else. But she kept returning to Nick.

"How's Andrew doing?" Simone called from the front of the car.

Come on, Simone. You know I don't want to be thinking about HIM now.
"Oh, he's fine. The doctor told him to elevate his pelvis, so all week long he's been lying upside-down on the couch with his legs going up the wall,

high on Vicodin."

Laughter ensued, and Brooke suggested that he probably could get a really good high that way, which Erica confirmed.

She gazed out the window at the dark mountains as they wound their way down from the 4310-foot Siskiyou Pass, the highest elevation on I-5. They were lucky the sky was clear with good conditions. During winter months it was often shut down for hours at a time due to heavy snows. People had been stuck up there, in their cars. Sometimes even having tire chains or a four-wheel-drive vehicle didn't matter. If the pass had been closed, no one would be allowed through.

Suddenly she noticed two tiny lights about fifteen feet from the freeway, off the pavement. They were deer eyes. Her heart skipped a beat.

"Deer!" she called out, alerting Gavin.

"Where?" he gasped.

"Off on the side; we just passed it. I didn't mean to scare you. It's just kind of a reflex of mine when I see one."

"A few years ago I hit a deer while I was on a motorcycle," Brooke said. "It was really scary. I came around a corner on a winding mountain road and it wasn't even in the road, it was on the side, and it leaped out at me as I passed and hit me like a dart. Dislocated my shoulder."

"Yeah, hitting a deer can really mess you up," Erica said, looking out the window again. One night when she was twelve, her mother had taken Caleb and her to an employee Christmas party. She was in charge of watching Caleb, but the food was good, and there was a TV with the animated *Santa Claus Is Coming to Town* playing on it. There were a few other children in attendance, and she was the eldest. All the adults seemed to expect her to be the babysitter. "Keep an eye on Casey for me, okay, Erica?" "Could you make sure Stephanie doesn't have too much candy?" She wondered if her mother had told everyone what a good babysitter she was, told them she'd be at the party, probably said she'd be glad to do it. She spent the entire evening watching the clock on the wall; the minutes ticked slowly by while the adults in the kitchen caroused themselves into oblivion. One by one, the littler kids fell asleep on the floor, including Caleb. He was five. He didn't really feel like a brother. He felt more like how she imagined having a nephew would feel, one she loved and protected. She thought of herself as Caleb's guardian angel and wished that she had one of her own. Then she smiled as she realized that Aunt Maggie had been hers, for a while. Aunt

Maggie had been hers before she was born.

Finally their mother, who had permed shoulder-length brown hair and was wearing a knee-length red polyester wrap-front dress and white plat-form heels, had socialized long enough and they could go home. They got into her little brown two-door car and turned on the radio to hear more Christmas songs on the way home. She was singing loudly (their mother). Maybe that's why she didn't notice the deer until it was too late. She'd also had more than a few drinks. Erica had seen it first. She was in the front passenger seat, and Caleb was lying across the back seat. She saw the deer in the middle of the road, and her eyes locked onto it. A second later she yelled, "Deer!" and her mother swerved hard to avoid it. But the deer began running the same way that her mother swerved, and they hit it on Erica's side. Time stood still as the side of the deer's head, with its glassy black eye, crashed onto the windshield for a second, a few inches from Erica's head, and then fell off to the side. But the worst part happened next. Because of her mother's hard swerve, the car leaned to one side, balancing on two wheels, and nearly rolled. But it didn't. *Good thing*, Erica thought now, as she remembered that none of them, including Caleb, had been wearing seatbelts. Of course, the back seat probably didn't even *have* seatbelts back then. For weeks, whenever Erica closed her eyes she could still see the deer's face right in front of her own. She could see it now, its wet, lifeless black eye staring at her.

Erica yawned to pop her ears, then closed her eyes to rest the remainder of the way to Mt. Shasta City. They passed by Weed and Erica felt a pang of regret realizing that she'd let a whole year go by since she'd last visited her mother and Caleb, who both lived there. It was only an hour away! Why didn't she just pop down for the weekend some time? She felt embarrassed about not visiting, which made it easy to allow more time to slip by. Caleb was her only sibling, the only person in the world who shared parts of her bewildering childhood. They had the same mother. That fact alone forged an enduring union.

Gavin played a tape of mixed '80s songs, and when they exited the free-way, she had David Bowie's "Modern Love" stuck in her mind, which had been one of her favorite songs in junior high, with its catchy rhythm and exuberant horns. They all sang it as they unloaded their bags from the car and walked across the parking lot of the hotel. "Don't believe in modern love!" Erica belted out. She felt the giddiness return.

Later, after checking in and dropping their things off in their room, they joined Nick, Isaac, and his brother in the hotel bar. "It's a 'lounge,'" Simone had protested with mock superiority, dragging out the word. But it was a comfortable lounge, at least, dimly lit, furnished with upholstered velour seating and a river-rock fireplace.

Erica leaned on the bar and ordered a rum and Coke. As she did whenever she went to any bar other than her own, she watched how the bartender made her drink. This one was a young, full-bodied blond, *probably just turned twenty-one,* Erica thought. Not that a rum and Coke was difficult by any means, but it was more of a habit with her to watch. And unless she was completely dissatisfied with any drink, she always tipped well. "Always take care of your own," she would say to anyone who was with her.

She made her way back to the table of her friends, their faces glowing from the light and warmth of the nearby fireplace. She sat at one corner, next to Nick, of course, and across from Isaac's brother Miles. Isaac excused himself to get another drink already.

"You're probably just going to ask the bartender if she wants to go up the mountain with us tomorrow," Miles said.

"Yeah, but first I'm going to ask her if she wants to go hot-tubbing with us tonight!"

Everyone laughed, and Erica thought, *Same old Isaac.* She had known him longer than she knew anyone else there. They had met three years ago at the French restaurant, where he had waited tables and she bartended. They had literally collided on her first day working there, and disentangling themselves had not been easy. Even though she felt comfortable around him, there existed this underlying sense of restlessness. She blamed it on his eyes, his intense, piercing black eyes sitting deep in their sockets, mysterious and enticing. He had a history of using them, and his tousled brown hair, to his advantage, and Erica knew firsthand how well that worked. Isaac was the type of person you couldn't stay mad at, for even five minutes. Charm oozed out of him. Amused, she watched how he approached the bartender to work his magic.

She glanced at Miles, forgetting how similar he and his brother looked. Same eyes, hair, rangy build. She had met him when he had visited Isaac two summers ago, after returning from six months of studying abroad in Greece, and she had enjoyed talking with him about his travel experiences and career plans. He seemed to possess the maturity that Isaac often lacked, and the ambition. Isaac seemed content to be a professional waiter for an indeterminate amount of time, with no college plans in sight. Not that it diminished his appeal in any way. But, a little, Erica had to admit now. She just realized, looking at Miles, that she had a tiny crush on him. *Maybe. Certainly not as big as the crush on Nick.* But she was still too nervous to start small-talk with him, so she turned to Miles and asked if he was still attending the University of Oregon.

Miles, in a handsome, composed voice, confirmed that he was, and would obtain his Master's in architecture in a year and a half. They discussed Erica's school progress and plans for a few minutes while sipping cocktails, laughed about Isaac still hitting on the bartender, and then Miles excused himself to go to the restroom.

Nick turned to her and her stomach leaped. His long, wavy blond hair was pulled back in a pony tail, and she couldn't help feeling like diving into his eyes, which were the clear light blue of a swimming pool. "So how many kids do you have?" he asked.

"Two: a boy and a girl. They're one and a half and three." Erica wondered if her having kids would be an issue with him, but she could find that out later. *Much later.*

"I bet they're really cute. What are their names?" He took a slow sip of his beer.

Every move he makes is so sensual, Erica thought. "Nathan and Eileen."

"Those are great names. How did you decide on them?"

Erica loved telling people about her children's names, because she had chosen them. She was delighted that Nick had asked! She told him how she'd chosen them from some of her favorite songs growing up: Nathan from "Nathan Jones" by Diana Ross and the Supremes, and Eileen from "Come On, Eileen" by Dexy's Midnight Runners. Of course, Elaine, Andrew's mother, had assumed that they named Eileen after her, and they didn't have the heart to correct her. Andrew had the idea of naming their daughter Georgia, after the Ray Charles song, and sometimes Erica wished she had consented to that, having grown tired of hearing Elaine refer to Eileen as "my little namesake" all the time. But, she could let it go. It wasn't that big of a deal.

Nick commented that naming children after songs was a cool idea and asked to see pictures of them.

How sweet of him to ask! "No, and I can't believe I don't! I'm such a bad mother for not carrying pictures of my babies! I'll put some in my wallet when I get home and show them to you next time we work together."

"Okay. And hey, you're not a bad mother for not carrying pictures around with you. You're just a busy mother. Don't be so hard on yourself."

He says all the right things, Erica thought. *And he's a business major with goals. And I could really get used to the sound of his voice. Not to mention gazing into his eyes.* "Thanks," she said.

TWO MONTHS LATER, Andrew finally found a job. Erica was glad, but on the other hand, she knew that having him go back to work would mean a big change for her. She would have to quit school for a while, which disappointed her because of all the momentum she had built up in the past year. But Andrew working was definitely a good thing. They could afford for her to move out in a few months, which she wanted to do now that she and Nick were getting involved. It turned out that he wasn't the least bit bothered by her having children; he actually enjoyed going with them on outings to the park, and they even had a picnic with the kids at the lake one warm sunny day. Erica felt very compatible with him, and it was getting too messy to keep assuring him that she and Andrew were only still living together for the sake of financial convenience. Which was the truth, but Andrew didn't seem to catch on to that. He seemed to think that they were just "taking a break." Probably because she kept assuring Andrew that Nick was just a friend. She didn't think he was ready yet to hear that she had a boyfriend.

Erica put down the book on Richard Avedon that she had been reading for a final paper she was writing for her photography class and stared out the second-story window of the college library. It was a cloudy late afternoon in March, and she would need to stop and go to work soon. Three days a week, she carried a backpack containing some work clothes for the days when she would need to go straight to work from an afternoon class. She would no longer have to do that for a while, and she wouldn't miss it. All the juggling she had been doing was stressful. Next week she had three final exams to take (the paper for the photography class was her fourth final), and then spring term would end and she would be home alone with the kids (mostly just Eileen, since Nathan was now going to Early Childhood Development Center three mornings a week) until it was time for her to go to work.

Gabriel, Andrew's father who had just retired, volunteered to babysit the kids two afternoons a week on the days when Erica had to leave for work before Andrew had returned from work. It was a relief not to need to put them in daycare, especially Nathan, since they knew that he would not do well in a typical noisy, bustling daycare situation.

Andrew would start his job in a little over a week. He had been hired as an office assistant for a small home-based order fulfillment and shipping company. There were no benefits, but at least they were flexible about when he needed to leave work early to be with the kids. Erica hoped the job would work out for him; their financial situation worried her. Their anticipated tax refund would have to all be put toward their debt, and even that would barely make a dent in an amount that seemed impossible for them to ever pay off.

They felt fortunate that the state paid for Nathan's ongoing therapy that he so desperately needed. They could already see some improvement in that he could follow directions better and was beginning to use the laminated cue cards to indicate wants and needs. Because of his emerging ability to communicate, he screamed a little bit less now at home, a welcome respite. And with the program's learning-through-play approach, his own play had begun to show signs of increasing creativity. Last week, Erica had poured some frozen corn niblets in a bowl for him to eat (he would not eat them when cooked), and he ate some and then went and got his stuffed Tigger doll and brought it to the table with him. He put Tigger's face into the bowl of corn to pretend he was eating it too. This was a huge step for Nathan. Erica, amazed at his progress, was glad that she had been home and able to see it. She walked over to the table and reinforced the action by saying, "Tigger's eating the corn, too. Nice sharing," as the teachers and therapists had instructed her to do during home visits.

Erica turned her attention back to her book and jotted down some notes. "Avedon is best known for his portraits," she wrote. "Called a 'reductionist.' Omits unnecessary aspects from his photos. Mostly head shots using flat, artificial light or plain daylight, exposing flaws and wrinkles."

She closed the book and realized she was just too mentally distracted to get any work done now. Maybe she could get off work early tonight and finish up at home.

My life is full of flaws and wrinkles.

Eight

"Here, Sam, you can start by opening up and sorting all this mail," the office manager said, dumping a bag of mail on the desk in front of Andrew. They had decided to call him Sam, short for Samuel, Andrew's middle name, because the warehouse manager was named Andrew (and also did not go by Andy) and the office manager was named Andrea, and that was confusing enough already.

"Okay," Andrew said, feeling a tightness at the base of his neck that would be a full-blown tension headache within an hour. His first day at the new job, his first day working at all in over three years, and it was not a strong start. He grabbed a thin metal letter opener and began ripping open envelopes.

He had lived in Ashland for eight years and never even knew this place existed until he saw the ad in the paper three weeks ago. "Office assistant needed; experience with phones; must have car." The "must have car" part was due to the fact that it was an office out of the bottom half of someone's home, and the home was located six miles outside of town, not accessible by any bus route. It was actually two miles past Andrew's mother's home, around the other side of the lake.

Andrew recalled coming up the long gravel driveway for his interview and parking around the back. In addition to what appeared to be the main house, there were three yellow buildings, two small, one large, scattered around the four-acre property. Andrew wondered if this was an old commune of sorts; the ad hadn't described what sort of business it was, and he forgot to ask when he called to set up his interview.

He tentatively got out of the car, straightened his khaki pants and light blue oxford cloth shirt, and began walking, looking around for anything that resembled an office. A German shepherd came bounding his way, and he froze, thinking that maybe he should just get back in his car and take off. *Forget the interview.* Then he noticed the dog's tail wagging, so he figured he wouldn't be mauled. He patted the dog's back and began walking down toward the main house when a tall middle-aged man with a full beard came around the corner and walked up to him. He wore faded, frayed jeans and a checked flannel shirt and walked slowly, shuffling his feet in his Birkenstock sandals. When he spoke, it was with a bit of a slur. He pointed to the dog. "That's Ginger."

Andrew petted the dog, then looked at what he figured was an old hippie who had done too many drugs in his day and never quite recovered. "I'm here for a job interview?"

"Oh. The office is right there," the man said, pointing to the bottom of the main house.

Andrew thanked him and walked away, wondering just what sort of office it would be. Some Northwest conservation organization? An organic trail mix company? Manufacturers of kaleidoscopes and tambourines?

Plenty of light streamed in the office through numerous windows, so it did not feel like a basement. It felt cheery and, well, normal as soon as Andrew met the two women in the office, Andrea and Lucy, who were definitely not hippies. They were dressed casually, jeans and long-sleeved knit shirts and tennis shoes. It looked like a typical office with computers, phones, four desks and chairs, filing cabinets, printers, a fax machine, and plants. The walls were covered in bleached wood paneling and had a few posters of tropical beach scenes hung on them. There was a pretty view of the lake, surrounded by rolling hills and low clouds, out the front windows.

Lucy, a quiet, petite woman in her forties with dark curly hair and small round glasses, conducted the interview. She explained that the owner, Gloria Wright, was in Los Angeles finalizing all the details of the new account that the person whose position they were hiring for would manage.

"Are you familiar with New Age concepts?" Lucy asked.

"Well, not very, but I'm open-minded about them and willing to learn." *What, like reincarnation?* he thought. That was all the New Age he knew.

"That's good that you're open-minded about it because most of our clients are New Age music labels, and part of our job here is to answer phone calls from customers who have questions about the products, so it's important to be accepting of the concepts."

Andrew then discussed his experience dealing with difficult questions when he had worked in the customer service booth at Payless Drugstore, and Lucy seemed pleased. She told him that he would need to come in for a second interview in two or three days, when Gloria would be back.

Upon his return, he was not greeted by the dog/old hippie combo, and he felt much more comfortable knowing where he was going. When he entered the office, Gloria, a blue-jean-and-T-shirt-clad, average-height woman with straight chestnut hair grazing her shoulders, warmly shook his hand and invited him to sit in a chair next to her desk at the rear of the office. He detected an accent, possibly Australian.

"So, you've met everybody?" she asked.

Andrew thought that was an unusual way to begin an interview. He thought it almost sounded like she had already decided to hire him. "I think so. And a guy with a beard introduced me to Ginger," he said with a smile.

"Oh, that was my husband, Pat. He's recuperating from major back surgery. He can't even walk unless he's on pain medication. He hopes to be going back to work in a few weeks. He's a real estate agent."

Pain medication. That would explain the slow walk and the slur, Andrew thought. *Real Estate Agent. Probably not an old hippie, either.*

They talked about Andrew's qualifications, repeating much of what he had said to Lucy in the first interview. When things seemed to be winding down, Gloria said, "So, if we decide to hire you, we'll probably need to call you by a different name. As you know, we have an Andrea in the office, and the warehouse manager is named Andrew, so in order to avoid confusion, would you mind going by your middle name?"

"No, not at all. That would be fine." *I just need a job*, Andrew thought.

"So Sam is okay?"

"Sure."

Gloria then gave him a tour of the rest of the property, including the warehouse, which was the largest of the three yellow buildings. The other two were storage sheds, he discovered later, not commune dwellings. Andrew met the other Andrew, a nice guy about his age, but a bit larger, with shorter, darker hair. He was calm with a subdued voice and a round, pale face that looked like a clock. He had probably met a dozen other Andrews over the course of his life; it always surprised him to see how different they were, as if nomenclature should determine physical appearance, characteristics, even personality somehow. It would be strange to be called Sam five days a week, but he realized in a small business like that it would be necessary.

Andrew focused on his task. He had all the mail opened but had no idea how he should be sorting it. Most of the envelopes contained what looked like order forms with checks for payment, and some envelopes were just checks alone. Then there were some envelopes containing little cards with names and addresses on them, requesting catalogs, and others with just letters in them. Andrew made four different piles.

"I think I've sorted everything," he said to Andrea, a pretty woman about his age with long, velvet brown hair and oval wire-rimmed glasses. Her hair actually looked a lot like Erica's when it was its natural color, and grown out, thick and wavy.

"Great," Andrea said, walking over to his desk.

"Gloria wants you to call the mail order customers and let them know that there will be a two-week delay in shipping their order due to the warehouse location being moved. The company you're going to manage, Valley of the Moon, had their warehouse in L.A., so now all their product is on its way up here, and we can't process or ship any orders until it gets here and is sorted by the warehouse and we have all their inventory counted. So just go through this stack of orders, and call and let the customer know about the delay in shipping their order," Andrea instructed.

"Okay," Andrew said. This didn't sound fun.

Andrea then showed him how to dial out and said, "Let me know if you have any questions" as she walked back to her desk.

Questions? Andrew thought. *Good God, I have no idea what to say to these people.*

He took a deep breath and dialed the first person. An answering machine picked up, to his relief. He said in a professional tone, "Hello, this is Valley of the Moon calling regarding your recent order with us. We wanted to let you know that there will be a two-week delay in processing your order due to our warehouse moving. We appreciate your patience. Thank you."

Well, that's the first one, Andrew thought. There were about twenty in the stack. He dialed the next one. A gruff-sounding old man answered.

"May I speak to Jeff Gibbons?" Andrew said.

"He ain't here. Who's this?"

Andrew rattled off his lines about the shipping delay, already hating the job.

"I don't know what the hell you're talkin about. What do you mean about a two-week delay? That's bullshit! I didn't order nothing. That's probably my lazy son."

Andrew bristled. "Could you take a message, please? I can give you a toll-free number."

"I'm ain't takin no goddamn message. You'll just have to call back later!" the man yelled and hung up.

Andrew's head throbbed. *Is that what this company's customers are like? That's abusive! This is just as bad as waiting tables. At least with that job I got tips.*

Andrew continued making calls, and fortunately none were as bad as the old man. But that call had thrown him off, and he never really felt "on" to begin with. He couldn't wait to take a break for lunch. Every time Andrea or Gloria had walked by his desk and called him Sam, it took him a second to respond because it didn't even seem like they were talking to him. Who was Sam? Sam Pavel? *That person doesn't even exist,* Andrew thought. *This is so weird.*

On his lunch break, he sat at his desk and ate his turkey sandwich while Gloria's three dogs, Ginger, the German shepherd, Maddie, the short-legged Cocker/Corgi mix, and Pugsley, a pug, crowded around for handouts and took turns sniffing him, since he was new. They were in the office constantly, along with a big long-haired tabby cat named Angel, who laid on his carpet-covered cat tree all day. Andrew could hear the chirping and squawking of several birds up the stairs in the main part of the house. He was glad he wasn't allergic to any animals. That was something Lucy had asked in the first interview, if he liked animals. He had given her an enthusiastic yes, not realizing of course, that he would be surrounded by them all day long. But it was actually more of a novelty for him. He had grown up with many cats and missed being able to have any now, since they were not allowed to have pets in their rental. And he liked dogs, too. He had to be careful not to trip on any of them while walking back and forth in the office, however.

While he ate, Andrew looked over the Valley of the Moon catalog so that he could start familiarizing himself with their products. Andrea had suggested that he take one of the catalogs home with him. It was full of subliminal self-help tapes and CDs, guided meditations, and books on past-life regression and other metaphysical concepts. They also did seminars about fulfilling your life's purpose, something he could certainly look into. He was starting to think that he might like this job after all.

After lunch, Andrea came over and showed him how to start entering catalog requests into the computer database. It was a DOS-based program called On the Money, and when Andrew logged into it, he was reminded of the old Apple computers he had worked on when he first started college, with their black screens and green letters. This program was a little better, but the graphics were nothing like Windows programs, which he was now used to working with on his computer at home. She showed him how to enter the customers' names and addresses, which was simple. He typed in several of them, liking the data entry part of the job much better than the phones.

Andrew hadn't realized how difficult it would be to get used to being away from the kids all day. When he stopped to think about it, he truly missed Nathan and Eileen. He stared out the window above his desk at the lower Cascade mountains that surrounded the property. It was certainly beautiful there. As long as most of the customers weren't as bad as that one, he could get used to it.

He suddenly became aware of someone's voice repeating, "Sam?"

It was Gloria, at her desk eight feet away from his. "Sam?"

Again, he didn't realize she was addressing him.

"Sam? Everything all right?"

Andrew jerked his head away from the window and turned to her. "Yes, Gloria, sorry. I'm fine."

This Sam business was going to be hard to get used to.

ERICA NEEDED THE car to go to the grocery store, so she dropped Andrew off at work that day. He was right: the place did look like an old commune with all the buildings, out in a rural area. *Why did he have to get a job way the hell out here?* she thought as she drove back on Highway 66, the winding road into town. *At least he's finally working. Maybe I can move out in a couple of months.*

She was slowly getting used to being home all morning, every morning, getting breakfast for the kids, doing some chores, reading or drawing a little, then fixing their lunch. No wonder Andrew went a little nuts without having the car.

They couldn't take them for a walk in the double stroller because they lived on a steep hill. There was no park within walking distance, just the old cemetery on Sheridan, the next street over. A couple of times a week they would walk over with the kids and let them toddle around in the grass while they looked at the old tombstones, some dating back to the mid-1800s. So many children's graves from those days! It was an odd place to take young children to play, but they had to make do with what they had.

The cemetery, however, charmed them for only so long, and Erica had to find something constructive to do with her time. It was hard for her to just relax and do nothing since she was used to having so much going on. One week of lying around the house taking a much-deserved break was enough for her. She still had work, of course, in the afternoons and evenings, but she had almost eight hours to fill from when the kids woke up to when she went to work.

They were out of milk. It was the best reason she could come up with to the have the car for the day, since she had the day off and could pick Andrew up when he got off at five. She pulled into the Safeway parking lot and tried to think of anything else that they needed while she was there. Maybe after she dropped the food off at home, they could go to the park.

Erica pulled Eileen out of her car seat and slung her on her hip. Then she went around to the other side of the car and took Nathan out, holding him by the hand. He wore his dark green hooded fleece jacket, as he did whenever he left the predictable environment of their home.

"We're going into the store now. You stay close to Mom, okay? We have to get some milk, and some lettuce, and some bread. Then we'll take the food home and we'll go to the park! Does that sound like fun?"

Her children were silent. Nathan's fingers were in his mouth, and Eileen pointed at a dog that someone had left near the entrance.

They went inside and Nathan instantly became tense. Erica and Andrew had discovered that he just couldn't process all the sensory input of a grocery store, so they usually left him home with one of them while the other did the full week's worth of grocery shopping. Erica had hoped that Nathan could handle it for a little while; she only had to get a few things. But he pulled on her hand, anxiety all over his face, saying, "Go!" every few seconds.

What could be bothering him so much? Erica wondered. There weren't too many people in there at that time of the morning, and often crowded areas set him off. *The fluorescent lights? The music over the speaker system?* It seemed low enough to Erica, but Nathan was now almost in tears, yanking to free his hand and saying "Go!" fifty more times and trying to head-butt her to express his dismay. He would often, when upset, squeal while putting his head down and his body into a charging stance, then ram his head into the thighs of whichever parent or adult he was trying to communicate with. Erica realized she couldn't carry a gallon of milk, and Eileen, and hold onto Nathan. If she didn't, Nathan would have bolted out the door into the parking lot; his anxiety level was so high.

She grabbed a half-gallon carton and balanced it between Eileen and her own chest, with Nathan still pulling on her. No way was she getting anything else.

"It's okay, Nathan, it's okay. We're going. We just have to pay the money for the milk, and then we'll go. Stop pulling on me. Just hold my hand." *No line, please no line.*

Erica walked quickly to the express lane and set the milk down on the belt. A man with a small basket of things was in front of them.

Please hurry, Erica pleaded in her mind. Nathan had at least stopped saying "Go!" for a minute. As long as they didn't have to do a price check on any of the guy's items, they might get out of there quick enough.

Suddenly, as jarring as an explosion came the sound of a motorized coffee grinder in the open customer service booth right next to them. In the split second that Erica thought *Oh, no*, Nathan had already begun screaming, shrieking at the top of his lungs. He threw himself on the ground in hysterics, writhing and kicking and howling, a look of insane fear on his poor little face.

Erica set Eileen down, but she couldn't pick Nathan up in that state. She just said, "It's okay, it's okay," until finally someone shut the grinder off and she told him, soothingly, "It's over, now. It's okay, it's over."

Nathan continued sobbing, gasping, and resumed his desperate plea of "Go!" every few seconds.

The suit-wearing guy in front with the basket turned and said, "Jesus Christ, what a tantrum!"

Erica felt the blood pulsing in her ears and began to shake. "Can't you see he got scared?"

"Yeah, right! Can't you shut him up?"

"I'm sorry, he's upset."

"Whatever," the guy said, grabbing his bag and leaving.

Erica's eyes brimmed with tears. She debated on yelling after him, "He has autism!" but could barely accept the concept herself, so how could she possibly explain it to anyone else? Especially someone who obviously wouldn't have given a rat's ass.

Nathan's sobs had subsided, but he was still pulling on her to go. Eileen, fortunately, stayed close to Erica's other side, although she had begun to whine, "Up!"

"I'm sorry for the disturbance," she told the cashier, handing over a few dollars.

"It's okay. I could tell that noise startled him. Do you want a bag?"

Erica left the store feeling defeated, like she had tried to prove something and failed. Or maybe it was because, more and more, she found that she could no longer deny that her son really did have autism. Nathan, at three and a half, rarely spoke, sucked his fingers, and twirled his hair almost constantly. Hair-washing was still a huge ordeal. He reacted to all mechanical noises as if they actually hurt him, and Erica was starting to think that maybe they did. Vacuum cleaners, blenders, even leaf blowers three blocks away bothered him. *He has to outgrow it someday,* Erica thought. But the new books on autism they had been reading said that autism could not be outgrown. What kind of a future was there in that?

She drove straight home, not wanting to attempt the park. Even if there wasn't the milk to put away, she didn't have the strength to deal with another scene in public and, hearing the dying remnants of Nathan's sobs coming from the back seat, Erica didn't think her son did either.

THE NEXT MORNING dawned dark and dreary for the first day of spring. Erica rose and began getting Nathan ready for school, as she now did three mornings a week, while Andrew got ready for work. Since he had started working, neither one of them were able to drive Nathan into Medford for school, so the school district provided transportation to and from school for him on one of the little yellow special education busses, called a "sped bus." In starting to deal with the local school district, they learned that Nathan was a "sped child" and they were "sped parents," members of an elite group, initiated with the first meeting/home visit/therapy session they had to attend, one of perhaps hundreds over the course of their child's life.

Nathan ate a bowl of organic cocoa ball cereal and milk, his habitual breakfast, while Andrew made himself a turkey sandwich to bring for his lunch. All three of them were quiet, their minds and bodies adjusting to having to function before they wanted to. Eileen stumbled into the kitchen, crabby. Not one of them was a morning person. *Must be genetic*, Erica thought. She certainly didn't recall either of her parents even being around in the morning. She got herself ready for school alone at an early age, then had to get Caleb ready when he was old enough to go to school. Andrew said he also remembered getting ready by himself quite often. His mother was in bed with chronic depression; Erica's mother was in bed with a hangover. His father had already gone to work; her father was off backpacking in Mexico or Alaska or something.

Andrew picked up his blue insulated lunch bag, kissed the kids goodbye, and left for work. He knew better than to expect a kiss from Erica; she had put an end to that two months ago, and also stopped wearing her wedding ring, which didn't go over well. "I thought we were just separated!" Andrew had whined. "That is so disrespectful to me. I'm still your husband!" *Only on paper*, Erica thought. "You know that us living together is just out of financial necessity," she told him. Andrew went on to accuse her of "crazy-making," a term he had picked up from his counselor, who he was now seeing only once a month. "It's not a separation if we're still living together!" She still couldn't bring herself to tell him about Nick. Why did everything have to be so complicated?

Erica brushed Nathan's teeth, squeezed out a warm, wet washcloth and wiped his eyes and mouth, then put on their jackets and waited for the bus to pull up their driveway. Eileen ate dry Rice Chex out of her bowl at the kitchen table and drank apple juice, her favorite. She seemed a little happier now. Erica wondered if it was because she knew that Nathan would be leaving now and she would have Mommy all to herself. She wouldn't put it past her. Eileen routinely threw tantrums during Nathan's home visits with his therapists because she knew that she wasn't the center of attention. The therapists were always thoughtful enough to make sure Eileen had toys to play with too, but she somehow knew that they weren't there to pay attention to her, and that bothered her. She became crabby and temperamental, disturbing the therapy session, and Erica would often have to take her to the bedroom, which propelled her into a full-blown tantrum behind the closed door.

The little bus pulled up and Erica walked Nathan out the door. Eileen, content to sit at the table, knew the routine. Nathan did too, fortunately. The first time Erica had put him on the bus, he screamed and yelled as she buckled him in the child safety seat, with a look on his face like he felt betrayed. The kind bus driver, an older Santa Claus-looking man, assured her that all the kids screamed like that the first few times, then they got used to it. It was the day before Andrew had started his new job, so he was able to stay home with Eileen while Erica followed the bus in their car, so that she would be there when Nathan got to school and not think that he had been abandoned. She remembered the state that Nathan was in when she helped him out of the bus: hiccupping from sobbing, shaking, his face blotchy with tears streaming out of his red eyes. Erica felt horrible that her son had suffered so.

By the end of the first week, Nathan was doing fine, the bus driver assured her. And by now, the end of the second week, he was a pro. He walked up the steps by himself and offered no resistance while Erica buckled him in, said goodbye to Nathan and the bus driver, and went back in the house.

Eileen broke into an impish grin as she walked in.

"Hey, silly," Erica said, smiling, kissing her sweet head. She stuck two pieces of bread in the toaster and poured a glass of orange juice.

Erica relished Eileen's rare smiles, recalling her difficult infancy. At any time during the day Eileen would start crying, and it could last for hours. They guessed it was colic, but colic, according to the baby books, happened in the evenings, and it wasn't limited to evenings with Eileen, although Andrew said those were the worst. She felt bad for Andrew; he dealt with most of it because she had gone back to work at that point, so even though she was exhausted with having to work, she looked forward to the break.

Yet, there were moments when Eileen would reward them with the sweetest laughter and the cutest little smiles. They nicknamed her their Jeckyl and Hyde baby, for she could be crying one minute and laughing the next. There was never any middle ground with her. And now, at one and a half, she was already throwing some first-rate tantrums. Erica wondered how many years it would be before she felt comfortable taking either one of her children out in public again.

Nine

oney, I'm home, Andrew said to himself as he got out of the car, then laughed.

He remembered the first time he had walked through the front door and called that out to Erica after they had just moved in together. It was a rite of passage he had long looked forward to, one that he felt he was now being denied. *Kids should grow up hearing that,* he thought. *Now mine won't.*

He walked through the front door. "Hi, Dad," he said to his father. He set his insulated lunch box on top of the entertainment center near the front door and gave his father a hug.

"Hi, Andrew! How was work?" Gabriel's round, balding, silvery head came up to Andrew's eyebrows. He smiled and embraced his son. The joke of the family was that Andrew got his "height," all five-foot-nine of him, from his mother's side of the family, since her father had been five-ten.

"Fine. How did everything go here?"

"Pretty good. Eileen took a little nap on the futon, and Nathan and I watched *Toy Story.*"

"Yeah, that's one of his favorites."

Andrew greeted his children, who were quietly seated on opposite sides of the couch, watching another movie, looking like they never caused any problems. Eileen put her little arms around his neck, but Nathan acted as if he resented the intrusion, craning his head around Andrew to see the TV.

"They both had a poop," Gabriel said, putting his blue canvas barn jacket on over his "U of O Dad" sweatshirt.

Why does he feel compelled to tell me that? Every time? "Okay," Andrew said. *It's as if now that I've reprimanded him enough about bad-mouthing Mom and talking about their divorce proceedings, he's reduced to talking about his grandchildren's bodily functions with me. Can't come up with any better topics.*

Andrew told his father how much he appreciated him watching the kids and suggested they have dinner together sometime, which was met with enthusiasm. They made tentative plans, around his father's bowling schedule, of course, and Gabriel said goodbye to his grandchildren. Eileen waved limply and Nathan stared at the TV, like he couldn't be bothered. Andrew wondered if that's what his father thought. It would be like him to assign an adult interpretation to the behavior of a toddler and an autistic preschooler. Gabriel hadn't been around his own children enough to know even typical children's thought processes. But he watched his grandchildren two days a week, from 2:45 to 5:15. Andrew had a feeling that his father was trying to make up for the fact that he wasn't around much when his own children were growing up, although that theory was never mentioned nor confirmed. Whatever the reason, it worked out well for all of them.

Come to think of it, with all the babysitting I had to do growing up, it's payback time, Andrew thought. *And I had homework to do; I was just a kid myself! God, I remember that time Sol was leaping from the top of the stairs all the way to the bottom while I was rocking Bern, kept doing it, over and over. Broke his damn arm. Couldn't do anything till Mom and Dad got home. And of course it was my fault. The oldest gets blamed for everything.*

Yet, Andrew also knew that being responsible for his siblings was what made him feel closer to them. He thought about it and realized that they were his best friends, especially his brother. He loved to talk to Solomon on the phone, act out the *Star Wars* scenes as they did while growing up, and analyze recent movies they had seen. They reminisced about stalking seagulls at the beach when they were kids, walking quietly behind the ever-elusive birds, attempting to touch them before they flew off, a contest that neither of them won. They discussed their lives, their parents, their futures. And Andrew felt fortunate to have a connection with his sister also, especially since they were eight years apart. Andrew loved that Bernadette shared an enjoyment of the outdoors since Sol did not as much. And even though he knew the two of them loved each other, he always felt like the link, as he did when they were growing up. They were the flowers and he was always the vine.

He went into the kitchen to prepare dinner. His children were veritable creatures of habit. Eileen, with the appetite of a flea, ate steamed carrot circles and squares of buttered toast for dinner. She alternated between that and hot dogs. Nathan, also a carrot lover, ate scrambled eggs, hot dogs, and, a developing trend, the occasional burger. Pizza, no. Macaroni and cheese, no. "All kids eat macaroni and cheese!" Andrew remembered Erica's mother saying when she had come to visit a year and a half ago, for Eileen's birth. Nathan proved her wrong.

He put their food on the table and, not feeling like doing anything elaborate for himself, opened a can of soup and poured it in a pot on the stove. He sat the kids at the table, leaving the TV on to distract them so they would eat.

Even to eat, I have to placate them, he thought. *That's going to be a hard habit to break—TV on during dinner.*

While the soup heated, Andrew went into the living room and stretched on the couch. Work was managable; it was just hard getting used to sitting at a desk all day, talking on the phone so much, being called by a different name. Sam—his alter ego. He had always liked Samuel as his middle name, but he just didn't identify with it as a first name. He didn't know if he would ever really get used to that.

He scanned the living room, stuffed animals and toys spread out all over the floor. The usual. His eye fell on the bottom shelf of the entertainment center, where he saw the spine of a book he had recently bought: *Mom's House, Dad's House: Making Two Homes for Your Child* by Isolina Ricci, Ph.D. The cover had a picture of two identical houses standing side by side with a tree in the middle, blue sky with puffy clouds in the background. Andrew had bought it to help them deal with the coming change of Erica moving out; no date set yet, but he knew it was inevitable. Andrew liked the book with its many helpful tips for communicating while going through the process and helping your children to handle their own difficult feelings. He purposely left it out for Erica to look through, even told her about it, but so far she hadn't commented on it. She hadn't commented on much of anything lately. He wondered what went on in her mind these days.

He was so much better! Couldn't she see that? The medication had made such a difference. He no longer peeled the skin off the bottoms of his feet, he was happier (at least, as "happy" as he could be, under the circumstances), and he certainly never rearranged the kitchen chairs anymore. He was working now, he would go out to a nightclub once in a while, he had snowboarded again after his injury healed. He wrote in his journal and started working on his book some more. He felt like he was getting back to being himself. Only now, he would be by himself. His marriage was ending, even if they did still have sex once in a while. Andrew clung to those times because they were his substitute for emotional closeness, and the only times that Erica would touch him. He longed to be back in her arms, her mind, her soul.

He jarred himself away from those thoughts to go check on his soup. Sometimes it was all just too painful to think about.

HOW DARE IT rain on Memorial Day? Erica thought as she drove home from work. *What if I'd gone camping this weekend? Ha! Yeah, right.*

Andrew had the day off and was home with the kids. He seemed to like his new job now, and it was a relief to be able to pay the bills without having to put their groceries on credit cards. Once in a while Erica would have to call him at work about something, and she always had to ask for him as Sam, which she thought was funny. Especially since Andrew said his mother acted like it was such a neat thing and would call him for no reason just so she could ask for "Sam." It drove him insane. But the job itself, he'd said, was okay. He said he pretty much knew what he was doing by now, even though he'd felt like he had to train himself. "Aren't most jobs like that?" Erica had said. She hadn't meant to sound argumentative, but Andrew took it that way. "Since when are you the authority on office protocol?" he jabbed. Any little thing set him off, and Erica figured it would only get worse, biding their time before she moved out.

It was Erica's usual day off, but she had wanted to go in for a bit to work on some bar inventory. Memorial Day weekend had depleted their stock, especially since Saturday night they'd been packed. No one had wanted to go anywhere, to camp, for instance, because of the weather, but that didn't stop them from boozing it up in town. She'd made a good haul in tips, which always made it worth her while to work on holidays. Fourth of July was another big night, and of course nothing beat New Year's. In all her years of bartending, she still couldn't believe how much money people were willing to spend just on alcohol. And why on earth would anyone want to start off a new year with a nasty hangover? Talk about bad omens. *Well, one person's misery is another person's paycheck.*

She phoned in her order to restock everything, then reorganized her shelves behind the bar and fixed the strand of tiny white accent lights underneath them that had fallen down. After lunch, she would meet Nick in Medford for a movie, and maybe afterward, dinner. Rain wouldn't spoil her day. She had invited Simone and Gavin to meet them at the theater, but they were three hours away at the coast for the weekend. Erica wondered if they got hit with any of the rain over there.

She went home and had to wait at the front door while Andrew unlatched the inside lock they had put on it to keep Nathan in. After Andrew unlocked the door, he stormed off to the kitchen without acknowledging her. She could see that the kids were just finishing up lunch, and Andrew wiped their hands and faces with washcloths. She briefly wondered what his problem was, then dismissed it, like she would a spider on the wall that was small enough to not need to be killed, deciding she could co-exist with it.

"Mommy!" Eileen called from her chair at the table. She eased herself down out of the booster seat and ran to Erica.

"Hi, sweetie!" *At least someone's happy to see me.*

Nathan walked straight to the entertainment center and grabbed a video, then held it out to Erica. "Yo?" he asked, his word for video. He had been interacting more lately, asking for help in his own way, indicating wants and needs. His progress had been so positive that he was now going to school four days a week, and would continue that through the summer. Erica put the video cassette in the VCR and turned it on. She set her small black leather purse and her cluster of keys on top of the bare wood entertainment center.

"*Lion King* again? Didn't you just watch that this morning?" she asked. Nathan turned to go sit on the couch, twirling the hair at the top of his head.

"Speaking of videos, I need to talk to you," Andrew said to Erica, motioning her into the kitchen. He crossed his arms and spoke in a snide tone. "Hollywood Video called this morning about *Wild Orchid* being late. I certainly don't remember renting or watching that, especially since you and I don't rent videos there. Then they asked me if I was Nick! Now, why would they do that, Erica? When I said no, then they asked for you, and when I said that you were at work, which I probably sounded like a fool saying, they said that you and Nick had an account together and left this number as the contact number. So I said I'd be sure and get the message to you."

Shit, Erica thought. "It's just a video account, Andrew. Nick and I watch movies together, so we just thought it would be easier if both our names were on the account."

"That's not the point, Erica!" Andrew's voice began to raise. "You've been telling me all this time he's just a friend! It sure doesn't sound like you're 'just friends'!"

Erica looked at the floor and sighed. "All right. We started off as friends, but it's a little bit more than that now. You and I have been separated, Andrew. It's just . . . time to move on." *Didn't envision having this conversation today.*

"Have you been sleeping with him?"

Shit. "Yes; just recently, though," she said quietly, bracing herself.

"You and I just had sex last week!" Andrew yelled.

"I know, Andrew, I'm sorry. I didn't want to say no to you. It was just so 'in the moment.' I did it for your sake." *That sounded bad.*

"Oh, so now I'm just a charity fuck?"

"Jesus, Andrew, you want the kids to hear?"

"Yeah, find something to blame me for. That's appropriate. You know, Erica, it's bad enough that you obviously don't want to be married to me anymore, but you don't have to be so disrespectful to me."

"I'm sorry, Andrew. I should be able to move out in about six weeks."

"Fine. Whatever," Andrew said, turning to the counter to clean up the lunch dishes. He began banging stoneware plates in the stainless steel sink.

God, I just wish this was over with, Erica thought.

As she turned to leave the kitchen, Nathan came walking into the room and stopped when he reached Erica. Obviously sensing the tension, he pointed to the front door and said, "Go work," thinking that since it was afternoon, it was time for her to go to work.

Erica blanched. Her little boy didn't want his parents home at the same time. She looked at Nathan. "Work is closed today, Nate. No work today."

Nathan squealed and tried to head-butt Erica. "No! Stop that! Not okay!" Erica said as she held him by the shoulders. Nathan spun around to get out of Erica's grip and, still squealing, ran to the kitchen table and tipped a chair backward so that it crashed to the floor. Then he ran to the side of the table and tipped another chair back, letting it crash. Andrew ran and held him back, picking up the chair and telling him, "No! You may not do that!"

"Maybe you shouldn't have started yelling!" Erica said, picking up the first chair.

"Why don't you just get out of here? He's so intuitive; he's totally reacting to the anxiety." Nathan continued squealing as he tried to wrestle himself out of Andrew's arms. "It's okay, honey. Mom and Dad were mad, but it's okay now. Do you want to watch more *Lion King*?"

Nathan relaxed a little as Andrew stood up and carried him back to the couch and sat down with him. Eileen sat on the other side of Andrew, quiet and tiny.

Erica walked into the bedroom and shut the door. She sat down on the edge of the bed, tears welling in her eyes. She had been so emotional lately and wasn't used to that. She wasn't sure if she was just feeding off of Andrew's moods or if there was something going on in her that was unrelated. She'd turned twenty-nine two months ago and she'd noticed that since winter, for a few days every month, she'd felt agitated, like all her emotions were right on the surface, dancing around. But then after a few days, she'd be back to her normal, detached, unflustered self. She wondered if it was PMS. She'd read that with many women it started or got worse around age thirty, as if turning thirty soon and going through a separation didn't give her enough to think about.

Just because I'm the one who wants to be separated doesn't mean it's easy for me! I'm not the bad guy here! I have tried so hard with him! I just can't do it anymore. I wish it didn't have to be this way, but there's nothing left. It's been over for a long time.

She stood up and reached over, putting her hand into the tissue box on the desk.

"Fuck," she said. Empty.

SHE DIDN'T TELL Nick about the confrontation of the afternoon. Who wants to date anyone with baggage, especially baggage that's still happening?

They met in front of the multi-screen movie theater in Medford. "I'm going to meet some friends for a movie in Medford," she had told Andrew.

"Meaning Nick?"

"He might show up."

Andrew snorted. "What are you going to see?"

"*Fear and Loathing in Las Vegas.*"

"Oh. Well. Let me know how it is," Andrew said sarcastically. "If I see you."

Erica knew he had wanted to see it. He was a big fan of Hunter S. Thompson since college. "Andrew, if you want to see it, just pick a day when I'm home with the kids and tell me. You never do anything. You have to make plans—"

"I never do anything because you're always doing something! I never have any free time!"

"Andrew, I've got to go. We'll talk about this when I get home."

"Sure. Fine."

Erica supposed it could be worse. Like if Andrew wasn't working. All things considered, he was dealing with it pretty well. They wouldn't have too much trouble setting up a joint custody arrangement after she moved out. With both of them working opposite schedules, it already seemed like they had set it up.

Her face broke into a grin when she saw Nick, sexy beyond all reason, leaning against the building watching her, smiling. His long blond hair, usually back in a ponytail, was loose, falling around his shoulders, skimming his black leather motorcycle jacket. His hands were in the pockets of his jeans, ripped at both knees. When she was close, he took a long stride toward her, wrapped his left arm around her, and pulled her beside him as they walked together in perfect sync. Erica enjoyed walking connected with someone who fit with her. It had always been awkward with Andrew, and she wished he had been a little taller.

Nick was flawless. His arm easily draped over her shoulder and enveloped her as they walked, and her arm was at the perfect height to encircle his waist comfortably. She reveled in the novelty of it and turned her face up to his for a kiss.

Afterward, without missing a beat, he reached in his jacket pocket, presented the tickets to the usher, and they continued into the theater.

"Want anything?" he asked.

"I'm fine. Maybe we can get something to eat after the movie?"

"Sure," he said, his full lips smiling and his blue eyes glinting. She could stare at his face for weeks. They found two seats near the middle of the half-full theater, and Nick excused himself to the restroom.

As much as she tried to distract herself, Erica found her thoughts plaguing her. She kept coming back to something Andrew had said earlier that really got under her skin. "You're not a teenager anymore. You can't just run away from your problems. It's not just you anymore; there are other people involved." She had been defensive at first, but later realized there was an element of truth to what he had said. But he couldn't fault her for running away at sixteen. Her mother's second husband hadn't hit them, but he was a bitter, verbally and emotionally abusive man. Bitter, Erica realized, because he was a disabled Vietnam vet, which made him think he had the right to make everyone else miserable. She hated the way he called Caleb "dumbass" all the time and would yell out "What are you? Shit for brains?" whenever either of them tripped or knocked something over or didn't know how to do something Bill thought they should, like change the car's oil or chop wood exactly the way he wanted it. His favorite thing to do was to start an argument every night when their mother came home about whether or not she was cheating on him. Erica had no idea why her mother married him. Even when they were dating, he seemed like a loser, barely saying two words to Caleb and her. He walked with a cane, and because he was short, he reminded her of Charlie Chaplin. But just for a minute. After the "wedding" at city hall, they moved into his trailer. "It's a double-wide," their mother had said, trying to sound positive.

Keep trying, Mom. Erica put up with Bill and the double-wide for a year before she just couldn't stand him anymore. Caleb was nine, and she wanted to stay for him, but she knew he'd be okay. Bill was an asshole, but he wouldn't hurt anybody. At least not physically.

"You just don't listen to him when he says mean things," she told Caleb the night she left. "You know you're smart. He's just mad because he's not. He's like a big baby, trying to make other people feel bad. Just ignore him." But she knew that Caleb would be able to ignore him just about as well as she did.

"I don't want you to go," he murmured.

"I know, and I'll miss you too. But I'm an adult now, and it's time for me to be on my own. Don't worry, I'll come see you whenever I can." That turned out to be once a year at Christmas. But Caleb never held it against her. He would leap onto her and throw his arms around her neck until the year when her knees buckled under his weight; he was probably twelve. Then they would wrestle on the floor. And they talked on the phone a lot more often in those years it seemed, contributing to their bond. Maybe he felt that she was the only person he could trust, even though she'd left him. Maybe somehow he understood.

When she left that night at age sixteen, heavy ski jacket on, full backpack weighing her down, she wondered if all her decisions in adulthood would cause such a bizarre combination of melancholy and elation. She certainly felt it now, thinking about leaving Andrew.

The previews had begun, and Nick returned and slid into his seat next to her. "Did I miss anything good?"

"No," she said. *Only a morose counseling session in my head.*

Ten

"We currently have four titles on CD, but we're working to put more on," Andrew said into the phone. He estimated that he handled at least forty customer service calls a day. He became aware of someone coming up behind his desk as he answered the next question. "We recommend that you listen once a day, either morning or night, whichever works best for you. Most people begin to see results in three to six weeks, but some people will sooner than that. And if you're not satisfied, just send it back for a refund or exchange . . . You're welcome. Thanks for calling."

He turned around in his chair to see Gloria, in a moss-green linen sheath, her hair up in a bun, holding a mug of hot tea. She had an elegant way about her, especially with her mild Australian accent. "You're handling those calls very well now, Sammy!"

She had started calling him "Sammy" lately, but then, she added an "-y" to any name she could, as an endearment, Andrew guessed. Her husband Pat, she usually called Paddy; even the dogs became Gingey and Puggy. Warehouse Andrew had stipulated that he didn't like Andy, so he became "Drewy." He didn't seem to have a choice in the matter. And Andy as a nickname was already taken for that matter: Andrea the office manager got it, whether she wanted it or not. But everyone liked Gloria's little nicknames; there was a sense of intimacy there that Andrew hadn't felt at any other place of employment. After all, they worked out of her home; she made them feel like they were family, offering cups of tea whenever she went upstairs to make one for herself. And he found that he actually liked being called Sammy better than Sam; he always envisioned the rock star Sammy Hagar whenever Gloria said it.

"Thanks, Gloria. I'm feeling more confident now. I think I sound like I know what I'm talking about!"

"You do! You sound great."

"Good, I'm glad to hear that."

Just then the pug came tearing around the corner to go up the stairs, hearing the other dogs barking up there. He leaped to get up the stairs and missed, which greatly annoyed him. "Ah, you dopey bugger!" Gloria said, making her accent a bit stronger for emphasis. They laughed as he regained his footing and continued up the stairs, barking maniacally. This would happen several times a day.

"So how are things going with Erica?"

Andrew had previously mentioned that he and his wife were separating. The close proximity of desks in that office made it next to impossible to maintain privacy, but Andrew didn't mind talking about it. It's not like he should pretend that everything was fine when asked, and then the next time he's asked, have to say, "Well, we're divorced," and have everyone be shocked and wonder why he never said anything, what he was hiding. He certainly had nothing to hide.

"Not very well, I'm afraid. She'll be moving out next month." He tried not to sound too pathetic.

"Oh, I'm sorry to hear that," Gloria said, and reached down to give him a hug. It was nice to have a sympathetic boss. Sometimes she seemed like a fairy godmother.

"Well, as much as I don't want it to, it needs to happen. She's got a new boyfriend now--"

"She does?!" Gloria's eyes bulged.

"Yeah, some guy she works with."

"Are they moving in together?" Gloria's voice had a gossipy urgency to it that was almost comical. Andrew wondered if it was still considered gossip when you were talking about your own life. He decided he didn't care and told Gloria that Erica didn't even sleep at their home anymore. She spent the nights with Nick and would come home at seven or seven-thirty in the morning when Andrew would be getting ready for work.

Gloria clucked and had a look of disgust on her face. She said it was terrible that he had to deal with that.

"The weirdest thing is going through it the same time as my parents," Andrew said.

"Oh, my God! Your parents are getting divorced?"

Andrew described the nuisance that was his parents' divorce, mentioning how both of them would call him up to complain about the other one, even though Andrew was going through his own divorce. Gloria remarked that one would think after all these years they would have figured out a way to deal with each other.

"They have a lot of deep-seated issues," Andrew said. He took a sip of water from the glass on his desk.

"Every marriage has them," Gloria said, resigned, accepting, certain.

"I heard a saying once that if everyone put all their problems in a suitcase and stood in a row together with their suitcases in front of them, and we could pick out any other person's suitcase, that in the end we would rather pick up our own suitcase of problems and carry on with that."

Gloria nodded and said that that was a good analogy. Then she asked how the kids were doing.

Andrew told her that Nathan was progressing well with his therapy and talked about positive points, such as Nathan reading signs while riding in the back seat of the car. "Bank," he'd say, reading the word off the sign out in front of a bank they'd never been in before. Nathan had never been in any bank before, probably didn't even know what one was. From playing with his alphabet blocks, at three and a half, he figured out that if he grouped letters together they formed words. He had taught himself to spell. But then Andrea, the office manager, would bring her son, who was the same age as Nathan, in the office, and he would say, "Hi, Gloria" and "Thank you" in the cutest, sweetest voice, not to mention talk in full sentences about what he got for his birthday. Andrew thought about Nathan, his squealing to communicate, knocking chairs over, head-butting, shrieking in public. Such a chasm of disparity in their abilities. Andrew felt like he had missed the parenting train. Or that he'd gotten on the wrong one.

But he didn't tell his boss any of that. Didn't want to be labeled a complainer. Instead he talked about how feisty Eileen was with her tantrums, and he laughed it off, saying, "But then, she's two," in a tone that conveyed his relief that there was something, one thing, in his parenting experience that was typical, that was acceptable.

Gloria commented that Eileen was probably reacting to the tension at home. "You've got a lot on your plate, Sammy. I feel for you." Her eyes conveyed a world of compassion.

"I'll be all right."

"Yes, you will. I see so much strength in you."

"Thanks, Gloria. Well, I better get back to work," Andrew said, turning back to face his computer monitor.

"Okay, Sammy," she said as she walked back upstairs.

But Andrew didn't feel all right. He didn't feel strong. He felt drained, empty, like a shell of himself. It was hard for him to smile these days. He had lost twenty pounds in the past eight months because his appetite was so low, compounded by anxiety burning up any food he did manage to force down. And he hurt. He hurt all the time. He ached to be close to Erica again, emotionally and physically, to not be rejected, to feel loved. She actually told him that for four years she'd been trying to be someone else, that it's not in her nature to be a partner emotionally, and she couldn't handle not being herself. So this woman who he thought was the perfect wife never really existed. He looked at her and saw a different person now. Just last night she'd told him (because he asked) that she thought she had regained her "sense of self" now. Andrew was sad that the person he loved was gone. He'd never had his heart broken before.

Now, he thought as he stared at his computer screen, *I know what the big fuss is about.*

NATHAN'S RADAR WAS up. He seemed to know whenever he was being taken somewhere he wouldn't like. Or maybe he just sensed Andrew's apprehension about how he was going to manage it. Nathan tugged madly at his hair and sucked his fingers audibly in the back seat of the car.

It was Erica's day off, and she was home with Eileen while Andrew left work early to pick up Nathan and take him to the Education Service District Audiology Department in Medford for his hearing test. Neither of them would have attempted to take both the kids at the same time. "You'd have to be insane," Andrew had said. "Suicidal," said Erica.

But, after putting it off for months, it had to be done. They knew there probably wasn't anything wrong with his hearing, but it had to be ruled out. And Nathan began his litany of "Go"s before they even set foot inside the older brick building in downtown Medford.

He pulled back on Andrew's hand as he walked with him through the clear glass doors into the foyer. It was empty save for what Andrew assumed to be the receptionist sitting in a little office behind old-fashioned sliding frosted glass doors at waist level. Andrew told her they were there for a hearing test, and, after checking her chart, the short, round-faced woman with short brown hair and reading glasses stood up and said, "Okay, come right this way," and opened a door on the side of the office for them to come through. There appeared to be no one else there. Sensing Nathan's mounting hysteria and trying to evade it, Andrew picked him up and carried him.

She led them down a dim hallway into an even dimmer small room that had thick, gray, soundproof acoustic paneling on all the walls and ceiling. Small speakers were attached to the two upper corners at the rear of the room, and the side walls had shelves with a few stuffed animals on them. Nathan continued begging to go, even though Andrew held him. The woman directed them to sit in the center of the room on a thinly upholstered chair, like one found in a banquet room at a lower-end hotel. Seeing Nathan's stress, she said it was okay for him to sit on Andrew's lap.

The woman turned to leave, explaining that she would administer the test from the next room where, through a window, she would watch Nathan's reactions to sound. As soon as Andrew began to sit down, Nathan began yelling. "Go! Go!" he cried and screamed, working himself into hysterics, even though Andrew held him securely and kept reassuring him, saying, "It's okay, it's okay." He wondered how on earth the woman would be able to get any accurate results with Nathan in this state.

Every ten seconds or so, the corner speakers would emit soft jingling-type sounds. Immediately, Nathan would lessen his wailing for a brief second and turn his head in the direction of the sound. After each short jingle interlude, he resumed his howling, convinced that something terrible would befall him in this room. Each time the jingling sound began again, sometimes even softer than before, he would stop and turn his head toward it. He didn't miss a single sound, even though he screamed the entire time.

It seemed to Andrew to last an eternity (probably to Nathan as well), but in reality the test took only about five minutes. When the woman opened the door of the room to tell them they were finished, Nathan had progressed to his hiccupping, residual sobbing phase with his tear-streaked face. Fortunately his fear-based outbursts were not lengthy, compared to Eileen's brooding tantrums, which were often over half an hour long. Nathan just didn't seem to have the energy for that.

"See, it's over," Andrew told him, getting up. "You're fine! Nothing happened to you. We can go home now."

"Go," Nathan said feebly.

The test administrator led them back out to the lobby and gave Andrew the chart with the results, briefly explaining the SRT (Speech Reception Threshold) and mentioning that Nathan's hearing was well within the normal range.

Well, one less thing, Andrew thought as Nathan led the way out the front door. He was so exhausted he couldn't even feel the relief he knew he should.

IN AUGUST, ONE week before Eileen's second birthday, Erica moved out.

The first day of the rest of my life, as the saying goes, she thought as she carried some boxes to the front door and stacked them along the wall under the window next to three full Hefty bags containing her clothes. Eileen watched her from the futon where she was performing her latest trick: slow motion somersaults. First she would bend over and stay in the somersault stance for a minute so she could look at things upside-down, smiling. Then she would throw herself over and lie on her back, laughing. Erica cringed as she realized that when Gavin arrived with his SUV, they'd have to roll up the futon and pack it. It was going to be her bed in the studio apartment she'd rented.

She'd found it by accident, walking home from Nick's house early one morning, which was two blocks away from it. She had almost passed the house, an old Craftsman style on B Street with many bushes in front of it, when she noticed the "For Rent" sign in the window, stopped, and walked up to take a peek in the window. She couldn't tell at first if it was vacant because she saw a couch and dresser in the living room area, but the walls were bare and it was immaculately clean, so she guessed it must be semi-furnished. It was like a studio-duplex, with the other half of the house appearing to be twice the size. It was small, but it was close to Dogma, and since Andrew would need the car to get to his job, she figured this place would work out. The kids would stay with her two nights a week, and they could all fit on the futon, just until she could afford a bigger place. She had a pen and some paper in her backpack and jotted down the phone number on the sign. After she got home and Andrew had left for work, she made an appointment to see the place that afternoon.

The landlord, a tall, thin man in his late fifties, seemed quiet and nice, and he rented the place to her on the spot after she exaggerated a little about her situation. Okay . . . she'd made Andrew out to be an unreasonable asshole, but it got her the apartment, and that would make him happy, she figured. And he'd never know. It's not like she said he was abusive, just that he gave her an ultimatum. In actuality, she was surprised that Andrew had been so reasonable about her staying most nights at Nick's place. He would greet her every morning when she got home like it didn't bother him.

Erica was even more surprised that Andrew didn't make any barbed comments as she went through the house packing her things. He seemed easier to deal with after the decision had been made that she was definitely moving out. And Andrew was almost cheerful after she got her apartment. The limbo phase of being separated-but-still-living-together had an end in sight. It would be better for both of them.

Nathan was another matter. While Eileen seemed to think this Saturday morning was no different from any other, Nathan tore through the house, trying to head-butt Erica, banging his head on furniture, making guttural growling noises, tipping the kitchen chairs backward so they crashed to the floor, and literally climbing the walls. Andrew took him back into his room for a while to calm him down; he was obviously disturbed by the boxes and bags in the living room, didn't understand what was happening, and didn't have the ability to ask, nor understand any explanation. Erica felt terrible for upsetting him, but she pushed back the negative thoughts and focused on the fact that she needed to be on her own; she'd been needing to do this for a long time. The kids would adjust in their own ways. She figured it had to be better doing it now while they were young enough to work through it faster.

Gavin pulled up the driveway and turned around in the parking area so that the rear of his vehicle faced their front door. He hopped out and Erica, standing in the doorway, greeted him with a hug.

"Thanks so much for helping."

"No problem."

Erica wished she was already in her new place. The thought of moving in was exciting, but it was the moving out that she was dreading. And her possibly-PMS hormone surge was affecting her, making her more emotional than she wanted to be. She wanted this to be over, to get through whatever drama awaited. Is this what actors feel on the opening night of a play they're in? No. There would be no applause from her audience when this play ended. Only boos. Boos and bad reviews.

They walked into the living room, and Erica was glad to see that Eileen was no longer playing on the futon. She explained to Gavin that they would probably need to make two trips because she was taking the entertainment center, and that would take up the whole back of his car. But she wanted to take the futon and everything else that was going in the first load before Eileen decided to play on it again. Erica couldn't help but see the sad truth that her daughter might be more disturbed by the futon's absence than her mother's.

Andrew came in the back door through the kitchen and said that the kids were playing in the backyard. He said hi to Gavin and together they rolled up and carried the queen-size futon out and slid it into his car. Other than saying hello, Andrew kept quiet, and Erica was glad he didn't make any negative remarks to Gavin.

Andrew went back outside to be with the kids since Gavin said he could manage the rest. Erica figured she'd say goodbye to them when they came back for the entertainment center. Andrew had already bought a new 27-inch TV, a VCR, and a dark oak armoire to put them in. It looked nice; Andrew had good taste in furniture, but Erica was incensed with the fact that he had put it all on a credit card. *How idiotic is that?! We can't even afford to pay the bills as it is.*

They pulled up to her new place and found Nick and Simone waiting on the front step with an open box of donuts. "You guys rock," Erica said. "I forgot to eat breakfast!"

Nick kissed her, then she unlocked the door and entered her new home. Her friends commented on how big it was for a studio, and what a nice kitchen it had with the raised ceiling, and how beautiful the light oak trim and molding was around all the doors and windows. Erica felt dazed, like she was on auto-pilot going through the motions. She had wanted to do this, but she couldn't identify what she was feeling. She wasn't having second thoughts, but she just felt strange, almost melancholy. Not how she had expected to feel when the day finally came. She allowed herself to be distracted by the jovial mood of her friends and enjoyed the donuts, orange juice, and coffee with them. Nick had brought a bottle of champagne for later.

It only took a few minutes to carry in everything from the first load, and then she and Gavin returned for the entertainment center. He and Andrew jockeyed it into the car while Erica said goodbye to the kids, who were already watching a movie on their new TV. Erica shook her head in disbelief, but then she realized that this would probably help them deal with the day better, having their routine to rely on. She thought of pausing the VCR, but she knew that would upset Nathan, so she just squatted down in front of the couch and told them that she would see them on Monday morning. *Just two days,* she said. Battling her own unwanted tears, Erica kissed her children and said goodbye.

Andrew came back inside, not looking at her. "I'll drop them off around eight-fifteen Monday morning," he said in a quiet, dry voice.

"Okay, see you later."

She took a deep breath and walked out of the home she had lived in for almost three years, shutting the door behind her. It was over. She had moved out. Trying to avoid the range of emotions she didn't want to deal with, she quickly got in the car next to Gavin.

"Got everything?" he said as he looked over at her.

"Yeah."

Gavin must have noticed her watery eyes. As he drove down the driveway he said, "You're doing the right thing."

"Yeah, I know. It's just that I didn't realize it could be so hard to do something that I wanted to do."

Eleven

It had been one month since Erica moved out. One month of Andrew dropping the kids off at her new place every morning on his way to work, and every morning after they got out of the car, Nathan, with his hooded jacket on, would plant his feet on the sidewalk in front of Erica's house and would not budge. He would yell his battle cry, "Go!" as Andrew tried to coax him up the walkway to Erica waiting in the doorway, picking up Eileen, who had run to her. "Go!" Nathan would insist. Andrew would get down on Nathan's level and remind him of the "Mom's House, Dad's House" book with the drawings of the happy, separate houses, and finally he would allow Andrew to gently pull or push him into the house as he moaned. He had done this every day for a month, except for Mondays and Tuesdays, because he was already there in the morning, having spent the night before with Erica.

Andrew would drop them off Sunday afternoon and pick them up Tuesday afternoon. Wednesday, Thursday, and Friday mornings he would drop them off on his way to work and pick them up on his way home. They did the joint-custody shuffle, and so far, it was working (except for Nathan not wanting to go inside his mother's home).

Andrew pulled up to the curb in front of Erica's house and parked right behind his father's new forest green BMW sedan, which he had bought for himself as a retirement gift. He had said that Andrew could drive it some time, and Andrew looked forward to it. It would be like a dream compared to what he'd been used to driving.

He knocked on the wood-framed screen door on which Erica had immediately installed a hook-and-eye lock high up on the inside to keep Nathan in. His father opened the door and greeted him. The kids were watching a movie and barely acknowledged him.

How was work? Gabriel always asked.

Pretty good, Andrew usually replied.

"Well, I think I'll use the bathroom before I leave," Gabriel said, heading toward the back of the house.

Andrew glanced around. The futon was rolled up under the window next to the front door; the entertainment center sat across from the couch that had come with the place, along with an old but nice wooden dresser that was along the wall behind the open front door. Erica had lined her books up along the top of it. Toys were strewn all over the plush, blue carpet, and Andrew began picking them up and putting them back in the entertainment center, which was where Erica kept them now. He picked up a Disney magazine and set it on top, and then he noticed a package of photos sitting there, near his dad's small brown leather bag. He reached in and pulled out the stack of photos and began to flip through them.

His heart began to beat faster as he looked at pictures of what was obviously a birthday party for Eileen, here at Erica's. His own daughter's birthday party. He hadn't been invited. There she was sitting on the couch with someone holding a cake in front of her, Nick handing her a big stuffed Winnie-the-Pooh, other adults—Gavin, Simone, Isaac, somebody's mother he hadn't seen before—all laughing, standing around behind Eileen and clapping.

Andrew's blood boiled. How dare Erica have a birthday party for Eileen and not invite him? Her own father! He shoved the pictures back in the envelope as Gabriel came out of the bathroom.

"Come on, guys, it's time to go!" Andrew said, putting Nathan's sandals on, then Eileen's. "Bye, Dad! Thanks! See you on Tuesday."

His father grabbed his bag and headed for the door. Andrew wondered if he had seen the photos. He might have thought that Andrew had been the one taking them, and that's why he wasn't in them. Maybe he didn't even notice.

"Bye, everybody," Gabriel called on his way out the door.

Andrew held the door open for Nathan and Eileen as they walked through, then shut it and went to go put them in the car. His adrenaline raced through him, fueling his anger. He sat in his seat, waiting for his father to pull out, and took some deep breaths to calm himself.

It didn't help much. As he drove off toward home, his jaw was set and both his hands clenched the wheel. He fumed inside. *She doesn't give a damn about me.*

"I hope she gets burned as badly as she burned me," he said aloud to the car in front of him.

"TIME TO GO to Mom's house!" Andrew announced on Sunday afternoon. His cheerful, excited tone not only helped to keep his children positive about the transition, it reminded him to view this time away from them as both a needed break and a chance to run some errands without them, instead of a time to mope around missing them. And it was getting easier. Each week, it got a little easier. Even washing Nathan's hair was somehow less of a battle, much to Andrew's surprise. He had dreaded doing it alone, wondering how he would be able to contain Nathan's thrashing body in the tub while successfully shampooing and rinsing his hair. Nathan still hollered at an ear-splitting decibel, his "child-protective-services scream," Andrew called it, but the kicking and thrashing subsided a bit. Andrew wondered if perhaps Nathan felt less threatened because he wasn't being held down; both of his parents weren't ganging up on him. Figuring out Nathan was harder than figuring out any other challenge Andrew faced: paying the bills, moving his wife out, dealing with feuding parents. Having an autistic child took the title for the most confounding element of his life.

Nathan still resisted going inside Erica's house. Andrew couldn't help but think maybe it had just become a routine for him to stabilize his little body in the front yard and say "Go!" a dozen times or more before allowing himself to be cajoled or coerced inside. It was a ritual now, a habit. He wondered how it affected Erica, since they never discussed it. Maybe she realized that this was Nathan's way of dealing with the transition.

In any case, she didn't pressure Nathan about it. Andrew felt confident that they were both similar in their parenting approach and in how they interacted with and disciplined their children. It was comforting to know that whenever they were with her, they were safe and loved. One Monday, just two weeks after Erica had moved out, Andrew stopped off at the little grocery store near her home on his way home from work. He picked up the few items he needed and made his way to the check stands. Suddenly, about thirty feet in front of him, he saw the backs of his family, his children and his wife, heading up to the check stands also. He froze, knowing that if the kids saw him, they would be confused and possibly upset, wanting to go home with him. It would not be good to disrupt their fledgling routine. He turned and walked down another aisle, then came back up and hid about ten feet behind them while they were in line to check out. Erica had Eileen on her hip, and Nathan examined the candy shelves as they waited. He seemed so much more at ease than whenever he was in Safeway. This small grocery store was quieter, with fewer people and dimmer lights and, most notably, wall to wall indoor-outdoor carpeting. He was certain that made a difference in Nathan's comfort level there. It muffled so much more sound than the bare floors of most large stores.

Nathan handed a candy bar to Erica. "No, honey, we're not getting that." Nathan squealed in opposition, and Erica leaned down to him and gently but firmly said, "Nate, stop. We have other candy at home, okay?"

Not only did it amaze Andrew that Nathan actually stopped squealing, it amazed him that Erica handled the situation exactly as he would have. It's not that he had any doubts; it was just affirming to know that his instinct had been right. She was a good mom.

She was not, however, helping him to get Nathan into her house.

For some reason he was a little more resistant today. Andrew finally resorted to picking him up and carrying him into the house, plastic grocery bags full of stuffed animals, toys, and clothes shoved up his arm and rustling as he wrangled his way through the door and set Nathan down. He immediately ran over to the rolled-up futon and lay down on it, sucking his fingers and tugging his hair.

Erica came walking out from the bathroom with Eileen trailing behind her. "Sorry I didn't help you with Nate, but I have to be careful of my leg. I, uh, had an accident the other night." Erica pulled up the cut-off leg of her gray sweatpants-turned-shorts, removed a large, white, taped-over bandage, and revealed a horrendous burn on her upper thigh near her groin. Andrew gasped as he stared at the pale white, charred skin with chunks missing: a terrible third-degree burn. He had never seen such a bad burn like that up close. He shuddered.

"I was making pasta Friday night and dumped a pot of boiling water on myself," she said, in a jovial 'silly-me' tone. "Nick took me to the hospital."

"Oh, my God. This looks bad, Erica."

"It's a third-degree. I'll be okay, though. The doctor told me how to take care of it, and I got some pain medication."

"Are you sure you'll be all right with the kids?"

"Yeah, as long as they don't climb on it! I'll be fine."

Andrew asked if she needed anything. Did she have enough food until Tuesday? Did she want him to run to the store for anything?

She said thanks but she was all stocked up, and Andrew told her to call him if she needed anything. He didn't feel it was right leaving them alone with her when she was injured, but then he remembered that he had been fine taking care of them with his groin injury when Erica went to Shasta. She could manage.

Nathan had adjusted and moved to the couch to watch TV. Andrew said goodbye and left.

Oh, my God, he thought. *I did this. I manifested this. I said I hoped she got burned but I meant emotionally, not physically. Guess I needed to specify.*

He got in the car and drove silently home. "Thoughts are things, and they create," he remembered reading in a book published by one of their clients at work. "There are no accidents. Your energy, translated into thoughts, words, and emotions, manifests your experiences."

Andrew, curious about all the materials put out by their New Age clients, had begun to acquaint himself with several metaphysical concepts, some of which were actually helping him to deal with his anger toward Erica. He was learning that he could not control Erica's actions; he could only control his reactions to them. He could decide to be upset, or decide to accept it and let it go. She wasn't going to change. He needed to let go of his expectations.

Having the intonation he had made about hoping she got burned come to fruition really shook him. He began to realize how powerful words and thoughts could be. He couldn't decide how he felt about it. A little amused, but a little scared, too, like the first time he'd held a butane lighter.

I manifested it, he kept thinking. *I put that out in the universe and I manifested it.*

ERICA'S WOUND HAD finally stopped throbbing. After a week, it was still a tender and vulnerable cavity, but she took care of it and went back in to see the doctor, who removed some dead skin and said it was healing fine. She'd had to sponge-bathe herself all week, which she was getting tired of doing and which also made her certain that any unpleasant odor she happened to get a whiff of must have come from her.

It was really Simone's fault that it happened. Erica had just taken the pot of boiling water and pasta off the stove to dump it into the colander in the sink when Simone came around the corner into the small kitchen. Not realizing, of course, that Erica was holding a pot of boiling water, Simone playfully pinched her butt. Erica jumped and tipped the pot onto herself, then slipped and fell back and the hot pot landed on her upper thigh. She had been wearing a pair of thin boxer shorts.

Screaming ensued, from Simone as much as Erica, and a chorus of "Oh-my-God"s, as Nick sprang up from the couch and orchestrated the trip to the hospital. In retrospect, Erica thought he had seemed a bit exasperated about the whole thing, as if it had been staged. He was angry with Simone, actually snapped at her and said, "What a stupid thing to do!" Simone kept crying in the back seat about how sorry she was, "didn't know she had the pot of water," et cetera. Erica just remembered feeling faint and nauseated and cold as she went into shock. She also remembered at some point Nick demanding, "Didn't you hear her behind you?" as if she might have avoided the accident that way. Later, she couldn't figure out if that was just the way Nick reacted in a crisis, or if he just found the whole thing to be a ploy for attention or drama. Either way, she didn't like it.

He did bring her flowers, although just boring pink carnations, and came over to check on her several times during the week to see if she needed anything, and he drove her to her doctor appointment. But really, she was almost insulted by the carnations; he knew her better than that. He never stayed long, either, not even to watch a movie with her. "I'll let you rest," he'd say, getting up to leave after fifteen minutes. Maybe he just feels uncomfortable around invalids, she thought.

Uncomfortable feelings aside, it was a beautiful early fall day—Indian Summer weather. Erica put on a pair of black and white checked Capri pants, black platform sandals, and a snug-fitting black off-the-shoulder top. She put on some eyeliner and maroon lipstick and decided to walk over to Nick's house. She'd had to work late the night before, and it was busy, with all the college kids back in town since school started. Security was busy too, with all the people they had to escort out of Dogma after they'd been cut off. One drunk idiot had tried to climb over the bar after she refused to serve him. And a huge fight had broken out on the dance floor involving plenty of broken glass. Tonight, a Saturday, would probably be even busier.

Nick had left work early last night, saying he had a fever and a sore throat, so Erica picked up a box of fizzing flu medicine from the small grocery store near her home to bring to him. She walked down the tree-lined residential street, glancing at all the old homes, mostly Craftsman and Victorians, some kept-up and some a bit neglected. It was a pretty town, and she had come to enjoy it, especially living so near the downtown area. She'd been in Ashland for five years now, and had come to love the small town with its gourmet restaurants, world-renowned Shakespeare productions, beautiful parks, and the friends she'd made. And she and Andrew were both glad that their kids would grow up here. Ashland felt so safe. "Safe and secure and surrounded by love," she said in a sing-song voice as she walked up to Nick's place. She and Simone had often joked that Ashland sometimes seemed like a pop-up storybook town with its painted, colorful Victorian homes, picturesque parks, and quaint downtown area, like the Disneyland of cities.

Nick and his roommate rented a two-bedroom house farther down on B Street, with a sparse lawn in front and a small, sagging porch. She let herself in through the waist-high chain link gate and walked up to the front door. She was just about to knock when, through the half-open blinds on the window next to the door, she saw bare flesh on the couch. Two bodies grinding. Nick's strained face and long blond hair swinging around.

Erica ripped open the door and stepped in. "Yeah, I can see you're really sick, you asshole!"

"What the fuck?" Nick yelled. He jumped up off the girl, whom Erica recognized as a waitress from another downtown restaurant, and said, "Erica! What are you doing?"

"I came to say hi and bring you some fucking medicine! But I can see you're feeling much better, you fucking liar!" she screamed, shaking as she slammed the door and stormed off the porch.

How could he do that to me?! Who does he think he is? He didn't even seem that surprised, really. It's like he wanted me to find him with someone else. Jenny Apostolo, stupid little slut.

Tears began pooling in her eyes, which made her even angrier. He wasn't worth crying over. "Bastard," she muttered, walking home to call Simone, crushing the box of flu medicine that was still in her hand.

Twelve

ndrew wondered if Nathan would ever be able to converse. He hoped so much for his son, and yet, it was not so much. It was something that parents of typically-developing children—"neurotypicals," a term that Sally, Nathan's therapist, used—took for granted. Most parents don't have to hope that their children will be able to talk with them, they just assume that they will. Or they complain that their child talks too much: "Can't get that kid to be quiet for one minute!" They take for granted being able to go to the grocery store, to a neighborhood pumpkin festival, to a family restaurant without having some small noise send their child into shrieking hysterics. And they assume that Nathan did it because he was behaving badly as a result of poor parenting, Andrew knew because of the negative looks he would get. Even Lucy, his co-worker, had exhibited a level of ignorance when he told her that his son had autism. "That must be easy," she said. Andrew wondered if she was being sarcastic. "Why do you say that?" he asked. "Because autistic kids are so quiet." Andrew was shocked, and decided right at that moment that as soon as he found the time to write, he would write about autism, getting the word out. Eradicating the myths.

All people change and grow, but I think I will spend my entire life learning about Nathan, Andrew had written in his journal the night before. *Who is this little boy? Part mystery, part genius, all loving. He is a wondrous person, a gentle soul.*

And he showed some emerging verbal skills. Whenever Andrew would film him with the video camera, Nathan would reach for it, saying, "Hold," and he was starting to ask for help when trying to open something or put something together. It sounded like "yelm," but it was a start. On his fourth birthday, Erica had helped him blow out the candles on his cake, and in his sweet, innocent voice he asked, "All gone?" He could say "yhine keen" for *Lion King*, his favorite movie, and tried to sing "The Bare Necessities" from *The Jungle Book*. But the most endearing phrase he uttered, one that he had heard since before his birth, was "I yuv-voo." Andrew and Erica knew it was echolalic, they knew he had learned to parrot it back to them when they said it to him, that the possibility existed that Nathan didn't even know what it meant, but the fact that they could hear him say it was a gift. Andrew clung to that phrase as he would a buoy in the middle of the sea.

And going out into the community was always a challenge. Even if there were no lawn mowers or leaf blowers at the park when they happened to be there, there was always the issue of not interacting appropriately with peers. One Saturday he went up to a boy who looked about five years old and started laughing in his face because he was trying to get him to play with him. Nathan had made the connection that when children play together, they laugh. So he must have figured that if he laughed, the other boy would play with him. The kid said in an angry voice, "Hey, how would you like it if I laughed at you?!" Andrew, rushing over to intervene, said, "He's not laughing at you; he's just trying to have fun. He's just trying to play with you." But the kid scowled and said, "Well, if he does it again, he'll be sorry" and walked away. *How can a five-year-old think that way?* Andrew wondered. He worried so much about Nathan going to school and having kids be mean to him because he couldn't interact like them. Kids could be cruel even to typical peers. How would they react to someone like Nathan? Andrew knew he was smart and could learn, so maybe he could learn socially acceptable ways to interact.

He had brought it up with Sally, who was at his house for a home visit, which Nathan still had twice weekly. "Yes, he can certainly learn how to interact with his peers in socially acceptable ways. Neuro-typicals also have to learn these things, but kids with autism take much, much longer, in general. Anything they need to learn has to be repeated many times before they really understand. That's one of the things we're working on with him. We're still seeing mostly parallel play, but he's indicating a desire to interact, and we're of course encouraging that and also modeling ways to do it that are socially appropriate. He's really doing well in the program," Sally said. "And we're also seeing more eye contact."

She pulled a clear, plastic rectangular container with a blue lid out of the big tub that they always brought for the home visits and put it on the floor in front of Nathan. Inside were four mini Mr. Potato Heads with attachable arms, shoes, hats, eyes, and mouth. No room for noses. Sally showed Nathan how to put them together, and he began to do them on his own. Eileen played with a standing marble maze made out of connected plastic ledges and tubes at the other end of the living room.

Andrew prayed that she wouldn't throw another tantrum as she had the week before when she had to be removed from the foam shape board that Sally was trying to work on with Nathan. She'd let Eileen have some time with it, but Eileen wasn't willing to give it up, and it was an essential therapy tool in Nathan's program. Andrew had to pick her up and carry her to the bedroom, howling all the way, which she continued for the remainder of the home visit that ended up being cut short because of her yelling. Sally, ever the flexible professional, elected to limit the use of the foam shape board to Nathan's school time, so that Eileen wouldn't have to see it.

Sally got up and went to the kitchen table where she had set her brown leather briefcase. She reached in and pulled out a stack of three-by-three-inch laminated cards and handed them to Andrew. "I finally made you the cue cards you requested. Sorry it took so long," she said.

"No problem," Andrew said as he flipped through them. They had previously given him some general cards to prepare Nathan for various outings, such as "park," with a black line drawing of a swing set and slide, "store," with a similar drawing of a shopping cart, and "go," with a drawing of a car. Andrew had requested some for around the house, including "rewind," with a drawing of a video cassette (since Nathan was always upset when he wanted to watch a video that needed to be rewound), "vacuum," "bath," "clip nails," "brush teeth," "wash face," "sit down," "no yelling," with a drawing of a head with lines coming out of the mouth and a circle with a diagonal line (crossing it out) superimposed over it, and "no hitting" and "no throwing" done in a similar manner. The most interesting card was labeled "different," and showed two arrows pointing in different directions. This one was used to indicate to Nathan when they would do anything that deviated from the schedule he was used to. For instance, occasionally they would spend a Friday night at Erica's house, and he was used to being at home with Andrew on Friday nights. It disrupted his routine and upset him. Sally had explained that whenever they have to do something that's not usually on his schedule at school, he reacted the same way, so they started showing him the "different" card and saying "Today is different," and he could assimilate the change easier. Andrew wanted to try it at home.

"Thanks; these are great," he said to Sally.

"You're welcome! Let me know if you need any others." She went back to working with Nathan.

The phone rang in the kitchen and Andrew answered it.

A curt male voice asked to speak to him. "I'm calling on behalf of Citibank credit department. We have a matter of an overdue payment for your account that we'd like to discuss with you."

Andrew blanched. He wondered when they would start calling. He'd been having trouble paying the bills with his slightly-above-minimum-wage job since Erica moved out. She had promised to help him pay their bills, but so far it had been over three months and he hadn't seen a cent from her. He hadn't been able to make a payment on their credit card bills for two months. His paychecks barely covered rent, food, phone, electricity, his school loan payment, and gas and car insurance. Cable TV? He never had it. Cell phone? Nope. There was nothing to cut back on. The situation was so bleak that he had recently called around to see how much it would cost to declare bankruptcy. He certainly didn't want to, but with his debt more than twice his annual income and no extra funds to pay even the minimum payments, it seemed like the only option. He would also need to move to a one-bedroom apartment, but that would have to wait until he got his tax refund in three months because he had nothing for first and last months' rent, plus a deposit. *How do you explain all of that to a creditor?*

"I'm going through a divorce and experiencing financial hardship right now. I'll pay as soon as I can." *There*, he thought. *It's the goddamned truth.*

"I can understand that, Mr. Pavel, but do you realize how this is negatively affecting your credit?"

"Yes, I do. There's nothing I can do about that right now." Andrew moved as far into the corner of the kitchen as he could and kept his voice low.

"If you don't begin making the minimum payment soon, your wages will be garnished. We'd like to arrange a payment plan with you to try to avoid that."

"I'm sorry, but can we discuss it at another time?" Andrew hoped that Sally couldn't hear him.

"It would be best to take care of it now, Mr. Pavel."

Mr. Pavel. God. "I'm not able to discuss it now," Andrew said, and hung up. He turned the ringer and the machine off. The bloodletting had begun.

"Erica," Andrew began as he picked the kids up from her house after he got off work the next day, "when you moved out, you said you would help pay the bills, and you haven't." He hadn't been looking forward to the confrontation.

Erica, getting ready for work, zipped up a pair of knee-high black leather boots. He sensed her become defensive. "I haven't had any money to give you, Andrew. I now have school loans to pay off, too, and I don't even have my degree yet."

"Your rent is one-third of what mine is!" he said. As soon as he said it, he realized how whiny he sounded.

She stood up. "Then move."

"I can't do that until I get my tax refund." Andrew looked at the kids sitting on the couch watching a movie. They didn't seem bothered by the discussion.

"Then I guess we'll have to file for bankruptcy." Erica walked over to her dresser and began putting on jewelry for work. She picked out a turquoise amulet on a short chain and silver hoop earrings to go with her black V-neck blouse that buttoned up the back and a dark paisley print mini-skirt. Her dark hair had grown out a bit; it bounced off her shoulder blades when she flipped it out to put on the necklace.

He told her how much it cost, that he had already looked into it, and that as soon as they paid the retainer fee he could get the creditors to stop calling.

"Have they been calling?"

"Yes. Yesterday one called while Nathan was having his home visit. It was really embarrassing."

"Well, after Christmas, I should be able to come up with at least half of the retainer fee." Erica stood by the door. "I've got to go to work now. You can hang out for a bit if you want."

"No, we'll go. I better get dinner for them," he said, putting Eileen's shoes on, then Nathan's.

"Okay. I'll see you tomorrow," Erica said, picking up her purse and keys off her dresser and walking out the door.

Andrew shut off the TV, put the kids' fleece jackets on, and herded them out to the car. His mind kept going over the situation as he drove home. He was insulted by Erica's calloused attitude about the bills. They were her bills, too, not just his. He had the kids more nights a week than she did, making him the custodial parent. Technically, she owed him child support also, aside from her share of the bills. If he filed for divorce, the state could enforce support. Erica didn't want to be married anyway; she had been blunt about that. Andrew didn't have any false hope of them getting back together, so why shouldn't he file? Why hadn't *she* filed yet? Why was she leaving it up to him? Ending his marriage was beginning to feel like a slow, painful death. An agonizing failure left out on the lawn to rot in the sun, like a gopher carcass a cat had killed. He couldn't deal with it sitting there anymore. It was time to clean it up.

One weekend night when Erica had the kids and he went out, he had run into an old roommate from when he was in college and they had a beer and got caught up, talking about their lives. "You need to get your house in order, Andrew," he had told him. Andrew knew he was right.

He got home, got the kids inside, and began getting some dinner for them. Nathan still insisted on eating uncooked frozen corn niblets. Andrew remembered when Nathan held Tigger's face into his bowl and pretended that Tigger was eating the corn. It was the first imaginative thing they had seen him do. And recently he had stopped lining up the toy cars along the back of the couch and staring at them. He had learned to push them around the floor and make car noises, almost like any other kid.

These small victories made Andrew feel like it wasn't worth it to make an issue out of what Nathan ate for dinner. At least he wasn't eating dirt or any other non-food items, like he had read other kids with autism did.

"You have to pick your battles," he said to his brother on the phone that evening, explaining how things were going with Nathan. He had called Solomon after the kids were in bed to talk about his concerns with the bankruptcy, his divorce, their parents' divorce. "It's so weird going through a divorce the same time as your parents," Andrew said. "Who would have thought?"

"Yeah," Sol said. "Are Mom and Dad both still bad-mouthing each other to you?"

"Not so much now. I had to lecture both of them about it. That was another funny thing: lecturing our parents!"

"Perfect! How'd that go over?"

"They were apologetic. And they've been better about it, but occasionally something slips out. I guess I can understand, going through a divorce myself, but I am bound and determined not to do that to Nathan and Eileen."

"That's good. I think our generation is just more conscientious about things like that," Sol said. Then he asked how things were with Erica.

"Well, we're getting along, but there's no chance of us getting back together. I have to be realistic about that."

"I'm sorry, Andrew. I know it's been hard on you. Are you okay? Are you still on Zoloft?"

"Yeah, I'm still on it, but I don't want to increase the dosage. That would just mask the feelings that I need to work through, you know?" Andrew talked about how his job was one of the best things in his life, how his boss was flexible if he needed to leave early to pick up the kids or go to an appointment.

Solomon gently asked if Erica had filed for divorce.

"No, neither one of us has yet. I'm going to, though. She owes me child support."

"How much does she make?"

"I don't know, but her expenses are lower than mine, and I'm stuck with all of our credit card bills. I haven't been able to pay them for two months and they've started calling. I'm going to have to declare bankruptcy."

Andrew felt the statement hang in the air like a football thrown out of bounds on a key play. Then Sol, in his diplomatic way, said that he was sorry to hear it, but reminded Andrew that bankruptcy no longer had the social stigma that it used to, that it probably wouldn't be so bad. A friend of his had declared bankruptcy last year; he'd already been getting credit card applications sent to him in the mail. "You won't be able to buy a house for a while, but it's not the end of the world."

"Yeah, it'll probably be seven years before I can buy a house anyway, so I may as well get it over with now."

"It'll probably be a relief to you," Sol said.

Andrew shifted position on the couch and, attempting to change the subject, asked what was new with Sol, who proceeded to tell him about his job at the Ahmanson Theater, where he had started off as an usher and had recently been promoted to lower management, with benefits. He had been taking acting classes as a hobby and met his girlfriend there. She worked in medical claims processing, but also loved theater and acting. She was smart and mature, and Sol sounded like he was in love.

"I'm glad to hear things are going well for you, Sol," Andrew said with sincerity. He wistfully remembered conveying similar news to Sol when he and Erica had first gotten together.

"Yeah, we're planning on taking a trip to Mexico next summer. She's half Mexican, but her family's been in the States for a while."

"Nice. Any plans for you coming up here any time soon?"

"Definitely next Thanksgiving. No matter what!"

Andrew said he would hold him to that, then told Sol he missed him, hoping he didn't sound too forlorn.

"I miss you, too, Andrew. We'll talk again soon, okay? I love you."

"I love you, too." It almost felt as if their roles had reversed, his little brother telling him things would be all right, giving advice, living and working in a big city. While in college, Andrew had always envisioned himself doing that, maybe in San Francisco, even New York, working for some big publishing company, working to accomplish his old, now-forgotten college dreams. Maybe the role-reversal was occurring because he subconsciously wanted to live vicariously through Sol, to follow a dream, even if it belonged to someone else.

IT WAS SO nice, so normal, to go to the grocery store and not have to deal with an episode of shrieking hysterics. To not have to worry that there might be one. It wasn't that Eileen was her favorite; no, Erica loved them both equally, more than anyone else in her life. And Eileen certainly had her fair share of prolonged tantrums, crying and carrying on in her room, sometimes for close to an hour, when she didn't get her way. At Erica's place, she would have her tantrums in the bathroom, since that was the only room in the studio apartment with a door. But Eileen was more predictable than Nathan, and she rarely started anything in public; it was almost as if, at two and a half, she somehow realized that the way her older brother acted was not okay. Or maybe it was just that she loved having her mom to herself while Nathan was at school.

And Erica loved having alone-time with Eileen. Usually, she could take her anywhere. She often took Eileen with her to Dogma in the mornings, when she did her inventory or scheduling, and Eileen loved going. She would dance by rotating her little body around on the dancefloor when

Erica turned on the new DMX radio system, and she could sit on the big, square, black vinyl seats of the barstools and have a soda. Then Erica would take her to the doughnut shop for a treat. It was their little secret.

They had just returned from the little grocery store that morning, since they had gone to Dogma the day before and didn't need to go again. Erica put a video in the VCR to entertain Eileen while she unpacked the two bags of food. Her thoughts turned to work, how smoothly things had been going since Nick had quit a month ago. She had refused to work with him after she had walked in on him with that girl. It was all the best fodder for the gossip mill that Ashland's restaurant industry was. Erica couldn't stand how all the little hostesses talked about Nick and her like she didn't know they were talking about them. As if the event were so huge it had become public domain; they had a right to talk about her personal life. They were entitled to it. And she just had to take it.

Simone had been an invaluable source of commiseration because she had, coincidentally, broken up with Gavin that same weekend. Erica had called her to lambaste Nick, and Simone launched into her own attack on Gavin, how she could no longer stand him: slobby, lazy, constantly stoned. Simone said she felt like she just woke up finally and saw the real Gavin, sexual prowess notwithstanding. "Being a good lay only gets you so far," she'd said. "Maybe he was trying to sleep his way to the top," Erica joked. "He's got to get a job before he can do that," Simone snorted. They had a good laugh then, since Gavin hadn't worked for so long and was still taking his time completing his bachelor's degree. "He's going to wind up on some-one's couch when his trust fund runs out, and it won't be mine," Simone stated. And regarding Nick, Erica could tell that Simone was making every effort not to say I-told-you-so. "I'm sorry, honey, but he's got player written all over him! What did you expect from a bartender? Oh-my-God! I'm sor-ry! I didn't mean it like that! I mean a guy! A guy bartender! Guy bartenders are like that! Shit, Erica, I'm sorry! I wasn't thinking!" Simone had touched a nerve, but Erica had to laugh at her backpedaling, even though Simone, of all people, knew better. Well, Erica had been through worse. And the gossipers would soon move on to a new drama, a new rumor.

She had just finished putting the groceries away when there was a knock at the door, and she felt an ache in her upper thigh where she had been burned. The wound was like an old war injury, predicting storms or warn-ing her of threatening situations. She opened the door to find a young male police officer standing there, envelope in hand. Her heart leaped and her pulse began racing; she didn't like cops, never had. She had been out with some friends one night when she was twenty-one; they had gone to a GBH concert, an old punk band. Afterward, they went to a Denny's, and it was there that one of her friends began having a bad acid trip. She started writhing on the floor, thrashing and yelling, knocking things over. Erica and two others in their group tried to restrain her and calm her down, but the cops were there so fast. They must have been sitting in the parking lot. One of them, a big, stupid, corn-fed looking 'good ol' boy,' made a beeline for her distraught friend and yanked her up by the arm. Erica flashed back to her abusive stepfather grabbing her little brother, and she snapped. She flew into a protective rage, vaulted toward the cop, and pushed him away.

"Erica Hudson?" the cop asked.

She jolted. "Yes?"

"I'm Officer Randy Davis here to serve a legal document to you. If you could sign here, please." He held out a clipboard with an attached pen and showed her where to sign.

Erica wondered if it was something to do with the bankruptcy, but Andrew would have told her if he had filed. No, she would have had to file with him. Her hand shook as she signed her name.

"Thanks; have a good day," the officer said as he left.

She shut the door and sat down on the couch. Her fingers slid under the flap of the large envelope which bore the return address of Family Legal Services in Medford. Erica pulled a stack of papers out and looked at them. They were divorce papers.

"In the Circuit Court of the State of Oregon for the county of Jackson, in the matter of the marriage of: Andrew Samuel Pavel, Petitioner, and Erica Jasmine Hudson, Respondent," Erica read, and stopped. She laid her head back on the wall behind the couch and stared straight ahead.

He did it. I can't believe he really did it. Guess I should have seen it coming.

She let out a long sigh. It had been one year since she had told Andrew she wasn't happy and wanted to be separated. Almost exactly one year.

Eileen came up to her then. In her little Bugs Bunny voice she said, "What's up, Doc?" and then, "Cookie?"

"Okay, I'll get you a cookie." Erica got up and went to the kitchen. Eileen didn't exhibit Nathan's sensitive hearing, but she definitely mimicked his speech patterns: repeating lines from videos, asking for something using one word. Erica wondered if Eileen might need speech therapy because of it.

She handed her the cookie and watched her walk back to the living room, her honey-colored hair skimming her shoulders and her little diapered butt wagging from side to side with her steps.

Nathan would be coming home soon on his little bus. Erica returned to the couch and sank into it. She picked up the papers and tried to finish reading them, but she couldn't concentrate. She felt empty, even though she thought she had wanted this. She had wanted her freedom, but now that it was so close, it seemed anti-climactic. Maybe because she had been robbed of achieving it on her own. Or maybe because she didn't want to face the fact that her marriage had failed, and she wasn't sure if she had done all that she could to save it. And a very small part of her, a part that she wanted to silence, wasn't entirely sure if she had wanted to save it.

Thirteen

"Come on, let's get in the car. We're going for a ride to see a new apartment," Andrew told the kids one Saturday afternoon in March.

He handed Nathan the "go" card with the drawing of the car on it, and he looked at it, said "Go," and went to get his shoes. He was now four and a half and in his second year at Early Childhood Development Center. The only time he spoke more than three words spontaneously was when he quoted a line from a video, but he had started to interact more appropriately with peers and had learned to cover his ears when a sound bothered him. Something so simple, covering his ears, had to be modeled repeatedly before he started doing it on his own. It had now become a reflex. And every day he wore his dark green fleece jacket with the snug-fitting hood that helped to muffle many sounds. He even wore it indoors because it helped him to feel more comfortable participating in activities that were previously too noisy for him. It seemed to be his own version of a security blanket—the "security jacket," Andrew called it. And it prevented him from tugging on his hair so much. But Nathan was growing out of it and Andrew would need to replace it soon.

He strapped Nathan and Eileen in their car seats and drove south two miles, through the downtown area, past Safeway, and turned down a street across from the college. He continued down a few blocks, and then turned into the parking lot of a single-story apartment complex. It had been built in the late sixties, Andrew guessed by the dark kitchen cabinets, aluminum-frame single-pane windows, and popcorn acoustic ceilings.

The complex consisted of five four-unit buildings, called quads, so each apartment shared only two walls and had no one above or below them, which greatly appealed to Andrew. It was also generously landscaped, with trees all over the property and in between quads, and a lawn area in the back near the on-site laundry facility. The ad in the paper had read "One-bedroom garden apartment in quiet complex," and Andrew had liked it immediately. Each apartment had its own little garden and side yard, where he could fit the kids' plastic Little Tikes play structure and store their tricycles and outdoor toys. It would work just fine.

He had filled out and turned in his application the same morning that he saw the place, and three nights later he went to the property manager's home to pay first, last, and deposit and sign the rental agreement. It was raining that night, pouring. He recalled how his parents used to say that rain was a sign of God blessing an event with His holy water. Whether he believed that theory or not (in fact, he believed it was only said to him as a consolation for rained-out Easter egg hunts and birthday parties), he still felt confident that this apartment would be the right place for him to be. He had just turned twenty-eight, and it was his first place on his own. The first time without roommates or girlfriends or a wife. But this time it was with his children, and it would be just right.

He got the kids out of the car and led them down the little walkway between two of the quads. His was number eighteen, off in a corner. He unlocked the door and entered the clean, empty apartment. After he shut the door, he said, "This is our new apartment. We are going to move here and live here." He wondered if they would comprehend that, but he figured it would be best if they saw it first so they could get used to the idea of moving.

Nathan understood. He immediately began wailing, crying, "Go! Go!"

My God! Andrew thought, running to comfort him. *How could I have put it differently?*

Eileen also began to cry, incited by Nathan. This would not make a good impression on his new neighbors. Thinking quickly, Andrew said, "Not today. We are not moving here today. On Saturday. Five days." He held up his hand with his fingers extended. "We go home to our house in a minute." Andrew wished he had a cue card for Nathan that could somehow explain it visually for him.

Knowing the move was not happening that day seemed to be enough to calm him. He stopped crying and began walking around the apartment, with Eileen behind him. Andrew was so glad he had been able to come up with something to assuage Nathan's fear. He recognized it: instinct. It was the same thing that had woken him one night when Nathan was nineteen months old and told him that Nathan was sleepwalking. Andrew just sat up in bed and he knew. Then he got out of bed and found Nathan walking down the hallway, whereupon he gently redirected him toward his bed. He had heard no sound; he just knew.

"See, this will be yours and Eileen's bedroom. Your bed will go here, and Eileen's will go here. And your dresser will go there, and your toys will go there," Andrew said, pointing out the designated areas. The kids actually smiled and seemed to be getting used to the idea.

It was a large bedroom with a window that had a view of Grizzly Peak, and on the first day Andrew saw it, sunlight streamed through the window and lit up the white walls of the room. Across from the window was a walk-through closet with plenty of storage space, and on the other side of it was the bathroom. Then he brought them back out to the living room and explained that Dad's bed and the TV would go there. He had decided to set up his bed as a couch during the day (the old red couch would be put in storage along with the washer and dryer). At night he would experience something he never had before: watching TV in bed. He'd never liked the idea of having a TV in the bedroom, but the situation here made it necessary. The armoire wouldn't fit in the kids' room, nor would he want it there. No, he would have to watch *The X-Files* in bed.

Andrew felt excited about the move. He was anxious to leave the duplex, and not just for financial reasons. Being there made him remember all the fun family moments, sharing family life with Erica. That's what he missed most of all. Parenting with someone. Well, he'd had it for a while, at least. And it was good. He had been packing a few days ago and packed up the KitchenAid stand mixer, remembering how Erica had used it to make chocolate mousse, her specialty dessert, for them.

I guess when things are too good they're too good to be true. Come on, man. You both made a hell of a lot more than the chocolate mousse with that mixer.

Andrew still felt lonely, wondering how long it would take him to get over Erica. He seemed stuck in the grieving process. He felt like he'd worked through the anger and blame, but the sadness remained. He missed all of them doing things together, being a family. He remembered how he and Erica, on her nights off, used to lay the kids down side by side on a blanket on the floor, and one of them would drag the kids around the house on the blanket while the other one would "chase" them. He wanted to be a family again. He wanted his best friend back. He'd felt hollow, three months ago, when he'd signed the divorce papers, not really wanting to, but knowing that he had to. It was the first step in getting on with his life.

The divorce wouldn't be finalized until after the bankruptcy, since they needed to file as a married couple. In January he and Erica met with a low-cost lawyer in Medford who specialized in bankruptcy, and they paid the retainer fee. They were impressed with his professional demeanor; he was not at all condescending or judgmental. He got the facts he needed from them, asking questions about their income, debts, expenses, and explained the fees and procedures and how things would progress. He advised them on how to fill out the forms, commenting on how dual residences was a plus, since it increased their fixed expenses. They signed all the papers and left without feeling completely worthless. The only problem was that they couldn't file until they had saved up enough to pay the rest of the fees. Andrew had used all of his tax refund to get into his new apartment, but because the rent was one-third less a month than the duplex, he figured that they'd have the rest of it within two months. Then they could officially file, and the court date would be scheduled for approximately two months after that. Then it would be all over.

Andrew couldn't help but realize how strange it was that he seemed to have an emotional attachment to his debt. But it was probably because he'd shared most of it with Erica.

ANDREW LOVED HIS new apartment. He loved it so much he told himself that he'd stay there until he was ready to buy a house. It surprised him that he felt that secure, especially after leaving the duplex, but after only one week he and Nathan and Eileen had settled into a comfortable routine. He could tell they were happy there, too.

He smiled as he watched Nathan climb up on the jungle gym and slide down the slide while he stood behind Eileen and pushed her on the swings. She was in one of the black rubber baby swings with the wide straps across the front and back. They were in a park, just two blocks away from the apartment, with a water play area and many swings, slides, climbing and ride-on toys. Beyond the playground were basketball courts and volleyball courts and acres of grass where groups of kids played soccer and football. The water play area would not run until May, but there were still plenty of activities. Nathan bounced from one jungle gym to the next, and Andrew was glad he was so surefooted. So far he hadn't laughed in anyone's face or done any other socially unacceptable thing, fortunately. He seemed to be comfortable around the twenty or so other children and parents who were at the park.

"Out," Eileen began to whine.

Andrew lifted her out of the swing, disentangling her shoes, which got caught in the black rubber straps. She made it worse by kicking while still stuck, and yelling.

"Be patient, Eileen." Andrew dreaded the idea of her going into a full-blown tantrum in public. They were bad enough at home, but here, there was no enclosed room for her to go to. And if he had to take her home, it wouldn't be fair to Nathan, since they hadn't been there long and he was in no way ready to leave. Then he would have two screaming, flailing children to deal with, dragging them home since they had walked there.

He finally got Eileen's legs out of the swing and stood holding her. Much to his shock, she slapped his face. "No, you don't, young lady! We don't hit! Now you need a time out. You sit with me on this bench for a minute. You don't ever hit anybody."

Andrew's mind turned as Eileen squirmed and kicked and yelled. Had Erica slapped her before? He certainly hadn't. Where else could she have learned it? His dad? His father had spanked them every so often when he was growing up, but he had never slapped them across the face. Maybe it was some innate impulse of hers that came with her temper.

"You be quiet, Eileen. No hitting."

Andrew looked around for Nathan. He didn't see him right away, so for a second he figured he was in one of the plastic tubes on one of the jungle gyms. But something felt wrong. Andrew shot up off the bench, Eileen in his arms, and ran around, his eyes darting back and forth around all the play areas. Nathan was gone.

Panic hit him in an icy wave. Immediately he scanned the ball courts with games in progress, then his eyes went farther, taking in the little soccer bodies running around on the grass, fifty yards away. He still didn't see his son.

Oh, my God, oh God, where is he?

Something propelled Andrew toward the street, beyond the grass fields where the soccer games were going on. It was East Main Street, busy even though it was only two lanes wide. He looked across the street, and then he saw Nathan, his little dark green fleece jacket with the hood up. He was walking, by himself, on the train tracks that ran perpendicular to the street. How he had crossed that busy street, and in the short time that Andrew had been preoccupied with Eileen, was beyond comprehension.

Without thinking, so ecstatic to see him, Andrew called to him. "Nathan!"

Nathan looked up, saw his father, and began running toward him.

Oh, my God! He'll run in the street!

Andrew still had Eileen in his arms. With his free arm, he held his hand up, trying to will Nathan to stop. "No! Stay there! Stop!"

But it was too late. He wasn't stopping.

Andrew couldn't even look at the cars. He didn't even know if there were any coming. He just looked at Nathan, how scared and confused he was. It was a terrible moment, burned in Andrew's mind forever, those few seconds with his son in the middle of the street.

Suddenly, he was able to react. He glanced both directions, and there were cars coming, but if Nathan came to him, he could make it. There was not enough time for him to go to Nathan and then come back. But if Nathan tripped, it could be a horrible nightmare. Nathan had never tripped. He walked at ten months and was running at thirteen. All of this Andrew realized in a fraction of a second. He knelt down as he waved Nathan to him, his arm in a large sweeping motion. "Come on, honey. Hurry to Dad!"

Andrew imagined his hope carrying Nathan across the street to him. And he made it. As Nathan reached him, Andrew found himself gasping with relief. He embraced his son, overcome with emotion. After a moment, he admonished Nathan for leaving the park and crossing the street to go to the train tracks without him. There was no way Andrew could deal with returning to the park, or going anywhere else for that matter. He needed the security and comfort of his apartment to recuperate. Shaking, he walked home holding his children's hands. Sensing the graveness of the situation, they offered no resistance.

By that evening, Andrew still didn't feel that he was functioning normally. He was still in a sort of automaton mode from the shock of losing Nathan, then seeing him run across a busy street. It was time for the weekly bath and shampoo number, and he really didn't feel up to it. Nathan still had issues with having his hair washed, and Andrew was still berating himself for risking his son's life by having him run across the street to him.

Why didn't I think? Why didn't I just go to him at the tracks instead of calling out his name? Why didn't I just go to him when he was in the middle of the street? What the hell was wrong with me?

Andrew filled the tub and then began bathing Eileen. He had an idea as he rinsed her hair while she reclined. He wondered if it was the tipping back, the reclining, that bothered Nathan. Some inexplicable sensory issue. He liked the baths well enough, and he didn't seem to mind when he was back upright while Andrew put the shampoo in his hair and massaged his scalp. It was when Andrew laid him back, even though he cradled him securely in the crook of his arm, that Nathan became upset. Maybe if he taught him to bend his neck back while sitting upright, and he poured water out of a cup onto his head, he wouldn't be so disturbed.

He towel-dried Eileen's hair and body and dressed her in sweatpants and a long sleeved shirt, both Nathan's hand-me-downs. Then he braced himself for Nathan and showed him the bath cue card while he undressed him. He didn't want to trick him, but he knew if he showed Nathan the wash hair cue card, he would begin shrieking, and the last thing he wanted was for his new neighbors to call Child Protective Services on him.

Nathan was one step ahead of him. "No wash hair," he stated as Andrew sat him in the tub.

"Nathan, your hair needs to be cleaned."

"NO!"

Andrew picked up the plastic tumbler he had set on the bathroom floor and showed it to Nathan. "See this? I'm going to just pour the water on your hair. No lying down. You sit up, and I'll wet your hair." He slowly poured water on Nathan's arms and back, working his way up to his head. He seemed fine as Andrew wet the back of his head.

"Okay, Nate, now lift up your chin, like this," he said, showing him how to tilt his head back. "Look up at the ceiling."

He did it. Andrew used his free hand to shield Nathan's eyes from the water as he wet the top of his head, and it worked. He seemed calm. No shrieking. No thrashing. Not even a squeal.

Andrew praised him while he lathered his head with a two-in-one shampoo/conditioner, the tear-free, no-tangle variety. Then he told him he was going to pour more water on him to get the shampoo out, talking in a soothing voice, crooning to him. Andrew rinsed the back, then told Nathan to look at the ceiling again as he used his hands to shield Nathan's eyes from the soap and finished rinsing the top of his head. It worked. Andrew couldn't believe it worked. He was almost laughing as he continuously applauded Nathan, called him a big boy, kissed his forehead. He handed Nathan some bath toys and told him he could play in the water for a while, and Andrew went to check on Eileen, who was watching a video.

Andrew sat down on the edge of his bed, in shock again, thinking that maybe, just maybe, the days of hair-washing hysteria were over.

"MY MOM," ERICA began, her voice faltering, "was driving drunk last night and she—she crashed into a tree," she told Andrew. "She died."

Andrew immediately wrapped his arms around her. "I'm so sorry, Erica."

She held onto him a minute, shaking, out on the sidewalk in front of her house. Her brother had called her two hours earlier while she was feeding the kids lunch. Erica was sad, but not devastated. Her mother had lost jobs because of her drinking, and this was not her first accident. Whenever Erica answered the phone and heard her brother's voice, she always wondered if he would say to her exactly what he had said today: *Mom died last night.* Erica somehow knew that her mother would meet with the same fate that her own mother had. It was an accepted but rarely discussed conclusion that Erica's grandmother, Jeanette, was probably drinking the night that she, according to the police report, "fell asleep at the wheel" and careened into an oncoming cement mixer on the highway, killing herself and her teenage niece, her sister Maggie's only child. Erica often wondered if Aunt Maggie's vehemence about taking her in was a mourning mother's attempt to create some karmic balance. If Jeanette's negligence robbed Maggie of her daughter, then Maggie's own vigilance for Jeanette's grandchild would somehow make up for it. Two wrongs don't make a right, but two rights can cover up a wrong. One right for taking care of her sister's grandchild. Two rights because she didn't have to. And she never complained. Erica never felt like the object of resentment, the stone in Aunt Maggie's shoe, the spider in her bed. She felt loved. She just never knew how complex that love actually was. But families of alcoholics were nothing if not complex. As the direct descendent of two to-the-grave alcoholics (three if she included her grandfather), Erica looked forward to ending her ironic, ill-conceived career as a bartender. Somehow, she had to get through college quicker, but she would have to figure that out later.

Erica called her boss, who generously offered to pay for her to rent a car so that she could drive to Weed for a few days. Her mother would be cremated, something she always made sure to tell them over the years. "And spread my ashes on Mount Shasta," she had said, whose majestic, 14,179-foot peak was visible nearly anywhere in Weed. She had said that the mystical qualities of the mountain appealed to her Native American heritage.

Erica had come outside to meet Andrew when he pulled up to pick up the kids, since it was Friday, the day he got off early. It felt good to be in his arms again for a moment; she found comfort in the familiarity. It had been so long, and she didn't think she had a right to miss it, since she was the one who had wanted to be separated. But she couldn't deny the fact that she still cared for him very much. He was the father of her children! And a good one. And she was starting to feel like they were becoming friends again, which she enjoyed, and had hoped for. No one else in Ashland had ever met her mother, knew her history, other than Andrew. She didn't even have to say anything, and she knew that he knew what she was feeling.

She could barely acknowledge it herself. Of course she was sad, but she also felt this strange combination of relief, anger, disappointment, and longing. She felt like she had missed out on so much because of her mother's alcoholism. She couldn't understand, even in adulthood, why her mother wouldn't stop drinking. And because of it, she would only talk to her once or twice a year. "Call me back when you're sober, Mom," she would say, and not talk to her for another six months, her attempt at "tough love" that never worked. Her mother never called her back. Erica wondered if it was because she was too embarrassed or if she just didn't want another lecture.

"I have to go to Weed for a few days," she told Andrew. "Mike offered to pay for a rental car for me. I'm leaving this afternoon, should be back Monday night. We're having a little memorial service on Monday, then I'll drive back."

"Are you okay?"

"Yeah, I'll be fine. I'll call you when I get back, and you can drop the kids off Tuesday morning. Sorry about Monday," Erica said.

"Don't worry about it. I'll work something out. Did you tell them?"

"No. They wouldn't understand, and they don't know her anyway. I mean, my God, Nate's only seen her twice and Eileen only once, as a newborn. You'd think she would have wanted to see more of her grandchildren."

"Well, I'm sorry, Erica."

"Thanks. Anyway, it'll be nice to see Caleb. It's been a while. Sucks that someone has to be born or die for my family to see each other. The last time we all got together was about eight years ago, when my Aunt Maggie died." She had gone in her sleep, ninety-one years old, still living in the same house where Erica had spent her first five years of life. And Maggie had still worked in her garden and taken care of her pets, a lab-shepherd mix named Buster and a brown rabbit named Alice, until the day she died. Erica always found it sad that her great aunt had died alone. Maggie's nephew, Willy, discovered her in her bed two days later on his weekly check-in visit. She was buried in the cemetery beside her daughter, Ava. Erica attended the funeral and brought Buster and Alice home with her, to her mother's house in Weed. Alice only lasted about six months, and old Buster lived another three years. He died in his sleep, right before Erica moved to Ashland. In dog years he had lived as long as Aunt Maggie.

"Well, I better get the kids so you can get going," Andrew said, walking into the house.

Erica embraced her children and told them she had to take a little trip, which didn't seem to affect them. *Well,* Erica told herself, *at least it's easier than them crying and clinging to my legs.*

Andrew hugged her again and told her to drive carefully. "And tell Caleb I said hi." He had always liked Caleb.

AN HOUR LATER, after her boss had picked her up and taken her to the rental office, she began the drive to Weed.

It's only an hour! she yelled at herself. *Why didn't I visit her more often? That might have made a difference. I just couldn't stand to see her drink herself to death. Poor Caleb. I left him to deal with all this shit.*

Erica hadn't seen her brother for about a year, when she had gone to visit him and his girlfriend Daisy when their son, Drake, was born. She remembered arriving at their apartment, one week after his birth, and asking if their mother had come to see them yet.

"I had to give Mom an ultimatum," Caleb said. "I told her she couldn't see her grandson unless she was sober."

"How did that go over?"

"She said she would try and hung up."

Six months later for Drake's first Christmas, their mother had shown up with a teddy bear for him. "At least she wasn't fully loaded yet," Caleb had told Erica on the phone. "That was her 'trying.'"

Erica shook her head as she realized that the last time she saw her mother was during a brief time 'on the wagon' when Eileen was born and she had come up to Ashland for a visit. That was nearly three years ago. Her eyes stung with tears as she navigated her compact rental car through the winding, mountainous section of I-5 in northern California. Erica saw Mt. Shasta and could no longer deny her grief. She pulled over at a rest stop for a few minutes and let herself mourn.

One hour away! Now she's gone!

A montage of memories flooded Erica. Her mother made the best homemade play-dough. She loved Halloween and went overboard with decorations and costumes every year. Erica might have lived in a tent for a while, but she always had a detailed homemade Halloween costume. And her mom had such a melodious, infectious laugh. True, being drunk so often might have affected the quality of it, but when she was sober it was magical. She wasn't the greatest mother, and she had horrible taste in men, but she loved her children the best that she could. It seemed that her drinking didn't get really bad until after Erica left home. Caleb would write her letters and tell her how he would come home from school and make sure their mother was out of bed and getting ready for work. She waited tables at a diner-type establishment while Caleb made his own dinner, did his homework, and cleaned the house, discovering empty bottles of vodka stashed in various places, including under the bathroom sink and behind the TV, but mostly under her bed. Erica wondered if someone (Uncle Willy? Aunt Maggie, perhaps? Maybe even Caleb?) had, at some point, warned her, chastised her, that if she didn't watch out she would end up just like her mother. Her life and her death had been a sad, self-fulfilling prophecy.

Erica finished the drive determined to keep things positive on this visit, for Caleb's sake as much as her own. She reminded herself of the last phone conversation they'd had, when Caleb called her six weeks ago on her thirtieth birthday. They had exciting news: Drake had started walking and Caleb had been promoted to shift manager at the grocery store where he had started out as a courtesy clerk when he was fifteen. She told him that Nathan had started to talk a bit more and screamed a bit less, but that when they had gone to obtain a medical diagnosis of autism so that he could continue to receive services, the psychiatrist had asked him his name and Nathan didn't respond at all. "Maybe he'll be a musical prodigy," Caleb offered in a jovial tone. He seemed to sense that she didn't want to talk about turning thirty. Frustrated by the fact that she was still working on her undergraduate degree, she had to remind herself that she had accomplished something else by age thirty that she hadn't exactly planned: she'd had Nathan and Eileen, worth more than any delay in her academic progress. Her birthday had fallen on a night when they were with her, and she slept between them on the futon, content to inhale the scent at the backs of their necks while they dreamed.

She entered Weed, still finding it funny that a city of only three thousand people labeled the south end of town 'South Weed,' like 'South San Francisco.' Not to mention all the jokes about the name of the city itself, especially from her pot-head friends in Ashland, whenever she mentioned where she had moved from.

She parked on the street in front of Caleb's apartment and got her bag out of the car. Caleb, barefoot, dressed in jeans and a plain green T-shirt, came out to greet her, and they embraced, commenting on how they needed to see each other more often.

For the first time, Erica noticed Caleb's father's intense look on Caleb's face, how he'd looked when he wasn't yelling at someone. On his father, it had been an angry look, but on Caleb, it was a pensive look, like a scientist in a research lab, a Buddhist monk in a garden, or a dignitary's face on currency, authoritative but familiar. Caleb was twenty-two and was also built like his father, sturdy, muscular. That was probably why their mother had fallen for the man. But Caleb was a completely different man than the alcoholic who died two years ago at age forty-seven of a cocaine-induced heart attack. Caleb didn't drink, and he was also much quieter, introspective. He wanted to be the opposite of his parents, but he wasn't bitter about them. Erica marveled at her brother's ability to forgive them and live his life free of the grip of resentment. "You only end up hurting yourself if you carry that around with you," he'd said before.

They went inside and she greeted Daisy, also twenty-two, who was Caleb's high school sweetheart and perfect for him. Being petite, she had to reach up to hug Erica, and her green eyes looked comforting, sincere. She had gorgeous, shoulder-length auburn hair and a little round face that reminded Erica of a doll. But Daisy, like Caleb, was serious and mature. Erica felt like she was the younger one whenever she visited.

"Hi, Drake!" she said to her nephew, getting down to his eye level. He looked like a baby-boy version of his mother, whose leg he ran to grab.

"He's in the separation-anxiety stage," Daisy said. "And he's about ready for a nap."

Erica glanced around the small, modestly furnished living room and sat on the denim slip-covered couch. The walls were rental-white and decorated with metal-framed photographs of the small family, some candid snapshots, some from a portrait studio, like JC Penney. Caleb brought her some orange juice and sat down with her while Daisy took Drake to the bedroom.

"How are you?" Erica said, realizing now that both of his parents were gone.

Caleb ran his fingers through his short brown hair. "I'm okay. I'm just sad that things didn't turn out better for her. She wasn't a terrible person; she just had this addiction, and it killed her." He sounded resigned, accepting.

"At least she's out of her misery. I called her on New Year's and she sounded like she wasn't doing well."

"She was probably hung over!" Caleb said, chuckling.

"Yeah," Erica said with a little smile. "But I mean, she had lost another job, and she just sounded . . . like she was ready to give up."

"I think she gave up a long time ago. I'm just relieved that she didn't take anyone with her."

They talked for a while, reminiscing about the strange upbringing they shared: wildly dysfunctional, sometimes abusive, with moments of wacky fun and genuine love thrown in. Daisy came out and joined them, contributing her memories of the woman she had helped take care of, the countless times she had to pick her up from the bar, help her into bed. Daisy spoke of her laugh, too, and how she was so cheerful most of the time.

"It was like she seemed to think if she stayed positive, her life would improve on its own," Daisy said.

"She was like that even when we were in the tent," Erica said. "You know, to this day, I hate camping!"

They laughed then, tentatively, and Caleb said he had been too young to have it make such an impression on him, but he understood. Then he got up and suggested that they go to the morgue.

A wave of dread came over Erica. *How do you say goodbye to your mother?*

Fourteen

It was Andrew's first week without Zoloft after a year and a half of his daily dosage. He had just run out of his pills and decided that he no longer needed them. He hadn't even talked to Jim, the counselor, for over six months; he had been on a plan they called "med-management," in which he went in once a month to check in with a nurse and get his next month's prescription. In fact, the counseling itself had not been all that beneficial due to some of Jim's unprofessional methods. Andrew remembered how, early on in one of his counseling sessions, Jim had said to him, "Don't worry about Erica. She'll come around. Sometimes women just want to assert their independence for a while." Andrew laughed at the memory. How can a counselor say that to an obsessive-compulsive man whose wife stated in no uncertain terms that she wanted to be separated? How could he justify encouraging false hope like that? Andrew had wanted to believe him for a moment, but he knew better even in his state of mind at the time. Nothing to gain from that sort of 'counseling.' The medication he had continued to need for a while, to keep him feeling balanced, but even that was no longer necessary. He called the clinic and canceled his appointment and told them he had decided to exit the program.

The main thing was that he felt better and knew that he didn't need antidepressants any longer. He had regained almost half of the twenty pounds he had lost due to the emotional stress of separating. He felt secure at his job, liked his new apartment, and had settled into a comfortable joint custody routine and level of pleasant civility with Erica.

But he was most optimistic about having met Robin. He had been going out dancing at Dogma every other Friday night, and that's where he met her. He was out on the dance floor one night, doing his thing, looking at his feet, and she was suddenly in front of him. It was instant, mutual lust.

She was tall (why did he always fall for the tall ones? he wondered), blond, Nordic-looking, statuesque even, wearing a black halter dress. Her azure eyes penetrated him when she introduced herself. He had to buy her a drink. She was a middle school history/social studies teacher, and he felt a little silly the next day thinking about the comment he had made: "All the boys in your class must have a crush on you," to which she had rolled her eyes. But he must have said something to redeem himself, because she gave him a lengthy good-night kiss and agreed to go to dinner with him two days later.

It's not like he wanted someone chatty, but he felt like he had to drag even general information out of her. Dinner was full of false starts and uncomfortable voids in the conversation; Andrew couldn't ignore their lack of social chemistry, but he wanted to. It was like they were playing tennis: he kept setting her up with these great serves and she just couldn't return them. Or maybe she wasn't interested in playing tennis. Maybe she thought he was playing golf. But she had a Master's degree, so he knew she was intelligent, and she owned her own home and was established in her career. He wanted someone who was settled like that, and mature. And, *God*, was she sexy. Maybe it just took her a while to warm up to new people. He had to give her a chance. He would kick himself later if he didn't, because the attraction was undeniable. She seemed to want him as much as he wanted her. And he knew he wasn't imagining it; she invited him back to her place after dinner.

The sex was good and he didn't even have to pursue it. Nice for a change, although it had also been that way when he and Erica first got together. It was hard not to compare women he got involved with. He felt like he shouldn't, mostly because he wanted to prove to himself that he was over Erica. Not to mention the fact that Erica had been seeing someone for about a month, and Andrew had been tired of his own subconscious whining—"What's he got that I haven't?" and "What's wrong with me?" It was pathetic and he wanted to kick his own ass.

But he was making progress; he figured Robin was a step in the right direction. She had called him that Saturday afternoon, when he had returned from the weekly excursion to the neighborhood park with the kids, and suggested that they all go out to dinner together as a way for her to meet them. Andrew had strong doubts about the success of being in a restaurant with Nathan's sensory issues, but he wanted to seem spontaneous to Robin, so he agreed that it was a "great idea," cringing inside. He had told her that Nathan had autism, but Robin's knowledge of autism was limited to older kids who had responded well to past therapy and were higher-functioning.

Andrew cleaned and dressed his children, wishing he had a restaurant cue card for Nathan, something to prepare him. He explained to him that they were going to a restaurant and would have to sit in chairs at a table and be quiet, but he might as well have been telling that to a puppy. He tried to be optimistic when Robin arrived, but she seemed a little miffed that neither of his children greeted her. Well, Nathan did, in his own way. He walked up to her in the doorway and exclaimed, "Balto!" which was the name of the video he had watched that morning. Andrew tried to explain, but Robin didn't seem to understand, and the odd first impression had already been made. He quickly offered to drive to the restaurant.

They had decided to go to Panda Garden for Chinese food, or rather, Robin suggested it and Andrew didn't feel like saying, "McDonald's would be a hell of a lot easier." So he drove to Panda Garden, wondering what he was setting himself up for, what he would even get for the kids to eat.

Andrew felt certain that if he felt nervous about how Nathan would do that Nathan would pick up on it and react to it, so he tried to be as relaxed as possible, but it didn't seem to matter. Nathan, right from the start, was anxious on his own. As soon as the hostess seated them and they began to look at the menus, Nathan, moaning, slid out of his chair and began writhing on the floor.

Oh, God, Andrew thought, *it's starting already?*

"Nathan, come on, sit in the chair, okay?" He reached down and gently pulled him back into the chair.

"Go," he said, and immediately slid back to the floor and continued writhing. The moaning escalated to whining, and Andrew feared the "Go"s would get louder. He also figured that if Robin didn't understand about "Balto," she wouldn't understand about the sensory issues causing Nathan to writhe on the floor. She probably thought he was behaving badly, having a tantrum.

Shit, Andrew thought.

Robin looked at him with her eyebrow raised. "If you think it would be easier, we can order to go and eat back at your place," she said.

"Yeah, I think this is too much for him to handle. He's anxious in new situations."

"Is that it?" Robin said, raising her eyebrow again as she went back to her menu.

Andrew, feeling exasperated, picked Nathan up off the floor and put him in his lap. "Just sit with me for a minute. It's okay."

Nathan, wriggling in his arms, began to squeal loudly.

Fuck autism, Andrew thought. He tried to remain calm. "I'm going to have to take him outside," he said, standing up. He pulled out his wallet and handed Robin some cash. "Um, I'm sorry, but if you could order me a number four combo and whatever you'd like, that would be great. I'll wait outside with them." He held out his hand for Eileen, who had been quiet the entire time, and she went with him.

As soon as they were out of the restaurant, Nathan was fine. Andrew slumped in the front seat of the car as the kids climbed around in the back. "And what," he said to the windshield, "was wrong with that restaurant, Nate? It wasn't noisy. It wasn't crowded. Sometimes I just don't get it. And I try. I really, really try."

A MONTH LATER, Andrew sat in a metal folding chair in the waiting room at Family Legal Services, pen and clipboard in hand. It was time.

He and Erica had gone the week before to court for the bankruptcy hearing, so that was finalized. It was strange, the two of them at the courthouse together. The last time they had done that was when they were picking up their marriage license, five years ago. Five years. Well, they had gotten in debt together, and they got out of it together. Their full debt, other than student loans, had been discharged, and all of their meager property was claimed exempt. Andrew was relieved to have that behind him.

He looked at the paperwork in front of him and closed his eyes. This would be harder than he thought. It had been a rough week already.

Two days before, he had gone with his co-worker, the other Andrew, to the coast with the kids. The other Andrew brought his daughter, who was a year older than Nathan. It was Andrew's first time being away from work and still being called Sam all day long, which felt weird. Nathan and Eileen were young enough not to notice. It was a two and a half hour drive to Brookings, however, and Eileen became violently carsick in the other Andrew's car. She was crabby the whole day, and Nathan was nervous, being with new people in a new vehicle. Andrew wondered why he bothered.

Was it worth it to try to be social? To do the things that people do to get to know each other, become friends, or just pass the time? He felt like he did in grade school, the new kid trying to make friends and be accepted, sitting in class or joining a game of kickball at recess, only now he had two children in tow, one who vomited and one who shrieked, making it all the more difficult. The worst was when, after they had been there for half an hour, Nathan had to go to the bathroom.

There were only permanent pit-style chemical toilets, and Andrew steeled himself for a battle. He managed to get a moaning Nathan in and locked the door. There was barely room for any adult to drop his pants and turn around, let alone contain a hysterical child. Nathan began shrieking, "Nooo-ooo! Nooo-ooo!" and tried to bolt, shaking the enclosure. Andrew managed to pull down Nathan's pants, amazed that his son had not wet himself.

Someone demanded from the other side of the door, "What's going on in there?!" and Andrew quickly, cheerfully called back, "He's okay! He's just scared of this toilet here!" hoping no one was calling the police.

He lifted Nathan, assuring him over and over that he would be okay, and held him over the opening with both arms around him to keep him feeling secure, if that was possible in his state. Andrew heard the trickle of urine during Nathan's still-terrorized screams. "Aaa-aah! Aaa-aah!"

Someone else tried to open the door. "Do you need help?!"

"We're fine! He's just scared!"

After what felt like an hour of Nathan screaming, he seemed to be finished, so Andrew stood him up, pulled up his pants, and opened the door to countless negative stares and shaking of heads as the people, like spectators at the scene of an accident, tried to decide if they should walk away. He had obviously just sodomized a little boy.

The other Andrew walked up and asked him, "Does he do that a lot?"

"He has a fear of public restrooms, so, yeah. Not much I can do about it." Andrew said it loudly, hoping others around might hear him.

"Wow. That must be hard."

"Yeah." *It's pretty fucking hard, man. Harder than you will ever know.*

The words rang in Andrew's mind again as he looked over the final divorce papers on the clipboard. *This is harder than Erica will ever know,* he thought. He took a breath and signed his name, so quick, so cut and dry. He wished his emotional divorce could be that way. So concrete.

NATHAN, AFTER ALMOST a year, finally walked into Erica's house without putting up a fight.

Erica had been sitting on the couch reading when she heard Andrew pull up to drop off the kids on a Friday night. The door opened, and instead of Eileen, Nathan walked in, like he had been waltzing through the door all along.

"Nathan! Hi, Sweetheart!" Erica went and embraced her son, who was wearing his usual hooded fleece jacket, although a new one in a larger size now, and navy sweatpants which he liked to wear while sleeping. Nathan walked over to the old laundry basket where some toys were kept and began digging through it. Erica was used to him not responding verbally, but at least he would accept a hug. He always did, even if it was with predictable rigor.

Andrew then walked through the door, carrying a surly, whining Eileen. "Sorry I'm a little late. She's crabby," he said. "I think she's coming down with something."

"Wonderful," Erica mumbled as Andrew set Eileen on the couch. Erica stood up. She brightened, remembering. "Did you say anything to Nate? He just walked right in!"

"I saw that! Isn't that amazing? Finally! I just set him on the sidewalk and said, 'Go inside; go open the door!' Maybe that was it, the 'open the door' part. I've never said that before."

"Well, it worked! He's been doing so great lately, even trying to say pronouns," Erica said, walking into the kitchen.

"Yeah, he mixes them up, but at least he's trying. He always says, 'You want cookie?' when he wants me to ask him if he wants a cookie," Andrew said.

"He does that to me all the time, too." Erica was happy. She felt ecstatic about her son finally accepting her home. And it worked out well for them there. She enjoyed sleeping in between her two children on the futon, and they had a yard to play in during the day. They were within walking distance of the grocery store, the Laundromat, and her work. She had been saving up a little money and was looking forward to taking a class or two in September when Eileen started preschool at Head Start, which accepted three-year-olds.

"Oh, I wanted to tell you about this book I saw at the bookstore the other day," Andrew said, leaning against the wall in the kitchen.

Erica noticed that his hair was gelled and he wore a dressy, blue button-up rayon shirt and chinos. She wondered if he was going out to dinner with someone.

"It's about autistic kids being put on dairy-free and wheat-free diets and how they've shown improved ability to talk and focus. The book says that in these cases the symptoms of autism are caused by a cumulative allergic reaction, even though the child craves and likes these foods," Andrew said. "I thought it might be worth a try with Nate. What do you think?"

Erica finished cutting up a peach and split it on two Sesame Street plates. She sighed audibly. Lately she'd been realizing that she could no longer deny that Nathan had autism, and a child psychiatrist had confirmed that it was true, that it had been true all this time. She still hoped that one day he would "snap out of it," but that hope was fading, replaced by the grim acceptance of an uncertain future. But he could read! He taught himself that letters have sounds and combining them forms words. He could read words he didn't even know! And Nathan continued to be affectionate, sitting close to her every night to read books together. Erica couldn't recall anything about Nathan's infancy that pointed to autism. There were no warning signs. Nothing that stood out. He never banged his head on his crib in the middle of the night, like she had read about other babies who were later diagnosed with it. He never screamed in grocery stores as a baby. Did he just somehow slip into autism? When was this hood of fear, ultra sensitivity, and social strangulation thrown over her son's head?

Erica turned to look at Andrew. She saw this diet as a rope dangling from a helicopter above her as she struggled to get out of a deep, narrow canyon. "I'll try anything."

Andrew actually looked relieved as he said, "Okay, well, I'll stop at the store and pick up some soy cheese and gluten-free bread when I leave. When did you want to start him on it?"

"We can start tomorrow, if you want."

Someone knocked, and a cold ache surged across the region of Erica's scar, as it did whenever she heard a child cry in pain, or saw someone fall, cut a finger, or be injured in some way. Her scar was a harbinger of danger, reacting to potentially uncomfortable situations, a primordial "fight or flight" response.

She had hoped that Andrew would have been gone by the time Jonah, her new boyfriend, came over. Not that she really believed Andrew would have caused any problems, but things were going so well with him lately that she didn't want to spoil it by an unexpected meeting.

Jonah was also a bartender, at another bar in town, so she had known about him, but she just started seeing him the weekend after she got back from her mother's funeral. It turned out that his father had died a few years ago, so he understood what she was going through, and the excitement of beginning a relationship helped to drown out her sadness about not having a second chance with her mother.

She opened the door and greeted him with a hug. He was her height and a bit rangy, like her brother, but he was about ten years older than Caleb. He had long, straight brown hair tied back with a black bandana and wore several silver rings on his fingers. He had a relaxed but expectant look on his angular, clean-shaven face; she had told him that Andrew might still be there dropping off the kids. In fact, he seemed to be a little early, as if he had wanted to meet Andrew, size up her ex-husband. Well, that was fine, provided Andrew didn't freak out.

Jonah came in and took off his black leather motorcycle jacket and laid it on the floor in front of Erica's dresser. Underneath, he had on the requisite old concert T-shirt, jeans, and boots. He possessed the bad-boy image that Erica liked, but was soft-spoken and intelligent. A poet, even! She wondered what Andrew would think.

"Um, Andrew, this is Jonah. Jonah, this is Andrew, Nathan and Eileen's dad." She stepped aside as Andrew walked forward to shake his hand and say, "Good to meet you."

Satisfied, relieved, she remembered the peaches for the kids and walked back to the kitchen. "You want anything to drink, Jonah? Or you, Andrew?" she called out. She surprised herself with her casual tone, frivolous almost, as if she expected her ex-husband and her new boyfriend to have a drink together upon first meeting.

"No thanks," Andrew said. "I have plans tonight, so I need to get going."

Jonah also declined her offer and sat on the couch. Erica set the plates down on the counter for the kids, who were being hugged by Andrew. A moment later, he called good-bye and let himself out.

That was easy enough, she thought. Probably having his own date made

Andrew more accepting of Jonah's presence. He wasn't left standing at the finding-a-new-relationship dance.

ANDREW WAS SURPRISED by Erica's words: "I'll try anything." It was strange to hear that from the woman who for nearly a year after Nathan's diagnosis was in denial about it. Not only was she receptive to the proposal of a radical diet change, it almost seemed like she was desperate for it. Andrew understood. There were many times when he feared that he resented the disability. He just wanted a normal relationship with his child. Without even discussing it, he knew Erica felt the same way.

He had just picked up some food for Nathan (soy cheese, milk, yogurt, and gluten-free bread), and the thought occurred to him while he was in the health food store that it felt like he was doing a science experiment. He wondered if changing Nathan's diet really would improve his communication skills. "I'll try anything," echoed in his mind.

He drove the few blocks to Robin's house, where he had been invited for dinner. On the way he smiled as he recognized Brooke, Erica's co-worker, walking down the street wearing one of Erica's dresses. It was one that he had always liked, a short-sleeved knit knee-length dress with all-over thin blue and green stripes. He called it the Sesame Street dress because it reminded him of the shirts Bert and Ernie wore. Brooke wore it with black boots, like Erica did, although it was longer on her than it was on Erica. Andrew waved as he drove by, and Brooke looked at him, but he wasn't sure if she recognized him. Erica had mentioned a few months ago that Brooke had stopped by with some toys for the kids, a Woody doll, the cowboy from Disney's *Toy Story*, for Nathan, which he slept with every night, and a used ride-on car for Eileen that she'd picked up at a garage sale and painted with flowers. Brooke also helped out with babysitting, and the kids felt so comfortable with her that Nathan actually addressed her by name. It was the only name he could say besides Eileen.

Andrew thought about Jonah; he seemed all right. The last two guys Erica had dated both had long hair; Andrew wondered why she had ever been attracted to him in the first place. His hair had never touched his shoulders, mostly because he just didn't like it falling in his face and would end up cutting it off before it got long enough to pull back. And bandanas just weren't his thing. *Erica must like them, though,* he thought. He'd felt self-conscious tonight for different reasons, and it caught him off-guard. Initially he'd been glad that he was on his way to dinner and that Erica would see him dressed up. He wanted to look good when he saw her, wanted her to look at what she cast aside and wanted her to regret it. Success is the best revenge. But then he felt uncomfortably overdressed in front of Jonah, who looked self-assured in his casual attire, the kind Erica was attracted to. Andrew felt like he'd worn a three-piece suit to a backyard pool party. Then there was the initial defensive thought whenever meeting one of Erica's new boyfriends: Andrew mentally threatening the guy that he better not lay a hand on his children. That Erica better be sure she can trust him around them.

He shook his head as he pulled into Robin's driveway, not wanting to think about the baggage of Erica any more. He focused on the house in front of him. Robin owned a cute little Craftsman-style two-bedroom bungalow near the downtown area of Ashland. She had screened in the porch and cultivated a cottage garden in the front yard with a mixture of perennials and wild flower beds edged with rocks. Two white Adirondack chairs sat off to one side and a sprinkler pulsed on the small lawn. Andrew knocked on the front door.

Robin answered the door in knit yoga pants and a tank top, cementing Andrew's anxiety about being overdressed. For a second he wondered if he had the wrong night.

"Hi. Come in," Robin said in her disjointed way. He followed her through her small but perfect house, which looked like it belonged in an issue of *Better Homes and Gardens.* She had Shaker furniture on wood floors with colorful rugs underfoot and quilts hung on the wall alongside dried lavender stalks and other floral arrangements. The house was over a hundred years old and she had restored it handsomely.

"I had to pick up a few things at the Co-Op on my way over here that will need to be refrigerated until I can take them home—just this bag. Do you mind if I put it in your fridge?"

"No, go ahead."

Andrew put the food inside and told Robin about the book he had looked at describing dairy-free and gluten-free diets for kids with autism. The first few minutes with Robin were usually awkward, he felt, so he was glad to have a topic to discuss with her. She offered polite interest.

"Well, before we eat, I was wanting to do some yoga. Would you like to join me?" Robin said, before he was finished talking about the diet. She looked at him expectantly, like that was a reasonable thing to suggest to someone in a button-up rayon shirt tucked into belted chinos.

"Um, sure," Andrew said. He followed her into a room where she had laid some padded mats on the floor. "Let me just take off my shoes." He had done some yoga before, having checked out a beginner's guide that one of their clients at work carried, so he was familiar with some of the poses, but felt uncomfortable doing them in the clothes he had on. While Robin went through an entire moon salutation, Andrew sat on the floor, separated his legs in a V, and stretched over to touch his toes.

She seemed so aloof, which intrigued Andrew more, but it made it so hard to get to know her. Andrew figured she just must be one of those people who needed a long time to open up. He hoped that she would soon. He felt such a void where a relationship should be. He wanted to love and be loved. In the year and a half since Erica had told him she wanted to be separated, he had only had one other pseudo-relationship, and that was with a girl who had told him right from the beginning that she was only interested in a "friends-with-benefits" type of relationship. And the "benefits" were great. He hadn't had sex in several months at that point and welcomed it. He tried not to let it bother him that the girl, Heidi, also told him she didn't want to be in a long-term relationship with someone who had kids from a previous marriage. He even told himself "at least she was honest." But Heidi was cute and sexy and really fun, and he was glad to have whatever short-lived attention he got from her, which lasted about two months. Then she told him she had met someone she thought she might want to get serious with. Andrew's heart leaped for a split second; he thought she might have changed her mind and was alluding to him (Andrew) in a playful way. At least he didn't make a fool out of himself and tell her he thought that. As soon as she said, "He's in one of my classes," he knew how silly he had been.

Dinner, a homemade lentil soup served with whole wheat rolls, seemed an odd choice for a summer night, but it was savory and filling. He did most of the talking and question-asking, making him feel like he was on a job interview. He hoped the conversation with Robin would get easier soon. He did like her and wanted this to work.

Andrew cleared the table while she made tea, and then they went and sat in the living room. To his surprise, she began talking first, blurting out, "So, do you just want to be friends?"

Andrew, shocked, thought that this was her way of making a joke. They had barely gotten started! "What do you mean?"

"Well, it just seems like we would be better off as friends," Robin said. Her voice was almost 'sing-songy,' like she was talking to one of her students.

How can she just drop it in my lap like that? She doesn't want to come out and say it herself, so she asks ME if I want to "just be friends." Andrew, taken aback, said quietly, "Well, it sounds like *you* just want to be friends."

A small, perhaps embarrassed smile crossed Robin's thin lips. "It's just that I'm having a little trouble with the extended family."

Oh. This again.

"Okay. Well, all right. I'm okay with being friends." *Fuck.*

"Good, because I'm realizing I'm just not sure how much I want to get involved," Robin said in a patronizing tone.

Andrew wanted to get out of there. He stood up.

"You don't have to go."

"Well, I've got some writing I'd like to get done," he said, walking to the kitchen. It was only in his journal, but at least that sounded important. He was glad he remembered Nathan's food, that he wouldn't ruin his exit by having to come back for it.

Fifteen

Erica had had enough of Nathan's home visits. After almost two years, twice a week, she had begun to resent them. As beneficial as she knew they were, she wished they weren't such an essential part of the program. Like smelly fertilizer on a new lawn.

It was just too much for such a tiny place. Once a week (the other weekly session was held at Andrew's apartment), she had three or four adults, her two kids, and two big tubs of therapy toys, games, books, and cue cards filling her living room, her whole apartment, really, and there was not enough room. She knew Andrew's place was small too, but having her even smaller space bombarded for an hour and a half every week for nearly two years was more than she could bear. Of course, she appreciated all the time and effort of the ECDC staff; she could see how Nathan had progressed. But being a single parent was hard enough; having so many extra obligations and having to calculate the success of her almost five-year-old child just going out in public was taking its toll on her. It wasn't supposed to be like this.

While an assistant did a stacking and counting activity involving tiny blocks with Nathan, Sally showed Erica the social story book about eating in restaurants that she had made. "Andrew told me about when he had taken Nathan to a restaurant and he didn't do very well with it," she said, showing Erica the book, made of laminated half-sheets of paper bound by two metal rings on the left side. It showed stick figures going to a restaurant, explaining the process of being seated, placing an order, waiting for it, listing all the possible noises and distractions of other patrons, having the meal brought to the table and eating it, and asking for and paying the check.

Erica thanked Sally. While Eileen sat at the counter and Erica poured her some juice, she told Sally about their venture with changing Nathan's diet to dairy-free and gluten-free, how they read it would be helpful.

"Yeah, Andrew mentioned in a note that you had started that. How has it been going?"

"Not well. It didn't seem to help him at all," Erica said, recounting the five weeks they had tried the diet with Nathan. Their poor little boy grew so lethargic and sickly-looking, had low energy, and, most notably, showed no signs of an increase in language or any of the other changes exhibited by the other children after a few weeks of being placed on this diet. He had actually regressed, and after a month they stopped the special diet, abandoning the idea that Nathan's autism was aggravated by a severe food allergy.

"Well, it sounds like you made the right decision. In Nathan's case, it's best not to continue since he didn't have a positive reaction," Sally said.

"We thought we'd try."

"I'm glad you did. You never know unless you try."

Sally went over to check on Nathan's progress, and Erica paid some attention to Eileen, who always had a hard time with the home visits, since they were focused on Nathan. That was another reason Erica was starting to resent them; she had to deal with Eileen's meltdowns afterward. Children who like to be the center of attention always know when they're not.

Erica thought about her plans to sign up for a class next month. Eileen had been accepted at Head Start preschool, which was more like daycare for three-year-olds, and since she would be turning three in a month, she could go. She still wasn't potty-trained, and Erica could not for the life of her figure out why. She had thought that, having a big brother who was potty-trained, Eileen would be motivated to be a "big girl," and wear "big-girl pants," but that was not the case. Whenever Erica sat her on the potty chair, Eileen actually laughed, which Erica found disconcerting. At first Erica thought it didn't make sense, but then she realized that Eileen was so intuitive, of course she wouldn't want to be like her big brother. Erica could see that, even at a young age, Eileen knew there was something different about her brother. It was only a matter of time before it became more of an issue. Maybe it was already, but Eileen didn't have the ability to talk about it. One good thing about Head Start was that there was a resident speech therapist there who would be working with Eileen, and she would be around typically-developing peers.

At any rate, Erica was thrilled to be able to take a class, which was another good thing about Eileen being in Head Start. It was only one, between ten and eleven-thirty, Tuesday and Thursday, but it was something. It was better than staying home all day watching stupid TV or going out for doughnuts, or sitting around for one week out of every month feeling her premenstrual hormones surging through her body like a poison. She knew now that that's what it was, PMS, that would fill her with either rage or sadness in what appeared to be her body making a surprise attack on her, a siege. She had actually slumped on the kitchen floor one night, crying, when she discovered that Nathan had taken several bites out of the last pear on the counter that she'd saved for herself. She never felt so irrational in her life, crying there on the floor, unable to stop. She'd always thought PMS was just some women's excuse for being irritable and eating junk food. She and Simone had laughed behind co-workers' backs about it. She couldn't tell Simone. Erica had to find a way to control it on her own.

Sally walked back over to her. "Oh, I had one other thing I wanted to ask you about. The other day out on the playground, Nathan was angry about having to go back inside and he said something like, 'It's my gun; you've got no right to take it,' and we were really stumped with that one! Do you know what he meant by that?"

Erica smiled weakly, wondering if they thought she or Andrew had a gun that Nathan had somehow gotten a hold of. Fortunately she had an explanation. "It's another one of his memorized phrases from a video. It's from a scene in Disney's *Swiss Family Robinson* when the two older brothers are arguing and one of them grabs the gun and the other one says, 'It's my gun; you've got no right to take it!'"

"Ohhh," Sally said, "that explains it! Especially since it's from a scene when they were angry. Our nickname for him is Mr. Association because of things like that! He associates situations well, better than most kids who exhibit echolalia. I understand completely now!"

That's great, Erica thought. *I wish I did.* Of course, she knew what echolalia was, but the fear, the realization, was beginning to grip her that this was not something Nathan was going to grow out of.

"Video," Nathan said, enunciating each syllable and pointing to one of the two videos Andrew held out in front of him.

"Okay, I'll put on *Aladdin,*" Andrew told him, in the habit of verbalizing his actions to help Nathan increase his vocabulary. He was five now, and communicating better than he did two years ago when he had entered Early Childhood Development Center's program, but Andrew still longed for the day, if it might come, as he always hoped, when he could converse with Nathan on a level higher than "Would you like a sandwich or scrambled eggs for dinner?" But for now, the fact that he could answer him was wonderful. At home, he rarely screamed as he used to. He could tell his father what he needed or wanted, even if not in complete sentences.

Nathan was beginning to talk. Now, at five years of age, he was finally putting two words together, sometimes more. From going to ECDC for the past two years, he had picked up general comments related to activities that he had heard the teachers and therapists say, both to him and to other children. "Good catching," he would say if he saw someone toss a ball to someone, or "good throwing," as well as "good drawing," "good sharing," and "good sitting down." And when he couldn't describe something specifically, he would say, "Good job in doing," which was Andrew's favorite phrase of Nathan's.

Mostly his word groupings consisted of repeating lines from Disney videos he had watched, and about half the time he used them in the correct context. Many times he didn't even understand the phrase from the video, and in trying to imitate it, he would produce nonsensical words like "yu-bee-ah-tu ME, NOW!" which was actually "You belong to me, now!" said by the evil octopus in *The Little Mermaid*. Nathan would usually use these mimicked phrases as a way to convey his emotions, especially anger or fear.

In spite of the echolalia, Nathan had come up with some phrases of his own, like "balling snowthrowing" for throwing snowballs and "circle chocolate cookie" for Girl Scout Thin Mint Cookies. Another positive development was that he communicated with Eileen much better than before, calling her by her full first name and sharing toys. Andrew recalled the pleasant shock of hearing Nathan call from their bedroom, "Eileen, come here!" It sounded so normal—another rare lucid moment. Nathan had even begun to reach over and twirl Eileen's hair when they sat next to each other on the couch while watching a movie, instead of just twirling his own. Andrew took it as a sign of bonding.

Andrew started the movie for him and turned to walk out of the room, nearly tripping on the step up out of the living room in his mother's new house. Bernadette, who was sitting in a thickly upholstered rocking chair at that end of the room, laughed.

"I just did that ten minutes ago!"

"Yeah, it's hard to get used to," Andrew said. It was also hard to get used to the fact that, for the first time in ten years, Thanksgiving dinner was in a different house. Their mother had just moved in three weeks before to a two-thousand-square-foot home at the south end of town. It was a beautiful tri-level home on a quarter of an acre with a trickling creek running through it, but it had been psychologically difficult for his mother to downsize from her large home on ten acres. Andrew had gone to the house the week before she moved to help her sort through some things and to say goodbye to it. As he walked through it, alone, so many memories flashed in his mind. Nathan and Eileen as babies, toddling around. All the holiday dinners, the graduation parties, and his wedding reception. He recalled the time that he and Erica had been there house-sitting for a week and had sex in the living room in the middle of the day, looking out at the lake while leaning on the couch, sunlight pouring in through the huge windows, bathing their naked bodies. And the time in college that he and Sol sat on their parents' bed and smoked a joint. He remembered how, even in adulthood, he enjoyed sliding in his socks across the wood floors down the long hallway to the guest room. He thought about how he would even miss seeing the lavender-tiled kitchen counter with the lavender grout.

It was strange for Andrew to have to drive by the old house every day on his way to work. He could see it from Highway 66, alone on a hill. It didn't look the same since his mother moved out. It looked darker, somehow tired. Uninviting. *Even houses have souls,* Andrew thought. It made him dream more often about owning his own home, giving it a soul. Hearing his children's laughter fill each room. Sliding across wood floors with them, making their own memories.

Andrew knew he would eventually get used to his mother's new house, and it helped that everyone was there to christen the first holiday in it. Bernadette and her boyfriend Colin drove down from Eugene, Sol and his girlfriend Gisela flew up from L.A., and Elaine even had her new boyfriend there. When Andrew wasn't preoccupied with the kids, he tried to catch pieces of conversations and observe interactions in order to formulate impressions of the new "halves." Colin seemed a little shy, but that was to be expected at a first family gathering. He looked clean-cut and appeared conservative for his twenty-one years with his short brown hair wet-combed like Andrew's mother used to do for him for many years of his childhood every Sunday getting ready for church, school pictures, and other such occasions. Colin was a business major, which initially raised Andrew's suspicions based on his own experience with some business majors he had worked with and partied with in college: superficial guys who cheated on their girlfriends and had the audacity to brag about it the next day. It was a fleeting prejudice, though, as Andrew quickly gauged Colin's love and respect for Bernadette, evident in every embrace, every gentle removal of a lock of hair that fell in her face, every admiring word exchanged.

Gisela was everything Sol had described, and Andrew could see that they adored each other. She gregariously contributed to the dinner conversation, very much a family-oriented person, and indicated a genuine interest in Nathan and Eileen. She even sat down and watched part of a movie with them, then pulled back her long, layered chestnut hair into a ponytail so she could set up a line of dominoes for them to knock down and applauded when they did. "You scored, bro," Andrew whispered to Sol, who grinned in response.

"So Dad's in Yosemite, right?" Sol asked.

"Yeah, he swears it's the most beautiful time of year to go. Cool weather, fewer tourists, more animals out, really peaceful."

"When did he leave?" Sol took a gulp of his beer.

"He drove down Tuesday, I think, and he's driving back Sunday."

"Seems like he purposely wanted to be out of town for Thanksgiving, which kind of sucks. I wanted to see him and have him meet Gisela."

"Well, he knew Mom was having everyone over for dinner, and if he was going to be alone on Thanksgiving, I don't think he wanted to be home, you know? He'll probably be making a trip to L.A. soon to see you." Andrew said. He knew that their father, still bitter over the divorce, would not have been able to be social with Elaine even on a major holiday. And he certainly wanted to steer clear since he'd heard that she had a new boyfriend. Gabriel wasn't ready to deal with that milestone at all.

But Andrew thought that Daniel, their mother's boyfriend, was good for her. He had met him over the summer when the three of them had rafted the Rogue River together one Sunday afternoon when the kids were with Erica, and he liked the relaxed way his mother seemed when she was around him. He had short, salt-and-pepper hair, wore oval wire-rimmed glasses and an oatmeal wool sweater with a black turtleneck under it. Andrew secretly wondered if he had ever been a beatnik, imagining him with the stereotypical beret, maybe even a goatee. But he liked the guy, especially the fact that Daniel could give his mother a hard time and get away with it. Before dinner, she had come in the living room and asked Colin to start a fire in the woodstove and kept hovering over him while he was doing it, saying, "When I start a fire, I usually put the newspaper in first." Daniel, from across the room, called out, "Would you let the grown man start his own fire!" Everyone laughed, and Elaine, hiding a grin, tiptoed out of the room.

Andrew enjoyed meeting and getting to know everyone, although Nathan would frequently get overstimulated with all the new people and Andrew would have to sit in a quiet room with him for some time to calm him down. During dinner he had to jump up from his chair every few minutes to check on Nathan in the living room to make sure he wasn't knocking anything over or getting too close to the woodstove or causing any other problems while he watched his videos. He had fed both Nathan and Eileen hot dogs before everyone else sat down to eat. There was no way either of them would have sat through a formal dinner, nor would they have eaten any of the food.

At dessert-time, Andrew had yet another movie going for the kids, since they would have nothing to do with pumpkin pie. Elaine brought up the fact that she was car-shopping, and Andrew mentioned that he also needed a new car. The week before he had been driving to work and the car died in the middle of a busy intersection. He couldn't get it started again and had to push it to the nearest gas station (which was right on the corner - the only upside to breaking down in an intersection) and had to call the other Andrew from work to come and pick him up. The mechanic called a few hours later to tell him it was an expensive electrical part that needed replacing.

"Again?!" Bernadette said. "It just broke down, like, six weeks ago when you came to visit!"

"I know, it's ridiculous! I've spent as much money every month on that car as I would for a car payment!" He had gone to visit Bernadette one weekend in October and left to drive home at around midnight. Half way between Eugene and Roseburg, on I-5, he broke down, out in the middle of nowhere without a cell phone. He spent the next seven hours in the car by the side of the freeway with only his father's thin old army blanket that he had found in the back to cover himself. When he got out of the car in the morning to try to find a house and call for help, he couldn't feel his feet. After stamping them back to life, he had to walk about a half a mile before he saw a house with a light on, and it took him about fifteen minutes of waiting to see some activity before he felt comfortable going up to the door. He didn't want to have a shotgun shoved in his face when the country folk opened the door. The middle-aged farmer that opened it when Andrew finally got up the courage to knock seemed nice enough, though, and even invited Andrew in out of the cold while he called a tow truck for him. It turned out to be that the alternator had gone out.

"Isn't it Erica's car?" Sol asked.

"Yeah. By the time I get a new one and give it back to her, I'll have made so many repairs on it that it'll run great and she probably won't have any problems with it at all!" He laughed at the magnanimous tone in his voice, as if he were making all these repairs to her car as a favor for her. Maybe deep down he just wanted her to feel some obligation to him, as if fixing her car would somehow fix their marriage, even though he knew it was beyond repair. They were divorced! It was truly over, and no amount of good-deed-doing could retrieve it.

Sixteen

Dad will be here soon to pick you up to go to Eighteen," Erica told Nathan while she helped him get on his shoes. Nathan called Andrew's home "Eighteen" since that was the apartment number. At least he no longer recited license plates when people walked through the front door, but calling his father's home a number was probably a carryover from that habit.

"Eighteen," Nathan said in his typically stoic, flat voice. It was not robotic, but it often lacked inflection. It was his way of saying, "I want to go to Dad's house."

Erica had started trying to teach him to tie his shoelaces, figuring he should be able to do it since it didn't involve talking or loud noises or tipping his head back. Sally had made a cue card of a line drawing of a pair of hands making two loops out of a shoelace on a tennis shoe. Nathan seemed interested and tried to do it.

"Very good!" Erica said, smiling, showing enthusiasm to motivate him. Nathan jolted; Erica hadn't meant to be so loud near his ear, and he didn't have his hooded jacket on yet. She put her arm around Nathan and apologized for startling him.

At least he didn't scream, Erica thought. He still squealed occasionally, but screaming at home rarely occurred.

Erica started getting Eileen ready to go, who pouted and resisted. She had been temperamental lately, whining almost constantly and having long tantrums in Erica's bathroom over simple things like not getting a second piece of candy. Erica wasn't too concerned; Eileen had never been what could be classified as a "happy baby" anyway, and she was used to her daughter's tirades. Erica had bought some healthy cookies and opted to bribe Eileen with one if she let her put on her shoes, which worked. While she was tying them, she remembered that she had a paper to write for her economics class, a general-ed requirement she had been taking since September. She loved being back in school, even if it was only one class, mostly because she was one class closer to finishing her degree. She couldn't let go of her dream. She would get there someday.

Jonah encouraged her, since he was also taking some classes, deciding two years earlier at the age of thirty that he had played around all of his twenties and it was time to get serious. He had longer to go than Erica, wanting to be a psychologist, but he could take more classes at once, so he would probably finish before she did. At any rate, she appreciated dating someone who had goals and was actually working to achieve them. And Andrew liked him too, which made things easier. Jonah had told her a few weeks ago that he had been out one night and ran into Andrew and they actually had a beer together. She was glad they liked each other but couldn't deny that it unnerved her a little, the thought of them comparing notes.

Jonah, not having any family in the area, accompanied her to Weed to visit Caleb and his family for Thanksgiving. Erica was determined to see them more often since their mother's death. She was glad she could talk about it with Jonah, how she'd felt going to see her mother at the morgue. He'd been through it with his father, that feeling of loss-too-early when a parent dies whose child is barely an adult, when the parent is nowhere near old age and it's too soon to say goodbye, too sudden. "I can't remember the last time I told her I loved her," Erica, crying, had said to Caleb as they stood over her body, her matted hair covering most of the gash on the side of her forehead. Her skin looked like a brownish, papery film covering butterscotch pudding. She'd never looked so closely at her mother's face before. Even in death there seemed to be no release, and Erica gasped as she realized with sadness that her mother's face portrayed not only a painful death but an entire painful life. Caleb enfolded his sister in his arms. "She told me once that the only love she could ever be sure of was yours and mine," he said. "She knew you loved her."

Initially, the plan had been to spread her ashes Thanksgiving weekend, but the weather was not cooperating, so they decided to attempt it again in the spring. "Come to think of it," she told Caleb, "Mom would have been appalled if we did it on Thanksgiving. Remember how she would always say that Thanksgiving was only second to Columbus Day as the most insulting holiday for Native Americans?" They laughed at the memory and spent a good hour swapping other stories, entertaining Jonah.

The only negative thing was that it was the first holiday Erica had not been with her children, and that was hard, especially watching Drake, her little nephew, running around. Christmas would be upon them in two weeks, and it would be the second year that she and Andrew would have to split the day with the kids. She was considering just going over to Andrew's apartment for lunch and spending a few hours with them there so they wouldn't have to be disrupted by being shuttled back and forth. It seemed easier on all of them that way, and she and Andrew were at such a positive level that it wouldn't bother her to spend time with him. Then she could have a quiet Christmas dinner alone with Jonah.

Andrew walked in through her front door with a blast of cold air.

"Hey," Erica said, "how are you?"

"Freezing! God, it's cold."

"Eighteen," Nathan said, walking to the door.

"Yes, honey, we're going to eighteen. Give Mom a hug goodbye first," Andrew said.

Erica knelt down and embraced a willing Nathan, then reached for a moody Eileen. Last week when Andrew had picked them up, he brought up the fact that he thought Eileen's anxiety was due to not liking Head Start. He had talked with her teacher, who was a very large, boisterous woman who probably intimidated Eileen (although not necessarily on purpose), and she said that Eileen would not participate in any activities and cried and yelled during transitions to different activities. She had also been pushing others and running away from the staff, and generally not doing very well there. Andrew also found out that Eileen was only seeing the speech therapist a half hour a week, and even that was time with other kids, not one-on-one. Her needs were not being met there, that was certain. And they both wondered if Eileen might have experienced some belittlement due to the fact that she was still not potty-trained. How would they know? Eileen, at three and a half, still slurred her words when she tried to talk and had a limited vocabulary, so they couldn't ask her what was bothering her at school.

Andrew seemed adamant about wanting Eileen to switch to Early Childhood Development Center, where Nathan had been successful. He pointed out that she would receive much more intensive speech therapy, which was what she needed. Erica couldn't deny that, but how could she have two children in special education? She didn't know if she could handle all the implications of that. Having one child in special education was difficult enough. How could she handle double the home visits, double the meetings, double the loss of having a normal child?

ANDREW HAD TO admit that his heart still belonged to Erica.

He had gone to Dogma for one of his every-other-Friday-night outs, and aside from a few glances at a hot girl here or there, he didn't feel compelled to pursue anyone. He began to realize that Erica really hadn't been his type physically, but it wasn't so much about that. It was about the shared history, or maybe the aborted future. And as much as he tried to tell himself he was over her, he was still as sad as he ever was.

More than two years have passed, and it still hurts just as much, he had written in his journal that afternoon. *I don't know what to do. How do I work through it? How much more time? Maybe it's taking so long because I see her almost every day, not like with a regular break up where you go your separate ways. This could take years, but somehow, I have to let go. I have to stop loving her. I still have my dreams, though. That's comforting. Anything can happen in them, anything I want, even if just for a moment. For a few minutes, I can have Erica apologizing and saying she wants to work it out. I can have Heidi or Robin say she's falling for me, kids and all. I can snowboard expertly. I can see my writing in print. I can have a conversation with Nathan. I can be in love again.*

Andrew gulped the last of his pint of hefeweizen and went back onto the dance floor. It wasn't very crowded, being the week before finals, as most of the usual patrons were writing papers and studying for exams. Next weekend would be packed with those who hadn't left town for Spring Break, and Andrew would just as soon stay home with the kids. He enjoyed having room to move freely on the dance floor, expressing himself. All he could think of was picking up his feet and moving his body in time to the hard, fast techno rhythms that pulsed through him. He forgot about Erica, forgot about having two children in special education, and forgot about his agitation at being called Sam eight hours a day, five days a week. It had been a novelty at first, but it was starting to irk him, having to answer to a different name and not being able to respond to his own. But he appreciated the fact that his boss was so flexible and understanding, allowing him to leave work if he needed to pick up the kids or go to a long meeting for one of them, which occurred at least once a month.

He focused on the music and danced the next two songs before he took a break and went to the bar to get a glass of water. He sat down at a barstool and looked around, noticing some of the same people who also seemed to go out on Friday nights. He saw a tall Asian girl he remembered seeing on New Year's; it had already been over two months since the new millennium began. New Year's Eve happened to be on a night when Erica usually had the kids, which was a nice coincidence. Andrew remembered the DJ that night calling out, "Okay, for one more hour we can still party like it's 1999!" and playing the corresponding Prince song amid much cheering. Silly as it was, he was glad to be a part of it. Making new memories without Erica was important. At midnight, he had kissed some girl he had never seen before 11:30 that night and would probably never see again. She was petite with long, silky straight brown hair and big, round chocolate eyes. She wore tight-fitting black pants and a silver sequined tube top. She was a little too bubbly, like the cheerleaders who would walk right past him in the halls of his high school, talking about which football player called them last night. But she was cute. She mentioned that she was from Eugene, down to party with her cousin, and left soon afterward to go to another bar. It was fitting, Andrew thought, starting the next thousand years by kissing a stranger.

Just then he noticed that Erica's friend, Brooke, had come up right next to him to order a drink. It looked like she had the night off since she wasn't carrying a tray with a white plastic cash box on it, as she did when she cocktail waitressed. Andrew, not expecting to, found himself attracted to her with her low-slung tight jeans and animal print tank top. Her sandy blond hair brushed across her shoulders when she turned to him. He noticed for the first time the sexy little freckles dotting the bridge of her nose. He noticed her hazel eyes, and her wide, shapely, enticing lips.

"Hi! You're Erica's ex-husband, aren't you?"

Shit. Why do I have to be known by that in this town? "Yeah, I'm Andrew."

"Oh, yeah, now I remember your name! I forgot for a second. I'm Brooke."

"Yeah, I know who you are. Erica always used to talk about you when she would get home from work. She said you kicked ass, that she was glad she hired you."

"Really? That was cool of her." She generously tipped the bartender and took a sip of the cocktail that he had put in front of her. "Mmm, this is good. Want some?"

Andrew smirked. *If you only knew,* he thought. "Sure. What is it?"

She handed him the glass and told him it was a White Russian. Andrew sipped the creamy, coffee-flavored drink and thanked her, trying to think of something to say next.

"So how have you been?" was what he came up with.

"Pretty good. Just working. I went to Cleveland, Ohio, to see Metallica and Kid Rock for New Year's! They fuckin' rocked!" Brooke said, becoming very animated as she talked about the songs they played and things Kid Rock said to the crowd, that it was the best New Year's she ever had.

Andrew remarked that it sounded cool and told her what he did for New Year's Eve, then about his new car. When Erica's old car had broken down in the intersection and he had to replace the electrical part, the mechanic told him that the timing belt would need to be replaced soon, and Andrew just didn't want to deal with any more repairs. He applied for a car loan through a company that handled bad-credit situations (since it had only been six months since the bankruptcy) and was approved for a car loan. He had already received his tax refund and used it for the down payment to buy a six-year-old mid-size SUV with low mileage (and a high interest rate, of course). He loved not having to worry if his car was going to stall when he came to a stop sign, or worry if it would even start in the morning. Brooke seemed more interested in the fact that Andrew had given Erica's old car back to her, commenting on how Erica had picked her up to give her a ride to work many times in it when she had first started working there.

The DJ called out, "Last call for alcohol!" and Andrew was surprised that it was so late, that the night had gone by that fast. And Brooke was still sitting next to him. He offered to buy her a drink.

"Sure. Hey, I heard there's an after-hours party tonight. Want to go?"

Andrew tried not to sound too eager. "Okay."

"Let me go talk to Jenny Apostolo. She knows where it is. I'll be right back," Brooke said. Jenny, Andrew remembered hearing, was the girl that Nick had cheated on Erica with, and he wondered if Erica knew that Brooke was friends with her. Not that it mattered to *him.*

Brooke hopped off the stool and Andrew watched her walk away, mentally undressing her. He figured she had to be interested in him, too, or she wouldn't have sat next to him for so long. He could tell by the way she walked away, swinging her hips.

They do that on purpose, he thought. *They say they don't, but I know they do.*

"WHAT IS WITH you today?" Andrew asked a whiny Eileen as she clung to his neck while they walked down a path in the middle of the Portland Zoo on a cool, clear spring day.

"Nathan likes the zebras," Erica said, focusing the video camera on Nathan, who walked ahead of them toward the zebra exhibit. She swung back around to Andrew holding Eileen. "Eileen doesn't like anything," she narrated as she filmed. Eileen had started going to ECDC a month ago, but they figured it was too soon to see any improvement. Erica was just glad that Eileen's attendance at ECDC did not require home visits since she was only receiving speech therapy.

Eileen turned her head away. "No!"

"Did you see that?" Erica asked Andrew, laughing in disbelief. "I didn't think she heard me! Eileen, don't you want to see the zebras? Like in *Lion King*?"

"No!"

"Well, at least Nate seems to be enjoying most of it," Erica said. The four of them made the five-hour drive to Portland the night before and spent the night in a motel; Andrew slept with Nathan, and Erica shared a bed with Eileen. It was the first trip they had taken together in two years, and so far there had been no problems. Erica felt relieved that Andrew could handle being friends and doing things together, which at this point was much easier than trying to do things alone with their children. Nathan often still had difficulty being out in public, and combined with Eileen's recent meltdowns and moodiness, Erica was reluctant to attempt more than a quick trip to the grocery store with both of them together.

Nathan enjoyed seeing the animal exhibits that were visible aboveground; he balked at even going near the metal doors leading to any underground viewing areas, but many of the animals were not visible from above. Finally, when they reached the elephants, he had been motivated enough to see them while they were eating, which required walking down a slope, through double metal doors, and into the underground viewing area. Andrew still held Eileen, who refused to walk, so Erica knew it was up to her to coax Nathan through the doors. She knew that once she got him inside he would be fine, that his anxiety was due to not knowing what was on the other side of the metal doors and not being able to verbalize his fear. Erica quickly walked ahead of Nathan and opened one of the doors wide while Andrew tried to corral him down to the entrance. Nathan was about ready to bolt when Erica distracted him by crying, "Look! The elephants!" and pointed through the open door. Nathan, intrigued although still nervous, caught a glimpse of an elephant through the glass-walled area beyond the doors. He smashed his hands onto his ears, averting potential loud noises even though his jacket hood was up, and whined a little but gingerly stepped through the door of his own accord. Erica and Andrew exchanged glances of surprise and walked in with him, assuring him that all would be well, that now he could watch the elephants eat. Erica suddenly realized that Nathan had probably been so afraid because he could not make the assumption that if they went underground, the animals would be separated from them. How could he have known it would be safe?

After a few minutes, Nathan removed his hands from the side of his head, turned around as Erica was videotaping, and quietly he said, "Nathan do it," holding his hand out to the video camera. Erica took in her breath, aware of what a huge breakthrough this was for her son, overcoming his fear, trusting his parents, wanting to become involved, speaking. She set the camera up for Nathan and held it up to his face.

"Eat," Nathan said in his usual flat tone as he held the camera to his eye and filmed the elephant in front of him.

Erica looked at Andrew, both of them with wide eyes, and smiled. Eileen still refused to be put down, but that was okay. Nathan, engaged in an activity of monumental proportions for him, held their gaze, and they reveled in it. They had learned to appreciate the small triumphs and take nothing about Nathan's development for granted.

After viewing the rest of the exhibits and taking a little train ride around the perimeter of the zoo (which to Erica's relief, did not upset Nathan, who covered his ears the entire time), they decided to leave by three in the afternoon so that they could be home before nine. Andrew took Eileen out to his car to change her diaper, and Erica found herself faced with the daunting task of taking Nathan into a public restroom.

The typical hard, bare walls and cement floors of these necessary build-ings produced an echo effect that Nathan had difficulty processing. The worst were those with air hand dryers; he would not even enter a public restroom if he saw that it featured any on the walls, which was the first thing he looked for when he poked his head through the entry. Erica, walk-ing through with Nathan pulling backwards on her hand, straining to be released and making nervous whining sounds, was glad to see that this restroom only had paper towel dispensers. When Nathan saw that, he no longer pulled on Erica's hand, but he still made his protesting sounds, in-dicating anxiety.

Erica led him into a metal stall and locked the door. Nathan pulled down his jeans himself and sat on the toilet. Then, because out of anxiety he had been leaning forward so far on the toilet, before he was even finished uri-nating the auto-flush sensor on the toilet sensed that he had gotten up even though he hadn't, and the toilet exploded as it flushed itself. It was enough to startle Erica, and it was so loud and violent that it threw Nathan into hysterics. He barely finished pulling up his pants while screaming, then began clawing at the door. Erica hurried to use the toilet herself, telling Nathan, "It's okay, it's okay," the litany she had sung so many times before that never seemed to help. Nathan screamed on as if in agony. Erica tried to hold him with one arm to comfort him while she pulled her pants up with the other.

She finished and opened the stall door to the stares of women and other children, and Nathan bolted for the door, still screaming. In her own mo-ment of duress, Erica tried to quickly wash her hands. She later wondered why she felt she needed to, with a screaming child. Perhaps it was a force of habit, or maybe a subconscious attempt to normalize the situation, to fol-low through with the process as if nothing were wrong. Erica didn't really know. *Sometimes,* she thought later, *when you have a child with a disability, you just can't think straight. When faced with a situation like that, you become paralyzed. You can't always make the best decisions when you feel like the world is crashing down around you.*

As she washed her hands, she tried to corral Nathan between herself and the counter with the sinks, but of course he jerked loose and began to writhe on the floor, still screaming. One middle-aged woman nearby stared for a particularly long time. Erica had grown accustomed to reactions like that, and often was exasperated by them. But this woman, non-threatening in her jeans and sweatshirt, round glasses and shoulder-length graying hair, did not seem as judgmental as other people, so Erica said to her, "I'm sorry for the disturbance. My son has autism."

The woman looked at Erica with such sympathetic, concerned eyes and just said, "I understand." Erica, stunned, wanted to thank her for that brief moment of support, of rare acceptance, but no words came to her. She hoped the appreciation showed in her eyes, in the few seconds they had connected.

After that, Erica gently picked Nathan up under his arms to stand him up and helped him walk out of the bathroom. One more distressing situation under her belt. One more tough moment that she survived. She was sure that Nathan, on some level, was thinking the same thing.

Seventeen

"Would you mind giving me a ride home?" Brooke asked Andrew one Friday night a few weeks later. They had spent the entire evening together, as they had been doing every Friday night that Andrew went out to Dogma, and even though they seemed to have good chemistry (Andrew's optimistic assessment), no more than a hug had passed between them. With Brooke being a friend of Erica's, Andrew just didn't know if it was a good idea to get involved with her. Or if Brooke wanted to, for that matter, possibly for the same reason. He couldn't tell. He did know that he enjoyed her company and she was fun to dance with, and it was all right if nothing progressed beyond the point of friendship. He liked being her friend.

"Not at all," he told her as they walked through the front door of Dogma out into the cool April night, saying goodbye to all the people they knew who had been there that evening.

The air felt good on his sweaty face, chest, and back, penetrating his olive green T-shirt. He had been dancing right up until the last song because the music had been really good that night. Dogma had a new DJ who had turned out to be a friend of Jonah's. Andrew had discovered that he liked Jonah, especially liked how he didn't think he needed to worry about how Jonah treated Nathan and Eileen, and he figured that if Erica was happy, that positive energy would only reflect upon his children when she was with them, so he had come to hope for her happiness as much as his own. He no longer pined away for Erica; he felt like he could finally focus on being effective co-parents, and maybe even friends.

He glanced over at Brooke, so cute in her short navy blue dress with tiny white polka dots that she wore with knee-high black boots and a black cardigan sweater. They had talked for quite a while earlier in the night; she told him some personal information that he figured she didn't tell everyone, a condensed version of her life story. She had grown up in Sacramento, the middle of three children, with a brother four years older and another one four years younger. Her father, while favoring her, had been abusive toward her brothers, much of which she witnessed, causing her to turn away from him. She got into drugs with her older brother and regularly skipped school, which she never liked in the first place, having had ADHD and dyslexia and not learning to read until age ten. Her truancy led to dropping out of high school her junior year, at which point she left home and lived with her older brother for a while. She worked in a pizza parlor for a few months before deciding that drug dealing was far more lucrative and fun. Cocaine became her livelihood and her life. It was all she cared about. Just when she was realizing that she had become an addict, her apartment was raided, too many packets of coke were seized, and she was sentenced to ten years in prison at the age of twenty-two. During her time locked up, she overcame her addiction, got her GED, and rebuilt her relationship with her father, who came to visit her every week. She was paroled after four years, but when she got out she found herself hanging out with her old friends, many of whom were smoking crack. She decided to move to Ashland, where her brother, who had cleaned up and now had his own family, was living. Then she met Erica through Gavin, her first friend in Ashland, and had worked at Dogma ever since.

Andrew felt drawn to her for reasons he couldn't identify. Sure, she was sexy and sweet, friendly and funny, but there was something else. A familiarity in her eyes, in the way she laughed with him. She reminded him of his first love in high school, that was it. Not in the way she looked, but in the way she interacted with him. Brooke's nature was bold and demure at the same time. He loved every minute he spent with her.

He pulled in the driveway of Brooke's little rented house, sandwiched in between two apartment complexes. It had a small yard with a few large trees that provided limited privacy. As they approached the house Andrew noticed the lights on, music playing from inside, and people in the living room.

"Looks like my roommate is having a party. Want to come in?" Andrew figured he would for a little while, since she offered. He met Felix, her roommate, a Native American in his early twenties with long black hair held back by a backwards baseball cap. "I told him he was like Felix from

The Odd Couple, but he'd never seen the movie before," Brooke said.

Andrew thought he seemed more like the character Oscar, with all his friends over for a party, cigarette butts and beer bottles everywhere, TV blaring. He followed Brooke around for a bit, glancing at faces to see if he knew anyone, found he did not. Brooke offered him a beer, and he declined.

"Thanks, but I think I'm going to head home. I'm pretty tired."

"Do you mind if I crash at your place?"

Andrew's heart raced. "If you want to."

"I don't really feel like staying here tonight," Brooke said. She put her sweater back on and followed him out the door.

Oh, my God! She wants to sleep at my place! What does this mean? What does she want?

He drove to his apartment, just a few blocks away, trying not to look at her for fear of spoiling whatever was going on. Brooke talked about how loud Felix's parties got and how nice it would be to have a quiet night for a change. "He's always got somebody over there," she said.

As they walked through the front door, Andrew explained his living arrangements with the kids (who were at Erica's that night) having the bedroom, and that he didn't normally have a bed in his living room, which made Brooke laugh. He loved how low and sensual her laugh sounded. He handed her a T-shirt and a pair of boxers to change into and told her he was going to take a quick shower.

Andrew jumped in the shower and lathered up as fast as he could while trying to come up with nonchalant things to say, deciding how to approach the subject of sleeping arrangements. There had never been any sexual banter between them, so it would have been presumptuous of him to think that she wanted to have sex. Maybe the fact that she was Erica's friend precluded any of that in the first place. He just didn't know.

After washing the sticky dried sweat off his body, he brushed his teeth, towel-dried himself, and put on a pair of gray knit boxers. He kept running over in his mind what to say, and when he walked out to the living room he just blurted out, "There's a futon in here I can sleep on, if you'd like the bed." He figured it was diplomatic enough, chivalrous even, although tinged with nervousness.

Brooke, in his clothes and sitting on the edge of his bed, said, "I don't mind sharing with you."

Andrew's heart flapped again. "Okay," he said as he climbed in beside her and turned out the light.

Now what?

"Well, goodnight," Brooke said, putting her arm around him to hug him.

Great. "Goodnight," he said, hugging her. *God. I should have known. That's what I get for getting all worked up.*

Brooke turned her back to him, and he couldn't help putting his hand on it, gently rubbing it. He just wanted to touch her. He lightly combed her hair with his fingers, just for a second.

She turned back around and put her hand behind his head and drew him to her. Their lips locked, fused together in a tingling kiss, and Andrew felt the blood rushing through his body, channeling to his groin.

Oh, God.

"You are such a great kisser," Brooke murmured near his ear before connecting with his mouth again. "I had no idea."

He dared to slide his hand up inside the shirt she had on and felt another surge through his body as he cupped her breasts and slowly turned her nipples, making them harden, while he kissed her. Then he brushed his hand around the small of her back and she sat up and pulled off the shirt. Her bare torso looked just as he had imagined, silky white curves glowing in the moonlight coming in through the window, shining on her hair. *Incredible.*

"God, Andrew, how come you never hit on me before?"

"I didn't know how you felt about me," he said, sliding his hands over her thighs. *This is so good.*

"Let me show you," she said, leaning over and connecting with his lips in another electrifying kiss.

ANDREW SHOVED HIS new tent, sleeping bags, camping pads, and backpacks containing a weekend's worth of clothing for himself and the kids into his car, wedging everything around the ice chest. It was a Friday afternoon, so he had left work early and picked up the kids from Erica's to go on their first camping trip. And the best part was that Brooke was coming.

They had been inseparable since that night at his apartment. Andrew got that silly, high school-lovey feeling whenever he was around her. At first it seemed like it would just be a fun thing, maybe for a few months. But as the weeks went by, he realized that he didn't really know what happened to him when he was with her. Sure, it was infatuation at first, but something stronger was developing, something he hadn't expected and could not yet verbalize.

Erica seemed to find it a novelty that Andrew and Brooke were dating, but she appeared to be comfortable with it, and she and Andrew shared a laugh about how incestuous the restaurant business in Ashland was. It was good to laugh with Erica, to be her friend again and not have any negative energy between them. Andrew hadn't felt this happy in years.

Eileen, now almost four, was finally potty trained, although Andrew had packed a couple of diapers for nighttime, and he made sure she and Nathan went to the bathroom one last time before loading them up in the back seat of the car with plenty of toys and snacks. He had set up his new dome tent in the living room a few days ago so that the kids would know where they'd be sleeping on the trip. They had rolled around in it, squealing "Tent! Tent!" and brought their favorite stuffed animals in with them.

And there was Brooke. She came walking up with a cute spring in her step, smiling, backpack and sunglasses on, wearing green cargo shorts with a gray tank top and hiking boots, her hair up in a pony tail. She looked much younger than her thirty years.

"Sorry I'm late," she said, kissing him.

"You're perfect."

They drove the two-and-a-half hour winding road to the coast, and just as it deposited them onto Highway 101 and they headed north toward Brookings, Eileen, carsick again, began to throw up. Without hesitating, Brooke turned around in her seat, reached back, and cupped her hands to catch the vomit and flung it out the open window.

Andrew quickly found a place to pull over. He couldn't believe that Brooke had been willing to do something like that! Even he wouldn't have done it!

"I've known these kids since they were babies," she said, pouring water out from one of the water bottles Andrew had packed, rinsing her hands by the side of the road, like it was nothing.

It's strange, Andrew thought, *dating someone who couldn't deal with the "extended family" and then going to someone willing to have my daughter throw up in her hands. Another thing to love about her.*

They continued on another half an hour up to Loeb State Park, a campground park located about ten miles inland from the southern Oregon

coast, where Andrew set up his new tent in the rain while Brooke enter-
tained the kids in the car. The rain didn't let up while he crouched under an
eave outside of the bathroom building and tried to boil a pot of water on
his propane-fueled cook stove so he could heat up some hot dogs for dinner, grimacing at the irony that they were camping and couldn't roast hot
dogs over a campfire. Couldn't even *start* a campfire, for God's sake, on the
kids' first camping trip. He laughed, thinking of his parents' adage about
rain being a blessing.

God is really blessing these hot dogs. And my new tent.

About an hour later, Andrew crawled into the double, zipped-together
sleeping bags he had borrowed from his father and spooned up against
Brooke, which was what he had been looking forward to all week. Nathan
and Eileen were in their own new sleeping bags to his left. He let them
play with their flashlights for a few minutes while he snuggled with Brooke
in her plaid flannel pajama pants and thermal shirt. He remembered the
morning after the first night they had spent together, his shock when she
had her back to him and he saw her tattoo—a crescent moon—in the center of her upper back, which was the first thing he saw when he opened his
eyes. It wasn't exactly like Erica's, but it was close enough to be shocking
first thing in the morning.

As he reclined next to her in the sleeping bag, Andrew reminisced about
some of his many family camping trips while growing up. He loved talking
with Brooke, sharing with her. He told her about the time at Lake Tahoe
in California, when he was about six, and he swore he saw a bear shadow
on the wall of the tent while lying in his sleeping bag one night. The next
morning they discovered all the boxes and bags left out on the big wooden
table at the campsite had been torn up and strewn about. But his mother
said that it was her sister, camping in her own tent the next site over, who
had been playing a joke on them, and that he had been dreaming about
seeing the bear shadow. Maybe, he thought years later, she just didn't want
him to be scared.

Then he told Brooke about the time in college when he had gone camping on the beach with a group of friends and they ate psychedelic mush-
rooms an hour before sunset. While the sun sank into the sea, they watched
from atop a ridge, commenting on how beautiful it was, the long, low
clouds tinged with shades of red and orange, even purple, as the glowing
orb of the sun melted into the smooth, dark Pacific. Andrew had said, "I

feel sorry for the people on the East Coast. They never get to see the sun set," and all of his friends laughed, making him realize how ridiculous he sounded. Brooke laughed then, her low, rolling laugh, almost like the purr of a cat.

Soon the kids fell asleep, and Andrew stopped talking and entwined his legs with Brooke's and buried his face in her hair, breathing in her scent on the back of her neck. All night long they listened to the sound of the rain pattering on the roof and in the trees. Andrew was pleased to note, the next morning, that his new tent was water-tight.

ERICA TRIED TO catch Andrew's eye. They were at yet another meeting for Nathan, and this one was approaching the three-hour mark. With two children receiving special education services, they found themselves lining up a babysitter and missing work at least twice a month for these meetings. Having just attended one the previous week for Eileen, Erica's tolerance for lengthy sessions was low.

Meetings were part of the teachers' job description; they got paid to be there, didn't they? Erica wasn't sure, but she did know that every afternoon conference she had to attend took time away from her hours at work, her minimum wage paycheck. And it was the same with Andrew.

Is that selfish? she wondered. *Don't I have a right to feel that way, after all I've already been through? Of course they've done wonderful work with Nathan, and he's made remarkable progress, but why must these meetings be so drawn out? It reaches a point where it almost seems like it's overkill. Like the meeting is an end in itself instead of the means to an end.*

"So, based on Sally's evaluation that Nathan would be most successful in a small, structured classroom with the use of visual cues and written information, the placement team (that's all of us here) has determined that the STEPS program at Stewart Elementary would be the most appropriate placement for Nathan," said the director of Early Childhood Development Center, who had not been present at most of the other meetings concerning Nathan, but attended this one because it was an exit interview. The eight people present, including the speech therapist, occupational therapist, new Kindergarten teacher of STEPS (Specialized Training in Education Program Service), Sally (Nathan's teacher for almost three years), the director, the regional autism consultant, and Erica and Andrew, all began taking turns signing their names to the Individual Education Plan—or IEP—for Nathan.

Erica felt guilty for her feelings of exasperation, for thinking negative thoughts about the caring, skilled professionals who tirelessly worked with her son. But did they realize how difficult this was, month after month, year after year, without an end in sight? Knowing that this may well be her son's fate for the rest of his life? To live with the knowledge that her son will have a life very different from most other boys, most other men? That to spend so much time in meetings, knowing that when she got home or tried to run an errand in town, she would have to deal with the same difficulties as always? Of course they knew, to an extent; of course they cared. But each of them felt that her area of expertise (*Why were they all female?* Erica had wondered) deserved the most attention; the occupational therapist had gone on for almost an hour, then another forty-five minutes for the speech therapist. Erica couldn't stand it much longer. She wanted to scream. *I know this! I live this! I know how my son communicates! I know what his strengths are! I know what his sensory issues are! I don't need to be in a three-hour meeting to discuss it!* She wondered if Andrew felt the same way.

There were, of course, positive points to having these meetings. The speech therapist had proposed a goal for Nathan of using six-word sentences with correct pronouns and word order to interact with adults and peers, which Erica and Andrew felt was far too ambitious at that point for him, and they had it reduced to a goal of using three-to-six-word sentences. And the occupational therapist was still working with him on grasping a writing utensil and teaching him to write. Erica believed that, because of Nathan's ability to read, once he learned how to write it would liberate him to no end.

There were many areas of communication, socialization, and sensory integration that he needed to work on. Nathan still said, "You want cookie?" whenever he wanted someone to ask *him* that, because *he* wanted a cookie, but that was more a force of habit in that situation. In other situations, the skill of using correct pronouns was emerging, although when talking about himself, he would usually say "Nathan want toast" or "Nathan is jumping." Erica was certain that it was the skilled intervention of the ECDC staff that had enabled Nathan to achieve what he had, and she wondered if he would be as successful in the new program, in a whole new school.

In spite of all Nathan's progress, not an hour went by that Erica didn't think about his disability. There were moments, only occurring at home, that Erica could just enjoy the life they did have, the accomplishments Nathan had made, and for a moment convince herself that their lives were not defined by autism. She could usually find some time each day when she realized that they had all been functioning at their own level of normal, and it wasn't so bad, at least if they didn't leave their home. In addition to that, once in a great while Nathan had these "moments of clarity" when Erica might ask him a question and he'd answer her, not in the rote tone of autism, but in his own sweet voice, with complete comprehension of what Erica had said to him. And he knew the simple words with which he chose to answer, not just a phrase he had memorized from a video that would fit within the context of the situation. And Erica could see in his eyes that it was really *him*—not the disability—that was communicating. Most of the time, Nathan could function and communicate on a basic level, even though he seemed vacant. In those moments, Erica believed the autism was talking, not her son. Unfortunately that was the case most of the time.

The meeting seemed to be winding down, much to Erica's relief. She always enjoyed when she and Andrew would drive back to Ashland together, rehashing the highlights of the meeting, since they were both of similar mind in that regard. It was good to be Andrew's friend. She had developed a great deal of respect for him for overcoming his problem with depression and for being willing to attain a good co-parenting relationship with her. She liked the ease with which they communicated now. She somehow felt closer to him divorced than she did when they were married. And it was an added bonus that he liked Jonah, which seemed strange to her because they were so different. Jonah was much more distant than Andrew, and while Erica always needed her own space, she craved a little more attention than Jonah was willing to give. It was a recurring issue for them, one that she was beginning to doubt could be resolved. And one that she wasn't ready to do anything about just yet.

The funny thing was that Andrew and Brooke were together. Erica couldn't imagine how that manifested, knowing both of them as well as she did. Brooke lived by the seat of her pants and Andrew, the kitchen-chair-arranger, was much more settled than that. She didn't think it would last, but she certainly didn't mind the fact that her ex-husband was dating someone who she knew loved her children. There was some security in that.

The speech therapist began talking about some article on autism that had been printed in a national parenting magazine, commenting how great it was that there was some exposure now helping to break the stereotypes, mentioning the controversial theory about mercury-based preservatives in vaccines being a cause of the skyrocketing number of cases identified in the 1990s. Erica remembered how, with more than one of Nathan's vaccinations in infancy, he had screamed all night with fever and pain, with his injected thigh red and swollen. For weeks afterward, the injection site remained a blueberry-sized hard pebble under his skin, until it finally dissipated, absorbed by his tiny, innocent body. The doctor had said that sometimes babies had reactions to vaccines, and there was nothing to worry about with Nathan. Nothing to worry about, he said with cheerful certainty.

I will worry the rest of my days about Nathan.

It seemed to Erica that the rest of the world still viewed autism as some bizarre curiosity that happened in asylums, that autistic people were quiet and rocked themselves in a corner all day, as she herself used to believe. So maybe an article in a well-read magazine would be helpful in shattering the archaic knowledge of the disability. But Erica couldn't get beyond her own prejudice toward the shiny national magazines ever since Nathan was a toddler, before he had been diagnosed. Erica would read all the articles on discipline and teaching manners and developmental milestones, but her child was so vastly different from those described in the articles that she came away from reading them feeling isolated and foreign. The concept of "time out" had always been lost on Nathan. He had always met or exceeded every physical milestone and had developed well cognitively, but socially and communicatively his level could not be evaluated using common guidelines. Erica had always thought that those parenting magazines needed far more articles on living with children with disabilities, not just for the sake of the parents who have them, but for everyone, so that others could understand. So that when they see a child writhing on the floor and screaming in public, it's not because he is poorly behaved, it's because he has a disability. Parents can't keep their children locked up at home for the rest of their lives just because their behavior is different and the potential exists that it might disturb someone.

"Let's get out of here," Andrew muttered in Erica's ear as he stood up from his chair.

They thanked everyone and made their obligatory polite goodbyes, to some for the last time, since Nathan would be moving on. He wouldn't start at the new school until September, and he would still attend ECDC twice a week during the summer. The home visits, it had been decided at the meeting, would end in one week, and as much as Erica would not miss them, it was strange to think that that era of her life was ending. Nathan "graduating," moving on, made Erica keep alive her private hope that one day he would just somehow snap out of autism. Not that Erica expected it; she just faintly hoped for it, dreamed of it, as if one of those rare moments of clarity would be enough to cause Nathan to "turn over," like starting an old, fragile car, and last forever.

Eighteen

Nathan, come down from there!" Andrew called out. His son had scrambled up a thirty-foot-high slope of football-sized rocks they had encountered along the half-mile trail from the parking lot down to the camping area at Endert's Beach on the northern California coast. He seemed to keep his footing well, never slipping or losing his balance, but Andrew, who was loaded down with gear, knew that he wouldn't be able to go after him if there were any problems.

He wasn't responding, so Andrew called him again, and Nathan slowly turned himself around and came back down.

"Thank you for listening," he said to him, relieved that he hadn't needed to put down all of the backpacks, sleeping bags, tent, and whatever else he had strapped to his body so that he could go up and get Nathan. Eileen trudged along behind, whining about having to walk, and Brooke skipped ahead with the pillows and bags of food. They would need to make a second trip for the ice chest, water, and a few other things before sunset, which would be in about an hour.

Andrew stayed close to the kids, making sure they didn't walk too near the far side of the trail, which dropped off a good forty feet down a rocky incline to the beach below. He had been here several times before and wanted to show Brooke how beautiful it was, but he hadn't thought about how nerve-wracking it would be to keep an eye on his children. In about three hundred feet, they would be beyond the high bluffs, and then he could relax a little.

Endert's Beach was a paradisiac spot of land where the redwoods met the sea. Andrew had camped there in college with friends and had also brought Robin for a day trip last year. He was glad to be back to camp again and looked forward to a relaxing weekend with his family. Nathan scampered on ahead with Brooke as Andrew verbally coaxed Eileen to keep up with him. Now four, she still exhibited a clingy, anxious, temperamental nature that made Andrew wonder if at some point she had undergone an entire personality shift. The possibility of its permanence alarmed him.

They continued down the trail as it sloped down into a lush, mossy, wooded glen at the bottom of the hill. Ferns brushed against them as they entered the small camping area, which had only six sites that shared one chemical toilet. Andrew remembered then that there were no sinks or running water, and he flashed forward to how filthy the kids would be by the time they left Sunday afternoon. Well, they would have fun.

"This is so beautiful!" Brooke said as he caught up to her.

"Isn't it great? It's so secluded," Andrew said. "There's a site over here that's really private. It's got bushes all around it." He led everyone over to it and unloaded the gear.

"Can I set up the tent? I love setting up tents!" Brooke said, her eyes sparkling.

"Sure, it's right here. I'll just take the kids for a quick walk on the beach, and then we can get the rest of the stuff out of the car."

Andrew took them along a trail that went up a small sandstone bluff, jutting over the sand, and then down to the beach. He loved being on top of the hill, looking down into the small green canyon filled with ferns and trees and a gurgling creek that slowly wound its way over fallen tree trunks and rocks, around the bluff, and out to the sea.

Nathan scrambled down the trail to the beach while Andrew picked up Eileen and followed. When they reached the coarse but soft sand, Nathan took off running and exploring, and he set Eileen down. Since there was no one else on the beach for the kids to disturb, and because he could easily keep an eye on them, Andrew enjoyed a few minutes of what he called "passive parenting." He watched them, of course, but he could relax because he didn't have to be vigilant, didn't have to be one step ahead of Nathan (or behind him, as was usually the case). He took off his sandals and let his feet sink deep into the dark, almost oily sand as he strolled a good distance behind them, watching them go up to the water as the foamy edges of the receding waves kissed their toes, and then run away squealing with laughter.

After about twenty minutes he managed to haul his reluctant children back to the campsite. He wished he didn't have to interrupt them, but they needed to hike back up to the car to get the rest of the gear before sunset.

Brooke, proud and beaming, had just finished setting up the tent and held Nathan's hand as they walked up the trail. Andrew, carrying Eileen, felt warm and complete.

During the hike back down from the car, however, Andrew lost his happy feelings when Nathan ran on ahead, racing past the open cliff drop-off area, ignoring Andrew's shouts to stay close to him, as Eileen whined behind him. He labored under the weight of the ice chest and the firewood piled on top of it, but he decided not to set it down and lose his momentum. Brooke, carrying the rectangular jug of water and another bag of supplies, offered to go after Nathan. Andrew figured he'd be all right since they'd already been to the campsite and Nathan had a good sense of direction.

As he reached the campground he heard Brooke calling for Nathan, and his pulse quickened. He rushed to their site, dropped off his load, and ran back to Brooke, who said that Nathan had run so far ahead that she hadn't even seen him. Andrew figured Nathan had gone back to the beach since he'd had so much fun there earlier and had not wanted to leave it. He told Eileen to stay with Brooke while he ran to check the beach. He was certain Nathan would be there.

He wasn't. Andrew peered up and down the beach as far as his eyes could reach. Nothing. He became concerned but remained calm. He figured Nathan must be wandering around the campground, looking for their site, so he went back and combed the campground, calling his name. Andrew checked the accessible areas of the banks of the creek, the chemical toilet, and back to their campsite. Then he got worried.

The sun was beginning to set, and Brooke said she would go around and ask other campers if they had seen Nathan. Andrew slung Eileen around his waist and went back to the beach, then back along some forks off the main trail behind the campground. He called Nathan's name over and over, hearing Brooke do the same, as his heart thumped faster and seemed to be jumping out of his throat. Eileen, constantly perched on his waist, joined in.

Perhaps it was not even a conscious thought, but Andrew started back up the trail to the car, shaking with every step, knots forming in his stomach. Although the south side of almost the entire trail was a rocky cliff descending forty feet to the beach, he trusted in Nathan's sense of balance and somehow knew that he hadn't fallen. But when he neared the parking lot and still hadn't found him, Andrew started to lose it, and he began to think that someone had taken him. That was his one fear—that some sick bastard had grabbed a beautiful, innocent little boy and taken him.

Andrew started to cry, and Eileen did as well. He rounded the last bend before reaching the parking lot, and there he saw his sweet baby boy walking toward him. For a second he thought he was hallucinating, that his mind was playing an evil trick on him. He stopped, looked at Nathan again, and got down on his trembling knees to stand Eileen on the ground.

"Dad," Nathan said, gasping and shivering. He had been lost almost an hour, and the sun had nearly set.

Andrew took him in his arms and kissed his tear-streaked, dirty little face. He held him and told him how scared he was that he was lost. In the back of his mind, he almost couldn't believe how blessed he was to have found Nathan, unharmed. The idea came to Andrew that Nathan must have thought they would go back to the car for another load of gear, but of course he wouldn't have understood if Andrew asked him that, nor been able to answer.

"I can't find Brooke," Nathan said, and for a split second Andrew marveled at both his correct pronoun usage and the fact that he had bonded so quickly with his new girlfriend.

After Andrew made sure Nathan was all right—just a few scratches on his legs, probably from clambering up a forty-foot rock face—they began walking back to the campground. Andrew couldn't remember when his legs felt so weak, but he focused on being thankful that he could hold both of his children's hands as they walked. He had both of them. It was okay. It was over.

Shortly after they began walking, Nathan looked up at Andrew and said, "Thank you for rescuing me."

It was one of those lucid moments that Andrew cherished so much. That might have originally been a line from a video, but not at that moment. That was Nathan talking. Nathan himself coming through, in a moment when autism was far away, suspended, erased for a few seconds. Andrew didn't know how or why those rare moments occurred, but they sustained him.

Tears in his eyes, Andrew said, "I'm so glad I found you."

THE ALARM CLOCK jarred Andrew awake. He bolted forward in the dark to shut it off and pulled on his sweatpants, which had been on the floor by the side of the bed.

It was six-thirty in the morning, and he had to get Nathan up and ready to get on the sped bus that would take him on the forty-five minute commute to Stewart Elementary, where he had been going to school for the past month. Andrew thought that seven-forty-five seemed too early for an elementary school to start, and Nathan was just in Kindergarten. It was grueling to have to get him up so early every day. The mornings that Nathan woke up at Erica's house (from having slept there the night before) were the most difficult; Andrew had to drive to Erica's house to pick Nathan up and have him back at his own house in time to get him on the bus at seven. They didn't want to wake Eileen by having Erica drive Nathan to Andrew's. "No rest for the wicked!" Brooke had teased, one of those mornings as Andrew shuffled out the door. "No rest for parents of children with disabilities," he grumbled in return.

But the STEPS class at Stewart Elementary already seemed to be working out well for Nathan, so the sleep deprivation was worth it. The teacher, a warm, younger grandmotherly-type, sent a notebook back and forth between school and home each day, communicating with Andrew about Nathan's progress and any problems, which were minimal. He seemed comfortable and never complained; a good sign, but Andrew hated having to drag him out of bed every morning in the dark and cold, dress him while he was half asleep, and watch him slowly spoon his cereal into his mouth as if in a trance.

Andrew trudged through the living room of his new house. Six weeks ago, he and Brooke had moved in together into a cute, older two-bedroom house on a steep hill up above the college. Built in the 1930s, it still had all of its old windows, doors, cabinets, and molding. Andrew liked its character as much as he liked the huge, quarter-acre backyard with lots of trees —apple, pine, maple—and a view of Grizzly Peak. The house had a laundry room that had been tacked-on at some point, which looked like a little shanty attached to the back of the house. It had probably been the back porch and someone just walled it in.

Andrew remembered the night that he and Brooke had decided to move in together. Earlier that day they had gone to a barbeque at Brooke's aunt's house, who lived in Medford, and she introduced him to everyone as her boyfriend, which made him feel proud. And all of her relatives treated the kids and him like they were family. They didn't even seem bothered by Nathan taking off his bathing suit when it got wet from the sprinklers (because of his tactile-sensitivity to wet clothing) and running around naked until Andrew stopped him.

"Wish I could do that!" Brooke's aunt had called out as everyone laughed.

Andrew easily relaxed there, realizing that he didn't have to worry about Nathan doing any socially unacceptable things that Brooke and her family couldn't deal with. He was so happy that he had to tell Brooke he loved her.

Why is it always so hard to say the first time? Andrew wondered, trying to find a good moment, the perfect situation, to make it seem effortless and unplanned. Finally it happened. Brooke, often accident-prone, tripped on the garden hose as she was bringing Andrew his burger from the grill and the plate went flying. As she got up and staggered over to him, she said, "I'm sorry! I don't know how you put up with me."

"Because I love you," he said, putting his hand on her upper arm and squeezing it while he looked into her eyes.

Brooke's face lit up. "Really?" she gasped. "You do?"

He assured her that he did, although he felt suddenly insecure because of her reaction. *That must have been too soon,* he thought. *I shouldn't have said it.*

But that night, while cradling her in his arms before they fell asleep, she told him that she loved him and that she loved Nathan and Eileen like they were her own. His spirit soared, and he felt like the luckiest man alive to have found the sweetest, prettiest girl who not only loved him, but his children as well.

"I want to move in together," Brooke said into his chest.

"That would be perfect," Andrew said as he slowly ran his fingers through her hair. Not only was he thrilled at the prospect of living with Brooke, he was also glad to be getting out of his one-bedroom apartment. He laughed to himself as he remembered the journal entry he had written a year ago in which he'd said something about staying there until he was ready to buy a house. That had certainly been a premature statement. In fact, he was going out of his mind not having a yard and, most of all, his own bedroom.

But that frustration was now behind him; he loved the house they'd rented and he loved living with Brooke. Her social nature brought new people into Andrew's home and life, friends of hers who became friends of his, specifically Gavin. It was good to have a friend again, since all of his college friends had moved away and he hadn't had many opportunities to get out and meet new people when the kids were babies. He'd isolated himself then, home alone with them, not even working. Now, being with Brooke, those days seemed far away, like trying to remember what you used to eat for breakfast ten years ago.

Brooke never ate breakfast. Andrew constantly tried to get her to eat something, but she told him that any food before noon made her sick to her stomach, as did not smoking a cigarette within ten minutes of waking up. She twitched her feet in her sleep, her toes actually, in some sort of a subconscious tapping pattern, moving like a court stenographer. Andrew figured it was an ADHD reflex of hers, nothing she could control. Her idiosyncrasies both amused him and endeared her to him further.

Andrew brought Nathan his toothbrush and brushed his teeth for him, which, much to Andrew's relief, was no longer met with notable resistance. Then he washed Nathan's face with a warm washcloth and put an overcoat on over his hooded fleece jacket. They waited by the front window until he saw the headlights of the sped bus pull up in front of the house, and he picked up Nathan's little backpack and walked him out into the cold, foggy morning, greeted the cheery female bus driver, and put Nathan in his seat. Andrew kissed him goodbye, told him he loved him, then got off and stood outside waving to him as the bus pulled away. Nathan, as always, looked straight ahead and never seemed to notice him.

"EILEEN, STOP WHINING. We're at Grandma's house," Andrew said as he pulled her out of her car seat. Nathan was already running up the front porch steps to ring the doorbell, which was something he enjoyed doing, a ritual for him. Andrew heard his mother open the door and greet Nathan as he picked up a sullen Eileen, shut the car door, and slowly walked up the stairs.

God, I am too old to party like that any more. I'm aging faster than a crack whore at sunrise.

For the occasion of his thirtieth birthday, Brooke had made sure that Erica had the kids that night so that she could take Andrew out, and Gavin joined them. They called a cab to drive them into town since they knew none of them would be in any shape to drive home. They went out dancing and carried on at an after-hours party until about five in the morning. But he was thirty, and that called for a hell of a night.

He knew he looked like it, too, glancing at himself in his mother's hall-way mirror, noticing his pale skin and dark circles. She gave him a big hug and the "I-can't-believe-you're-thirty" speech and then went to set the kids up with a video in the living room, instructing him to have a seat in the kitchen.

Andrew saw that his mother had her white ceramic soup tureen out on the dining room table with the matching large, low soup bowls she had always had as far back as he could remember. She joined him a minute later and he reminded her of the time during his childhood when she had served split pea soup for dinner and had worn a caftan with long, flared sleeves. When she had leaned across the table, and her bowl, to give a spoonful to Bernadette, she scooped up split pea soup in her sleeve, to everyone's ma-niacal laughter.

"You all thought that was hysterical," she said now, rolling her eyes as she ladled some chicken soup into his bowl.

Andrew spread some butter on a warm whole wheat roll and took a bite. "That's what you got for wearing a caftan," he said.

"They were in style then!"

"Maybe in the Mediterranean," Andrew said, enjoying the banter while he sipped the warm liquid. He chuckled at the ensuing protest and contin-ued eating the savory homemade soup.

"So," his mother began a moment later, "do you feel any different?"

Yeah, Mom, I feel like I got dragged behind a chariot last night. "You mean, being thirty?"

Elaine rolled her eyes. "Yes!"

"Not really. I'm very fulfilled being a father. I wish I had more time to write, but I know when the kids are older, I'll be able to focus on that. And I'd really like to own a home soon. I just feel like I'm throwing away thou-sands of dollars a year by renting. And it's just something I've wanted ever since I was a little kid. Remember how Sol and I used to look at the Sears catalogs when we were little and pick out stuff we liked? Not just toys, but household stuff?"

"Yes, I remember. Part of me thought that was a strange thing for little boys to be doing, but then I remembered that I used to do that as a child, so maybe it was some genetic trait, this longing for a home of your own. It'll happen soon enough, Andrew. You've been through a lot the past three years, so just be patient with yourself. But that's certainly a worthy goal."

Elaine took a bite of bread and told him that she had decided to go to college, that she wanted to get a degree in psychology and maybe go into counseling work. She was fifty now, apprehensive about diving into the world of academia, likening it to Erica's experience with her father "teaching" her to swim. Andrew, supportive, told his mother she'd be fine, that Erica had mentioned recently how many older students she'd seen around campus; she'd even heard of some parents going to college the same time as their kids (which of course their kids hated).

Andrew was glad that both of his parents were pursuing new interests, keeping themselves busy instead of being bitter. His father had just informed him that he had gotten a seasonal job working in Yellowstone National Park at the front desk of one of the lodges, where he had dreamed of working since he was a boy. He would be moving there in two months to be trained, then work until October.

"That'll be good for him," Elaine said, when Andrew had told her. "He always did love the national park trips we took." Gabriel's passion, aside from bowling, took them all over the western United States, a different destination each summer, with a few repeated trips to favorite spots. The Grand Canyon was one, and Yosemite. They had also been to Yellowstone, Crater Lake, Lassen, Zion, Rocky Mountain, Glacier, Sequoia, and even as far away as Mt. Rushmore in South Dakota. They'd ridden mules on a narrow, switch-backing trail into the Grand Canyon, rafted the Snake River in front of the Grand Tetons in Wyoming, hiked Vernal Falls in Yosemite and to the top of Mount Lassen, a dormant volcano. They'd swam in Crater Lake, one of the deepest lakes in the world, nicknamed the Gem of the Cascades with its blue so rich, so dazzling, it was hypnotic.

"Glacier was my favorite," Andrew said. They had camped there when he was seventeen, the last trip they'd all taken together.

"Yeah," Elaine said in a wistful tone. "Remember that gorgeous sunrise?"

Andrew nodded and closed his eyes. It had been the most glorious sight, beams bursting forth over the mountains, filtering through the trees, coloring the wilderness around them with a light so vibrant it seemed like it was a celebration. He felt the energy, the reawakening. His whole life was beginning anew.

"I DON'T WANT to put a four-year-old on antidepressants!" Erica exploded.

"I don't either," Andrew said. "I'm surprised they suggested it."

Erica relaxed a little. She should have known that Andrew would have resisted the proposal of the teacher and caseworker he'd had a meeting with that afternoon. They'd been unable to get a babysitter, so Erica stayed home with the kids, and he stopped by her apartment on his way home from the meeting to tell her how it went.

"They said that Eileen's anxiety has really become a problem. She's been crying at the door for almost an hour every morning wanting to go home to you, she won't participate in group activities, and she can't handle transitions," Andrew said, keeping his voice low in the kitchen so the kids, who were watching TV ten feet away in the living room, wouldn't hear. She was at least talking more, passing up Nathan in his fledgling language development, often stringing together six-word sentences. But her pronunciation needed work, making her slur words together like a miniature barhopper. Erica had to turn her head and laugh on many occasions when poor Eileen had tried to make an excited comment and ran her words together so that they were barely recognizable, like the drunk-talk Erica heard every weekend at work. "You're cut off!" she'd said to Eileen one time, sending Andrew out of the room laughing. They'd had a speech pathologist examine her palate and tongue formation to rule that out as a possible cause for her impediment, and he'd said she was normal.

"She's been at ECDC for almost a year and she's still having the same issues she had at Head Start," Erica said, leaning against the counter wearing jeans and a black T-shirt. It was Thursday, and she had scheduled herself for the late shift from now on since Gabriel had left for Yellowstone and couldn't watch the kids anymore. She didn't have to work until nine o'clock, but she did have a final exam next week to begin studying for. She always felt vindicated at the end of the term: another class under her belt, another three credits toward the hundred and eighty-six she needed to graduate. She would always visualize the builders of Stonehenge, celebrating as each monolith slid into the ground with a resounding thud.

"I know. I keep hoping it's something she'll outgrow, but it's like she went through an entire personality shift. It's been going on for so long. I can't figure it out."

"Maybe she's not happy being so far from home," Erica said.

"Head Start was close to home."

"That's true. Maybe she doesn't feel comfortable with the teacher again." Eileen's teacher at ECDC was physically the polar opposite of her large, boisterous teacher at Head Start, but her nervous, meticulous demeanor and the fact that she seemed to take it personally that Eileen had so much anxiety might have made the anxiety worse.

"That could be a possibility," Andrew said. "Eileen's probably feeding off of her. God, she was nervous today, just talking about Eileen. Wringing her hands, wrinkling her forehead. And she's got such an annoying voice."

Erica laughed. "I know! I mean, I feel bad because I know she tries really hard and it's obvious that she cares about Eileen, but sometimes I just want to tell her to relax!"

"Yeah, she seems too uptight to be a preschool teacher," Andrew said.

"I think we might have figured out at least part of the problem," Erica said.

Feeling confident that medication was not the answer, they decided to just wait it out, anticipating that Eileen might mature some over the summer, might outgrow the anxiety, and might be happier going to Kindergarten in Ashland with a more relaxed teacher. Erica then helped to get the kids ready to go to Andrew's house and walked out to the car with them.

"I'm glad we agree on so many parenting issues," she said. She couldn't imagine how hard it would be if they had vastly different ideas about how to raise their children. *At least we don't have to deal with that,* she thought.

"Yeah. It makes things easier," Andrew said. "See you in the morning."

Erica, barefoot, tiptoed back into the house and closed the door behind her. Just as she sat on the couch and picked up her *Principles of Design* book to begin reviewing for next week's final exam, the phone rang.

Somehow she knew it would be her father. She figured he would be returning from his annual two-month trek along the Pacific Crest Trail, and she was right. He asked how his grandchildren were doing, and she inwardly laughed, thinking that she could say anything and he wouldn't know the difference. She talked to her father about three times a year, at the most. He usually called her in March for her birthday, although he often missed the day, actually debating it with her ("I'm sure it's the twenty-first, because I always remember it three-two-one," he'd said three years in a row, as she assured him that her birth certificate said it was the twentieth, as did her mother). Then he usually called in August, and for Christmas. He insisted on talking to the kids even though they didn't have a clue about who he was, having never met him. They probably thought he was Gabriel on the phone.

But he was her last living parent, and Erica found that she loved him in spite of his faults, his emotional idiosyncrasies. When she was sixteen and left Weed, she decided to look him up in Santa Barbara, and he took her in. She stayed with him in the modest room of the hotel, owned by an old friend of his, in which he lived and worked as the manager. Every night he smoked a joint, squeezed his hulking Scandinavian frame into the recliner, and watched nature shows on cable TV. She would come home from waiting tables at a local Italian restaurant, trying to save money to get her own apartment, and he would tell her about the diet of the "flat-billed scooper fish" or the mating rituals of lions. And she would feign interest for five minutes, yawn without restraint, turn to face the wall, and go to sleep on her cot. On her days off, while her father worked the front desk or drove the hotel van to pick up guests from the airport, she would study for her GED, sketch or paint, or go surfing.

"How's Andrew?" he asked her.

"He's fine. He was just here, picking up the kids."

"I always liked Andrew. I still think of him as my son-in-law. How are you guys getting along?"

You must have liked him, Erica thought. *He's the only guy I've ever been with whose name you actually remembered. All the rest of the guys were always "Bud." And my female friends were all called "Sweetie." Hell, I'm lucky you remembered my name.* "We're doing great, communicating really well. I think we get along better divorced than when we were married."

"That's good," her father said, making her wonder how much of what she'd said had registered with him; he had probably already blazed up. He asked her if she was seeing anyone and she told him about Jonah, and that they had recently broken up. She remembered what Jonah had said to her: "Our chemistry has evaporated." *Evaporated? Leave it to a psychology major to come up with something so non-confrontational it doesn't make sense,* Erica thought. *My tolerance for your bullshit has evaporated. That's what's evaporated.* But she hadn't said that. She just nodded, let him say whatever verbiage made him look sensitive, empathetic, when in reality he had been the most emotionally distant guy she'd ever dated. Of course she didn't tell her father any of that. Owen was the epitome of emotional distance, so how would he, how *could* he, empathize? She did wish, however, that her father knew Simone, and knew Isaac, so that she could share a laugh with him about the incredulous fact that the two of them had gotten together. Simone, the ambitious career-ladder climber, with Isaac, the content career-waiter. She was shocked when Simone told her. "We just realized that we'd always been attracted to each other," she'd said. Erica laughed. "Isaac's always been attracted to everybody." "Hey," Simone admonished her. "People mature. People can change." Erica refrained from denoting the pitfalls of wishful thinking.

There had been no pitfalls in breaking up with Jonah, she was certain. The most beneficial result of it was that she would have more time to focus on school since she wouldn't have to devote that energy to keeping alive a one-sided relationship. And she began to toss around the idea of completing her degree at Cal State Long Beach, with its reputable graphic design department. She had to achieve her goals, and she realized more and more that she was just treading water in Ashland, that even if she attained her degree there that she would probably still be bartending, getting by but not getting ahead. How many times can you say "Enjoy your drinks" before it sounds insincere, robotic even? She'd grown weary of the trade, weary of barely paying the bills, weary of going nowhere.

Her father was supportive of such a big move, but then he liked cataclysmic events. His favorite video was a documentary on earthquakes. "You need to get out of that small town," he said.

"Well, I think at this point, since the kids are older, Andrew should be able to handle it if I move."

"Of course he can! He's a great father! And then he might want to move, too. There are probably plenty of good schools for autistic kids in L.A."

"Yeah," Erica said. *But he probably wouldn't be able to move for a long time. And how could I leave my children? How could I go more than two days without holding them, kissing them, being their mom? How could I be like my mother?*

Nineteen

Look, there's another one," Andrew said to Brooke, pointing to the car in front of them with an American flag taped inside the rear window. The two of them were driving over to the coast for the weekend, feeling strange going on a little weekend pleasure trip that they had planned over a month ago when now, because of what happened on the other side of the country, there was tremendous loss and sadness. So many cars had American flags on them. Every time Andrew looked at one, he felt a surge of pride that got stuck in his throat.

Three days before, he and Brooke had woken up unusually early (a little before six) the morning of September 11, 2001. Brooke had begun groping him, and they fumbled around in the dim light for a while. Afterward, Brooke said she couldn't get back to sleep and wanted to watch a little MTV.

"Oh, my God. Andrew, look at this."

Andrew, lying on his back in bed, picked up his head and stared at the live news report. He saw one of the Twin Towers on fire, and then he saw a plane crash into the other one.

"Oh, my God! What is happening?!" he said, standing up and putting on his sweatpants. "Is this supposed to be a joke?"

The frantic newscasts quickly convinced him of the terrible truth, and he held Brooke as she cried.

Work had been eerie. How could he focus on processing orders? It was suddenly so unimportant, so miniscule and banal. In shock, he answered a phone call in the usual way. "Thank you for calling Inner Peace Music. How may I help you?" The woman, from South Dakota according to the caller ID on the phone, shouted at him, "What are you doing open? Don't you realize what happened today?!" and hung up. *What are you doing call-*

ing, then? he wondered. *Wanting to check on your order? Are the CDs really that fucking important today?*

Gloria decided to close early, and Andrew found himself at home for lunch, trying to choke down a turkey sandwich while watching a news report about a man who had survived falling from the eighty-ninth floor. He recalled the summer when he was ten that his family had taken a trip to the East Coast to see all the historic sites and buildings in Virginia, Washington, DC, Philadelphia, Boston, and New York. He remembered distinctly how he and Sol stood on top of the World Trade Center, whispering because it was so impressive. "We're almost up to the clouds!" eight-year-old Sol had said. And their mother leaned over, hand tight on the railing, and said, "Take a good look around at everything. You never know if you'll ever be able to come back here and see this again." So they looked at all the buildings spread out before them, and felt the wind on their faces and in their hair as they squinted in the sun and pointed at tiny things and talked about what would happen if someone threw a penny over the side. "It would be so heavy by the time it landed that it would split someone's head open," Andrew told a wide-eyed Sol. They were silent then, not daring to think of it.

Andrew slid his sunglasses on his face as he navigated the car over the winding road to the coast. He still felt weird taking this trip, enjoying themselves. It didn't feel right. But they'd had to make extensive arrangements to be able to go, four different people (Erica, Brooke's brother, and both of Andrew's parents, separately) were taking turns watching the kids for them, and they would have been charged a hefty cancellation fee if they didn't go.

Brooke seemed to have worked through whatever feelings of sadness and shock she had experienced. She acted even giddier and goofier than her usual self, singing songs with the radio and jumping from topic to topic. There were times at home when Andrew had to visibly slow her down, holding his hand palm-down and slowly lowering it from his chest to his waist, saying, "Brooke, relax. You're getting all wound up." "I know, I'm a little ADD," she would always say, as if it were the first time telling Andrew that she had Attention Deficit Disorder.

But this, in the car, was over the top. "What is with you?" Andrew asked.

"I'm just excited! We have a weekend to ourselves!" she said, hopping in her seat.

When Andrew suggested stopping for an hour to see the Trees of Mystery, a grove of redwood trees along the northern California coast, Brooke nearly became hysterical. "No! We can do that tomorrow! I made dinner reservations at the seafood place next door to White Cliff! We can't be late!"

That's a surprise, Andrew thought. She'd never made any reservations of any kind before; he always did.

Within half an hour they had arrived at White Cliff Resort, a cluster of two dozen single-wide, cedar-sided manufactured homes, each with one bedroom and a loft, and wooden decks with private hot tubs. They were on a cliff overlooking the beach right on the border of California and Oregon. Brooke had found out about the place from a co-worker, and Andrew had made the reservation for two nights. They checked in with just enough time to wash up, change, and go to dinner, with Brooke rushing things the entire time.

They were seated at a white, linen-covered round table overlooking the water, which glinted from the start of the sun's descent. Brooke got up a lot during dinner, saying her stomach was bothering her, and barely touched her food. She talked a lot though, about their families, about how much she loved Nathan and Eileen, as if they were her own, and again, for about the hundredth time, told Andrew he was the best thing that ever happened to her. Andrew couldn't figure out if this was her ADD affecting her or if she was going to tell him that she was terminally ill.

Finally, when they had finished dinner (or rather, when Andrew had finished, after Brooke had returned from getting up for the seventh time), she begged to have a bottle of champagne.

"We hardly ever have champagne; I'd really like some," she said, sitting on her hands and rocking slightly.

"I thought your stomach was bothering you."

"I think the bubbliness will help it."

And when the waiter brought out the bottle and set it in front of Andrew, draped around the neck of it was a sterling silver necklace with half a silver heart engraved with his initials and half a phrase that he couldn't make out at first glance. His eyes popped out of his head and a chill came over him as he realized what this was, what was happening. He barely heard Brooke say, "I don't know if it's proper for a girl to get on her knees to do this, so I'll just look you in the eye and hold your hand and ask if you'll have me for your wife."

Andrew, in shock, tried to meet her gaze and gasped, "Yes!"

Brooke stood up and announced, "He said 'Yes!'" to the applause of all the diners and staff. Andrew, in a daze, kissed and hugged her in disbelief, feeling like he had won the lottery or reached the summit of Mt. Everest. He felt almost like he did when his children were born, tearfully joyous, filled with awe and wonder and excitement.

The waiter popped the cork and poured, and then Andrew toasted, "To my wife-to-be" as they both sipped and cried a little, to more applause.

Brooke, nearly hyperventilating, told Andrew all that he knew she had gone insane over not being able to tell him: where she had the necklaces made, who of their friends knew (Erica knew, for one, and Gavin), and all the crazy dreams she had been having since she started planning this. "I had all these different dreams about how you would react when I proposed: in one, you laughed, in another all the people in the restaurant laughed, in another you were really nice but you said no. It was torture! I'm so glad it's over!"

They were too excited to finish the champagne, so the restaurant let them take it back to their cabin. It was dark, and they decided to go for a flash-lit walk on the beach before retiring to the hot tub.

Andrew contentedly walked with his arm around Brooke, barefoot in the sand. *She proposed to me! How cool is that? I'm so in love with this girl.*

They stopped and he enfolded her in his arms as he kissed her, and then she fit the two silver heart halves together again and read the inscription, "One love, one heart, let's get together and feel all right," from her favorite song by Bob Marley.

He kissed her again and looked out over the sea at the storm that was off on the horizon. First they could see nothing, just the black of the sky all around, and then a flash of lightning would illuminate the water, and for a second they could see the miles of choppy water beneath the black sky, and then everything would go black again. Then a few seconds later would come a roll of thunder. Andrew thought of his parents' adage about rain being a blessing as he watched the storm, wondering if the rain would come, as he hoped.

ERICA COULDN'T BELIEVE whose arms she was in. The Sunday morning sunlight filtered in through the blinds and crept across her sheet-covered naked body and slowly over the floor. She had no intention of getting up and gently nuzzled her face into the shoulder blades of the sleeping naked man who had just turned over.

She had run into Miles, Isaac's brother, at the small grocery store near her home. Erica had come around the corner and there he was, at the other end of the bread aisle, looking sultrier than she had remembered, in his blue jeans and snug-fitting oatmeal henley shirt, his bowling-style shoes. His dark, straight hair was longish, with layers falling over his ears and his eyebrows, grazing his shoulders. He looked like a model, and Erica, of course, was in her yoga pants and a ratty old tank top, unkempt.

"Hey!" they said to each other, set their shopping baskets down, and hugged. It had been over a year since they'd seen each other, since Miles had been living in Los Angeles for almost three years, working in an architecture firm, and Erica didn't usually see him when he came up to Ashland for visits. They agreed to have dinner that night, and Erica hurried home to call someone in to work for her so she could have the night off. This was big.

She wore a knee-length, kelly green chintz vintage dress with brown high-heeled sandals and wore her long hair down. When she opened her front door after Miles knocked, she thought she saw his eyes widen for a second before he smiled and told her how stunning she looked, and that's when she made the connection. His eyes looked just like the wolf eyes on her arm. Not wild or lustful or vicious, but deep, evocative, searching. Pensive, yet impelling. Dark and noble.

He kept touching her hand during dinner (at a small, intimate Italian place where Isaac worked) as they talked and sipped a luscious Zinfandel, discussing not just the past three years, but everything that had come before. At one point, Miles laughed and said, "I feel like I should be telling you my favorite color and things like that," and it just happened to be green. He told her about his job, how even though it was stressful, he loved it. He asked her how she was doing in school; she told him how she felt she was stagnating, wasting her life away. She felt like a withering flower in a vase, petals dropping unnoticed to the table below. "Ashland is a vortex," he agreed. "You get too comfortable, and then it's hard to accomplish anything here." She told him about Nathan having autism, and how Jonah had found him to be a novelty, being a psychology major, and how that infuriated her. She told him that Brooke was now engaged to her ex-husband, that they had been living together for a year, and that the relationship had lasted much longer than she thought it would, but that she was happy for both of them. They talked about what an even bigger surprise it was that Isaac and Simone had gotten together and were going to have a baby. "Fatherhood will be an interesting venture for him," Miles said. "I think he's ready for it." He talked about what it was like growing up with Isaac in Arizona, having a truck-driver father and a coffee-shop waitress mother, being the children of a living cliché. Their parents had divorced long ago, but neither of them ever remarried, and they often celebrated holidays together. "You know how lots of kids whose parents are divorced wish they would get back together? Mine did sometimes."

When the restaurant closed, they picked up another bottle of wine at Safeway and went back to Erica's apartment. They walked joined at the hip, like they had been together for years, in perfect sync, her arm encircling his waist and his arm around her back, like a Yin and Yang symbol.

And when they reached her apartment, they curled up on the couch with a glass of Australian shiraz. Erica had discovered by process of elimination that certain substances exacerbated her PMS symptoms, even triggered them, and red wine unfortunately made the list, which also included caffeine and red meat. She made it a point to avoid these foods for ten days prior to her period starting and was often able to reduce the debilitating effects of PMS, sometimes avoiding them entirely. Erica was relieved to finally have the hormonal surges under control. And she'd just finished her period that week, so she would not need to concern herself with regulating her food intake during her visit with Miles. The wine flowed, the filet mignon was medium rare, and dinner had been a lovely reunion and first date at the same time. They talked about the old days, when he was a waiter at Dogma during the summers and they would flirt with each other, never knowing how far they could take it, how much the other felt comfortable with.

"I feel really comfortable now," she said.

"So do I," Miles whispered as he leaned in to kiss her.

There was no turning back. Thus began a frenzy of flailing arms and legs, an overturned floor lamp, spilled wine, and even torn clothing ("The price of passion," Miles had said, eyeing his linen shirt during a breather). And yet, mixed in with the animalistic urgency was an explorative tenderness, a longing to know every muscle, every crease of skin. Miles slowly brushed his fingers across her scar, sending an ache through her body like sugar on a dental cavity, making her shudder.

Erica felt she had never wanted anyone so much, like she had an insatiable hunger that grew with each touch of his hand, his lips. With each kiss she was already thinking that she loved him, deciding, knowing. It was beyond her control, a combination of a parent's consuming love for a newborn and the ninth grade infatuation of someone wanting more, no longer content to lace fingers while walking to class.

"We deprived ourselves of this for so long," she said, lying naked beside him on the floor and slowly running her fingers through his chest hair.

"It was worth the wait," Miles said, turning in to her, kissing her again, electrifying her as she felt his skin all over her. She loved his scent, his Greek skin, musky and toned. She wanted to absorb it, to fill all her pores as she rubbed her limbs around him.

She awoke with a fuzziness from the wine, but it was nothing unmanageable. What was unmanageable was the fact that she and Miles lived almost seven hundred miles apart. This was too strong a connection to be a fling. She knew she had to be with him. She was already in love. She had stared down the demons of unrequited love and abandoned dreams and emerged with a second chance, an acceptance of past mistakes and the promise of a fulfilling future, all in Miles' eyes. She could not deny herself this love. People make mistakes. It doesn't mean they don't deserve a shot at happiness.

Twenty

Nathan had been complaining that there were "dead people" under Central Elementary School in Ashland. He had been going there over a month, and he was having a terrible time adjusting to it. Andrew had been ecstatic that he no longer had to drag Nathan out of bed at six-thirty in the morning (much less himself) for the long bus ride to Stewart. And now there was no bus ride at all, because Central was right down the street from Andrew's house. And Eileen had started Kindergarten there, which Andrew found highly convenient.

But Andrew's elation over his children's school transfers, as well as his engagement, was soon replaced by the anxiety of reality taking over and things not going well. Nathan and the dead people. Brooke doing drugs and staying out all night long acting like it was no big deal. The only one who seemed all right was Eileen, whose mood had changed for the better since she had started Kindergarten. At least there was that.

Andrew, on his lunch break, had to drive to the school for weekly meetings with Nathan's teacher, the school principal, and various district consultants and therapists. In the six weeks since Nathan had started at Central, they constantly pulled him out of class to go to the resource room due to his disruptive behavior: yelling, knocking things off shelves, pushing other children. It was a vicious cycle. He knew that if he acted out, he would get to leave class, and it was at a point where they were sending him there first thing in the morning and he stayed there nearly the whole day. He had regressed socially and academically.

Andrew figured the dead people thing had something to do with the fact that the school was an old two-story building with a raised foundation, creaky stairs, and echo-filled halls. It probably had an effect on Nathan similar to the reverberation of public restrooms that had always tormented him. And he didn't have the verbal skills to explain what he meant by dead people being under the school. He didn't say that he had seen them. He had only said that they were there. The issue could not advance further because Nathan could not elaborate. It wasn't the first time that Andrew had to just acknowledge something and let it go.

Nathan's adjustment problems, however, had to be addressed. But going to meetings every single week was not what Andrew had bargained for. Nathan had done so well at Stewart, despite the commute. He had even started *writing* near the end of the year. He began by printing his name, laboring over the small h, until he decided, on his own apparently, to make a capital H instead because it was easier, so that his name read "NatHaN." But within three months, he was writing full sentences, writing more than he would speak, short "letters" even. "Dear Dad, Dad get string cheese, Love Dad," Nathan had written on a small piece of paper and handed to Andrew one day. After praising Nathan for his writing, Andrew tried to explain that he needed to sign the letters "Love, Nathan" so that people would know who they were from, but when he saw Nathan's confused look, Andrew realized that he probably was thinking, *Why wouldn't they know who it was from? I just handed this to you, so you must know it's from ME.* He had also started drawing, which thrilled Erica. The first things he drew were little cars with smiley faces. He drew houses and traffic lights. Then he went through a sign-making phase and was putting signs up at both Erica's and Andrew's homes, including "Warning: Do not let Dad out of the house," on Andrew's back door and several "Missing: Stuart Little" signs all over the living room when he couldn't find his *Stuart Little* video. Nathan also loved playing and writing on the computer, both at home and at school. His progress report said that he was improving with social interactions and Andrew and Erica, wanting him to be around typical peers so that he would learn from them, had felt positive about him transitioning to a regular classroom at Central, but their hopes were unrealized. He had made all this progress at Stewart, and now it was as if that had never happened.

Andrew parked his car and walked up the steps to the school. He checked in at the front office, then walked down the empty hallway toward the meeting room. About fifty feet away, at the end of the hall, he saw a child running back and forth, and then he realized that it was Nathan.

What is my son doing running through the halls?!

"Nathan!" he called. "Nathan! Come here!"

Nathan, with a wild, unfocused look in his eye, saw Andrew and bolted through the double metal doors going to the playground. He tripped on the threshold and went sprawling down the cement stairs right outside the doors. Andrew ran to get him, shocked and livid that his child was allowed to run through the halls. He picked Nathan up, and as he went back inside with him, the educational assistant assigned to work with Nathan came jogging over, looking bewildered and sheepish.

"Why was he running through the halls?" Andrew demanded. Nathan writhed and pulled on Andrew's hand.

"He just gets away! He won't listen!" the small-boned woman said. Andrew had seen her several times before at the previous weekly meetings. She struck him as a quiet, bird-like woman with a pointy nose and no lips who hated conflict and took a job working for the school district because she told herself that she liked kids but didn't have the credentials to be a teacher. She had graying hair which she had dyed a yellow blond and sprayed and coiffed it into a bulletproof style. Andrew had an urge to take a pair of clippers and shave her head. No wonder Nathan ran from her.

"He has autism! You have to let him know what his limits are! He needs visual boundaries!" Andrew tried to calm himself, but it was difficult. He wondered if she had even worked with autistic kids before. *Probably not.*

"We've been trying! He's not responding."

"This never happened at the two other schools he's attended!"

"I'm sorry. I can understand you're upset. Let's go to the meeting and we can discuss ways to avoid this," the assistant said as Andrew followed her into the resource room.

Andrew dragged his reluctant son into a room with eight adults sitting around a table, all looking at them as they entered. It was unnerving enough for Andrew, and he sensed Nathan's anxiety surge. He walked him over to a corner with some toys and books, and then Andrew went and sat at the table.

Nathan, still agitated, instantly jumped up and ran around the room squealing and tipping chairs over backwards. Andrew noticed the wild look again in Nathan's eyes, but something else beneath it, surfacing. A pleading look. *Help me, Dad,* it said. *Something here is not right.*

Andrew stood up and went over to hold his son. "It's okay," he whispered in his ear. To the table, he said, "This is not acceptable. He knows we're talking about him and he's disturbed by it. He needs to be where he'll be more comfortable."

The district special education coordinator, a friendly woman in her thirties who had worked with Nathan at ECDC for a time, took him into her office, and to Andrew's relief he went willingly. He returned to the table, where the educational assistant had started describing Nathan's problem behaviors in the classroom, and then his teacher looked at the principal and actually rolled her eyes. Andrew saw it.

How dare you roll your fucking eyes! My son is not a nuisance for you to tolerate! Why don't I say something? Why don't I say, 'You have no right to communicate that way about my son!' This is your job! And this is my child, not an animal you're training!

Andrew was furious with the teacher, but he was angrier with himself that he didn't say anything. The realization hit him that this school was not working out at all and he didn't know what to do. He was shocked at the calloused attitude of this teacher, who had been highly recommended because of her experience working with special-needs children. She was older, with short, permed, undyed gray hair and round glasses. She was probably burned out on teaching by now. But she still had no right to be that insensitive in his presence. Andrew looked at her; she was smiling and laughing as if it were a humorous triviality to pull parents from their low-paying jobs for weekly meetings and discuss their children as if they were annoyances.

You need to retire, crone.

ANDREW HAD TAKEN his first sick day in over a year, fighting a nasty flu that came on him like a truck. He hated missing work because there was so much to catch up on when he got back, but he'd had a fever of a hundred and three degrees the night before and was still very weak. Luckily, the kids were with Erica that night, so he didn't have to tend to their needs and was therefore able to get some rest. He couldn't afford to miss any more work since it was November, a huge month in the mail order business. One more day off and he would have really fallen behind.

He camped out on the couch in the living room and sipped a cup of chamomile tea, toying with the idea of writing in his journal. But it was getting late and he felt like he should go to bed early. He also wanted to avoid the melancholy frame of mind that journal writing usually put him in. Eileen was okay, but Nathan was slipping away. He had responded well to the intensive therapy for almost three years, but all the progress he had made during that time had diminished during the two months he had been at Central. Lately Andrew had seen behavior in Nathan that he hadn't seen for almost two years: chair tipping, head-butting, squealing. He had read of children with autism who seemed to show great potential only to regress later for unknown reasons, and it terrified him that it could happen to Nathan, that it was happening to Nathan. He felt helpless.

The stereo suddenly blared from the bedroom. Brooke entered the living room, wearing jeans and a sexy, low-cut black sweater, sashaying to an old Sammy Davis Jr. record she had found in her father's basement after a recent visit. She belted out, "The Candyman can!"

She must be tone-deaf, Andrew thought. *And so inconsiderate.*

His head pounded and his throat ached. Brooke didn't seem to be aware of how sick he was, having spent the entire evening wanting to talk or have sex, actually sitting on him earlier and pretending to give him a lap dance, then getting mad when he had nudged her off. She attributed his lack of talking to "moodiness" and told him to snap out of it because he was "wasting" an evening that they had to themselves. She continued to sing loudly, and when the song ended she ducked back into the bedroom and started it again, turning it up even louder. Andrew stood up slowly.

"Brooke, I'd really like to go to bed. Can you please shut it off?"

She wheeled on him then. "It's all about you, isn't it? I just want to listen to one song! All I wanted to do was listen to a little music. How often do I listen to music? You don't like music at all, that's the problem!"

Oh, my God. I don't like music. Of course! "I'm sick, Brooke! I've been telling you all night, I'm sick! My head hurts and my throat hurts and you've got the music up loud! Please understand!"

"Fuck you!" Brooke yelled, jamming her middle finger in Andrew's face. Then she stomped into the bedroom and shut off the stereo.

Incredible. "I'm going to bed," Andrew said.

Brooke stomped over to the TV in the living room. "Fine! You can have it your way!" She flicked it on and threw herself on the couch.

Andrew was too weak to make an issue of it. He sunk into bed, dreading the post-nasal drip and bodyache that would make it hard to sleep. He thought about the fact that it had not even been two months since he and Brooke had gotten engaged and she had become a different person, like she felt free to let down her guard, let it all hang out. She would stay out all night and get mad at him the next morning when he would ask where she was, as if as her fiancé he had no right to know. He knew she spent a lot of time with Gavin, and that was fine because Andrew trusted him, but it was the drugs Gavin always had around that alarmed Andrew. Knowing Brooke's history of addiction, he didn't think it was too smart for her to be around any drugs. "None of your business!" she would sneer at him in the way that someone who had something to hide would say. Less than a week ago she'd shot it out of her mouth as soon as she walked through the door, before Andrew even had a chance to say anything. He knew then that she was high.

Brooke stuck her head in the door. "Aren't you glad you got your way?"

She didn't wait for a response and pulled the door shut. Andrew turned on his other side, trying to ignore the TV blaring in the next room and hoped that Brooke would fall asleep out there. How could being with her have come to this? An easy dream had evolved into an anxious nightmare. He felt like he was falling through darkness, dreading the jolt at the bottom.

ERICA FIGURED THAT telling Andrew she was getting married would be difficult. After all, she had only gotten together with Miles two months ago. She hardly believed it herself. Talk about whirlwind.

Miles had stayed another week after they ran into each other at the grocery store, even though he was supposed to leave to go back to work in L.A. the next day. "It's not every day you fall in love," he'd said. He went with her when she took Eileen to her first day of school, which Erica found so endearing, and he had bonded with Nathan by watching *The Swiss Family Robinson* with him twice. "I always loved that movie when I was a kid," he'd said. And Miles had worn his jacket with his hood up whenever he was around Nathan because he had read, on his own, that mimicking autistic kids helps to engage them.

Erica realized how true the adage is—you find love when you least expect it, when you're not looking for it. And it seemed to be the best kind. On his third visit in six weeks, Miles brought her a ring and proposed to her in the bread aisle at the little grocery store. "This is where our life together actually started," he said. She threw her arms around his neck, tears in her eyes, not believing that she could ever feel so emotional about someone other than her children. She remembered the night after she had come home from the hospital after having Nathan, and she had just finished breastfeeding him and put him in his crib in his room down the hall. She climbed back into bed with Andrew, and he embraced her and said, "I never thought I could love someone so much," and she said, "Me, too." But, she found out years later when he brought it up, that he had been talking about her, and she had been talking about Nathan. He seemed sad when she told him, but what could she have said? How can you create feelings that are not there? She loved him, but he loved her more. That was all. There was nothing that could have been done, and she felt bad about it too.

But now she had Miles. And she was on a plane (finally, after airport security check delays in both Medford and San Francisco) to Vegas, in a daze, wondering how she had managed to throw together a wedding in three weeks' time. A long-distance wedding, no less. She had driven three hours to Eugene to find her dress: a long, cream-colored silk charmeuse sheath, simple but elegant. Simone, her maid of honor, was with her and picked out a similar dress in emerald green, in a larger cut to accommodate her four-month-along belly. Miles had gone online and picked out a chapel with an Elvis impersonator to perform the ceremony, which they figured would be fun. He had also booked five rooms at the Bellagio, one for them, one for Isaac and Simone, his father and mother (who agreed to share), one for Erica's father, and one for Caleb and Daisy. Erica was glad that they could all make it on such short notice.

The plane landed and she felt the butterflies again. She had felt them almost non-stop since she first saw Miles at the store. Every time he kissed her, every time he called, every time he said her name. Her phone bill for the past month had been absurd, and even at that it did not come close to the minutes on Miles' bill: over two thousand. They had a good laugh over that.

She called Andrew five days before she left. She felt tears form again (damn PMS) because he was so supportive, so positive. "I'm happy for you, Erica. You must really love him." Of course, she figured his reaction might not have been as pleasant were he not engaged himself. But it was affirming nonetheless. And she loved him for it. He was the father of her children and she would always care for him. His own proposal to her had lacked the romantic flair that Miles displayed, though, having said one night, "Are you opposed to the idea of marriage?" and she said, "No, not at all," and that was it. She had expected a little more from a writer, a creative person! But she had to cut him a little slack. He had proposed to her a month after she told him she was pregnant, after diffusing the shock of impregnating someone who had said that she couldn't have kids. He didn't feel tricked at the time (like she would have done that!); that notion came to him when they were separating. At first he had talked of Nathan as their "miracle baby," and thought he would be the only one. Then, shortly after his first birthday, she conceived Eileen and marched herself to the doctor to discover that her ovaries seemed to now be in fine working order. Rare, after having ovarian cysts, but possible.

The seatbelt unfastening announcement came on; she stood up and grabbed her purse, hoping that her suitcase with her dress in it would not be lost.

God, that would suck, she thought.

But nothing would spoil her weekend. And minutes later there was Miles, striding toward her, a bouquet of tiger lilies in his hand. She hadn't even told him that lilies were her favorite flowers.

"But, I graduated."

That's what Nathan had said in his flat tone when they told him that he would be going back to Stewart Elementary. It was one of those lucid moments that stunned them, not a memorized line from a video tape, not a garbled mess of incorrect pronoun usage and wrong verb conjugation. And he *had* graduated. They had a little ceremony in the classroom, complete with cardboard-and-paper tassel caps and rolled up diplomas and a cake with their names on it, when he finished Kindergarten six months ago. Erica had looked at Andrew from across his kitchen table, realizing that Nathan was expecting a response.

Think fast, she thought. *We don't want him thinking that he's being sent back, that he failed.*

Andrew spoke first. "You graduated from Kindergarten, Nate. Now you're in first grade, but you can still be in Sharon's class. Sharon's class has first grade, too."

Erica remembered how relieved she felt that Andrew had come up with that, and it seemed to satisfy Nathan, who walked back out to the living room without comment. It had been "decided" by the "committee" at the last weekly lunch meeting at Central (which Erica had been able to attend, having made arrangements for Eileen to stay at Kindergarten an extra twenty minutes) that due to Nathan's regression and the imminent stress on him due to Erica's upcoming move to L.A., that he would "feel more comfortable" in a familiar place. Erica believed that was a euphemism for the school just not wanting, nor knowing how, to handle a child with autism. But, she also believed they were right. Nathan was having his last day at Central that day, and then he would return to Stewart, and the grueling commute, after the two-week Christmas break.

And so Erica was packing, planning to leave in one week on Christmas Eve. Everyone she knew recoiled when she told them the actual day she was moving, but she explained that after she had spent the morning with her children, she would spend the evening with her brother's family in Weed, and then make the bulk of the nearly seven hundred mile drive on Christmas Day, when there would be no one on the road. It seemed like a good plan. At least that's what she told herself.

She also told herself that she had to do this. She had to do this or she would end up like Andrew had been, pulling out hair, peeling skin, and arranging chairs around the table all day long. Couldn't he see that? Maybe he could. He had not uttered one word of dissent, not made one disparaging remark about her decision, not created any hint of a guilt trip, and for that she was grateful, even loved him. If anything, he had been openly supportive. It did seem like he was better, more like the Andrew she had briefly been in love with. There were moments in recent years, yes, when she questioned her divorce: maybe she should have stayed with him? He did get better. But ever since she had fallen in love with Miles, she realized how much better he was for her, how much more alive she felt with him. Every day with Miles felt like an escalator ride up to the next level of a large department store. With Andrew it had felt like being in a long, snaking line in the grocery store, wishing you had chosen the line next to you that was moving faster.

She wrapped a glass candleholder in newspaper, a large cobalt votive holder that flared out at the top like an upside-down bell with long, serrated edges. It had been a wedding gift from Isaac and Simone, and she remembered the day with a pensive smile. How her father had told her that she looked beautiful right before walking her down the aisle, told her that he regretted so much that he wasn't around when she was growing up and that he wished he had been a better father and that he felt honored that she asked him to do this. And the sentiment from that exchange caught Erica by surprise; she hadn't intended on joining Miles at the front of the chapel with a tear-streaked face, "Love Me Tender" crooning over the speakers and a man in a sequined jumpsuit standing in front of them saying, "Dearly beloved, we are gathered here today to witness this man and this woman joined in holy matrimony." She had carried the bouquet of tiger lilies that Miles had given her at the airport the day before.

"Honey, stop that," Erica said to Eileen, turning around as she heard her kicking the boxes in the living room.

Erica shoved a stack of paperback books in another box and went over to pick up Eileen, who looked up at her with an angry, contorted face on the verge of crying.

"Don't move away, Mommy. I don't want you to go!"

Oh, God, Erica thought. *Why does everything I decide to do have to be so difficult? How can I go through with this?*

"Come here, sweetie," she said, sitting on the couch and cradling Eileen in her lap, who burst into tears and buried her face in Erica's chest.

Why is life so fucking hard?

"It'll be okay, I promise," she said, gulping, and then she couldn't say anymore so, silently crying, she rocked her daughter. She could think of nothing positive to tell her; there was no lemonade to be made from this lemon. What does "finishing college and getting a better job" mean to a five-year-old? How could she understand that her mother was moving away to provide a better future for her and her brother? Even if she were only gone for three or four years, it would seem like forever to them.

ERICA LOCKED THE front door and put the key in the "Key-per" rock provided by the landlord and set it to the left of the front steps, where he had requested she leave it. She peered in her front window at the studio apartment she had inhabited for over three years, where she had slept on the floor with her children, had sex on the floor with her boyfriends, dumped boiling water on the floor (and herself), lined up wooden blocks on the floor with Nathan when he was learning to spell, swept the floor with a broom because she couldn't afford to buy a vacuum cleaner and was too proud to borrow Andrew's. The floor could tell her story. How she had left an unhappy relationship, made a cocoon for herself there, loved her children fiercely, and tried to achieve her goals.

She sat in her old car a moment, staring at the dashboard, wondering, for a second, if it would even make it to L.A.

This is temporary. I'll finish school in a year, then work for a couple of years until I can go freelance and then I can move back here. I will not be away from them for too long.

She had spent the morning loading up her car, including a hard plastic cargo box strapped to the roof of it. Then she cleaned the studio (which didn't take too long). That was the easy part. Now it was time to say goodbye.

She had spent time with Isaac and Simone, who was now six months along, the night before, sharing a bottle of wine at the Italian place where Isaac worked. Simone, easily assimilating her role of expectant mother, sipped white grape juice. They toasted her move like it was an exciting adventure, perhaps trying to distract her from the part about leaving her children. Like skydiving with an instructor who can't get the chute to open but yells in your ear, "Look at this view, though!"

She pulled up to Andrew's house with a sense of dread, a brick in her stomach. She pulled out the gifts she had bought for Nathan and Eileen and walked to the door.

Eileen opened the door, announcing with excitement, "Mommy!" and the lump grew in Erica's throat. Then Eileen threw her arms around her and exclaimed, "Presents!" with the same enthusiasm.

Andrew's home smelled of the fresh noble fir he had cut down in the hills up behind Ashland, and the little white lights on it glowed steadily around the old ornaments she remembered from when they were married, most of them passed on from Elaine. He had taped Nathan's paper-plate snowman and Eileen's cotton-ball snowman on the living room wall, and stockings hung from a shelf with framed family photos along it, including Nathan and Eileen's first school pictures. Andrew got up from the couch and greeted her in a subdued but pleasant tone. She wondered if he hated her for moving and was just putting up a front.

Nathan entered the room without any greeting, as usual. Erica embraced him and handed them their gifts: a stuffed pug for Nathan and a stuffed orange and white tabby cat for Eileen. "It's Milo and Otis!" they said, hugging the main characters from their recent favorite movie. Then they unwrapped a hardcover picture book of *Peter Pan* and Erica sat on the couch with them and read it, trying to sound enthusiastic. It was the Disney version, so they recognized all of the characters from the movie, which they owned. Erica thought about all the videos her children watched on a daily basis, how watching them signified watching their lives. The videos had helped her children learn how to talk, how to live, even, especially in Nathan's case. He had progressed from no speech, to echolalic speech, to emerging independent speech, and also learned various types of social interaction along the way because of the videos. Of course most of it was all from fantasy worlds, but many times Erica felt that Nathan's autism had put them in some sort of a fantasy world, and she was just waiting for that story to end so they could start a new one. "Think of all the joy you'll find when you leave your world behind and bid your cares goodbye . . . you can fly!" she sang to Nathan and Eileen as they read about John, Michael, and Wendy flying out of their bedroom window.

When she had finished the book she stood and said she had to go. "I promise I'll see you very soon. You'll come and visit me in L.A. and see my new home." She looked at Andrew, who was standing close to her. "I think I should just leave and not drag this out," she said quietly.

"Okay," he said, and she hugged him. "Have a safe drive."

Then she knelt down and gave Nathan a squeeze, saying she had to go because she had a long drive. She looked at his blank face and wondered how much of this he comprehended. Probably more than she thought. She kissed his forehead, quickly telling him that she loved him; he was already squirming. But before she released him, before he darted away, he did manage to say "I love you" in his soft, flat voice. His beautiful voice. Part of her knew that he had learned to say that when they said "I love you" to him, that now it was something of a habit, but the fact that he could say it, and that she could hear it from him, mattered more.

Then Eileen, with wet eyes and a quivering little mouth, hugged her tight and said, "Mommy, I'll miss you."

Erica's throat tightened and she lectured herself. *Don't cry, don't you fucking cry now, you have to get out of here. Don't let her see you cry!*

Erica breathed in. "I'll miss you, too. But I'll see you soon, and I'll call you tomorrow on the phone. Big hug! I love you, honey!" And she stood up and she couldn't look at her baby. She just couldn't. "I gotta go," she said to

Andrew as she blinked away the tears.

"Bye," Andrew called as she walked briskly to her car, turning back to wave to Eileen when she was far enough away that Eileen couldn't see her face.

"Bye, Mommy," she called from the front door, waving her little hand and trying to smile.

My little angel, she's trying to smile for me. Oh, this is agony.

Erica drove off, wiping her face with her hand, and turned on the music: Siouxsie and the Banshees, her comfort music from high school. She tried to sing along to distract herself. "Dazzle! It's a glittering prize . . ."

She drove for about forty miles, her little old car laboring over the Siskiyou Pass, trying not to think, just singing along, listening to every note that she knew so well, and then pulled off at the Mount Shasta vista point, parked the car, covered her face and sobbed.

Twenty-one

She's gone. She's gone and I don't know what I'm going to do. I am now a full-time single parent. Oh, there's Brooke, but that's more like having a teenage daughter than a partner. She loves the kids, but she's also one of them. How could Erica do this? How could she leave? She was with Miles for a month! So impulsive! Who leaves their children? What mother leaves their children? I'm not looking forward to them crying about missing her. Somehow I don't think telling them "It's okay" is going to cut it.

Andrew wrapped a few last minute gifts in the bedroom and brought them out to put under the tree. It was after midnight; Brooke was watching TV, and he started to fill the stockings.

"I had fun at your aunt's house tonight. I'm glad it was her co-worker's kid who knocked over the big plant and not Nathan!"

"Yeah, but it wouldn't have been a big deal," Brooke said. She got up and turned off the TV. "He seems like he's feeling a lot more comfortable there." Nathan was also feeling more comfortable being back at Stewart Elementary, Andrew was pleased to note, and his transition had been problem-free. His regressive behaviors ceased, he talked more, and Andrew felt confident that sending him back had been the right decision.

"He is; I can tell." Andrew began stuffing miniature candy bars, small books, stuffed animals, and a new video in each of the stockings.

Brooke stretched. "Well, Erica's gone. How do you feel?"

"I'm fine. A little nervous, but fine."

"I'll help you out whenever you need it."

"Thanks. I just hope Eileen does okay at the Y." Andrew had to put Eileen in the YMCA's after school program, in which they would pick her up from Kindergarten and take her to the Y, so at least he wouldn't have to leave work to do that. But he would have to leave at 2:30 to pick her up there at 2:45, then be home by 3:00 to get Nathan off the bus. His father, doing volunteer work leading nature walks at Lithia Park to prepare for being a tour guide in Yellowstone, was no longer available to babysit, his mother was now enrolled at the college, and Andrew had to cut back to part-time so he could be home with the kids. He felt fortunate that Gloria had been so understanding and flexible to allow him to do that.

"She'll be fine," Brooke said, eating a piece of candy.

"Well, she has a lot of anxiety about new places."

"I'm sure she'll like it." Brooke crouched down by the presents under the tree and looked at the tags.

Andrew gathered up all the trash and walked to the kitchen to throw it away. "I'm more worried about finances than anything else. I'm so broke it's scary."

"Well, when my garnishments are over, I'll be able to help out more," Brooke said.

"Yeah, speaking of which, I really think you should take out a draw or something for your share of the bills. I've been paying my share plus half of yours for the past three months and I just can't cover it anymore, Brooke. Especially with Erica being gone now and I'm working part time because Nathan can't be in daycare."

"I said I would help as soon as I could!" Brooke stood up and put her hands on her hips. Her eyes, bloodshot from drinking at her aunt's Christmas Eve party, glanced defiantly at Andrew.

"It's not 'help,' Brooke. It's not extra. It's your share of responsibilities, and I can't continue to cover it until your garnishments are over. I mean, you've got three or four more months, right?"

"I don't know! Maybe six! I'm giving you all I have after the garnishments!" Brooke's voice rose.

"Well, it's not enough! You should take on a second job part-time," Andrew said.

"Okay, I'll start looking! I didn't think it was such a big deal."

Andrew noticed that her eyes weren't really focusing and she slurred some words. That didn't stop him. "It is! I make as much as you do, and I have two kids to raise, and I'm buying you new clothes because you don't have anything nice to wear for Christmas dinner tomorrow!"

"Well, if my wages weren't being garnished, I would have money to buy clothes!" Brook shot back.

"Well, if you had paid your bills, your wages wouldn't have been garnished."

Brooke exploded. "They were medical bills from when I was in the hospital! I didn't have enough money to pay them!"

"You just pay a little at a time, instead of not paying anything. You set up a payment plan. Now you have to pay double what you originally owed because of the fees!"

"Well, I didn't! Nothing I can do about it now! And just don't buy me anything!"

"I already did. At least you could be appreciative."

"I don't care about the fucking clothes now!" Brooke, in a stupor, stumbled into the bedroom and came out wild-eyed a moment later with a new beige linen dress. "See this dress?!" She tore it in half down the back. "That's what I think of the dress!"

Andrew, infuriated, lowered his voice almost to a hiss. "Stop it right now, Brooke. Just stop it. My God. It's Christmas Eve. Look at what you just did. I can't believe your immaturity. It's ruined now."

"Good. Because I never want to wear it." She stormed off to the bedroom and shut the door.

Andrew sunk into the couch. It was almost one in the morning. He stared at the tree, the white lights glowing like headlights on the freeway, coming at him.

Fuck. Now I have to sleep on the couch.

ANDREW WAS RIGHT. Within a week he had found Eileen crying by herself in her room, and "I miss Mom!" was the mantra of the month. He found himself writing in his journal more often than usual.

How could she do this to me? To them? This wasn't how it was supposed to be. It's bad enough she didn't want to be married to me, then she leaves me with heartbroken kids I have to raise alone. All of our acquaintances say "she'll be back" as some sort of consolation to me, like they can't wait to good-naturedly chide her for moving back, like they know her so well to assume that she would. But I know. She won't be back.

Andrew wound his way down from the Siskiyou Pass, with its bare pavement, a bit of luck for January. Erica had been gone a month, and he was taking the kids to visit her for four days. They had agreed to meet at the junction of I-5 and Highway 12, just north of Stockton in central California, which was about the half-way point. Andrew would drive five and a half hours, eat lunch and drink lots of Dr. Pepper, then turn around and drive five and a half hours home. But he would have a few days to himself, and he planned on snowboarding one of those days. It would be his first day of the season so he would be too rusty to attempt the Bowl, but by Spring Break, when the kids would be with Erica again, he thought he might be ready to try it finally. It was a minor goal, but one he'd wanted to achieve for a long time. He felt a little wave of excitement as he visualized himself going over the edge and heading down. It was an anticipated thrill, like waking up during childhood on a day his family had planned to go to Disneyland.

His own kids had such trouble falling asleep the night before from the excitement of getting to see Erica. But that was a good thing. The rest of the time, they'd have trouble falling asleep because they missed her. "I miss Mom!" Andrew heard ten times a day. A few days after she left, he had started singing "The Happy Dream Song" when tucking them in bed every night, since Eileen had begun complaining about nightmares. Completely off the top of his head, he'd come up with his own catchy little tune to which he sang, "And Eileen will have happy dreams about—" and he would pause long enough for her to say "Mom!" and then he would sing, "And Nathan will have happy dreams about—" and pause for Nathan to say "Mom" in his stoic voice. Then Andrew resumed the song by singing their itinerary for the next day: "And tomorrow you'll go to school. And then you'll come home on the bus, and then you can have a snack. And then you can watch a video, and then it will be time for dinner. And then it will be time for a bath, and then it will be time to brush teeth. And then we'll read some books, and then it will be time to go to bed. And I'll sing you 'The Happy Dream Song' again!"

And so went the first month. But they were surviving! Nathan was still doing well back at Stewart. He seemed even happier in spite of the fact that his mother was gone. Andrew wondered if Nathan had relaxed because now there wasn't the daily shuttling back and forth between his and Erica's homes. He surmised that Nathan felt more settled than he had in a long time. And Eileen actually liked the Y! The instructor said that she fit right in and wasn't showing any signs of the previous anxiety problems that Andrew feared. It was such a relief. He wondered if Eileen somehow realized that it wouldn't do any good to sulk because Mom wasn't there to sit with her at circle time or come and pick her up from school when she cried at the door. Whatever the case, it was one less thing for Andrew to deal with. And he had plenty to deal with concerning finances. He'd lost a fourth of his income by going to part-time, and he gained the expense of Eileen's daycare, plus two more days a week of feeding the kids than he'd had before. And with Erica not working yet, he wasn't receiving any child support. He was still having to carry some of Brooke's weight, plus his car payment. He was stressed.

Eileen announced, "My feet are tickling, Dad." It was her way of saying she was carsick.

"Okay, hold your bucket. Nathan, can you get the bucket for her?"

Nathan didn't respond verbally, but Andrew was aware of him leaning over to pick it up and hand it to his sister. He could certainly follow directions when he was motivated! Andrew knew that Nathan wouldn't want Eileen throwing up all over the seat.

She barely made it. "I got some on my pants, Dad."

"That's okay. I'll stop as soon as I can, honey."

He pulled into the next rest stop, cleaned her up and the seat. Nathan held his nose. "Why you throw up?" he said to Eileen.

"Sometimes people get carsick, Nathan," Andrew said. "It's an accident. That's why I tell you guys to watch the road. If you can see it, that will help you not to get sick." He had a feeling that Nathan would be reminding Eileen to watch the road every five minutes the rest of the trip. They seemed to have a good connection, and even before Nathan began developing some verbal skills, he and his sister had their own way of communicating. And now that he could talk a bit, the perfectionist in him loved to correct her, especially since she was still receiving speech therapy for her own language delay and problems with phonetics. One night at dinner, Andrew had served their turkey burgers on whole wheat buns, and Eileen asked, "Dad, what is this fred?" Andrew said, "It's a bun." "There are bun freds?" she asked. Nathan immediately interjected, "Not 'freds,' BREADS. Not an F, a B." Andrew had turned his face away, chuckling to the wall.

It was raining when they got back on the road. Andrew had gotten them up at seven, fed them cereal for breakfast, cleaned them up, got them dressed, finished packing last minute things like toothbrushes, pajamas, favorite stuffed animals. Then he cut and cored two apples and packed a bag of snacks for all of them.

"How much longer?" Eileen whined.

And so it begins, Andrew thought. "A couple more hours. Here, I'll put on the *Little Mermaid* CD."

The rest of the trip did not feature as many curves in the road, which they all appreciated. Nonetheless, as soon as they pulled into the parking lot at the meeting point, Eileen vomited again.

"I'm sorry you don't feel good, honey," Andrew said, cleaning her up again, "but pretty soon you'll see Mom!"

They got out in front of a McDonald's and stretched their legs while Andrew called Erica. She had passed the junction a little while ago, so he told her where they were, and she would get off the freeway as soon as she could to turn around. She arrived fifteen minutes later and Eileen ran to her. Even Nathan solicited a hug.

"I missed you guys so much!" she said, holding them to her. Andrew could tell she was fighting back tears.

They went inside to eat, and she talked about her classes, how everything was going, assuring him that she would get a job as soon as the kids went back. Andrew told her again how well the kids were doing (they talked a few times a week on the phone), and didn't mention finding Eileen crying. He didn't want Erica to hurt any more than he knew she did.

Then he helped load the kids in her car, which was Miles' green Jeep Cherokee, and kissed them goodbye. A moment later, he watched Erica get in the turning lane for I-5 South as he turned onto the onramp for I-5 North. His eyes began to water as he realized that this was the first of many times that he would say goodbye to his children and drive home without them.

IT WAS NATHAN and Eileen's last night with her, and Erica was glad for the relief from her own nights of sobbing, of wishing that the kids could live with her, of missing them like she would miss her arms. But she was beginning to realize how unrealistic having them live with her would be, especially with her in school. She and Miles were in a one-bedroom apartment and couldn't afford a bigger place until she started working. But at least they were with her for a short while. Now when she talked to them on the phone, they could visualize where she lived.

It was a small but open, airy third-floor apartment in a brick building built in the 1930s, located at the base of the hill on which Griffith Park Observatory was located. The apartment had nine-foot ceilings edged in the original crown molding, painted in shiny ivory, as were the walls. The living room, hallway, and bedroom had orange shag carpeting that should have been replaced two decades ago; Erica was just glad it wasn't avocado green. The best part, though, was the east-facing wall of windows in the living room which flooded most of the apartment with brilliant light. Erica had begun collecting plants and enjoyed the soothing tropical feel they gave the room. She had African violets, aloe vera, bamboo stalks, spider plants, a cactus, a miniature palm, and large, leafy plants whose names she couldn't remember. They helped to camouflage the signs of city life, the sounds of strangers passing by below them, walking, driving, talking, yelling. The smells of dumpsters nearing trash day, vehicle exhaust, the neighbors fried onions. Concrete, metal, glass, asphalt all around. Telephone poles and wires. Billboards advertising beer that will make you look sexy, upcoming movies, the hottest new hotel in Las Vegas, and abortion hotlines. It was a different world from southern Oregon. She hoped that Nathan and Eileen could adjust to it.

She wondered if they would think about the sirens and car alarms constantly blaring, the freeway traffic so bad it was like sitting in a parking lot, the smoggy sky that never allowed any stars to penetrate it. She wondered if it bothered them to sleep in the walk-in closet in the hallway that she had set up as their "bedroom." She wondered if they would like anything about visiting L.A., living with her. Oh, there was the zoo, and Disneyland, but you couldn't do that every day. In the summer they could go to the beach. Erica hoped they would like that as much as she always had.

She boiled some hot dogs in a pot for Nathan and Eileen and stirred the pasta that would be Miles' and her dinner. From the living room (which was just around the corner) she could hear Nathan trying to sing "The Bare Necessities" from the video of Disney's *The Jungle Book* that he and Eileen were watching and was reminded again of the parallel between their lives and the videos the kids watched. She thought about the necessity of love and that it was all she could offer them now. Love and phone calls.

Erica heard Miles enter the room and sigh and say in a chiding tone, "Another video? You guys watch too many videos."

She stuck her head around the corner and reminded Miles that it had been raining that afternoon, and they had already painted pictures and read books, and what else were they going to do?

She pulled the hot dogs out of the water with a fork and put them in the buns and got the bag of mini carrots out of the refrigerator. Miles had been on edge for the last three days. She knew he cared about her children and meant well, but he couldn't be a full-time parent, and she realized that now. There was a reason why he never had kids. He needed a lot of space, both physical and emotional, and time for himself. He would quickly grow to resent them, and her, if they were there full-time. Nathan seemed to be improving again at the STEPS program back at Stewart, and Eileen seemed fine, so having them stay in Oregon most of the time would work out better. Summer would be a challenge, because she wanted them for at least six weeks. She would just have to remind Miles that it was temporary and give him plenty of space and free time, and not put too many demands on him. It would be okay. And, she hoped, they would be in a bigger place by then.

She called the kids to the table and placed their plates in front of them. "Well, guys, tonight is your last dinner here until the next time you visit. Tomorrow we get up in the morning and drive back to Oregon."

"Aw, we like it here," Eileen said before she bit into her hot dog.

Erica's heart leaped. Did she dare hope that they felt comfortable here after all? She wanted to believe that somehow their fragile minds could look past the strange environment and see only her love for them, burning bright as the sun usually did through her living room windows.

"DUDE, IT'S GOT a bunch of old '80s stuff on it I downloaded that I know you'll like," Gavin told Andrew as he handed him a computer-recorded CD. Andrew had come to accept Gavin as what he called a novelty friend. He didn't have any other friends aside from his siblings and Brooke, and he found that unhealthy, inadequate. Gavin was shiftless and slobby, but Andrew liked his creative mind that came up with unusual ideas for books, including disease-ridden, apocalyptic island settings and murder mysteries with intricate plot twists. They were just ideas, but it was an escape of sorts to listen to Gavin's exuberant ramblings, and Andrew figured it was good to have a male friend, whatever the source.

"Thanks, man."

"Yeah, happy birthday. How have things been going?"

Gavin had called him about ten minutes before to tell him that he'd burned him a CD for his birthday (his thirty-first), and Andrew said he'd run by and pick it up since he was on his way to the grocery store anyway. Brooke, who had the night off, stayed home with the kids. Andrew could tell by looking at him that Gavin was high on either coke or speed. His jaw was set and he chewed the inside of his mouth. He was also wide-eyed and evasive and talked fast. Andrew had been around him enough to know.

"Things are okay, but I don't know about Brooke. I know she's been your good friend for a long time, but lately she's been verbally abusive, showing signs of being violent. She tore her clothes, threw a boot into the wall, screamed obscenities in my face . . ."

"I've been talking with her about that. She's going to go to anger management classes, Andrew. She really loves you and the kids," Gavin said, rocking from his heels to his toes, chewing his lip.

"I know she does, but I can't help but think about the fact that even when Erica and I were at our worst, going through our separation, even then she was never verbally abusive like Brooke is."

"Yeah, but Erica sure had problems with the concept of fidelity," Gavin said, looking at the ground.

"I know about Nick. She was sleeping with both of us at the same time near the end. I've dealt with that."

"I'm talking about before that. I hate to tell you the bad news, but there's something you should know, Andrew. I think it was like in '95 or something, Erica had an affair with Isaac and got pregnant. Simone took her to have an abortion . . ."

Andrew felt his blood go cold as Gavin's voice faded. His knees felt weak and his heart started racing. "I've got to get going," he said in a hollow voice. He turned around and walked out the door, ignoring Gavin calling him. In shock, he drove to Safeway, his breath quickening.

She slept with Isaac. She was pregnant and had an abortion! What if it was mine? Oh god oh god oh god. How could she have done that?!

He parked the car and got out, not remembering what he needed at the store, trying to calm himself from the rage that filled him. His ears were ringing as he wrenched a cart out of the stall and began pushing it around aimlessly. He felt a bizarre combination of anger and sadness that he finally identified as betrayal. Even when he'd found out about Nick, he didn't feel this way. *Nick was nothing compared to this. This is—*

Fuck grocery shopping! What the hell am I doing?!

He wanted to shout out to all the patrons, "Ever been cheated on badly and not find out about it until seven years later? Ever feel like a fool?" All the "hikes." All the "working late." All the "I need to go to the library to write my paper." How trusting he was! How blind! He always believed her, never doubted her. Always defended her.

Andrew, adrenaline-addled, managed to pick out a few essentials—milk, bread, lettuce—went through the check stand, got back in the car and drove home in a daze. So many thoughts flooded his mind. No wonder when they were married she never wanted him to go to Gavin and Simone's house. No wonder sometimes after being gone on a four-hour hike, her clothes and even her socks were perfectly clean. No wonder she had flinched when he told her that Isaac had approached him at Dogma and he'd wondered aloud how Isaac would have remembered him. No wonder. It was like he could finally see the huge, shaggy grizzly bear that had been sitting in the center of the room all along.

When he got home, he glanced at the kids watching a movie and walked straight to the kitchen to put the food away, where he found Brooke near the phone.

"Did Gavin call you?" he demanded.

"Andrew, I'm so sorry. I never knew. Honestly, I never knew." Brooke looked at him with sympathetic eyes.

Andrew found it hard to believe her, but wanted to. "I just feel so fucking betrayed. How could she do that to me?!" He slammed the milk in the refrigerator.

"I don't know, babe. That really sucks."

She tried to give him a hug, but he shrugged her off, muttering, "I have to get the kids in bed."

He walked out to the living room, shut off the TV, and went through the motions of getting his children ready for bed, trying to sound cheerful but ending up sounding so fake that he wanted to laugh at himself. He brushed their teeth, got their pajamas on, set out their clothes for school the next day, put them in bed and rushed through "The Happy Dream Song." He cringed inside as they both said "Mom" when he prompted them, not wanting to disrupt their routine.

Then, feeling overwhelmed, he went out to the laundry room and shut the door. He punched the old, thin wall of the room until his fist broke through. The anger, the grief, finally took over and he began to sob.

"Why? Why did you *do* that?!" he cried.

Brooke found him then. She put her arms around him and held him, sat with him there on the wooden floor of the laundry room. "It's okay," she said softly. "It's okay."

Twenty-two

rica sat at the computer desk in the bedroom she shared with Miles. She had photocopied and reduced an old pen-and-ink stylized drawing of a spiral shell she had done years ago and was scanning it into the computer for a project for her Advertising Design class, her favorite of the six she was taking at Cal State Long Beach, and the most useful, she thought. She was using the shell to design the logo on a brochure for a fictitious natural history museum. Erica had not attended college full-time before, so it was a bit of a challenge to get used to sitting in class so much and having multiple projects to do at the same time. But she wasn't working yet, so that helped with the transition, leaving her more time to focus on school; she was determined to finish as quickly as possible. Erica was glad to find that she didn't feel too comfortable at the sprawling, urban campus of Long Beach, and she figured that would motivate her to graduate sooner.

She had drawn the original shell ten years ago, and looking at it reminded her how different her existence had become, how many cars had crossed the intersection of life since then. She had been living with her mother, who was single again, when she painted that shell, and was taking her first college art class. And she got her first bartending job at the local pub that her mother frequented, much to her embarrassment. Caleb was in high school, focused on Daisy. They were fifteen and already talking about moving in together. It seemed like a lifetime ago. Now, they had recently had their second child—another boy, named Liam. Erica had rocked him when she visited them at Christmas. He was a colicky baby, reminding her of Eileen.

She almost didn't pick up the phone. Something was telling her not to, but she did anyway.

She heard Andrew's voice, low and angry. "I know about you and Isaac. And you kept me in the dark for almost seven years, making a fool of me. I worked so hard to get to a positive level with you, and be your friend, and helped you whenever you needed it, and defended you whenever anyone said anything bad about you, and someone just got tired of hearing poor Andrew defending his cheating ex-wife and finally told me the truth. You had an abortion, Erica! When we were married! It could have been mine!"

Nausea overcame Erica. Her heart beat faster; one of the things she feared the most had happened.

Oh god oh no oh fuckfuckfuck. Simone would never have told him. Not Isaac. It must have been Gavin. Oh shit, this is bad. This was not supposed to happen.

"I'm sorry, Andrew, but it wasn't yours. It happened during a time when we didn't have sex for over a month. We were all sick, and I was working late a lot—"

"Yeah! You were 'working late!'"

"I'm sorry, Andrew. I can understand your anger, and all I can do is apologize."

"Someday this pain will subside and I'll be able to talk to you without feeling like my insides have been ripped out. But that's a long ways away, Erica. I can't even talk to you now," Andrew hissed and hung up.

Erica punched the bed several times, then shoved her face in her pillow and cried.

Okay! I made a mistake seven years ago! Does it have to haunt me for the rest of my life? Am I such a horrible person? God damn it. Fucking Gavin. Fucking tweeker. Years of work rebuilding a friendship—all down the drain. God, he better not freak out and keep the kids from me!

Erica looked up and took a breath. "I'm sorry, Andrew!" she yelled at the ceiling. "I'm sorry!"

DUE TO THE fall-out from Gavin's bomb, Andrew had become some overnight Ashland celebrity. The phone rang day and night with every minor acquaintance wanting to know the sordid details of his ex-wife's affair and abortion. "How did you find out? When did it happen? Who was the father? Was it maybe yours? Have you talked to Erica yet? What are you going to do?" they all wanted to know. With Brooke working at Dogma, it seemed the whole town knew in the space of one hour. The top story.

No one had said anything helpful or supportive, other than Brooke that first night. His mother had said, of all things, "How could you be so surprised? I tried to tell you I thought she was having an affair." It was true. She had tried to tell him twice, seven years ago, that she had run into Erica around town with her arm around some other guy, desperately trying not to catch Elaine's eye. Of course it was probably Isaac. At the time Andrew had told his mother he was sure it was "just a friend." Maybe his mother had never experienced blind love. She was never blind to his father's idiosyncrasies, but then, he never cheated on her. She had the luxury of a loyal, albeit absent, spouse. Of course, Andrew always believed he had a loyal spouse, too. His father, when told of Erica's affair, had said, "Well, she better start paying child support soon," as if that had any bearing on the issue of infidelity.

Andrew pulled into the YMCA parking lot after getting off work to pick up Eileen. Last week when he entered the classroom to get her, she took his hand and brought him over to meet Connor, a little blond boy she had been calling her "boyfriend" for a few weeks. Very properly, with excitement in her voice, she said, "Connor, this is my dad. Dad, this is Connor." Andrew smiled and said, "Hi, Connor. I'm glad to meet you," and bent down to his level. He was seated at a table, drawing, and did not look up. He did not acknowledge Andrew or Eileen. Andrew saw her poor little face fall as she turned and said, "C'mon, Dad, let's go." Maybe Connor was just shy, but Andrew didn't think too much of him for being the first boy to hurt his daughter.

She was fine, though. The next day she came home talking about Connor again. *So quick to forgive,* Andrew thought. It had been two weeks and he still couldn't talk to Erica. She had called within a week of the confrontation, and after he'd said, "Hello?" she rapidly spit out, "I just called to talk to the kids," and he'd handed the phone to Eileen and said, "It's your mom."

He was still processing things. Remembering things. He'd be washing dishes and suddenly remember another night that she came home later than she should have, smelling differently. Not the usual bar smell on her clothes, on her skin, even after she'd showered. He figured out that his birthday had fallen right around the time when she was having the affair with Isaac. After the kids were in bed he'd lit a rare fire in the fireplace and arranged lots of pillows in front of it, put some sexy music on. She got home from work and flopped down on the floor with him and listened while he described an elaborate sex-on-the-beach fantasy for her, and then she got up and said she was "really tired" and wanted to go to bed. She wouldn't even make love to him on his birthday. He wondered now if it was because she had left work early and already made love to someone else.

The memories plagued him. He didn't want to remember any more. What he knew already was enough. Acquaintances called, telling him they knew of other affairs she'd had. He really didn't want to know. He didn't have the strength for it. It was such a game to them, and that disgusted him. Were they that insensitive?

This is my life! he'd wanted to yell at them. *Not your fucking soap opera.*

Andrew ran up the steps at the front of the Y, and at the top of them, he ran into Jonah, who said he was going to do some swimming.

"How are you doing, man?" Jonah said, looking concerned. "I heard about Erica's affair with Isaac."

"Yeah, everyone has."

"One slip in a small town and everyone knows. Man, you're not the only one. There was one night I'm pretty sure Erica cheated on me, too, also with Isaac. She's got some strong connection with him."

Andrew wondered if that was supposed to make him feel better, the possibility that she'd also cheated on Jonah. He wasn't married to her. He didn't have two children with her. How could Jonah possibly compare his alleged experience to Andrew's?

Jonah continued, "And now she's married to his brother. Pretty twisted."

"Yeah. It is." He recalled the night at Dogma that Isaac had introduced Miles to him, the secretive, knowing look that had passed between the brothers. Andrew seethed as he realized that Isaac had spent the past six years going out of his way to approach him, introducing him to people as his "good friend," instead of having the respect to keep his distance. Every time he thought of Isaac now, Andrew envisioned curb-stomping his head, beating him down without mercy, without remorse. Rage consumed him like a choppy, swollen river, its damage uncontrollable, unchecked.

NATHAN WAS ALWAYS the first one in the household to change the calendars on the morning of the first day of a new month, without fail. Andrew had noticed that, for the first two weeks of December, Nathan had seemed anxious whenever Andrew showed him something on the calendar, even though he was excited about Christmas coming. Andrew had thought it was because he was anticipating Erica's move. Then, mid-month, Andrew brought home a 2002 calendar and showed it to Nathan. Instantly his face lit up and he said, "Now we have a calendar for January!" He had been anxious because there was nothing for him to visually refer to after December for coming events.

He then told Andrew on which calendar days to write "No school," from a list he had memorized all the way through June. At that moment, Andrew had a brainstorm.

I'll move closer to Stewart! Then Nathan won't have to get up so early to commute, and I can probably find a better-paying job in Medford.

And he could get out of the rumor-ridden, back-stabbing, incestuous circle of acquaintances by which he'd found himself surrounded.

After noting Nathan's days off, Andrew set him up with a video, looked in on Eileen, playing with her dollhouse from Christmas, and went in his room to look at the classifieds online. His excitement grew. This was a great idea! Why hadn't he thought of it before? Why was it so important for his children to go to school in Ashland? To grow up in Ashland? Why should that have mattered?

He felt liberated as he turned on his computer, like he'd broken out of some mold, a vise. His line of thinking had been too restrictive, and he finally realized it. But within minutes his elation began to subside when he discovered that the average rent for a two-bedroom place near Stewart Elementary was just as high as it was in Ashland. He had hoped to find something he could afford on his own, what with Brooke's latest blowout.

She took him out to dinner the weekend after his birthday, which was enjoyable, but then she discovered that she had locked her set of keys in his car because she had driven that night. It might not have been so bad if she had not done that just the week before at Wal-Mart when she'd borrowed his car, and the week before that at Gavin's house, which exasperated Andrew to no end. In retrospect, he was sure it didn't help matters to tell her that she was irresponsible, as they stood in the rain in the bank parking lot in the middle of downtown Ashland. "I'm a little ADD!" she shot back at him.

You're a little bit of a stoner, as well, Andrew thought. *All your trips to Gavin's house for "salad." Your nightly excuse, "It helps me relax from a busy night at work!" Couldn't be that affecting your brain, could it? Get stoned and watch TV every night. What are you doing with your life?*

"How many times is it going to take, Brooke? Who's going to walk home to get the spare key this time?"

"I'll ask someone at Dogma to give me a ride home! That's what friends do!"

"You're so dependent on other people to bail you out! Don't you feel bad about bothering them?"

The argument escalated to Brooke accusing him of being perfect and never locking the keys in the car, to him reminding her that she had done it three times in as many weeks, to her screaming that he must think she did it on purpose, to him suggesting that she must be so embarrassed, to her jamming her middle finger in his face with the accompanying verbal insult.

It was then that Andrew remembered that he had his set of keys in his pocket. In retrospect, he could see why that made her angrier, but he was glad that he had made his point first: She was negligent and it was at other peoples' expense. It happened all too often and he was tired of it. He could easily not have had his keys on him since he didn't drive.

He'd spoken calmly as he opened the driver's door and got in, then unlocked her door and said, "Come on, get in. Let's go home."

His calmness seemed to infuriate her further; she yelled that she wasn't getting in the car with him, called him an asshole, and stormed back across the street in the direction of Dogma, where they'd had dinner. He called after her, telling her she was being ridiculous, and suggesting they just go home and talk about it at home.

"Fuck you!"

So Andrew drove home without her. What was he supposed to do, drive around the block all night playing this stupid game with her? Continue to encourage her scene?

She ended up getting a co-worker who was just getting off work to give her a ride home and came crashing through the door about fifteen minutes later, knocking over a lamp and shouting, accusing him of leaving her downtown.

"You refused to get in the car!"

"Why would I want to ride with you? I don't even know why I bothered to pay for dinner anyway. Not like I thought I might get laid tonight for a change!"

Andrew thought it best to ignore the remark, not wanting to rile her up worse and wake the kids. And he was relieved that his mother had left quickly, even though he'd had to lie about Brooke's absence. He refrained from pointing out to Brooke that most nights she passed out on the couch in front of the TV. It tended to put a damper on their sex life.

Somehow he got her quiet and into the bedroom. He just couldn't have the kids waking up, and that was the only way to prevent it. Sometimes damage control was harder to do with Brooke than it was with Nathan.

And with Nathan happy back at Stewart, Andrew had fewer problem episodes to deal with. He knew he should move, but he didn't know if he could afford to on his own, now that he'd gone online and researched the rent situation. Discouraged, he leaned his head on one bent arm and reclined at his desk.

The phone rang and it was Brooke, calling from work, asking what he was doing. After he told her, she asked in a meek voice, "Will that include me?"

"Well, Brooke, that all depends on your ability to manage your anger and communicate better. At this point, I honestly don't know."

"I'm going to anger management classes, I promise. I really want to be a part of your life, and a part of your family. Can you please give me another chance?"

"We'll see. I'm not making any promises. I have to figure out what I need to do."

"Okay. Well, I have to get back to work," Brooke said. She paused before tentatively continuing. "I love you."

Andrew sighed. "I love you, too." *That's what's making this so hard.*

Twenty-three

*O*nce upon a time there was a hard-working, well-meaning girl who was married to a responsible, intelligent guy, and they had two beautiful children. But the beautiful children had developmental delays and the responsible, intelligent guy stayed home to take care of them, and he became depressed and developed obsessive-compulsive disorder. And the hard-working, well-meaning girl tried for so long to be positive for both of them. And at last she grew to resent him and couldn't handle the darkness he projected. And she found solace at work in the company of a handsome, lively guy, and that brought her some happiness, some relief, during a negative time.

And because condoms slip off, unplanned pregnancies occur. And because no one wants a scandal in a small town, nor an unexpected mouth to put on food stamps, handsome, lively guys pay for abortions.

Erica had been dwelling on the past far more than she liked to. She was all about learning from mistakes and moving on. But this had plagued her. It plagued her when she lived through it, and it plagued her now. Who plans an affair? Maybe some people do, but she didn't. How many people can really say, 'I would never do that'? How many people know what it's like to work your ass off and come home night after night to a sullen, despondent spouse who glares at you when you say you're glad to be home? And pretty soon you're not glad to be home and you put off going home because it's so terrible. And there's someone fun and upbeat at work who makes you laugh and expresses an interest in you. Who can say that they wouldn't prefer the company of that person over the other? At least for a short while, to feel alive again?

People are so quick to judge. Like I felt good about having the affair. Like I enjoyed the guilt. Like I still do. I needed a lifeline, okay? I was weak and stressed and vulnerable. I did not have the strength to resist Isaac. I know that doesn't make it okay. But that's what happened.

Erica was grateful for Miles' support. He had known about everything years ago; Isaac had told him. When he had come home from work the day that Andrew had called her and confronted her, he held her as she cried. "It will be all right. Andrew will work through it. He's not going to keep the kids from you."

And he didn't. But when she had gone three days ago to pick up the kids at the McDonald's half-way point for Spring Break, Andrew had been icy. He talked to her, exchanged necessary words with her and was even civil, but he would not look at her. He looked at the table, the ground, or over her shoulder when they talked. Probably he needed more time, she realized. That's the way it had always been with him, mentally processing something like a grist mill. She could wait. She'd always had to wait for him to do anything if he had to get used to it first.

But the kids were with her again, and that was comforting. She could hear them playing in the closet while she got breakfast ready. That was always the easy meal: cold cereal and milk. Not only was the preparation easy, but because both kids, especially Eileen, were such picky eaters at other times, it was a relief to have one meal that they would just sit down to and eat. Dinner every night was a showdown. Miles couldn't stand the fact that they wouldn't try any new food. Every single dinner had him coaxing Eileen into eating something she didn't want to eat, trying to reason with her, even bribing her. Nothing worked on that stubborn child, and one time Miles actually stormed off to the bedroom because he was so frustrated.

She thought about the plans for the day. They were going to the Natural History Museum, which she knew Nathan would enjoy. He had developed a keen interest in dinosaurs, and an obsession with weather, storms, and natural disasters of all kinds, prompted by the movie *Twister*, which Andrew had let him watch. It was a good thing, though. It gave Nathan topics for conversation, which was an emerging skill for him. He realized that one way to talk to people was to ask them a question, only he asked them questions to which he already knew the answer. "What's a twister?" he would say, and some people (relatives he hadn't seen in a while, friends of the family) would begin to tell him, thinking he'd asked because he didn't know. Erica wondered if he just liked to hear what other people said, or if he felt like he was making a connection with them because he'd said something and they responded. Who knew? Yesterday he'd asked Miles, "What's an apple?" to which Miles retorted, "You know what an apple is!" Nathan said, "No. I don't." Miles said, "Yes, you do, and I'm not going to tell you," and walked out of the room. Maybe Nathan was actually wondering how apples grew, or something else about apples, but he didn't know how to formulate any other questions. At least he was trying. He was seven and a half, and he was finally talking. Erica, relieved at his progress, remembered how he had regressed just six months earlier, how powerless she had felt not knowing what to do, especially knowing that her move would probably exacerbate it. But Nathan was fine back at Stewart Elementary, and Eileen was adjusting even better than they'd hoped, so Erica felt validated. Her move had been successful, or at least tolerable. She had just finished her first full term and would start the next in about a week, after she took the kids back to Oregon. It would be her first visit back since the move, and she would be staying with Simone and Isaac and their new baby, Sadie. Simone had had a Caesarian after a long, problematic labor, but Sadie was healthy and Simone was recovering and Isaac was in love with both of them. And, regardless of the past, they were Erica's closest friends, family really, and they always would be.

"Come and eat breakfast!" Erica called, and the kids came out, hair standing up on one side, sleep in their eyes. She kissed the tops of their heads good morning and went to start making her own breakfast. Miles was at a yoga class, which he attended every Saturday morning.

"Mom!" Eileen said, wide-eyed. "I forgot to look under my pillow!" She got out of her chair and ran back to the closet.

Last night they'd had pizza for dinner (another easy meal), and Eileen had lost a tooth. She washed it and put in a plastic zipper-sealed bag under her pillow. It was not her first, but it was the first time that Erica got to play tooth fairy, which was a fun rite of passage. She waited until she heard their slow, rhythmic breathing, then reached in (over Nathan, since they slept right next to each other) pulled out the bag with the tooth, and slid two dollars under the pillow. What to do with the tooth? She knew people who actually saved all of their children's teeth in little glass baby food jars. Well, she wasn't going to do that, but she wasn't ready to throw this one away yet. It was so cute, and it reminded her of her own teeth coming out when she was a kid. The tooth fairy rarely came to her house, but she liked looking at her self-extracted teeth, with the sharp top edges and the redness inside. She stuffed Eileen's tooth in the back of one of her dresser drawers and decided to deal with it some other time.

"Two dollars, Mom! I got two dollars!" Eileen came around the corner waving them.

"Wow, that's great!"

"The tooth fairy in Oregon only gives one dollar!"

Oops.

PHOENIX, OREGON WAS probably the polar opposite of Phoenix, Arizona. To Andrew, the name of the small town he ended up moving to was almost uncanny; it was beyond a doubt a fresh start for him, a proverbial rising from the ashes like the mythical bird.

In an effort to get as close as possible to Stewart Elementary, Andrew found himself in Phoenix, a small city of under five thousand people that required most residents to have a post office box because most homes did not have mail receptacles. It was the type of town in which you didn't dare yell at someone who accidentally cut you off in the grocery store parking lot because she could easily turn out to be your child's teacher, or your neighbor.

Andrew did not realize before moving to Phoenix that even though it was close to Medford, it was not part of the school district for Stewart. It was part of its own little district with Talent, another neighboring small town. Nathan could still have been classified as a transfer to be able to remain at Stewart, as he had been while living in Ashland, but his teacher said that he was doing so well that she recommended mainstreaming with a support aid. Andrew was very nervous, what with their last attempt at mainstreaming being sorely unsuccessful. But he called the small district office's special education coordinator, was impressed with her demeanor, and decided to go to the meeting to discuss Nathan's transition and hope for the best. He recalled some of the New Age meditation programs he had worked with while going through his divorce, especially the one called *Positive Thinking*, which had subliminal messages like "All that I seek is seeking me" and "Positive solutions abound." He also recalled what Erica had said when they had tried altering Nathan's diet: "I'll try anything." He'd read that it was a common refrain of many parents of autistic children. A battle cry.

And the meeting went better than he could have dreamed. He was so affected by the combination of professionalism (They knew what they were talking about! And the meeting lasted only one hour!) and empathy (indicating genuine concern and interest about Nathan's individual needs instead of rolling their eyes), that he knew he was in the right place, that even though it was an accident of sorts, he had been meant to move to Phoenix. They even provided a printed map of the school when Andrew suggested it would help Nathan prepare for the transition in the fall. Central Elementary did not have a map. They didn't even have a fence! No visible boundaries. No wonder Nathan had felt so out of control there.

They moved into a two-story, two-bedroom duplex with a large side yard on a cul-de-sac with several kids, which was beneficial for Nathan's socialization needs. It was a simple side-by-side rental with humble wood siding painted glossy white and royal blue trim around the windows and front door. In spite of the requisite whiteness, both inside and out, Andrew somehow felt comfortable there, and the reality of marching up and down stairs all day had not yet set in. The kids liked them, of course, novelty that they were, and Eileen enjoyed bringing her new friends upstairs to the bedroom she shared with Nathan, showing them all her toys. She and Nathan both liked playing in the yard and in the neighborhood. Andrew would often sit out on the front lawn and read a book while his kids played with the neighbor kids, just to ease his mind that none of them would be mean to Nathan.

And Brooke moved with them. Andrew wasn't ready to call it quits with her yet. They were still engaged, after all, and that meant something. With so many other major changes in their lives, it was comforting to still have each other, even if Andrew had major doubts about their long-term compatibility. It was easier to stay in his rut, noting with relief that the frequency of her outbursts had decreased.

He was hanging his framed Yellowstone poster in the living room when the doorbell rang. He went to the white-painted metal door that matched the white walls, wondering how many coats of paint the walls of this forty-year-old rental held up, what they had witnessed. At least the carpet, a low-pile brown and tan pattern, was in good condition.

He pulled open the door and there stood one of the neighbor mothers, a short, stout Latino woman in her mid-thirties who lived next door with her two young daughters. Her expression was serious, disgruntled, and Andrew inwardly winced. Nathan stood next to her, a strange towel wrapped around his waist. The neighbor handed Nathan's clothes to Andrew.

"He got a little wet from the sprinkler and took off all his clothes out in the street. All the kids were laughing at him, so I thought I'd bring him home. And I don't need my three-year-old daughter asking me questions about penises yet." Her raspy tone indicated displeasure, but not contempt.

"I'm sorry. He has autism. He doesn't realize that it's socially unacceptable to take off his clothes in public," Andrew said, burning inside. He took the clothes from the woman and pulled Nathan beside him.

"That's okay. I just thought he should come inside."

Andrew managed to thank her and shut the door. Just when he thought it was going to be okay! He dared to think that they could live like normal people! That Nathan could just play with the neighborhood kids and he'd be fine. Poor Eileen! She must be mortified. What must it be like for her having an older brother who does things like that?

"Nathan, you can't take your clothes off outside or around other people. It's not okay. You only take your clothes off in the bedroom or the bathroom. If your clothes get wet outside, you come in the house first and then take them off."

Nathan made a dissenting guttural noise. Was he ashamed? Frustrated? Non-comprehending? Andrew thought that Nathan didn't know either, probably would never be able to tell him anyway, even if he could ever identify his own feelings. Autism hides so much.

"You need to stay in your room for the rest of the day as a consequence. Then you will remember not to take your clothes off outside." Andrew preferred the word consequence to punishment because he wanted to teach his children that all of their actions had consequences, both positive and negative. At this point, however, he suspected that his choice of words made no difference to the kids. He began leading Nathan upstairs to his room, with Nathan pulling back on his arm with so much force that he feared they might both fall backward down the stairs. The thought occurred to him then that either of the kids could fall down the stairs, especially Eileen. He hadn't considered that possibility yet.

"No room!" Nathan protested.

"Yes, you will stay in your room the rest of the day."

More guttural noises. His son sounded like a possessed wolverine.

TWO WEEKS LATER, Andrew and Brooke reclined together on the couch and watched the series finale of *The X-Files*. Andrew told Brooke that he had started watching it when Nathan was a baby. It was the only TV show that he had ever watched regularly in adulthood. And now he felt like it was the end of an era. He had watched that show religiously since Nathan was one week old, for seven and a half years. It seemed strange that a weekly TV show could regulate his life, set the pace, maintain consistency. It actually sustained him and got him through his years of depression and obsessive-compulsive disorder. *One more thing to move on from.*

Andrew thought about when he came home from running errands on Saturday and turned down the cul-de-sac and saw a bunch of kids riding their bikes. And then he saw Nathan, riding his own bike with the training wheels off! Andrew had never seen such a look of elation on his son's face. He whizzed by, keeping up with the other kids. Andrew pulled in the drive-way and Brooke came up to him, excited because she had taken the training wheels off for Nathan. Andrew thanked her, but he was disappointed because he'd missed it, he wasn't the one to do it. He remembered one of the few things his father had done alone with him—he had removed Andrew's training wheels and taught him how to ride a bike. Andrew remembered that day vividly, how momentous it was. He'd wanted to experience it as a parent. Brooke was defensive; she thought she was doing something good, thought Andrew would have been happy. "I am, Brooke. I'm happy that he's riding his bike. He looks great! I can tell he's really enjoying himself, and he feels like he belongs. And that's the most important thing." *But I missed it. I can't miss anything. Don't you understand?*

The show ended, and Andrew jumped up, remembering that Eileen had lost another tooth and that he needed to play tooth fairy that night. He shook his head as he scrounged around for two dollars. "Dueling tooth fairies," he muttered.

In June, after school was out, they visited Gabriel in Yellowstone National Park, where he had achieved his long-time goal of working as a tour guide. It was nearly a thousand-mile drive to get there, and they split it into two days. Andrew was surprised that Eileen hadn't thrown up yet on the trip.

They entered the park on the west side and began the hour-long drive to the Old Faithful area, where they would be staying in a cabin. Brooke remarked that she wished they could have camped. "Look at all these campers and RVs!"

"This isn't the easiest place to tent-camp with bears and bison. I just want to relax in a cabin after this long drive." Andrew had to drive the entire trip because Brook had lost her license for three months due to receiving a DUI. He also had to drive her back and forth to work in Ashland every day, which exasperated him and used up twice as much gas in his car. He didn't enjoy being an unreimbursed chauffeur. And Brooke couldn't pay her share of monthly expenses again because she had fees and court-ordered classes to pay for. Andrew felt drained emotionally, financially, and mentally. He looked forward to the paid week off. He had been at his job for four years now and had earned it.

From the West Entrance, a consistent stream of cars meandered around the bases of foothills that, forty miles to the south, would become the Grand Tetons. To their right flowed the dark Madison River, dotted by fishermen in waders and a few elk drinking from the grassy banks. Various pines and firs created a mosaic of greens that contrasted with the regrowth of blackened areas that had been damaged by the fire of 1988, which Andrew, as a teenager, had seen with his family the summer of that year. He remembered how dark the smoke-filled sky had been, how the sun presented as a blood-red ball.

But the sky was clear and blue that day as he came around a curve into a little meadow. Just then a whole herd of bison, maybe thirty of them, began crossing the road in front of them. Andrew stopped and got out the video camera while they all watched, gasping as the huge, molting beasts passed within two feet of their car.

"I must film the bisons," Nathan said in a flat but determined voice.

Andrew, thrilled at how well he asked, handed Nathan the camcorder for a couple of minutes until Eileen demanded to have a turn. Nathan handed it over without protest.

"I see them! I see them!" Eileen exclaimed as she looked through the viewfinder.

It took about ten minutes for all of the bison to leisurely cross the road, including several scampering calves. Andrew continued driving until they reached the Old Faithful area, where Eileen threw up. After a cleaning session, they went to the lodge to check in. Gabriel, in his park uniform, greeted them warmly in the lobby. Andrew could tell how thrilled his father was that they had made the trip. He seemed at peace, like he was finally working through some of his resentment, letting go of it, like when the last stubborn leaves still clinging to a tree in late autumn finally detach and plummet to the ground, as if they didn't know what they were waiting for.

Gabriel suggested they go to the cabin to drop off their things and rest for a bit, and then walk over to watch Old Faithful erupt, which would be in about forty minutes. The "cabin" was luxurious by cabin standards: a large room with two queen beds and a large bathroom, but still rustic-looking with exposed beams and a western motif. They brought all of their stuff in, used the bathroom, unpacked a little, then headed out to see the geyser.

Andrew was as impressed as he had been the first time he'd seen it, holding Bernadette's hand years ago. This time, he held Eileen's hand. The geyser began spurting, and within thirty seconds it was about sixty feet high, then continued for another minute before receding. Brooke, as Andrew feared, took his camera and snapped pictures every ten seconds, and he dreaded having a whole roll of geyser photos. When it was over, Gabriel told them that the next geyser over, called Beehive, was also supposed to erupt, which usually only did once or twice a day. Old Faithful erupted every ninety minutes or so.

"I don't want to go to the beehive," Nathan said.

"There are no bees there, Nathan," Gabriel said. "The name of the geyser is Beehive because the ground around it is shaped like a beehive." Nathan accepted the explanation but warily kept his distance as they watched it erupt. The cone that the steam shot out of really did look like a beehive, and it was more powerful than Old Faithful, with a gushing force that lasted about three times longer.

They ate burgers for lunch and then went to tour the original Old Faithful Lodge, built in 1903. Andrew marveled at the stair railings made of thick, knobby, polished tree branches and the huge, three-story stone fireplace in the center of the lobby. Gabriel was in his element, heaping facts and trivia on them at every turn, giving them their own private tour, but Andrew didn't mind. He was glad to see his father so happy, living his dream. He bubbled over himself talking about some things he had planned for their visit: Yellowstone Falls and the canyon and a real stagecoach ride! And he offered to babysit the kids that night so that Andrew and Brooke could go out to dinner in the lodge.

Then they began the walk to the Morning Glory pool along a six-foot-wide wooden boardwalk that passed by many thermal features. Signs urged visitors to stay on the boardwalk as the ground could be unstable, and Andrew worried that Nathan might step off, so he kept him close. It was a good thing he did, because they encountered a swarm of gnats in the middle of the boardwalk and Nathan screeched and tried to bolt, but Andrew held him tight by his side and shielded his head. Nathan stopped screeching, much to Andrew's relief, and agreed to walk in that manner, his head under Andrew's arm, pressing against his side. He overcame his fear and trusted his father, and Andrew silently rejoiced.

After a while, Nathan poked his head out, realized the gnats were gone, and continued on his own, a few feet ahead of Andrew. They then came upon a small geyser erupting, and the wind carried the fine droplets of warm spray toward them, hitting Nathan in the face. He screamed and started to bolt to the side. Andrew was not near enough to grab him. Gabriel had told them stories of people being burned, falling through the thin, crusty ground.

"Nathan! Stop!" he commanded. To his surprised relief, Nathan did, and Andrew leaped to him and held him. "You have to stay on the walkway! The ground has very hot water under it so we must stay on the walkway to be safe! Here, walk close to me again." Nathan immediately hid his face in his father's side.

Andrew berated himself. *Was it right to bring him here? Was it responsible?* He just wanted to do normal things with his children. He had such wonderful memories of vacationing in national parks when he was growing up, and he wanted to enjoy them again with his own children. He didn't think it was too much to hope for.

ANDREW LAY ON his back and looked up at the ceiling as he recalled the vivid dream he'd had of Nathan and Eileen. This was not his first dream of the kids since they had been in Los Angeles for the past two weeks, and would be for four more. Almost every night he had been plagued by nightmares, sometimes horrible: finding them in a gutter somewhere, half-naked, dirty, hungry, alone. It was hell having them gone.

In a little over a week he would be flying to L.A. to visit them for one day and one night. For the past two weeks he had been distracting himself by never being home except to sleep, and he wasn't doing much of that (to avoid the nightmares). Often he would leave work and go over to Gavin's house. Gavin was a trust fund baby who didn't have to work, and once he graduated from college, he sat around trying to figure out what to do with his degree in sociology, hoping to avoid having to go to grad school. While he sat around watching daytime talk shows and soap operas, he alternately smoked pot and snorted coke, and welcomed friends to do it with. Andrew found either method a good way to numb his melancholy spirit, and Brooke was only too happy to join him. He no longer had the will to try to stop her.

Andrew dozed off for the few remaining hours until it was time to get up and get ready for work. He tried to ignore the dull pain behind his left eyeball. By the time he got to work, it had become a sharp, stabbing pain spreading across the whole left side of his head. He called his chiropractor and made an appointment for the next morning. Within an hour his vision was blurred slightly in his left eye and he left for home, covering that eye while he drove. At home, he took some ibuprofen and lay down. He woke up an hour later fully into the migraine, so intense he could not even walk upright. He could not even crawl. His vision and equilibrium were off, his hands were numb, and his head felt like it was about to explode, like his brain was swollen so much it was going to burst out of his skull. The pain was incredible. He slid to the floor slowly, every movement causing the pain to surge again. He pulled himself prone along the floor to the medicine cabinet and steeled himself for the certain excruciating pain that came as he slowly raised himself upright to grab the ibuprofen. Then he sank to the floor again and crawled to the bathroom and went through the same agonizing process to get a cup of water. He took eight hundred milligrams of ibuprofen and crawled back to bed, where he writhed in pain for another half an hour until the medication barely took the edge off and he was able to sleep.

"Well, your C-2 is definitely out of alignment," the chiropractor announced the next morning. Dr. Phillips, a tall, broad-chested man in his early fifties with soulful canine eyes and the crooning voice of a minstrel, stood behind Andrew where he lay on his back on a vinyl-upholstered table. He placed his hands on the sides of Andrew's head, lifted it an inch and jerked it to the right, causing a quick series of cracks. "But stress and sadness can also bring on migraines for those who have a history of them."

Andrew had told him how he'd had migraines as a child, that they abated only because of chiropractic treatment. He'd begun seeing Dr. Phillips three years ago at the encouragement of his boss, Gloria, who had been a long-time patient of his, but Andrew could only afford to see him a few times a year since his insurance didn't cover chiropractic care.

"But I haven't had one for almost twenty years!"

"Well, you're lucky then, because thoughts and feelings can really affect our bodies."

"I'm so emotional right now that I get choked up over life insurance commercials," Andrew said as Dr. Phillips chuckled. "I'm surprised I never had a migraine during my separation and divorce."

"Maybe it means that the relationship with your children is the most important one in your life."

"Yes, it is," Andrew said wistfully.

"When do they come back?" Dr. Phillips asked in a sincere, gentle voice.

"Well, I get to see them next weekend; I'm flying down for a quick visit. And then they come home three weeks after that."

"That's good. Try to relax; you'll make it."

After work, Andrew went home and put on his swim trunks. He had bought a three-foot-deep wading pool last summer, and he had set it up in May so the kids would have time to enjoy it before they went to L.A. He reclined on a raft and just floated for an hour, trying to find enjoyment in the solitude, wanting to avoid the state of mind he fell into at Gavin's house. It was time to face the negative feelings, acknowledge the misery of missing his children and work through it.

He decided to go out that weekend, and every weekend after he got back from L.A. until the kids returned home. He figured he should try to get some enjoyment out of this period of free time, and being out of the house and social was a healthier way to distract himself.

"THERE IT IS. Umpqua Skydivers," Andrew announced as he pulled into the parking lot. He saw Bernadette and her now-fiancé Colin standing outside their car, and he parked next to them. He and Brooke got out and exchanged hugs and "Are-you-ready-for-this?"s with them and they went inside. Neither Bernadette nor Colin seemed nervous, and Bernadette wondered aloud if she could get her tandem partner to let them somersault out of the plane. She thought that would be "way cool." *As if skydiving with a conventional plane exit wasn't exciting enough*, Andrew thought. He had forgotten that Bernadette was such a daredevil, that her name meant "brave as a bear" and she always lived up to it.

It had been Brooke's idea to go, and Andrew had always wanted to try skydiving. Bernadette had previously expressed an interest as well, so they decided to meet there the weekend before Nathan and Eileen came home. Brooke had done it before, so she was not as nervous, but it was the first time for everyone else. She enjoyed embellishing the account of her first experience while they waited in the "lobby" area of the warehouse-looking building.

They paid the fee and received a five-minute instructional talk about the procedures: how to put the harness on, connect it to your tandem partner, and signals to communicate with them. Then they got into their harnesses, taped their shoelaces down, and everything happened so fast that Andrew didn't have time to be nervous. They all climbed into a small plane and it took off and they circled up twelve thousand feet.

Andrew's tandem partner, a short, balding guy who was the owner of the company, explained that they'd connect their harnesses with metal carabiner clips, inch forward to the end of the seat, crouch together sideways in front of the open side of the plane, then lean out. He told Andrew that they'd freefall for about ten seconds, then he would hold two fingers in front of Andrew's face as the signal for Andrew to pull the chute chord.

Colin was the first one out, then Bernadette, then Andrew. There was no time to think! He leaped out and then he was flying! There was no feeling of his stomach falling out, as he had feared. Just the wind rushing past his face, and the ground, with its patchwork fields of the rural outskirts of Eugene in central Oregon, getting closer. Then—the fingers! He grabbed and pulled the chute chord and it opened with a whoosh, pulling Andrew upright.

As soon as the chute had opened, there was absolute quiet. They could have whispered to each other if they wanted to. Andrew, awestruck, stopped breathing as he looked all around; his vision was unobstructed because the tandem partner was behind him and doing all the navigating. He saw the fields, mountains, highways, the curve of the earth. He tried to let all of the negativity go: the strain of being a working, low-income, single parent, the heartache of having a child with autism, the shock of finding out his wife had cheated on him, the stress of the rumors and moving, finding out the kids would have to attend a different school. The nightmares and sadness of missing his children. The horrible migraine. He let it all go for those moments as he flew above the earth, his tandem partner expertly steering as they neared the ground.

NATHAN AND EILEEN were back home, playing in the front yard with their neighborhood friends. Andrew didn't even have to drive eleven hours to pick them up; Erica and Miles had come all the way up so they could visit "friends" in Ashland. They didn't mention any names, but Andrew knew they would be staying with Isaac and Simone. The shock of Erica's and Isaac's affair had begun to ebb, and he no longer visualized kicking a prone Isaac with his combat boots, but the wound still throbbed at the thought of his children spending a weekend with Uncle Isaac, coming home and talking about him, saying they loved his house with the "real" pool in the ground, how much fun they had there. Andrew saw a black cloud whenever Isaac's name was mentioned.

Andrew looked out the living room window, checking on the kids. Nathan, riding his bike, jumped curbs now, and Eileen had learned how to in-line skate. She had just turned six, and Nathan would be eight in October. Andrew felt secure now that they were home. He recalled how Nathan had cried when Andrew had to leave after his quick visit with them last month. It broke his heart to see Nathan hiding his face in the couch as he walked out the front door of Erica's apartment, crying that he wanted to go back to Oregon, probably hoping, maybe expecting, that Andrew had come to L.A. to bring them back, even though he explained to them several times that he just came for a visit.

Eileen had been somewhat distant since they returned, having a hard time transitioning, Andrew figured. He made the mistake of having a birthday party for her the day after they got back. Small, just family, but Eileen hadn't had enough time to re-acclimate yet. When people started arriving, she hid in her room and refused to come out for the first hour—the girl who used to throw tantrums if she wasn't getting all the attention. Finally, Andrew carried her out of her room, held her while everyone sang Happy Birthday to her, and had to blow out her candles for her. Andrew made a mental note for next summer to wait a week after they got back before having a party.

He walked back upstairs to his and Brooke's bedroom, where he had also managed to squeeze in his large desk and computer, and sat down to continue filling out the application he had received. He had heard about the government home-buying program from some friends of Brooke's who lived in Talent and used to work at Dogma. He knew that if they qualified, he would, and he was anxious to get the process started. With any luck, he'd be able to buy a home in a few months.

While filling out the information on dependents, he suddenly remembered that Eileen's new Kindergarten teacher was coming that afternoon for a home visit so they could meet before school started. He looked at the clock and realized she would be arriving in ten minutes.

It had been decided at Eileen's IEP meeting in May that it would be best for her to repeat Kindergarten, and Andrew, much to his disappointment, had to agree. He wasn't disappointed in Eileen at all; she had done quite well, he thought, considering the fact that her mother had moved seven hundred miles away in the middle of the school year. By the end of the year, she was participating in all of the group activities and exhibiting far less anxiety and few transitioning problems. Andrew's disappointment lay in the school. The bottom line was that Eileen was in no way academically prepared for first grade. She could barely write the letter E and didn't recognize any others. He didn't believe that it was merely a reflection of her intellect. Kindergarten at Central had been more like another year of preschool; they called it the "developmental approach" to education.

Whatever they called it, Eileen hadn't learned a damn thing.

At least, if she had to repeat Kindergarten, it would be at a new school in a new neighborhood, and she wouldn't have to see her friends continue on while she was held back. In spite of that, she did ask Andrew why she was going to have another year of Kindergarten. "You had Kindergarten in Ashland; now you're going to have Kindergarten in Phoenix. And here they will teach you all of the letters so you'll be ready to start first grade." That had seemed to satisfy her.

Andrew stuck his head out the front door and told Eileen to come inside and wash up, that her new teacher was coming to meet her. Eileen flopped down on the front lawn and complained that she didn't want to go in; she wanted to play. Andrew went into coaxing mode. He walked out to where she had planted herself and sat down next to her.

"You had lots of time to play. Now it's time to come in to wash your hands. I told you your new teacher is coming in a few minutes."

Suddenly, Andrew saw a mean look replace the stubborn one on her face.

"So. I don't want to be a part of your family. I want to live with Mom."

Andrew bristled. *Oh, this is starting far too early.* "This is where you need to live to go to school. You can't live all the time with Mom because she has to work at night and won't be there to take care of you. Maybe when you're older you can live with Mom."

"Well, you took me away from Mom!"

"No, I didn't, honey. She moved away." Andrew hated to put it in those terms. She missed her mother enough; there was no sense making Erica look bad, making Eileen feel worse.

"Well, you took me out of L.A. and brought me back to Oregon," she continued, tearing up handfuls of grass.

"Eileen, your mom and Miles drove you back to Oregon, remember?" Andrew said, relieved that he could say that this time.

Eileen skipped a beat, and Andrew knew that her mind was turning. Then she shot out, "Well, I don't want to be a part of your family!"

"That's not a nice thing to say to someone who loves you very much. We don't say mean things to people we love."

"I don't love you," Eileen said in a challenging tone.

It really did feel like a knife in his heart. She was six! He expected this wanting-to-live-with-Mom maybe when she was ten or so.

"That makes me sad, Eileen. You don't ever say that. You come in the house now to get ready to meet your teacher," he said in a low voice as he stood up.

Eileen got up, pouting with tears in her eyes and a trembling lower lip, and went inside. *How could she be like that at this age?* Andrew thought. He figured that she was displacing her anger toward Erica, without even being able to identify that she was angry with her for moving away.

She's taking it out on me because she feels comfortable with me. This could be a lifelong thing.

ALREADY GOODWIN ELEMENTARY had called to say that Nathan was being disruptive and that Andrew needed to come and pick him up. He had been yelling, screaming, hitting, kicking his desk and knocking things over in the classroom. The old sinking feeling returned, the one that Andrew felt whenever Central called him at work for the same reason.

Will Nathan ever be able to be successfully mainstreamed? Can't I get a break?

But Goodwin handled the situation much better than Central had, which was a relief. Nathan's educational assistant, Rosa, a big-boned Italian woman in her mid-forties with a commanding but pleasant demeanor, came up with a motivating idea to help Nathan not be disruptive, listen to his teachers, and focus on his work. Since his latest obsession was *E.T. the Extra-Terrestrial* (due to the recent release of the movie on DVD), Rosa suggested giving E.T. "tickets" to Nathan at the end of the day if he tried hard and earned them through his behavior. When he had fifty tickets, Erica would take him to Universal Studios to go on the E.T. ride the next time the kids visited her. A great, spontaneous, effective idea, just like that. No weekly meetings, no Nathan running through the halls, no teachers rolling their eyes. Andrew allowed himself to feel some confidence that this was already working out much better than last year. The teachers at Goodwin had been so patient. Already Nathan had reacted physically to a boy who had made fun of him; he grabbed him by the shoulders and swung him around and threw him on the ground. Another time he threw a pinecone in a friendly girl's face. He had chased kids with sticks in his hand. He had knocked desks over and screamed in class. He had shouted at his enduring teacher, "You're fired!"

These people deserve a medal, Andrew thought. *And so do I.*

He pulled into the school parking lot, got out and walked to the double glass doors to wait for Nathan. Soon he saw the outline of Rosa's large frame walking toward him, Nathan next to her, holding a ticket. She always tried to walk down the hallway with him before the rest of the classrooms were dismissed because the loudness in the halls with all the other students upset Nathan.

"Much better today, for the most part," Rosa told him, smiling, black eyes sparkling. "See you tomorrow, Nathan!"

As usual, Nathan did not reply, and Andrew put his arm around him and began walking across the street to the daycare to pick up Eileen, where her teacher took her and several other students every day after school. It was expensive but convenient. By the time Andrew paid the daycare for the three hours a day she was there, he ended up making about two dollars an hour for over half of his day. It was maddening, but he didn't have a choice. At least Erica had finally started paying child support, which helped a bit.

Suddenly, Nathan looked up at Andrew, and in his own lucid voice he asked, "What's wrong with me, Dad?"

The feeling in Andrew's body as he heard those words stunned him. Those words set off a knot in his stomach, chilled him. He knew the day would come, since Nathan's verbal skills had developed, that he would wonder, and ask. Andrew was not prepared for it that day, one month into second grade. Too soon, too sudden.

Andrew stopped for a second and looked down at his son, whose gaze had returned to the ground. "We'll talk about it when we get home, Nate," he said. "We have to pick up Eileen now."

At home, Andrew set Eileen up to watch a video downstairs and took Nathan up to his room and sat on the bed with him, wondering how to begin. He berated himself, thinking, *Why, when he asked me what was wrong with him, didn't I say, 'There's nothing wrong with you, honey.'*

How do you explain autism to your eight-year-old autistic son?

Andrew started off by saying, "Some people have a disability in their eyes and they can't see. And some people have a disability in their legs and they can't walk. A disability is something that makes it hard for people to do things. You have a disability in your brain called autism. Autism makes it hard to talk, and it makes your ears sensitive so they hurt when you hear air dryers in bathrooms or leaf blowers or vacuum cleaners." His voice sounded hollow in his head. He wasn't sure if Nathan comprehended anything of what he had said, or if he was even listening. Andrew continued by telling him that his teachers and family will help him with understanding autism, and that there are some good things about autism too, like learning to read early and knowing how to read maps, as Nathan liked to do. Andrew told him it's okay to have autism.

Nathan seemed fidgety at that point and asked if he could go back downstairs to watch the video. Andrew gave him a hug before Nathan left the room. Then he got up, went to his computer, and wrote "Nathan's Autism Book." He wrote it in the first person, starting with, "My name is Nathan. I like to run, read, laugh and play like other kids. But there is something different about me. I have autism." Then the book talked about the various difficulties of having autism and how it affected him. Things like, "Sometimes I don't know what to say and I say something from a video. I like to watch videos. But other people do not know words from my videos. First I will tell them what video I am talking about when I say something from a video." After mentioning the positive aspects of Nathan's autism that he had discussed with him moments ago, Andrew ended with "Other people have autism too, other kids and other adults. Someday I can meet them." Andrew printed each page with a few sentences in large print at the top and left space below for pictures. Then he put the pages in plastic sleeves and bound them together.

He went downstairs, turned off the TV, and read the book to Nathan and Eileen. Nathan spent the rest of the day carrying his book around and later stated that he wanted to take it to school. He had such a relieved look on his face that Andrew chastised himself for not preparing the book before telling Nathan he had autism. Of course! He needed something visual in order to gain some understanding of this huge bomb he had dropped in his lap. Now he had an explanation. Something he could show to other people because he couldn't explain it in his own words.

ANDREW FORMED TWO patties in his hands from the ground turkey he had seasoned with Worcestershire sauce and pepper and placed them on his mini grill on the kitchen counter. His children would now eat three different entrees for dinner, and he rotated them: burgers, hot dogs, and pizza. All were served with baby carrots every day, the only vegetable they would both eat. Nathan still liked uncooked frozen corn, and Andrew occasionally indulged him.

While Andrew washed his hands and put away the rest of the meat, he thought about the letter he had received from the Federal Housing Administration people saying that his application was on hold for six months. Apparently, one of the credit reporting agencies had incorrect information on his credit report, stating that two of his credit card debts that had been discharged with his bankruptcy were still open accounts in bad standing. Both showed delinquent balances due of several thousand dollars. Fortunately the FHA office was giving him the opportunity to have the errors corrected instead of just rejecting his application. Of course, he wasn't pleased with the six-month delay in his home-buying quest, and contacting the credit agencies and sending them all the paperwork involved was just one more thing he really didn't have time to fit in.

Brooke was finally holding up her end, which was a relief. She was working full-time and had paid off all of her garnishments and fines for the DUI so she could contribute more to household expenses. She also had Mondays off and picked up the kids from school on that day so that Andrew could stay later at work since that was his busiest day of the week. And he appreciated that. The main problem was that he wasn't feeling fulfilled in the relationship due to her incessant TV-watching and her stunted intellect. He had thought that someone who watched that much TV would know what a bar mitzvah was! She actually asked him one day, "What's a bar mitzvah?" and he had thought she was joking. When he laughed and walked away, she'd said, "No, really. What's so funny?"

But he still loved her, and he could have fun with her. She made him laugh, even if it was unintentional at times. She had been his best friend for two and a half years now, and that was hard to walk away from. So was the sex. Good sex was damn hard to walk away from. He decided that his intellectual needs could be neglected for a while longer.

The good news was that Nathan was doing much better at school and seemed more relaxed. He had settled in, especially after Andrew made sure he realized that returning to Stewart was not an option. The autism book that Andrew had written for him made all the difference. Nathan brought it to school two weeks ago and even read it to his class, which was his own idea. Rosa told Andrew when he picked Nathan up that day that all the kids listened so well while he'd read it and both she and the teacher had tears in their eyes. Andrew was so proud of his son for reading it to his class. The wonderful thing was that, by reading it to them, three major issues were addressed. He introduced them to disabilities at a younger, more accepting age; he informed his peers about the reason behind his sometimes odd actions and speech; he eased his anxiety on his own and validated himself. The special ed consultant made two copies of the book to keep in the library for the rest of the staff and students. "Nathan's Autism Book" was the most important thing that Andrew had ever written. He told himself that if he published nothing as long as he lived, he had helped his son with his writing.

Another positive effect of the book was that it had encouraged Andrew to write an article. He had called it "Autism in the Rogue Valley," and wrote about how autism affected the area, gave a thorough description of autism (characteristics, behavior, treatments), and outlined the local programs available for children with autism. He also included two sidebars: myths about autism and a listing of resources, both local and national. Two days ago, he had finished the two-thousand-word article and submitted queries by e-mail to two local parenting publications. One had responded the next day, saying they would love to run the piece, but due to lack of funding had to recently cease publication. They offered to contact Andrew should they resume publication in the future, which he found encouraging.

The burgers were done, and Andrew set the kids down at the table to eat. Nathan began eating without comment.

"Yuck, lettuce!" Eileen wailed, making a disgusted face and yanking out the tiny piece that Andrew had hoped she wouldn't notice.

He ignored her remark and the removal of the offending vegetable. *You pick your battles,* he thought.

"Okay. I'm going upstairs to work at my desk for a little while. You guys eat your dinner."

Andrew walked up the stairs, remembering how the second week they lived there Eileen had tripped and pitched head-first down them, but aside from a rug burn on her chin and being scared, she was unharmed. Then Brooke had overshot a step and slipped backward, bruising her tailbone. A pile grew at the foot of the stairs of things—shoes, toys, laundry—that needed to be taken up when they had the energy to do it; Andrew vowed their next dwelling would be one level. He entered his room, turned on his computer and opened his e-mail program. His stomach leaped when he saw a response download from the second publication he had queried.

Relax, he told himself. *It could be a polite rejection.*

But it wasn't. Andrew wooted as he read the e-mail.

"Dear Andrew," the editor wrote, "I would love to review your article for publication. I worked at a Waldorf school in San Francisco where we had several autistic children, and I've always been interested in running an article about autism. Feel free to e-mail the Word document to me."

Andrew's heart raced and he pumped his fist in the air. He was going to be published!

Twenty-four

Erica's feeling of validation was like nothing else. She was graduating. She tilted her head to feel the spring sun on her face, breaking through the light fog, as she sat and awaited her name to be called for her Bachelor of Fine Arts in Graphic Design degree. She wouldn't receive her actual diploma that day, but she would rise and cross the platform, and her family would be there to witness her achievement.

Her father was there, and Caleb, and of course, Miles. She wished somehow that Nathan and Eileen could be there, but a two-hour ceremony was beyond their tolerance level. And they would be there soon for the summer anyway. She had talked to them on the phone that morning, tried to explain the significance of graduating from college. They had both "graduated" from Kindergarten, so there was some recognition of the term. She reminded them of how she would often tell them that she couldn't play, she had to study, and now she was finished studying. Now, she told Eileen, she would be a "working" artist, called a graphic designer. "Where will you work?" Eileen had asked.

Erica, for the past six months, had had an internship with an advertising agency, which she liked well enough, but her dream was to work for Disney. They did not have any current openings for graphic designers, but she thought that maybe with her recent experience with the ad agency, she could start in the marketing department and be there for the next internal hire. She would stay on where she had the internship for now; they offered her a part-time position, which would be convenient while the kids were there for the summer. Then maybe when they went back to Oregon, she could apply with Disney.

Last year she'd taken the summer off and often took the kids to the beach, and they'd had swimming lessons. Nathan did even better than Eileen, much to Erica's surprise. And they had a fun summer. But she felt bad because her children had to sleep in a walk-in closet. She had wanted to move to a bigger place last spring, before they came down for the summer, but moving in L.A. was not that easy. Most people, once they found a place they liked in a decent neighborhood with affordable rent, stayed where they were. It wasn't like Ashland, she had told Andrew, where any neighborhood is a good one, and it doesn't matter so much where you end up. She would work as much as possible after the kids returned to Oregon, maybe even pick up some bartending shifts somewhere, saving money to buy a house. Miles, of course, wanted to design his own, but they'd agreed that he should do that when they moved back to Oregon, and they weren't ready to do that yet. She would be the "ghost parent" for another year or two.

Last summer, when Andrew had come to visit the kids in July, he took them to Disneyland with his brother and stayed at a hotel that night. He dropped them off at her apartment the next day because he had to fly back and could only get the weekend off work. And after he hugged the kids and kissed them goodbye and left, Nathan curled up in a ball on the couch and cried. "Go home with Dad," he sobbed. "All done L.A." "It's okay, honey," Erica said, her heart aching as she sat next to him and caressed his head. "You'll be back in Oregon soon." Nathan stopped crying and said, "It's a sad song when someone moves away."

Erica marveled at how Nathan could talk now, especially expressing such insight. She wasn't sure if he meant that he was sad when she had moved, or that he was sad when he was with her and away from his dad. Maybe that was his way of communicating his emotion surrounding both situations. Or maybe it was his way of noting that they were all sad because she'd moved away. She wondered if the kids ever cried for her. If they did, Andrew never told her. She remembered all the nights, during the first few weeks after she had moved, that she had cried as Miles held her, missing them, wishing there was another way. Wishing she could be two places at once. She had already missed some milestones: Nathan learning to ride a bike, talking more, Eileen in-line skating and learning to read. So many sacrifices she'd had to make to achieve this goal. At least she got to take Nathan to Universal Studios for Spring Break when he had received fifty E.T. tickets for good behavior at school, which had taken him four months to collect. He was so proud, smiling the whole day. He had worked hard to earn the tickets, and she praised him. And she was so glad to be able to share that special day with him.

It was time for the Art Department now. Her moment was here. She thought about that morning, while she was getting ready, wearing a sleeveless black linen sheath and putting on mascara, and Miles came in the room and told her she looked beautiful, and that he was so proud of her, proud to be her husband. He knew how hard she had worked, how much she had wanted this. When she had spoken to Nathan on the phone earlier, she wished she had thought to remind him of how he felt that day at Universal Studios as a way of explaining to him the importance of her day.

Her Aunt Maggie would have been proud. "You see? You keep drawing like I tell you, and look at you now," Erica could hear her say in her rich, deep voice that she still remembered so well. Then the realization hit her that she would be the first in her family, perhaps on both sides, to obtain a Bachelor's degree. She thought of her mother then, wishing she could be there, hoping that somehow she knew, somehow she was watching.

This is for you, Mom. I love you.

And then, for the Bachelor of Fine Arts in Graphic Design, she heard her name announced, "Erica Jasmine Hudson," and she was walking, and the sun was shining, having burned off the fog, and she could hear her family cheering. Her heart swelled with pride. It had taken her almost twelve years, but she had her degree. No one could ever take that away.

"I WANT IT," Andrew told Pat in a determined whisper. He and his real estate agent had stepped outside of a house they were viewing.

Andrew couldn't contain his thrill that he was now house-hunting—to buy, no longer to rent. He felt as if he were being initiated into some private club. His agent was Gloria's husband, Pat, who had long-recovered from the back surgery that had caused him to shuffle and take medication that made him slur like the old hippie Andrew had, at their first meeting five years ago, thought him to be. They were both disappointed when the first place they made an offer on, a cute, newer three-bedroom in nearby Talent, fell through. A cash offer came in one hour after Andrew's offer, and Pat said they couldn't blame the seller for taking it. It was without a doubt a seller's market that spring, and hardly anything new was on it, at least not in Andrew's price range. He also had to worry about finding a place within the six-week eligibility period for his federal loan. If it expired and he hadn't found anything yet, he would need to get back on the waiting list for at least another six months. He wanted to own a home too badly to have that happen.

He had burst into the house the day that his application had been approved, picked up Eileen and twirled her around, saying, "Now we can own our own home and we can have kitties!" "Yay!" she squealed. He had explained to Nathan and Eileen that the houses that they'd lived in were all rentals—someone else owned them and made the rules about whether they could have pets or not. Renting a house was like renting a video from the store, he'd said. It seemed odd to him to have to explain it to his children. When he was growing up, his parents always owned the homes they had lived in. As a young child, he just assumed that everyone owned their own home.

Less than two weeks before Andrew's eligibility period would expire, Pat called him at work about a four-bedroom in Phoenix and Andrew drove over to see it immediately. It was an older ranch-style home built in 1971, the year Andrew was born, which he took to be a sign that it was meant to be his. It had a big backyard with a deck and was close to the elementary school. Not wanting to take any chances of losing it, they wrote up an offer that afternoon for the full asking price.

Unbeknownst to Andrew (although it had probably been in the fine print he hadn't had time to read), the Federal Housing Administration had certain requirements that all homes approved for loans must meet, mostly involving energy efficiency. They required all of the single-paned aluminum-framed windows in the house to be replaced with double-paned vinyl-framed windows, and the insulation in the floor and attic had to meet the highest standards. They also required the home to be repainted, which the seller had already agreed to do. That was fortunate, because the funds for every other upgrade had to come out of Andrew's pocket. He was relieved to be able to borrow the money for the repairs from his parents. The frustrating thing was that Andrew's case manager informed him that the entire mortgage depended upon "availability of funds," and that, even after all this work had been done, and Andrew had paid his own money to meet their requirements for repairs, it could still fall through. Andrew was a wreck.

The forty-five-day escrow period was filled with the stress of trying to coordinate all of the repairs, and Andrew felt like he was on auto-pilot, trying not to think about the fact that it might not happen. How could they tell someone, *'Yes, you're approved for a loan. Go out and buy a house, but at the end of escrow, the money might not be there, so don't get your hopes up'?* This was not the typical *'Get pre-approved for a mortgage, go out and buy any house you want for that amount, sign some papers and it's yours!'* home-buying process.

One good thing was that the seller had also agreed to replace the carpet, but that needed to coordinate with the floor insulation upgrade, which of course had been delayed. The windows went in without any problems, thanks to Pat. He went out of his way to get the best deals he could find through his contractor friends for all of the repairs that Andrew had to pay for. The seller painted the house as he said he would, and things started to come together. Then, when finished, the work had to be inspected by FHA and meet with their approval—another hurdle. Andrew trusted that everything would work out. Somehow he knew that he was supposed to have that house. He couldn't get this far and have the rug ripped out from under him, he thought as he went to sleep one night. Then he had to laugh at his unintentional pun the next day when he drove by the house on his way home from work and surveyed the exposed sub-floor where the old carpet had been removed.

With escrow closing in three weeks and things almost on schedule with the repairs, Andrew started packing. He went up to the kids' room while they were outside playing and sifted through books on their bookshelf that they had outgrown. Andrew pulled out the *Pat the Bunny* cardboard book, Sesame Street ABC books that even Eileen no longer needed, thanks to the academics-focused Kindergarten at Goodwin Elementary, and a hardcover picture book about having a brother with autism that was written from a four-year-old's point of view. Eileen would be seven in two months, and she was too old for it now. Andrew looked at it, wondering if he should donate it to the school, and then he had a brainstorm: donate it to Early Childhood Development Center! They worked with kids in that age group, so it would be perfect. He decided to do it before they closed for the day.

He got the kids in the car and drove to the main office, where he had gone years ago to hear that his son had autism. He had been back since, for other meetings, but that one stood out in his mind. That meeting, a harbinger of both unending challenge and unexpected joy, had determined the course of his life for the past five and a half years. And would continue to. It was not the typical parenting process, that was certain. It was a cross-country road trip without maps, a Himalayan trek without guides. A journey not for the easily daunted.

Andrew walked in with Nathan and Eileen, who played with a wooden ball maze in the entry area while he talked to the friendly receptionist. She assured Andrew that the book would be a welcome addition to their library and thanked him. On their way out, he noticed a rack by the door that held some copies of the local parenting magazine to which he had submitted his article. They hadn't notified him when they were going to run it; they'd said that they just couldn't fit it in the April issue, which disappointed him because April was National Autism Awareness Month, but Andrew liked reading it so he picked up a copy and started walking back out to the car with the kids.

He stopped short in the middle of the parking lot, staring at the headline that read "Autism on the Rise" listed in the Featured Articles box. Shaking, he frantically flipped through the magazine and found his article! And the picture of Nathan that he'd submitted! His article! The editor had changed the title, but his name, "by Andrew Pavel," was in print.

Ecstatic, blood tingling, he managed to get the kids in the car and rushed home to call everyone.

EVEN WITH ALL of the planned packing, boxes upon boxes stacked in each room of the house, Andrew still found himself doing what he called a "Hefty-bag move." The night before the move he resorted to flinging clothes, towels, toys, stuffed animals, sheets, pillows, shoes, and anything else unbreakable into big black Hefty bags and lining them up by the front door. He laughed as he remembered how many Hefty-bag moves he'd done while in college. All of them, really. Seemed funny now that he had bought a house and was settling down for a while that he would still be shoving his belongings in plastic bags at midnight.

In the two weeks since the kids had gone to visit Erica, Andrew was so busy and distracted with packing and work and inspections on the house that he felt guilty for not having time to miss them. It was certainly easier this summer, being so preoccupied, and he was glad not to have a repeat experience of the misery of last summer. He talked to them on the phone every three or four days, assuring them that he was packing all of their toys.

They had seen the new house before they left, so they knew where they would live when they got back, but they had seen it with the carpet ripped out, and Eileen told him one night on the phone that she'd had a dream that there was no bathroom in the new house and they had to pee and poop outside. Andrew told her that there were *two* bathrooms. "You don't have to worry, honey. By the time you get back, it'll be perfect."

Escrow closed three days later than expected, so he had to pay the seller three days' "rent" in order to move in on the day he had reserved the U-Haul truck. Since he had to move on the same day that escrow closed, he had to run out to Medford in the middle of unloading the truck to meet Pat at the title company for paperwork signing.

Sweaty and dirty-clothed, he ran in, shook hands with Pat and the escrow agent, both in suits and ties, and sat at a conference table with them.

"Oh, right!" Pat said, eyeing his attire. "You're moving in today!"

Andrew was surprised not to feel uncomfortable, looking unprofessional, but after everything he'd had to go through to get to this point, the stress of not knowing if the loan would even be approved or the repairs completed on schedule and according to FHA's requirements, this was nothing. He relished signing his name eighteen times, seeing his name printed on the property deed, and then rushing back to finish unloading the truck so he could return the U-Haul on time. He'd bought a four-bedroom home. His real life could begin now, albeit in filthy bluejeans and a T-shirt from a local microbrewery.

"Mom, we got two kitties!" Eileen told Erica on the phone, nearly screeching with excitement. "We got them at the shelter. Mine is a tabby cat called Tabby, and Nathan's is a gray one called . . . what is it called, Dad?"

"Isis," Andrew told her as he threw a pizza in the oven.

"Isis," Eileen repeated into the phone as she walked off down the hall into her bedroom. "I don't know; Dad thought of it."

It had actually been Sol's idea, many years ago. When they were growing up, he had started calling all of their cats "Isis" as a nickname. Andrew wasn't sure why, or where it came from, but it became something humorous for them, and he vowed that when he had his own cat, he would name it Isis for real. Nathan didn't seem to mind.

Summer had elapsed quickly, filled with unpacking and settling in, putting up towel bars (Andrew's new home was strangely without them), drapery rods and blinds, and pictures on the walls. And in a four-bedroom house, there were many more walls than Andrew was used to having. In the entryway he hung a small mirror for good feng shui, warding off negative energy, and framed postcards of national parks on the other side. To the left of the entry was a classic 1970s-era kitchen with dark cabinets and mismatched laminate countertops, butcher block on one side and white with gold-flecked swirls on the other. Andrew wondered how long he would have to live with it before he could afford to remodel it. The living room had a functional wood stove in one corner and French doors leading out to the deck and the backyard. To the right of the entry began a long hallway by which four bedrooms, a bathroom, and a closet were connected. He set up his office across from the master bedroom, which had its own bath, and he hung family portraits on both sides of the hallway, which, along with the rest of the house, was covered in a low-pile fawn-colored carpet that the seller had just installed. Andrew loved to lie on it staring up at the ceiling, which had recently been scraped of its popcorn acoustic texture and repainted an off-white color, the same as the walls. White walls again. But at least he could change that, whenever and however he wanted.

Andrew had gone to visit the kids at the half-way point, and this time he and Brooke drove down together and took the kids on an overnight trip to Legoland near San Diego. He had decided to stay with Brooke a little while longer; what with the move and all, it just wasn't a good time for a break-up. Was there ever a good time for one?

Andrew, happy to have the kids back home, felt that the house had been so empty—too big—without them. And he was completely relieved that Eileen didn't have the transitioning problems of last year. He wasn't sure if he could continue to deal with the heartbreak of his precious little girl telling him that she didn't love him just because she was angry with her mother for moving away. He wasn't sure if Eileen had worked through her anger or if she actually had the maturity to realize that it wasn't fair to take it out on her dad. Whatever the case, he hoped it was behind them.

Andrew could hear Eileen's voice from her room telling Erica how things were going at school. It was October, and they'd been back in school a month already. Eileen was seven and in first grade. Nathan was in third grade and would be nine in two weeks. He was doing so well, everyone told Andrew; parents who were able to volunteer in the classroom, whose children were in the same class as Nathan last year, and Rosa, his educational assistant, told Andrew how much calmer Nathan was this year. He had a male teacher, Mr. Russell, a gentle but purposeful man with a full head of graying hair who seemed to pick up on the fact that Nathan bonded faster with men than with women. He'd also had his eye on Nathan last year, and remarked on his progress every afternoon when Andrew picked Nathan up at the classroom door.

"Had the hood off today!" Mr. Russell greeted him in a boisterous whisper one day last week. "He came in from recess and I said, 'Nathan, aren't you too warm with your hood on? You can take it off now that you're inside.' And he did it! Looked just like any other kid. Had it off the rest of the day!" Andrew found it endearing that Nathan's teacher seemed so excited about his developmental coups. And he was impressed that Nathan trusted his teacher enough to do something he had never done away from home: remove the hood on his fleece jacket that he still wore every day, the 'security jacket.' It was the same type as what he had started wearing when he was three, just upgraded every year to a larger size. Andrew poked his head in the classroom, and there was Nathan, sitting at his desk with the hood off, his short, thick, wavy, dark blond hair sticking up. He did look like any other kid, and Andrew drew his breath in sharply.

There's my son. He's doing okay.

Nathan was also, at home, using Andrew's old computer that he had put in Nathan's bedroom. He loved to do CD-Rom programs about Greek history and read about natural disasters on the encyclopedia CD-Rom. Andrew was glad that Nathan was no longer watching so many videos, that he had another avenue of interest, and of learning.

And then Eileen handed Andrew the phone. "Hello?" he said. Sometimes the kids would hand him the phone just to hang it up, and Erica would already be off the line, but sometimes she was still there, so he was never sure.

"Hey, how's it going?" came Erica's familiar, cheerful voice.

Things were better now between them. It was hard because Andrew knew that whenever she and Miles came to Ashland for a visit, they took the kids to spend a night or two with them, and it was always at Isaac and Simone's house. Andrew felt it was disrespectful to him, but what could he do? Isaac was Miles' brother; he had to accept it. And Andrew tried to remind himself of the New Age teachings he had learned through his work, and he tried to allow himself to be influenced by his higher self, telling himself that in a roundabout way, Erica's happiness directly affects his children's happiness, so he might as well not wish her harm. Might as well not harbor any resentment, which would only do *him* harm. Things weren't quite at the positive level that they had been before he'd learned of the affair, but he'd forgiven her in his mind and was doing his best to let it go. It made him feel better, anyway. Learning the truth about Erica's affair, though extremely painful and, for a time, devastating, had liberated him. He was finally able to let go of the hold she still had on him, and on his heart. He loved to remember how she had come in the bedroom and kissed his cheek as he lay in bed one morning when she thought he was sleeping, shortly before she moved out. Before he found out about the affair, he still weakly hung onto that memory, which encouraged his moments of useless fantasizing, wishing that things could have been different for him and Erica. He was glad to be free of it, to move on.

"Good, really good!" he told her, sounding a little too enthusiastic to his own ear. "The kids are doing great in school, and next weekend we're driving down to San Francisco for Solomon's wedding. We're setting up Halloween decorations today."

"That's cool. Oh—Miles and I will be up for Halloween and Nathan's birthday. We'll be driving up on Thursday, and I'll come over on Friday to spend some time with them. Can I have them Saturday night?"

"Sure. I'm having a big party Friday night, both Halloween and Nate's birthday together, so you guys are welcome to come. If you want to take them trick-or-treating, feel free to come earlier. 'Cause I'll be busy setting things up."

When Andrew finished making arrangements he went back out to the front yard, where he had been making tombstones out of plywood and screwing stakes onto them and pounding them into the grass under the big cottonwood tree. He did six of them, and they wrote silly names and dates and drew skulls and used red markers to make blood drops on them.

Then Andrew hung up rubber bats under the rain gutters all around the front of the house, lined the front cement walkway with plastic skulls he'd bought at Wal-Mart, and hung a ghost in the cottonwood tree, spreading the sheet out like arms, floating above the tombstones. Andrew liked the creepy, fun effect.

Satisfied, he went into the house to wash up and take the pizza out of the oven and check his e-mail. He walked down the long hallway of his ranch-style house, still marveling at how big it was. The first night he moved in, he felt like a king in a castle. Four months later, it was still a novelty.

An e-mail downloaded with a 'from' address that he didn't recognize, and the subject line of 'Help!' Curious, he opened it and discovered that it was from the editor of *Shasta Parent*, telling him that she had read his article "Autism on the Rise," and asked if he would be willing to revise it with resources for the northern California area, and she would pay the reprint fee. The catch was that she was nearing her deadline and needed it in less than forty-eight hours.

Andrew, thrilled because the request had been unsolicited, finally felt like a real writer and spent the rest of the day working on the revision.

IN TWO MONTHS it would be two years since Erica moved to L.A., and Nathan and Eileen still wanted Andrew to sing the Happy Dream Song to them every night as he tucked them into bed. Now when he prompted them to say what they wanted to have happy dreams about, they would say "Dad" instead of "Mom" all the time. It made Andrew feel a little better. And he was sure it meant that they were more used to being away from their mother. Even so, there were many days, usually after they hadn't seen her for two months (as was the case right then), when Eileen would say "I miss Mom" out of the blue. Andrew would always offer to call whenever Eileen wanted to talk to her, but the last time he did, Eileen just said, "I miss her body, not just her voice." Andrew couldn't imagine how difficult it was for her.

How is this affecting them long-term? he wondered. *This long-distance co-parenting. Having two homes. Are they going to grow up angry about it?* Would they resent him for not moving to L.A. so they could be close to their mother?

Eileen had also said to him recently, "I have two lives, Dad. My life with you and my life with Mom."

"I know, honey. Sometimes I feel like I have two lives, too. My life when you're here, and my life when you're in L.A. and I'm missing you. But it's okay to feel that way. It's okay to have two lives."

"But it's not okay with me," she'd said, glassy-eyed, as she walked away.

How could you possibly respond to a seven-year-old who feels like she has two lives? She does have two lives! And an autistic brother! Poor kid. She'll probably grow up and write a book about all of it.

But she seemed happy enough, excited that her mother would be there in six days for a visit. She couldn't wait to show Erica her witch costume. Andrew kissed her goodnight and went across the hall into Nathan's room.

"Dad? How big is the Mariana Trench off the coast of Guam?"

"Nate, if you know the Mariana Trench is off the coast of Guam, you know more about it than I do." *What nine-year-old kid knows about the Mariana Trench? Or Guam, for that matter?*

"But how big is it?"

"I don't know, honey. Maybe tomorrow we can find a book about it at the library. Right now it's time for bed, okay?" Nathan willingly got into bed and requested "The Happy Dream Song."

His children in bed, Andrew turned his attention to relaxing on the couch with his latest read, Shakespeare's *The Tempest*. His favorite line had always been Caliban's "When I waked, I cried to dream again." Dreams held such universal power, full of mystery and adventure, beauty or terror. No wonder Nathan and Eileen still insisted on being ushered into tranquility with his little nightly song. He wondered if they dreamt of the same things he did when he was a child, the good dreams of flying over acres of brilliant green grass, then landing and rolling down the hills, laughing, or the bad dreams of trying to run on legs that wouldn't move, shouting to Sol to run, gasping and crying because a murderer was coming after them with a knife.

The phone rang, and he heard Brooke's slurred voice say, "Hey, will you come pick me up? I'm at Lupe's."

Brooke had spent the evening at their previous neighbor's home, half a mile away. Lupe was the one who had brought Nathan home in the towel the day he took off all his clothes. After such an unusual meeting, Andrew and Brooke had become friends with her, and their families often had dinner together, making tamales from Lupe's grandmother's recipe. Since the move, Brooke often went back over for late visits, which usually involved playing shot-glass checkers and various other drinking games.

Andrew told her that the kids were already in bed and it was a school night and suggested that she spend the night there or walk home; it wasn't far.

"It's not that late!"

"I'm not going to get them out of bed, Brooke. Just spend the night there."

"Fine. Whatever."

God, I hate it when she's drunk.

Andrew recalled how embarrassing she had been at his brother's wedding, falling down on the dance floor, then ripping foliage off of the hotel's landscaping to decorate Sol's car.

But the wedding had been beautiful, with a sense of belonging and deep love permeating the air, and Gisela's family really knew how to celebrate. Andrew thought about how proud he'd felt standing next to his little brother as his best man, how happy. Sol was thoughtful enough to buy special favors for the kids—little Lego sets to play with at the reception while they waited for the food. And their parents did well together, were cordial even, which Andrew was glad to see. In fact, he was pleasantly surprised, given the fact that Daniel had accompanied his mother. His parents had made progress.

Nathan had wanted to talk on the microphone. He went up to the stage while the mariachi band was taking a break, and Sol adjusted one of the mic stands down to his level, and Nathan put his right hand around it and spoke slowly in his stoic voice.

"It is a happy day of this wedding of my Uncle Sol and my new Aunt Gisela. Well, my mom and dad were married, but they got separated and divorced. It was like the book *Mom's House, Dad's House.* So everyone just has to remember to get along. Thank you for letting me talk on the microphone." Then, to the applause of the entire room, he stepped down and walked back to their table. Andrew's breath caught in his throat. That was his son. His autistic son, speaking his own words. On a stage, to a room full of people, hazy and quick, like a dream.

Andrew suddenly heard a thumping sound coming from the attic. He put his book down and walked quickly through the house, trying to ascertain what it could be.

What the hell is that?

The sporadic thumping continued, and as he walked to the back of the house, he realized it seemed to be coming from the laundry room, past the kitchen. He went in and discovered that Brooke had been banging on the outside door. He ripped it open.

"What are you doing? Why didn't you come to the front door?" he demanded.

"Because I didn't want to see you! It would have taken you two minutes to come and pick me up! Two minutes!"

"I told you, the kids are in bed and it's a school night," Andrew hissed, walking back through the house.

Brooke leaped onto his back. "I'm tired of always being second-best to you!" she yelled as she yoked his neck with her right arm, making him almost fall backward.

"Get off me!" He tried to pull her arm away from his neck and when, after a struggle, he succeeded, Brooke dropped to the floor with a thud.

"You wanna throw me down?!" she yelled. "That's abuse! I'm calling the cops!" She got up and staggered down the hallway, crashing into the wall and knocking a picture down.

Nathan came out of his room.

Oh, God.

Andrew ran to him. "It's okay, it's okay," he said.

He heard Brooke in the kitchen, yelling their address into the phone, saying to hurry. She came stumbling back down the hallway. "You're going to jail!" she yelled.

Nathan began to cry and Andrew held him.

"Stop it, Brooke!"

"You're going to jail!" she repeated, continuing down the hall.

Andrew shut Nathan's door and sat on his bed with him, cradling him, assuring him that he wasn't going to jail, that Brooke was wrong. He hoped that Eileen had slept through it. After a few minutes, he got Nathan to lay down next to him and tried to get him to go to sleep, praying that Brooke had been faking the call to the police and that she had gone and passed out in their bedroom. He didn't hear any more from her, and was relieved when enough time had passed and the police hadn't come.

It was bad enough all the times when it had just been the two of them, when the kids had been with Erica, but now she had done it in front of Nathan. He had to end it, but how could he afford all the bills alone now that he'd bought this house? And they were having a big party in six days, with Brooke's aunt and brother and his kids all coming, and he didn't want to ruin Nathan's birthday party. He couldn't kick Brooke out. And then the holidays were right around the corner. He couldn't end a three-and-a-half year relationship, break an engagement, in one night.

What is this combination of anger and paralysis? he wondered. *Resignation?*

Twenty-five

Erica pulled into the short driveway of Andrew's home and parked next to his car. It seemed odd to be doing that, like she lived there, but his small, quiet street did not have curbs; the asphalt of the road ran right next to the grass of everyone's front yards, so she couldn't park on the street.

She sat in her car a moment after turning it off, exhausted but happy to be there. She and Miles had begun the nearly seven-hundred-mile drive after she had come home from work and had dinner last night. They had figured on rush hour having died down by 7:30, but apparently half of L.A. was getting out of town for the weekend, so it was a busy night on I-5 North, like a log jam. They crawled up and over the Grapevine and saw a river of red taillights in front of them, inching down the mountain pass.

Erica had hoped to leave that morning, so they wouldn't have to drive at night, but she had a deadline for a project at work and couldn't get the extra day off. It had been only a month since she'd been hired at Disney's marketing department and wanted to maintain the good impression she had made. They liked the fact, mentioned in her interview, that she had worked at Disneyland before, even though it was long ago. "Working for Disney again would feel like coming home," she'd said in her interview. And it was true. She felt like she belonged there, like she was part of something meaningful. And now she could tell her own kids that she worked for Disney, and see their little faces glow in awe, excited to tell their friends at school. And they might be satisfied to think that maybe, maybe it was okay for her to move to L.A. Because if she still lived in Oregon, she wouldn't be able to work for Disney. But Erica knew that she was trying to trick herself, trying to justify something that still made her ache, even though she knew she'd had to do it. Could she hope that, when they were older, the kids would understand?

She walked up to the front door, which had a four-foot-long skeleton hanging on it. She felt happy for Andrew that he had been able to buy a home, as he had wanted for so long. And it was a nice place, something to be proud of. It had traditional wood siding painted off-white, not brand new but not too old, with a good amount of character. A large front yard with a big tree. Inviting, stable, attractive. She liked how he decorated for Halloween, the homemade tombstones and the ghost hanging in the tree, bats strung up. It reminded her of how her mother loved Halloween and the time she had made a coffin out of plywood and put a skeleton in it and had it by their front door. She would have loved how Andrew set this up.

No sooner had she knocked when she heard Eileen from inside shrieking, "Mom's here!" and her daughter flew into her arms. Erica picked her up and held her, which she loved to do and was glad that she still could. Nathan was too heavy for her to do that now for any length of time. Eileen wrapped her arms around her neck and clung to her. "I missed you," she said.

"I missed you too, honey." It was so good, so fulfilling, to have her close, to be in her presence. Over her shoulder she saw Nathan coming out of his bedroom, and she put Eileen down to greet him.

"Mom," Nathan said, coming into the entryway, "look at this." He held out something made of Lego.

"First you say, 'Hi, Mom,' and give her a hug," Andrew prompted as he approached from down the hallway. Erica had also found herself saying something similar to Nathan whenever friends and family came over. Greetings were difficult for him, for some reason. At least he no longer stood and stared at people while sucking his fingers. She and Andrew had been able to get him to stop when his permanent front teeth were growing in; they had told him that if he sucked his fingers his teeth would grow crooked. They had been amazed that he was motivated by mere aesthetics.

"Hi, Mom," Nathan said in a flat voice. Then he put his arms around her waist and squeezed. He seemed a little taller than when she had last seen him. She rested her chin on his curly head for a moment, then pulled away to look in his beautiful hazel eyes.

"Hi, sweetheart. What did you make?"

"A catapult," he said, holding it in front of her face.

"That's cool, Nate," Erica said. She turned to Andrew. "Has he grown?"

"Yeah, I bought him several pairs of pants two months ago and his ankles are already poking out of them," Andrew said. He stepped aside as Eileen led Erica to her room to show her the witch costume.

"Where's Miles?" Eileen asked.

"He's at Simone and Isaac's house. He'll come over tonight when we go trick-or-treating, and then after the party we're all going to spend the night at their house. Wait 'til you see Sadie! She's gotten really big!" Erica had looked at the floor when she said Isaac's name. A quick wave of shame passed through her, making her scar ache for a second. It wasn't the first time she had mentioned his name in Andrew's presence since the day, almost three years ago, that Andrew had learned of the affair, but she still felt self-conscious, sensitive to Andrew's feelings. He had worked through his resentment, and for that she was appreciative, respectful. She knew it could not have been easy for him to do, and she made it a point to keep any mention of Isaac to a minimum.

But he was her brother-in-law, and that made his and Simone's daughter her niece. Sadie, almost two, had the same eyes as Isaac and Miles. Eyes that looked like they saw through to your soul. She loved them on the brothers, but on this toddler, they were mystical. And she was talking. Erica was amazed to watch a typically-developing child. She felt wistful, watching Simone interact with her daughter, seeing what she had missed out on, seeing what autism had robbed from her. She remembered one summer day last year, when Nathan was seven and a half, and she had gone to the post office to send out a package, she saw a boy about his age get out of his parent's car that had pulled up to the curb, jog inside, insert the P.O. box key into the correct slot, take out the mail, close and relock the box, and jog back to the car. *Can seven-year-olds really do that?* she'd wondered. She was certain that she had at that age, or could have. But as a parent, she had adapted to her son's level of capability and accepted it. It was only when she saw other children do something that he couldn't that she realized how different their lives were. But it was okay. There were just some things, some memories, she wished they could have had, and some she wished they hadn't.

But doesn't that make me the same as any other parent?

When Eileen put on her Halloween costume, it reminded Erica of an old photo from when she was about Eileen's age and had also dressed up as a witch. Her mom had made the hat out of black felt, and Eileen's was store-bought nylon, but the effect was the same. Oh, she wished she had that photo. Who knew what happened to it? She and Caleb had gone through everything of their mother's and found plenty of other photos, and some things they wished they hadn't found, like syringes and snorting tubes among the empty bottles, but Erica had not seen the old witch photo of herself.

She'd take pictures tonight. One of Eileen by herself in the witch costume. That one wouldn't get lost.

Erica sneezed then, and, as if on cue, Tabby made a valiant leap off of Eileen's bed and out the bedroom door. She sneezed multiple times as she went across the hall to the bathroom for some tissues, cursing her allergy. She hated to cut the visit short, but she could feel her throat starting to close up.

She'd have time to recuperate, though, before coming back to take the kids trick-or-treating. Trick-or-treating was always her "thing" to do with them. Andrew accompanied them the first year, but every other year he had bowed out; she sensed because he realized that Halloween was always a special day with her mother. She remembered the first time, when Nathan had just turned six, and she was concerned that he wouldn't understand the purpose, be scared by a noise on someone's porch, freak out in some way, run in the street. But he surprised them, as he often did. By the third house, he was running up the steps, ringing doorbells and yelling "Trick or treat!" like anyone else. Erica had been so happy. Eileen loved it too.

Yes, tonight was her night with them.

"I'LL BE BACK in about an hour," Andrew called out the door to his mother, who was babysitting. She finally no longer required extensive instructions, much to Andrew's relief. Being a full-time college student seemed to have the same effect on Elaine that it had on most people, regardless of age: her self-confidence increased in proportion to how well she did and how much she learned. She became more open-minded and learned how to keep things in perspective. She came to realize that the world was not to be feared, it was to be experienced. That you don't always know all the answers, but you'll be all right with the ones you do. "Take your time!" she'd said as Andrew left. He smiled at her nonchalance, so different and welcome.

He was on his way to his first IEP meeting of the year, and it was already

May. There hadn't been one for over six months, and he was glad that they no longer held them once a month, or once a week, as they had in Ashland. He would have to go to another one next week for Eileen, but that was okay because it would be the last one. Her teacher had recommended, and Andrew agreed, that Eileen no longer needed speech therapy. After nearly seven years of meetings for two kids, he couldn't wait to sign those papers.

Third grade, Nathan's second year at Goodwin Elementary, brought significant progress. He rarely had the hood of his jacket up; if a noise bothered him, he just covered his ears. He hadn't had any episodes of disruptive behavior all year requiring a call to Andrew to come and pick him up. He usually interacted well with the other kids and did his work as long as his educational assistant hovered about to redirect his attention when it wandered. He could read at a fifth grade level and his math skills were improving. He could participate in P.E. with the other kids, even in the loud, echo-inducing gym. Andrew felt elated that Nathan had adapted, was learning and growing as he'd only dared to hope. Outings to the grocery store, doctor's office, and restaurants were almost issue-free. Even the use of public restrooms had become easier as Nathan learned to filter out disturbing sounds, sounds that only a year ago would have caused him such agony.

Again he spoke on a microphone to a room full of people, this time at Bernadette and Colin's wedding, which had been in March. Andrew coached him beforehand not to talk about divorce on the microphone since he did that already at Uncle Sol's wedding. So Nathan said, "This is my second wedding I ever went to. And I like the cake. It has Greekan columns on it. They are called Corinthian style. And I like them. Thank you." Then Eileen wanted to get in on the act. "Hi, my name is Eileen, and, um, I don't know what to say; I just wanted to talk on the microphone. Thank you!" The proud grandparents loved it. They were seated at different tables of course, but Andrew was impressed by the fact that they had both walked his sister down the aisle together, as she had requested. It was a long way to come for two people who used to have difficulty being at a grandchild's birthday party at the same time.

Andrew had relatives asking him when it was his turn, remembering that he and Brooke had been engaged for a long time. Sol and Bern had gotten married within six months of each other—the family's novelty of the year. He tried to be casual in response to his aunt's inquiries: "Oh, we're not sure; we just don't have the money right now; maybe next year." The truth was that he had planned on ending things with Brooke as soon as the kids went to L.A. for the summer. She had, of course, apologized for her tirade in front of Nathan—what she remembered—but it didn't change anything. On Christmas Eve, she had gotten drunk at her aunt's house again, stumbled into their house when they got home, used half a roll of wrapping paper to wrap the box of slippers that Andrew had requested as a gift, and then passed out in bed. He played Santa by himself, disappointed that his partner had to get drunk every holiday, every weekend, even during the week. And, even without the drinking, he knew that Brooke just wasn't right for him. He'd grown tired of narrating movies she didn't understand, fixing or replacing things she'd broken out of clumsiness or drunkenness, defining simple words she didn't know, and having her interrupt him every five minutes while he was trying to write when the kids were in bed. He remembered that there had been no rain on the beach the night of their engagement. Not a drop.

He parked in the school parking lot, shaking his head thinking about the new household items he had hidden in the closet until after Brooke would move out. He'd bought a matching nightstand for the other side of the bed, and a stained glass lamp to put on top of it, a new phone since Brooke had thrown the old one into a wall, and a new chenille blanket that she probably would have spilled wine or orange juice on. It amused him that he was more concerned with his girlfriend ruining things than his children. They were responsible for a few spills on the rug, but they'd never broken anything.

Andrew walked through the open classroom door into the resource room, where Nathan rarely spent any time, thanks to the competent teachers and assistants at the school. Andrew felt optimistic, cheerful even, as he greeted Mr. Russell, then the speech therapist, who was a thin, quiet woman, and the district special education coordinator, a middle-aged woman who reminded Andrew of a teddy bear. She told him that the new regional autism consultant would also be attending the meeting. They sat in kids' chairs around a low, round table.

A minute later, Andrew could not contain his elation as he saw Sally McIntyre, Nathan's first therapist from almost seven years ago, walk through the door. Her hair was long now, but he recognized her immediately, and got out of his chair to hug her. "It's so great to see you, Sally!"

"I see you two are well-acquainted!" the district coordinator said, smiling broadly.

"Hi, Andrew, it's good to see you too! I got to see Nathan this week; came and observed him in the classroom. He's like a different child now!" Sally said, sitting across from Andrew, breathless, excited, her round face flushed.

"Yes, he really is," Andrew said, taking his seat.

"It's so great to see how well he's progressed."

"He feels really comfortable here."

Andrew loved the fact that Sally was excited about his son. He was thrilled to have their paths cross again. They talked about the goals on the IEP, made a few changes, and reminisced about how Nathan used to be.

"Yes, he has certainly come a long way," the district special education coordinator said. "But we're not out of the woods yet. He still has autism."

Andrew deflated a little. *I know he still has autism; I know the reality of his disability and I accept it. But "not out of the woods yet"? If that's the case, we must have been in a deep ravine in the woods, and now we're just in the woods. We're out of the ravine with the sharp rocks and dark, swirling water that sucked us down time and again when we didn't know which way to turn and lost our footing. We're out of the ravine and now we're walking through a grove of beautiful birch trees. Those are the woods we're in now. The sun is filtering through the leaves, and we're walking purposefully, with our heads up looking straight ahead.*

ONCE UPON A TIME, a responsible, intelligent guy had gone through an unwanted divorce. And because his two children had developmental delays, he discovered that the women he dated didn't want to get involved. And he grew vulnerable, tired of being alone all the time. He longed to be in someone's arms again. And then he met a pretty, sweet girl who loved his children as much as she loved him. And he fell in love with her. And the pretty, sweet girl fulfilled the emotional needs of the responsible, intelligent guy.

But, over time, the responsible, intelligent guy realized that the pretty, sweet girl had a drinking problem and became verbally abusive. And he realized that, even though she loved him more than anyone ever had, love was not enough. Love is not all you need.

Andrew pulled in his driveway after grocery shopping. His food bill was so much lower when the kids were in L.A. He had driven them down to Stockton a week ago, the half-way point where Erica met them. It was their third summer in L.A.

The time had come to have the talk with Brooke. He wanted to sit in the driveway and prepare himself a little longer, but she was sitting on the front porch, in cut-off jean shorts and a black tank top, smoking a cigarette, watching him. He grabbed the four plastic grocery bags by the handles and walked in the house, telling Brooke hi.

"I'll be in in a minute," she said as she exhaled.

Andrew set the bags down on the kitchen counter and began to unpack them. He thought about when they went camping together for the last time, two weeks ago, and it rained. "What does this remind you of?" he asked Brooke as they rushed to get the tent set up.

"Our first time camping," she said with a laugh.

Four years with her, Andrew thought. Four years of laughter, that was certain, and love. But also four years of frustration, and rationalizing. He knew she felt it, too. A couple of times she had even threatened to move out. They were just too different.

The kids played in the light rain at lush, green Seacrest State Park in Washington, about an hour from Mount St. Helens National Monument. They had planned on taking a helicopter tour into the crater the next day, and Andrew had brought earplugs for Nathan, not sure how he would do with the sound.

With a clear sky the next morning, they drove out to the place that gave helicopter tours. While waiting for the next tour, they looked around the gift shop, buying silly shot glasses (*"I got lit at Mt. St. Helens!"*) and socks for Brooke, who had forgotten to pack any, and *The Fire Below Us* documentary DVD for Nathan, who seemed to have inherited a love of natural disasters from Erica's father. Andrew enjoyed the fact that he didn't have to constantly shadow Nathan in a store any more. He knew he wouldn't wander or cause any problems.

Soon it was time for them to go down to the airstrip and watch a short instructional video. Andrew put in Nathan's earplugs, a skull cap hat on his head, and his hooded jacket over that, and they walked out to the helicopter. Brooke held Eileen's hand, and Nathan held Andrew's hand as they walked around the painted white lines in the landing area.

They climbed in, first Eileen, then Nathan, then Andrew, with Brooke in the front seat next to the pilot. He told them to put on their headsets, and Andrew could feel the kids' excitement building.

Nathan turned to him. "Uh, Dad? I don't need these," he said, handing Andrew the earplugs that he had taken out by himself.

"Okay," Andrew said, stunned.

But there was no time to marvel about Nathan; they rose into the air then, lifted as if by puppet strings. Andrew looked at the thin river below with banks about fifty feet or higher that had been scoured by the mudflows. The river continued across flat land with a few elk wandering around. The aerial view reminded Andrew of *Wild Kingdom*, a TV show he'd watched as a child, in which they often filmed herds of animals from a helicopter.

Nathan asked the pilot what his favorite natural disaster was. "The eruption of Mt. St. Helens!" he said. "What's yours?"

"The eruption of Mt. Vesuvius and the destruction of Pompeii. It was an ancient Roman city," Nathan said. He seemed pleased with himself that he had asked his favorite question with an appropriate audience.

They entered the mile-wide crater, bare rock filled with snow and ice, and the pilot told them that the world's newest glacier was inside, that it was six hundred feet deep. It was so new it hadn't been named yet. As they turned to go back to the airstrip, Nathan and Eileen both said that they wanted to be pilots when they grew up, that this was the best trip ever. Andrew envisioned telling his family about it at his mother's house on Thanksgiving. He loved having that to look forward to.

Finished unpacking the groceries, Andrew sat down at the kitchen table as Brooke came in. "I need to talk to you," he began.

She sat down. "What is it?"

Andrew sighed. "Brooke, I'm sorry, but I really need to be on my own for a while. We're just very different people. And I also want to focus on my writing, because I want that to be my career, and I wouldn't be able to do that every night and have a relationship, with you or with anyone."

"You're dumping me?"

"Brooke, 'dumping' would be if I had someone else I wanted to be with instead, then I'd be 'dumping' you for someone. But that's not the case here. I just need to be on my own." Andrew paused and glanced at her. He felt a pang as he noticed her eyes watering. "I'll always care about you. And you'll always be a part of Nathan and Eileen's lives. You can see them anytime."

"Yeah. That's the hardest part," Brooke said between gasps. "I love those kids. I love them like they were my own!"

Andrew looked at her desperate, contorted face. He wondered if that's how he had looked when Erica had told him that she wasn't happy in their "relationship." He'd vowed that he'd never make anyone feel the way Erica had made him feel—so rejected, worthless, and sad. But now he knew, he understood. You can't plan love. You can't predict who you'll fall in love with, how long you'll stay that way, and what the other person might do, how they might become, that will affect the outcome. Love offers no guarantees. But it's still worth it, no matter how unpredictable, like skydiving, like snowboarding the Bowl, like anything else in life that's worth the risk.

"I know. And they love you, too." Andrew got up and hugged her. "I'm sorry, Brooke. I know this is really hard. Part of me wishes we didn't have to do this, but I think we both know that in the past two years we've had a lot of problems, and that's made me feel differently about you. I'll be your friend, but I can't be your fiancé or your boyfriend any longer."

"Okay," Brooke said, tears streaming down her face. "I want us to be friends. Because I want to be a part of your life for as long as I can. And I will cherish it for however long it is." She broke down then, and Andrew held her—this girl, who he had once loved deeply, when he had wondered if he'd ever be able to fall in love again.

"IT'S SO GREAT that they can get themselves ready now," Andrew said to Erica as she got a Pepsi out of the refrigerator and set it in front of him on her kitchen table. It was July, time for his annual mid-summer visit. He had spent the night at his brother's house when he arrived in L.A. the night before and had come over to take Nathan and Eileen to the beach for the afternoon, and they were brushing their teeth and getting dressed. Brown boxes were stacked all over Erica's kitchen, as well as the rest of her apartment. She had hoped to move before the kids arrived for the summer, but it had taken Miles and her a while to find a good place. At least there would soon be an end to all of them being cramped in that one-bedroom apartment.

"Yes, finally. We certainly put in our time waiting for that to happen," Erica said. She sat down across from him. "So how've you been?"

Andrew talked about how he had started writing an article on autism that he intended to submit to a national magazine, like *Child* or *Parents*.

Erica, glad to see him motivated, said she thought it sounded like a good idea. Then he told her that Brooke was moving out, that he broke up with her.

"I'm sorry to hear that." *But I'm surprised it took you this long,* Erica thought. *You guys are so different.*

"Well, it's for the best. I've been wanting to end it for a while, but there just never seemed to be a good time. She's just not right for me. It's like she's thirty-five going on nineteen. I felt like I had a teenage daughter. Even Nathan commented to me recently that Brooke was like 'the third child,' he said. He's so intuitive sometimes." Andrew took a sip of his soda.

"Yeah, he is."

"I'll probably tell the kids tonight, so they have some time to get used to it before they come back to Oregon."

"I'm sure they'll be okay with it," Erica said. She picked up the can and drank. "So how was your visit with Solomon?"

Andrew told her that they enjoyed catching up, that his brother was still working at the Ahmanson Theater, doing well. The big news was that Gisela was pregnant, due around Christmas, and everyone was thrilled to have a new member of the family on the way. Sol said he'd talked to their father a few days ago. Gabriel was glad to be back in Yellowstone, completing requirements to become an assistant park ranger, and he'd started dating one of the other tour guides. She even liked bowling! Sol said that he sounded content for the first time in years.

"I'm glad to hear that," Erica said. "I always liked your dad."

"Have you talked to Caleb lately?"

Yes, she told Andrew, *just last week as a matter of fact.* His younger son, Liam, who was now three, had just been diagnosed with autism. She felt a jolt when Caleb said it, felt empathy for him, because she knew what lay ahead: years of therapy, meetings, shrieking in public, not being able to talk with your child. Autism affects people differently, but no matter what, it's always difficult, especially the early years. There's just so far to go and no guarantees. You can't see the proverbial light at the end of the tunnel because it's so long, but also because it never ends. The tunnel of raising a child with autism never ends.

"Oh, my God," Andrew said, stunned. "It's so much more prevalent these days."

"Yeah. He's pretty sure they're going to move down here to have access to better therapy and schools for Liam."

"That's good. We were lucky to have ECDC in southern Oregon. Nathan did really well there," Andrew said.

"Yes. Caleb and Daisy are coming for a visit in two weeks, and it'll be good for them to see Nathan so they can see what Liam's potential is. It sounds like he's about the same level of severity that Nathan was at that age. It'll be good for them to see how different he could be seven years from now."

"A lot of it had to do with a good response to good therapy," Andrew said. "But I also think it also had a lot to do with us as parents. It really helps that we have similar parenting styles. We must be doing something right!"

They laughed together—an unreserved, hearty laugh that made Erica feel good. They had these two kids together, and there was quite a bond in that. Nothing could change that.

"Andrew, I just wanted to say thanks. Because I really appreciate you being so understanding when I moved, and dealing with the major changes so well. I know it wasn't easy, and I'm sorry. But I'm glad you're their father. I wouldn't want to go through all we've been through with anyone else."

"I feel the same way," Andrew said, looking at her. "And I'm okay with the past. I forgive you." He got up from his chair then, holding his arms out to her, and she got up and embraced him.

"Thank you. That means a lot to me," she said, swallowing back tears. Not wanting to give in to the strong emotions she felt, she pulled away then and suggested that he and the kids better get going to beat the traffic. There was a volleyball tournament at Hermosa Beach that day, so she had printed out directions to go to Manhattan Beach instead.

Andrew called to the kids: Had they gone to the bathroom? Got their swimsuits and sandals on? Got their towels? Then they came running, and he stuffed their towels and sand toys in the big straw tote bag that Erica had provided, and she handed him a stack of coins for the parking meter, and Andrew thanked her, and they left.

Erica closed the door behind them and walked back into her sun-filled living room. As much as she looked forward to being in a bigger place, she would miss this room. And packing wasn't fun, either. But in cleaning out her dresser drawers she'd found Eileen's little tooth, the only one she had ever lost at Erica's home. Something in her wanted to save it. *Why? To give to Eileen some day? What do you do with a tooth? Put it on a necklace, like a shark tooth? What does an adult do with a childhood tooth?* Erica knew what she would do with one of her own. Hold it in her hand and remember who she was all those years ago. Remember the little girl who had learned not to trust and tell her she didn't have to be that way anymore. Sometimes all you can do is trust. Trust that you're doing the right thing and that it will all work out in the end.

Erica took in a jagged breath as she surveyed her plants and noticed that the cactus was blooming, a soft pink. She smiled as an image flashed in her mind of the day that she and Caleb spread their mother's ashes around the base of Mount Shasta and how they had laughed about the fact that she never did anything there. She didn't ski; she didn't hike. She'd had practically nothing to do with Mount Shasta while she was alive. And yet, she was part of it now. There were probably flowers that had grown where her ashes fell. Maybe orange poppies. She could see them now, their petals fluttering in a gentle breeze.

THERE ARE SOME things that no apology can fix. That time might heal, but not completely. That's what Andrew had thought for the longest time. He didn't know if he could ever get over the knowledge of Erica's affair, if he could ever feel comfortable with her again, laugh with her without feeling insincere. But he knew that if he didn't work through it, the negativity would compromise his well-being. And he wrote in his journal, *She did something thoughtless, and hurtful, but it doesn't make her a terrible person. It doesn't mean I can't still care about her, and love her as the mother of my children. That's what forgiveness means to me.* And he thought that she might need to hear it, maybe as much as he needed to say it.

But caring about Erica didn't change the fact that he was still on his own at home, still facing the same challenges. Like being a LISP, Gavin's coined acronym for Low Income Single Parent. But Andrew decided that he preferred the acronym SLIP: Single Low Income Parent. Or 'Super Like-able Intelligent Person.' And 'Severe Love Induced Paralysis,' his favorite. *Slip.* He wondered if women actually wore slips anymore; no one he'd ever dated had. Erica certainly hadn't. He remembered his mother used to walk around the house in her slip every Sunday morning while everyone prepared for church. Her slip symbolized being almost ready to go, but not quite. Something just beneath the surface, providing substance. Andrew had felt like that for most of his life. But he was content with that.

He merged onto the 405 freeway then. The traffic was as light as his mood. He thought about the flying dream he'd had a few nights ago. He could feel himself soaring up into the air, slowing to change direction, like in Disney's animated *Peter Pan*. He had this power; there were people standing forty feet below him, looking up, marveling. It felt natural and real. Peaceful.

Andrew could hear Nathan in the back seat singing along to the Elvis song on the stereo: "Devil in Disguise." Andrew smiled, never taking for granted that he could hear Nathan's voice, that even though he would have autism his entire life, he could find enjoyment in singing along to a song, and so many other things.

Boogie-boarding turned out to be one of them. Andrew watched in proud amazement as Nathan jumped and dove in the surf, rode the waves in on his stomach, arms outstretched grasping the front of the board, smiling as he stayed on until the board stopped in the sand. Then he would get up and run out to do it again. Erica had said that he was doing well with swimming lessons this summer, and maybe next year he would be able to try surfing. Andrew thought that Nathan looked like a natural. He'd even started taking showers to wash his hair. Nathan, the child who, seven years ago, shrieked and thrashed in the tub when it was time to wash his hair, now loved to take showers and dive under ocean waves. Andrew was continually surprised by his son's ability to adapt to his sensory issues. It was so encouraging that Andrew allowed himself to speculate about how Nathan might be when he grew up, that he could go to college, hold down a job. He loved books and reading, learning historical and geographical facts, possessed a photographic memory. Maybe he would enjoy being a librarian, and would be a good one. Or maybe he'd be a surfer. Or maybe both.

Eileen loved the water too, although she didn't dive into it the way her brother did. She jumped the smaller waves and rolled in the shallow surf, laughing like she'd never been happier.

Andrew joined them, and it reminded him of when he was a kid, water up to his chest, jumping the waves and feeling his body sway with them. He'd stay in so long that he could still feel the motion of the waves while riding home in the car. And at night, in bed, he'd close his eyes and he could still feel it, still taste the saltwater and feel the sand between his toes.

Eileen said she wanted to build a sandcastle, so they came back on shore and Andrew got the plastic shovels and molded turrets out of the tote bag. He looked at them then, with their wet hair slicked back, droplets of water and clumps of sand on their tanned skin. They began digging a moat in the damp sand near the water.

Then Andrew spotted the dolphins.

"Look! Look, guys! Dolphins!"

Nathan and Eileen stopped digging and watched in awe as several dolphins swam in front of them, cavorting in the waves just thirty feet away.

"I see them!" Eileen said.

"Aren't they beautiful?" Andrew said. He glanced around the beach and realized that it had grown quiet, and that of the hundred or so people in the immediate area, every single person was transfixed on the magical beings playing before them.

"Do you think they're a family, Dad?" Eileen asked.

"I think so," Andrew told her.

"There's five of them," Nathan said, still looking out at the water.

"Families can be of any size," Eileen said.

"Families are who you spend your life with. Who you love," Andrew said, putting his arms around his children as they watched the dolphins.

"And who you're happy with," Eileen said.

"Those dolphins look really happy playing in the waves," Nathan said. It was one of the longest sentences Andrew had heard him say.

"You know what?" Andrew said, looking at his son. "So am I." *The three of us—conversing! This is wonderful!*

The dolphins swam off then, and they watched until they could no longer see them. All about them, people resumed their activities, and Andrew kissed the tops of his children's heads as they continued their digging. Fully content, he sat back on his towel and leaned on one arm, watching them.

Nathan spied a seagull several yards away and got up, wanting to investigate. Slowly, cautiously, he approached. Andrew noticed that Nathan got closer to the bird than he and Sol had ever gotten when they were kids. He hoped that Nathan could do it, that he could touch the bird, just as all boys who go after birds wish they could do. Then, just as Nathan reached out, it flapped vigorously and flew off. Nathan, seemingly unfazed, watched it go for a moment, and then he began walking back to his father and sister.

I used to dream about what Nathan would be like if he did not have autism, how our lives would be different. But that is not our path. He will forge his own path, and grow and learn, and succeed on his own terms. And his family will be there, every step of the way.

Slip

A Reader's Guide

TANYA SAVKO

Questions for Discussion

1. Although the main focus of *Slip* is parenting a child with autism, a few other topics are addressed. Marriage, infidelity, and divorce are present throughout the story and shape the lives of the main and supporting characters. Do you see any parallels between how the adult children react to their parents' divorce and how Nathan and Eileen react to Andrew and Erica's divorce? What differences are there between their divorce and Andrew's parents' divorce?

2. Another theme in *Slip* is the importance of family, even if it's broken. What do you think of the different styles of single parenting (Andrew's, Erica's, and Erica's mother) portrayed in the story? How did the roles and personalities of Erica's mother, father, and great aunt shape her? How did the roles and personalities of Andrew's parents shape him? What is the significance of the title (*Slip*), other than "Single Low-Income Parent" mentioned in the last chapter? Do you recall any other references to the word "slip" in the book?

3. In the beginning, Erica was in denial about Nathan's diagnosis and resistant to the labeling. How did her views evolve throughout the story? Did she move away because she was subconsciously repeating her mother's pattern of leaving her children? Or do you think Erica moved away because it was difficult for her to be a full-time parent of a special needs child?

4. Alcohol has played an ominous role in Erica's family history with several members' alcoholism and three deaths as a result of drunk driving. Is it ironic that Erica is a bartender, or is it, as she calls it, just an "ill-conceived career"? Is it merely her way of trying to prove that she is in control of the alcohol in her life? In what other ways does she exert control in her life?

5. After his divorce from Erica, Andrew becomes involved in a long-term relationship with a person who has obvious alcohol and substance abuse problems. Why is he so reluctant to leave Brooke, even given her verbal abuse toward him and the chaos of her addiction? Is it codependence? Andrew's own vulnerability? Does he believe that it would be hard to find anyone else who could accept and love his children as much as Brooke does?

6. Andrew is openly devastated after he finds out about Erica's affair with Isaac, and Brooke comforts him. Given that Andrew found out about Er-

ica's infidelity more than three years after their divorce, does it appear that he is not emotionally over her yet? Does his reaction indicate that he is still in love with Erica? Later, in the fight with Brooke when Andrew refuses to pick her up from Lupe's house late at night, Brooke yells, "I'm tired of being second-best to you!" What do you think she means by that? Is she thinking that Andrew's heart still belongs to Erica, or is Brooke referring to Andrew's constant focus on his children?

7. How much did you know about autism before reading *Slip*? Has your view changed at all? If you saw a child screaming in public, like Nathan did in the store with the coffee grinder and in the bathrooms at the zoo and the beach, would you assume it was a regular tantrum, or might you think that it could be a sensory meltdown? Do you know someone who has a child with autism or any other disability? There are several statistics indicating that a high percentage of marriages affected by autism end in divorce. Do you think that that was the case with Andrew and Erica? Why or why not?

8. The characters in *Slip* are heavily influenced by family dynamics. Despite different upbringings, Andrew and Erica share an emotional ambivalence toward their parents, yet they feel very close to their siblings. What are the reasons for this? Is there a correlation between Andrew having to be responsible for his younger siblings while growing up and later being the custodial parent of his own children, as his counselor had suggested? Andrew enjoys talking to his brother Sol and seems to live vicariously through him. Do you think that Andrew has any regrets about the choices he made in his life?

9. During the course of the story, Eileen gets to a point where she begins to wonder about her brother and his differences. She is also more directly affected by her mother's long-distance move. When she lashes out at her father, telling him that she doesn't love him and doesn't want to be a part of his family anymore, is it just because she's upset about her mother living far away, or is she also starting to become embarrassed by her brother's behavior?

10. Cars and driving often appear as metaphors throughout the story. Erica makes a comment at the end of chapter 17 about hoping that one day " . . . one of those rare moments of clarity would be enough to cause Nathan to 'turn over,' like starting an old, fragile car, and last forever." At age five, when Nathan finally starts holding a pencil and drawing, the first things he drew were little cars with smiley faces on them. What is the symbolism

of the nearly 700-mile drive to visit his mother? For the first half of the story, Andrew, being the custodial parent, drives Erica's old car, which is constantly breaking down and needing to be fixed. How symbolic is Andrew's purchase of a new car?

11. Water is also a metaphor in *Slip*, from the beginning scene with Nathan's bath to the last scene with seeing the dolphins at the beach. Andrew must come to the realization that it's not the water that Nathan can't handle about the baths; it's the sensory issue of leaning back to have his hair rinsed. What is the symbolism of Nathan enjoying boogie-boarding at the beach? Andrew comments a few times about his parents' adage of rain being a blessing. How does Andrew apply that to events in his adulthood?

12. In writing *Slip*, Tanya Savko drew from her experience with raising her autistic son. She is also a single parent of two, lives in southern Oregon, and went through a divorce at the same time as her parents. Many parents of special-needs children who write about their experiences choose the memoir genre. What are the advantages or disadvantages of writing a novel versus a memoir? How do you think *Slip* might have differed if it had been written as a memoir?